"Your sister thinks you should marry…"

Bethany's face grew hot. "Husbands don't exactly grow on trees in New Covenant."

"Anyone you chose would be getting a fine wife."

She looked up to study Michael's reflection in the glass, but it wasn't clear enough to let her see what he was thinking. "Are you making me an offer?"

"You would be getting a very poor bargain if I was."

She turned around so she could look into his eyes. "Why do you say that?"

"Because it's the truth."

There was so much pain in his voice and deep in his eyes that she wanted to hold him and promise to make everything better.

She couldn't. "What's wrong, Michael?"

"Nothing that you can fix."

"How do I know that if you can't tell me what troubles you?"

"Trust me. You don't want to know." He turned and walked down the hall and out the back door.

He was so wrong.

Bethany wanted to know everything about Michael Shetler.

After thirty-five years as a nurse, **Patricia Davids** hung up her stethoscope to become a full-time writer. She enjoys spending her free time visiting her grandchildren, doing some long-overdue yard work and traveling to research her story locations. She resides in Wichita, Kansas. Patricia always enjoys hearing from her readers. You can visit her online at patriciadavids.com.

Vannetta Chapman has published over one hundred articles in Christian family magazines, receiving over two dozen awards from Romance Writers of America chapter groups. She discovered her love for the Amish while researching her grandfather's birthplace of Albion, Pennsylvania. Her first novel, *A Simple Amish Christmas*, quickly became a bestseller. Chapman lives in the Texas Hill Country with her husband.

USA TODAY Bestselling Author

PATRICIA DAVIDS

*An Amish Wife
for Christmas*

&

VANNETTA CHAPMAN

*Amish Christmas
Memories*

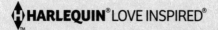
❖HARLEQUIN® LOVE INSPIRED®

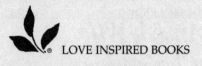 LOVE INSPIRED BOOKS

Recycling programs for this product may not exist in your area.

ISBN-13: 978-1-335-22980-9

An Amish Wife for Christmas and Amish Christmas Memories

Copyright © 2019 by Harlequin Books S.A.

An Amish Wife for Christmas
First published in 2018. This edition published in 2019.
Copyright © 2018 by Patricia MacDonald

Amish Christmas Memories
First published in 2018. This edition published in 2019.
Copyright © 2018 by Vannetta Chapman

This edition published by arrangement with Love Inspired Books.

www.Harlequin.com

Printed in U.S.A.

CONTENTS

AN AMISH WIFE FOR CHRISTMAS   7
Patricia Davids

AMISH CHRISTMAS MEMORIES   229
Vannetta Chapman

AN AMISH WIFE
FOR CHRISTMAS

Patricia Davids

This book is dedicated with great admiration to my longtime and dare I say long-suffering editor, Emily Rodmell. I'm sure I have tried your endless patience far more often than any other author, but you have never failed to help me get back on track. During the bleak moments of my personal life and in some weird and crazy times you have remained confident in my talent and pushed me to write a better book even when I wasn't sure I wanted to go there. Thanks for your faith in me. Here's hoping it isn't misplaced. Onward and upward.

That he would grant you, according to the riches of his glory, to be strengthened with might by his Spirit in the inner man; That Christ may dwell in your hearts by faith; that ye, being rooted and grounded in love, May be able to comprehend with all saints what is the breadth, and length, and depth, and height; And to know the love of Christ, which passeth knowledge, that ye might be filled with all the fullness of God.
—*Ephesians* 3:16–19

Chapter One

❧

"Your brother's behavior reflects badly on you, Bethany, and on our community. Something must be done."

Bethany Martin sat across from Bishop Elmer Schultz at her kitchen table with her head bowed and her hands clasped tightly together in her lap. Her dear friend Gemma Lapp sat beside her. Bethany was grateful for Gemma's moral support.

"We Amish are newcomers here," he continued. "We can't afford to stir ill will among our *Englisch* neighbors. Don't you agree?"

Bethany glanced up and met his intense gaze. She nodded slightly. An imposing man in his midfifties, the bishop had a shaggy gray-and-black beard that reached to the middle of his chest. A potato farmer and owner of a shed building business, he was known for his long and often rambling sermons, but he was a fair man and well liked in their small Amish community. Bethany didn't take his visit lightly. She prepared to defend her brother.

"Ivan isn't a bad boy. It's just that he misses his grandfather. He's angry that God took Elijah from us

and he feels guilty. The two of them were very close."
Her heart ached for her troubled brother.

"Time will heal this," Gemma added.

The bishop sighed. "Your grandfather Elijah was
a fine man, Bethany. I have no doubt that he kept the
boy's high spirits in check, but Ivan has quickly put one
foot on the slippery slope that leads to serious trouble.
He needs a firm hand to guide him and mold him into
an upstanding and righteous man."

"I can do that," Bethany assured him. "I've raised
Ivan from the time he was five and our sister, Jenny,
wasn't much more than a newborn babe." She might be
their sister, but she was also the only mother they had
ever known. Both mother and father to them after the
man who bore that title left his family for the fourth and
final time. Bethany's anger surged to the surface but
she quickly brought it under control. At least her mother
had been spared knowing about his final betrayal. She
had been positive he would return to care for his children after she was gone. He hadn't. Bethany brought
her attention back to the matter at hand.

Gemma waved one hand. "Ivan is almost fourteen.
Boys that age get into mischief."

It was a weak argument and Bethany knew it. Her
brother's recent behavior was more than mischief, but
she didn't know what to do about it. He seemed to be
done listening to her.

The bishop's expression softened. "Bethany, your
grandfather was concerned that you have sacrificed
your chance to have a family of your own in order to
care for your siblings."

She drew herself up straight. "I don't feel that way.
Ivan and Jenny *are* my family."

The bishop laced his fingers together on the table. "I am the spiritual leader of this community and as such I have a duty to oversee the welfare of all my flock. Normally I would leave the discipline of children to their parents. In this case I feel duty bound to step in. Elijah was my dear friend. It was his vision that founded our new community here. It was his desire to see it grow. For that we need the goodwill of our *Englisch* neighbors."

"I'm aware of that. I spent many months helping him search for the best place to settle. New Covenant is as much my dream as it was his." She didn't like the direction the bishop seemed to be going.

"Then you agree that we can't let the reckless actions of one boy ruin what has been created."

"He isn't trying to spoil anything." Bethany was compelled to defend Ivan, but the truth was she didn't know what was wrong with him. Was he acting out because of his grief or was something else going on?

His schoolwork had suffered in the past weeks. His teacher had complained of behavior issues in class. He had been in several scuffles with non-Amish boys earlier in the year but they weren't anything serious. It was his recent secrecy and withdrawal that bothered Bethany the most. How could she help him if she didn't understand what was amiss?

She lifted her chin. "There is no proof that he damaged Greg Janson's tractor or that he is responsible for letting Robert Morris's cattle loose."

Bishop Schultz leveled a stern look at her. "He was seen near both farms at the time and he'd been in fights with both the Janson and Morris boys."

"That's not proof," she insisted.

The bishop pushed back from the table. "I have written to your uncle in Bird-in-Hand."

She frowned. "To Onkel Harvey? Why?"

"Elijah mentioned that Harvey and his family plan to visit you this Christmas."

"That's true. We are expecting them to stay a week as they were unable to come to the funeral."

The bishop rose to his feet. "I have asked your uncle to take Ivan with him when the family returns to Pennsylvania."

Bethany's mouth dropped open. "*Nee*, you can't send Ivan away. This isn't right."

"It was not an easy decision. I know your intentions are *goot* but the boy needs the firm guidance of a man. You are too easy on him."

"Because he's still a little boy." The situation was quickly slipping out of her control. They couldn't take her brother from her. Fear sent her pulse pounding in her temples. "Please, Bishop, you must reconsider."

"I will not."

Bethany pressed both hands to her heart. "I promised my mother before she died that I would keep the family together. I promised her. Don't do this."

The bishop's expression didn't change. Her plea had fallen on deaf ears. Men were the decision makers in her Amish community. The bishop had the last word even in this family matter.

He took his coat and hat from the pegs by the door and put them on. "Bethany, if you were married I wouldn't have to take this course of action. Your husband would be the one to make such decisions and discipline the boy. With Elijah gone, I see no other choice. I must think of what is best for all, not just for one."

He nodded to her and left. Bethany wanted to cry, to shout at him, to run after him and beg him to change his mind, but she knew it wouldn't do any good.

"I'm sorry." Gemma laid a hand on Bethany's shoulder.

"What am I going to do? There has to be a way to change the bishop's mind."

"Why don't I make us some toast and a cup of coffee. Then we'll put our heads together and come up with a plan."

"We're out of bread and I don't want any coffee."

"What Amish woman runs out of bread?"

"This one. There has been so much to do since Daadi's passing I haven't had time to bake. If Ivan straightens up and starts behaving, if he apologizes to the bishop maybe he'll be allowed to stay. It's five weeks until Christmas. That's enough time to prove he has changed."

"Or you can get married. That will fix everything."

Bethany gave her friend an exasperated look. Gemma knew Bethany's feeling about marriage. It wasn't for her. "It's unlikely that I could find someone to wed me before Christmas, Gemma."

"If you weren't so particular, maybe not. Jesse Crump holds you in high regard."

Bethany wrinkled her nose. "Having a conversation with Jesse is like pulling teeth. He's a nice enough fellow, but he never has anything to say."

"Ack, you're too fussy by far."

"You marry him."

Both Gemma's eyebrows shot up. "Me? Not a chance. Besides, it isn't my brother that is being sent away."

Bethany battled her rising panic. "I wish Daadi were still here. I don't know what to do."

Gemma slipped an arm around Bethany's shoulders and gave her a hug. "If your grandfather was still alive we wouldn't be having this conversation."

"I know."

Ivan's troubling behavior had started when their grandfather became ill early in the fall but it had gotten much worse since his death. Her gaze moved to the closed door leading to her grandfather's workroom. Their grandfather had happily spent hours repairing clocks and antique watches during the long winter months in his tiny shop. With the door open she used to hear him humming or muttering depending on how a particular project was progressing.

The workshop hadn't been opened since Ivan found Elijah slumped over his desk barely breathing. The boy ran to find help but by the time it arrived Elijah was gone.

She should have mailed his unfinished works back to their owners before now but she couldn't bear to enter the room. The grief she tried so hard to control would come pouring out when she did.

Tears stung the backs of her eyelids, but she quickly blinked them away. The quiet strength and unquestioning love of her grandfather had seen Bethany through the worst times in her life. It was still hard to accept that she could never turn to him for guidance again.

She drew a deep breath and squared her shoulders. He would tell her prayer and hard work solved problems. Worry and regret never did. There had to be a way to keep her family together and she would find it.

Perhaps her uncle would side with her. She would write her own letter to him and plead her case.

She slipped into her coat. "Thank you for coming today, Gemma, but I'd best get the rest of my chores done."

Gemma followed her to the door. "I don't know how you'll manage this farm without Elijah and Ivan."

"One day at a time and with the help of our neighbors if I need it."

"I've never known you to ask for help." Gemma moved to put on her black bonnet and coat.

"I asked you to sit with me when the bishop came today, didn't I?"

Gemma rolled her eyes. "Okay, you have asked for help one time. I wish I knew what to say but I think it is all up to Ivan. I'm surprised he wasn't here this morning."

"He's at school. I didn't want to take him out of class."

The New Covenant Amish community was too small yet to have their own school. The five Amish children in their church, including her brother and sister, attended the nearest public school. It was far from ideal but the teachers and school board had taken great pains to accommodate the needs and customs of the new Amish pupils.

The two women walked outside together. Gemma pulled on her gloves. "Do you want me to come over this evening when you talk to him?"

Bethany shook her head. "*Danki*, but I think it's best I speak to him alone."

"All right. I'll stop by tomorrow and you can tell me

all about it." The two women exchanged a hug. Gemma climbed into her buggy and drove away.

Bethany's breath rose as puffs of white mist in the chilly mid-November morning as she crossed the snow-covered yard to the newly completed red barn. It was the latest building to be added to the new community. The bulk of the structure had been raised in a single day with the help of an Amish community from upstate New York. Thirty men had traveled all night by bus and worked feverishly to complete the barn before taking the long bus ride home again that night. Someday the people of New Covenant would return the favor.

Her grandfather had had plans for half a dozen additional structures to attract more Amish families to New Covenant. It had been his dream to form a thriving Amish district in Maine, far from the tourist centers in Pennsylvania. To him, fewer tourists meant less money but more time to spend close to God and family without worldly influences. If only he could have lived to see his dream grow and thrive.

Bethany fed and watered the chickens, gathered the eggs and then fed and watered the geese before heading to the barn. Her mind wasn't on her chores. Her conversation with the bishop replayed in her head as she fed and watered their two horses. Outside the milk cow's stall, Bethany paused and leaned on her pitchfork. "I've got trouble, Clarabelle."

The cow didn't answer her. Bethany pitched a forkful of hay to the family's placid brown-and-white Guernsey and then leaned on the stall door. "The bishop has decided to send Ivan to Bird-in-Hand to live with Onkel Harvey. It's not right. It's not fair. I can't bear the idea of sending my little brother away. It will break his heart and Jenny's, to say nothing of mine. We belong together."

Clarabelle munched a mouthful of hay as she regarded Bethany with soulful deep brown eyes. The bell around her neck clanked softly as she tilted her head to allow Bethany to scratch behind her left ear. Bethany complied. As a confidant, Clarabelle was unassuming and easy to talk to, but she was short on advice.

"Advice is what I need, Clarabelle. The bishop said Ivan could stay if I had a husband. Someone to discipline and guide the boy. I don't believe for a minute that is the solution but I'm getting desperate. Any idea where I can get a husband before Christmas? And please don't suggest Jesse Crump. Jedidiah Zook might be a possibility if he smiled more. Maybe he just needs a wife to make him happier. What do you think?"

"I doubt your cow has the answers you seek but if she does I have a few questions for her about my own problems," a man said in an amused drawl.

Bethany spun around. A stranger stood in the open barn door. He wore a black Amish hat pulled low on his forehead and a dark blue woolen coat with the collar turned up against the cold. He carried a duffel bag over one shoulder and he leaned on a black cane.

The mirth sparkling in his eyes sent a flush of heat to her cheeks. How humiliating. To be caught talking to a cow about matrimonial prospects made her look ridiculous.

She struggled to hide her embarrassment. After looking the man up and down, she stabbed the pitchfork into the hay again and dumped it into Clarabelle's stall. "It's rude to eavesdrop on a private conversation."

"I'm not sure talking to a cow qualifies as a private

conversation but I am sorry to intrude." The man put down his duffel bag.

He didn't look sorry. He looked like he was struggling not to laugh at her. At least he was a stranger. Maybe this mortifying episode wouldn't become known in the community. She cringed at the thought of Jedidiah Zook hearing the story. "How can I help you?"

"Mind if I sit here for a minute?" He pointed to a stack of straw bales beside the barn door.

She wanted him to go away but her Amish upbringing prevented her from suggesting it. Any stranger in need deserved her help.

He didn't wait for her reply but limped to the closest bale and sat down with a weary sigh. "The bus driver who dropped me off said New Covenant was a little way along on this road. His idea of a little way does not match mine."

"It's less than half a mile to the highway from my lane."

He rubbed his leg. "That's the farthest I've walked in six months. How much farther do I have to go?"

"You have arrived at the south end of our community."

He tipped his head slightly. "I thought New Covenant was a town."

"It's more a collection of houses strung out on either side of the road right now, but it will be a thriving village one day." She prayed she spoke the truth.

"Glad to hear it. I'm Michael Shetler, by the way." He took off his hat and raked his fingers through his thick dark brown hair.

She considered not giving him her name. The less he knew to repeat the better.

He noticed her hesitation and cleared his throat. "It's rude not to introduce yourself in return."

She arched one eyebrow. "I'm being rude? That's the pot calling the kettle black. I am Bethany Martin," she admitted, hoping she wasn't making a mistake.

"Nice to meet you, Bethany. Once I've had a rest I'll step outside if you want to finish your private conversation." He winked. One corner of his mouth twitched, revealing a dimple in his cheek.

Something about the sparkle in his blue eyes invited her to smile back at him but she firmly resisted the urge. She stabbed the pitchfork into the remaining hay and left it standing upright. "I'm glad I could supply you with some amusement today."

"It's been a long time since I've had something to smile about."

The clatter of hooves outside caught her attention as a horse and wagon pulled up beside the barn and stopped. She caught a glimpse of the driver through the open door. He stood and faced the barn. "Ivan Martin, are you in there? It's Jedidiah Zook. I want to speak to you!"

Her gaze shot to Michael. His grin widened. Her heart sank as he chuckled. "I may not have given Clarabelle enough credit. It seems your preferred beau has arrived. It was Jedidiah Zook you hoped would come courting, right?"

She glared and shook a finger at him. "Don't you dare repeat one word of what you heard in here."

Michael couldn't help teasing her. The high color in her cheeks and the fire in her eyes told him she was no meek Amish maid. He wagged his eyebrows. "Do you need a go-between? Shall I speak on your behalf? I'll be happy to help any way I can."

"If you say anything, I'll… I'll…" She clamped her lips closed. The sheen of unshed tears gathered in her eyes, but she quickly blinked them back and raised her chin.

Teasing was one thing. Upsetting her was another. He held up one hand. "Relax. Your secret is safe with me. If the cow spills the beans, that is not my fault."

"Stay here." Bethany rushed past him out the wide double doors. "*Guder mariye*, Jedidiah. Ivan isn't in here. He's at school. Can I be of any help?"

"Your brother has gone too far this time."

The man's angry voice brought Michael closer to the open door to watch. Bethany faced Jedidiah defiantly with her head up and her hands on her hips. "What has he done?"

"Two thirty-pound bags of potatoes and a ten-pound bag of dried beans are missing from my cellar."

"What makes you think Ivan took them?"

"Because he sold a bag of potatoes to the general store owner just this morning."

She folded her arms in front of her. "That's not proof he took them. Maybe it was one of our sacks that he sold."

"Was it?"

"I'm not sure."

"You tell him I came by and that I'm on my way to report this theft to the bishop. This has gone beyond what can be ignored. It must stop. If you can't control the boy someone else will have to." He lifted the reins, turned the wagon around and headed down the lane.

Michael limped out to stand beside her. "Not a very jolly fellow. Are you sure he's the one?"

She shot him a sour look. "In spite of what you think you heard earlier, I am not in the market for a husband."

Why wasn't she married already? She was certainly attractive enough. Not that he was in the market for a relationship. He wasn't. He might never be. He sobered at the thought. The men who shot him and robbed the store he had worked may have robbed him of a family, too. He had no idea if his PTSD would get better living in the isolation of northern Maine, but it was his last option.

Bethany brushed past him into the barn, a fierce scowl marring her pretty features. "I need to speak to my brother and get to the bottom of this. You are welcome to rest here."

He was glad he wasn't the brother in question. She went down the aisle and opened the stall door of a black mare with a white blaze. She led the mare out, tied the horse to a hitching post and began to harness her.

"Let me do that for you." He took a step closer.

"I can manage," she snapped.

He took a step back and held one hand up. She didn't need or want his help. In short order she had the harness on and then led the animal outside, where she backed the mare in between the shafts of the buggy parked in a lean-to at the side of the building.

"May I?" he asked, pointing to the buggy. She nodded. He finished securing the traces on one side while she did the other. He buckled the crupper, the loop that went around the mare's tail to keep the harness from sliding forward on the animal, as Bethany finished her side and came to check his work.

"Danki."

She thanked him like it was a chore. Bethany Martin was clearly used to doing things by herself.

Michael realized that he hadn't looked over his shoulder once since hearing Bethany's voice. That had to be some kind of record. He glanced around out of habit but there was nothing sinister in the farmstead and empty snow-covered fields that backed up to wooded hills on either side of the wide valley. All throughout his trip to New Covenant he'd been on edge, expecting danger from every stranger that came close to him. He'd spent most of the bus ride from Philadelphia with sweating palms and tense muscles, expecting another attack or a flashback to overtake him at any second. They never came when he was expecting them.

He rubbed a hand across the back of his neck. For the first time in weeks the knots in his neck and shoulders were missing. Maybe he was getting better. Maybe this move was the right thing, after all. He prayed it was. Nothing here reminded him of the Philadelphia street or the shop where his life had changed so drastically.

Here the air was fresh and clean. The next house was several hundred yards up the road. Nothing crowded him. He could start over here. No one would look at him with pity or worse. He had a job waiting for him in New Covenant and a place to live all thanks to the generosity of a man he'd never met. He needed to get going, but he was reluctant to leave Bethany's company for some reason. Her no-nonsense attitude was comforting. He pushed the thought aside. "I should be on my way. Can you give me directions to Elijah Troyer's farm?"

She shot him a startled look and then glanced away.

"This was his farm," she said softly with a quiver in her voice.

"Was? He sold it?" Michael waited impatiently for her to speak.

She kept her gaze averted. "I'm sorry but Elijah Troyer passed away three weeks ago."

Michael drew back with a sharp intake of breath. "He's dead? That can't be."

He fought against the onrush of panic. What about the job? What about the place to live? Were his hopes for a new life dead, too?

Chapter Two

Bethany watched as Michael limped away and sat down on the hay bale inside the barn door. He rubbed his face with both hands. She could see he was deeply affected by the news of her grandfather's death. Sympathy made her soften her tone. "I'm sorry to give you the sad news. Did you know my grandfather well?"

Michael shook his head. "I never met him."

If he didn't know her grandfather, why was he so shaken by his passing? As much as she wanted to stay and find out Michael's connection to Elijah, she had to speak to Ivan as soon as possible. If he had stolen the potatoes and beans as Jedidiah claimed, the items would have to be returned at once, but there had to be some mistake. Her brother wasn't a thief.

Please let it be a mistake, Lord.

The bishop would never reconsider sending Ivan to live with Onkel Harvey if Jedidiah's claim was true.

She slipped the reins through the slot under the winter windshield of the buggy. "I'm sorry you didn't have a chance to meet my grandfather. He was a wonderful man."

"He offered me a job working for him. Is that job still available?"

"I know nothing about such an offer. Are you sure it was my grandfather who promised you work?"

"Elijah Troyer, in New Covenant, Maine. That's what the letter said. Is there another Elijah Troyer in the community?"

"There is not. I don't know what my grandfather had in mind, but I can't afford to hire someone right now."

"I was also told I would have a place to stay. I reckon if there's no job there's no lodging, either?"

Was he talking about the small cabin that sat at the back of her property? Her grandfather had mentioned readying it for a tenant before he became ill, but she didn't know if he had finished the repairs. Besides, she wasn't ready to host a lodger. Nor did she want to leave Michael Shetler like this. He appeared dazed and lost. Her heart went out to him.

"You should speak to our bishop, Elmer Schultz. I'm sure he can help. He won't be at home this time of day, but I can give you a ride to his place of business."

"It seems I don't have much choice. *Danki.*"

Michael slowly climbed into the passenger seat. Bethany walked around the back and got in on the driver's side. She picked up the reins. "The school is about three miles from here."

"I thought we were going to the bishop's place of business."

"We are but I must stop at the school first. I hope you don't mind."

"As long as I don't have to walk three miles I don't mind."

From the corner of her eye Bethany noticed him rubbing his leg frequently. It must pain him a great deal. This close to him she noticed the dark circles under his eyes, as if he hadn't slept well. He was pale, too. She sat silent for the first half mile of their trip but her curiosity about Michael got the better of her. "Where are you from?"

"My family lives in Holmes County, Ohio. My father and brother have a construction business in Sugarcreek."

"Did you work in construction with them?"

"Nee." He didn't elaborate.

"I've heard that's a large Amish community. Do you have a lot of tourists who visit there?"

"We do."

"Like where I am from. Bird-in-Hand, Pennsylvania. My grandfather wanted to start a community that wasn't dependent on tourism. Don't get me wrong, he knew how important the industry is to many Amish who can't make a living farming, but it wasn't the lifestyle he wanted to live."

Michael pulled his coat tighter. "There had to be warmer places to settle."

She chuckled as she looked out over the snow-covered fields that flanked the road. "The coldest part of the winter has yet to come."

"So why here?"

"The price of land and the ability to purchase farms large enough to support big families were more of a consideration than the weather. Plus, we were warmly welcomed by the people here. Many local families have been here for generations. They like the idea that we want to be here and farm for generations, too. A lot of the elders in the community remember farming with horses when they were children. Folks are very independent minded in Maine. They know what hard work is. When someone has to sell farmland they would rather sell it to the Amish because we will live on it and farm it as their grandparents did. They consider it preferable to selling to a large farming corporation intent on grabbing up as much land as possible."

"What do you grow here besides snowdrifts?"

She smiled. "Potatoes. Maine is the third-largest producer of potatoes in the United States. Broccoli grows well in the cool climate as do many other vegetables."

"As long as you don't get an early freeze."

"That's true of farming in Ohio or almost anywhere."

"I guess you're right about that."

The main highway followed the curve of the river and after another mile Fort Craig came into view. Bethany turned off the highway into a residential area at the outskirts of town. The elementary school was located in a cul-de-sac at the end of the street.

As she drew the horse to a stop in front of the school she noticed several of the classes were out at recess. She stepped down from the buggy and caught sight of her sister, Jenny, playing with several other girls on the swings. Jenny spotted her and ran over. "Sister, what are you doing here?"

"I've come to speak to Ivan. Did he get on the bus with you this morning?"

Jenny shook her head. "*Nee*, he said Jeffrey's mom was going to bring him to school."

"And did she?"

"I don't know. Sister, I have *wunderbar goot* news."

Bethany crouched to meet Jenny's gaze. "Have you seen Ivan today?"

Jenny screwed up her face as she concentrated. "I don't think so. You should ask his teacher."

Bethany stood upright. "That's exactly what I plan to do."

"Don't you want to hear my news?"

"In a minute."

Jenny's happy expression faded. Michael got out of the buggy. He took several stiff steps. "I just need to stretch my legs a little."

"Who is that?" Jenny asked in a loud whisper.

Bethany was inpatient to find Ivan but she made the introduction. "This is Michael Shetler. He's a newcomer. This is my sister, Jenny."

He nodded toward her. "I'm pleased to meet you, Jenny. I'd love to hear your news."

"You would?" Jenny asked hopefully.

"Sure. It must be important. You look ready to burst."

Jenny smiled from ear to ear. "I got picked to be in the community Christmas play. I'm going to be the aerator."

Bethany looked at Michael. He returned her questioning gaze and shook his head slightly. Jenny was bouncing up and down with happiness.

Bethany smiled at her. "That is *wunderbar*. What does the aerator do?"

"I get to tell everyone the Christmas story in English and in Pennsylvania Dutch while the other kids act out the scenes. Ivan is going to sing a song by himself."

From the corner of her eye, Bethany saw Michael rub a hand across his mouth to hide a grin. Bethany was afraid she'd start laughing if she looked at him again. Learning English as a second language was difficult for many Amish children who spoke only Pennsylvania Dutch until they started school. "I'm sure you will make a *goot* narrator if you practice hard."

"I'll practice lots and lots if you help me."

"You know I will."

"I need to have an angel costume, too. I'm going to be an angel aerator."

"Angel *narrator*," Michael corrected her in a gentle tone.

"Narrator," Jenny replied slowly. He nodded and she grinned at him.

Bethany patted her sister's head. "We'll talk about it when you come home from school this evening."

"Okay." Jenny took off to rejoin her friends.

"Cute kid," Michael said, still grinning. "How many siblings do you have?"

"Just Jenny and Ivan. Excuse me while I check on him." Bethany headed through the front doors of the school. She found the eighth-grade room and looked in through the open door. Ivan wasn't in his seat. His best friend, Jeffrey, was missing, too.

A bell sounded in the empty hall, startling her. The boys and girls in the room filed to the back to gather their coats, mittens and hats from hooks before rushing past her to get outside. After the last child exited the room Bethany stepped inside. "Ms. Kenworthy, may I have a word with you?"

The teacher looked up from her desk. "Miss Martin, of course. Do come in. I was just getting ready to write a note to you."

"About Ivan?"

"Yes. I hope he is feeling better. He's missed almost an entire week of school. I have a list of homework assignments for him to complete and hand in when he returns."

Bethany's heart sank. "My brother is not sick at home."

"I see." Ms. Kenworthy opened a desk drawer and pulled out a sheet of notebook paper. "Then I assume you did not write this note?"

Bethany removed her gloves, took the note and quickly scanned it. It informed Ms. Kenworthy that Ivan would be out of school for a week due to his illness. It was signed with her name. Bethany sighed heavily and handed the letter back. "I did not write this. It is not my signature."

Ms. Kenworthy took the letter and replaced it in the drawer. "I thought it was odd that Jeffrey was the one who delivered it to me and not your sister. Do you know what Ivan has been doing instead of coming to school?"

"I wish I did. He doesn't confide in me these days."

"He was close to his grandfather, wasn't he?"

The understanding in the teacher's eyes allowed Bethany to unburden herself. "They were very close. Since Elijah's death Ivan has refused to talk to me about what's troubling him. He's changed so much. I was hoping he might have confided in you."

"I am deeply sorry for your loss. Elijah was well liked in this community."

"Thank you."

"Your brother's grades were not the best before your grandfather passed away. Since that time, he has earned nothing but Fs for incomplete work. Even when he is here he seems withdrawn until someone speaks to him. Then he's ready to start a fight over nothing. Unless he does extra-credit work and turns in his missing assignments, I'm afraid he is going to flunk the semester. I know that according to your religion this is his last year of education, but I still have to follow state guidelines. That puts me between a rock and a hard place. If he flunks the semester, he'll have to attend summer school."

Bethany shook her head. "Ivan will be needed on the farm this summer. I don't see how we could spare him even a few hours a day."

"In that case he will have to repeat this grade next year. Talk to him. Try to make him see what's at stake." She removed a folder from another drawer. "Give these assignments to him. Hopefully he can finish most of them over the weekend."

"I will. Thank you." Bethany was angry with Ivan for his deceit, but she was more disappointed in herself. Where had she gone wrong? How had she failed him? She tried to be a parent to her siblings but without her grandfather's help she didn't know how to reach Ivan. Maybe letting him return to Pennsylvania would be for the best.

Except that it didn't feel like the right solution. She loved her brother. She couldn't imagine life without his annoying habits, constant teasing and his hearty laugh. She had to make him see that his actions were tearing the family apart.

But she needed to find him first. Clearly Jeffrey was in on whatever Ivan was up to. His parents lived a mile farther up into the woods from her home.

Bethany left the school building and saw Michael sitting on the buggy step. She'd forgotten him. A thin yellow hound lay a few feet away from him. The dog wagged its tail tentatively as it watched him. Michael pulled his gloves off and took something from his pocket. He held it toward the dog. The animal crept a few inches closer.

"Good girl," Michael said, tossing the item at the dog's feet. She snapped it up. At the sound of Bethany approaching, the dog darted for cover between two nearby parked cars.

Bethany stopped beside Michael. The dog grew bold enough to peek out from between the cars but didn't approach. "I see you made a new friend."

He rose to his feet. "She was sniffing at the trash cans and trying to get them open. I could see she was looking for a meal. I had a little leftover jerky I picked up on the bus ride here. She appears to need it more than I do. Is your brother at school?"

"*Nee*, but that doesn't prove he stole provisions from Jedidiah."

"You're still giving him the benefit of the doubt?"

"Of course. He's my brother."

"I hope your confidence isn't misplaced."

"I pray it's not but I will admit I'm at my wit's end. His teacher says he hasn't been to school all week. His friend gave the teacher a note that was signed with my name that said he was sick at home. I have to find out what's going on. He's left each morning to catch the school bus with his sister and he's walked home with her each evening, yet he hasn't been in school."

"Don't think too badly of him. Boys his age are sometimes impatient to grow up and live their own adventures. Then they make foolish mistakes because they aren't as smart as they think they are."

"Are you speaking from experience?"

"I am. My own."

"How many forged notes did you send to your teacher?"

A wry grin curved his lips. "My teacher happened to be my mother's youngest sister, so none."

"I'm afraid of what the bishop will say when Jedidiah tells his side of the story."

"If the bishop is a reasonable man he'll listen to your side of the story, as well."

She was grateful for his reassurance, but he didn't know how serious the situation was becoming. She held on to the hope that her uncle could be persuaded to let Ivan remain with her. "I will take you to see the bishop now."

"I appreciate that." He moved to open the buggy door for her and took her hand to help her in.

His grip was firm but his hand was soft. His skin lacked the calloused roughness of a man who made his living farming the land or woodworking. It wasn't the hand of a laborer, yet she found his gentle strength oddly comforting.

Perhaps he was a shopkeeper. Her grandfather had had plans to open a small grocery in New Covenant. Maybe that was the job he had promised Michael. It didn't matter. Her grandfather was gone, and she wasn't in a position to continue his work. At least not yet.

She looked up and met Michael's gaze as he continued to hold her hand longer than necessary. There was a profound sadness in the depth of his eyes that she didn't understand. What troubled him? What was he thinking?

Michael stared into Bethany's light blue eyes as the warmth of her touch went all the way to the center of his chest and warmed a place that had been cold for a long time. He studied her face, trying to find out why she triggered such a strong reaction in him.

Her pale blond hair was parted in the middle and worn under a white prayer covering. Her skin was fair with a scattering of freckles across her dainty nose. She was an attractive woman, too attractive for his peace of mind.

He let go of her hand, stepped away and limped around the back of the buggy, letting the pain in his leg remind him of why he had no business thinking about how perfectly her small hand had nestled in his. If things had been different, if he wasn't so damaged he would have enjoyed getting to know her better, but things weren't different. He had to accept that.

He also had more serious things to think about. He needed a job and he needed somewhere to live. Preferably a good distance away from other people in this remote community. His neighbors wouldn't appreciate being awakened in the middle of the night by the screams that sometimes accompanied his nightmares.

Thoughts of his dreams filled him with apprehension as his pulse shot up. He quickly scanned his surroundings. A car drove past the school, the tires crunching on the snow. Children were playing on the playground. He could hear their laughter and shouting. Someone stood at the corner of the school building. He thought it was a woman but he couldn't be sure. The person was bundled in a parka with the hood up. Perhaps a teacher watching the children. He struggled to convince himself that there was nothing sinister here but he couldn't shake the feeling that something bad would happen at any second. His heart began to pound as tightness gripped his chest.

The dog ventured out and came to stand in front of him. He focused on her unusual golden eyes. She looked to be part yellow Labrador retriever and part pointer. Her white-tipped tail wagged slowly. He held out his hand and she sniffed it. It was a shame he didn't have more to feed her. She retreated again and he got in Bethany's buggy.

Inside the small space he started to relax. No one could get behind him now. He glanced at Bethany. She was watching him intently. Could she see how anxious he was? He needed to divert her attention. "Are you waiting for something?"

"Nee." She turned the horse and headed back up the street. The clip-clop of the mare's hooves was muffled by the snow that covered the road. It was the only sound other than the creaking of the buggy. He discovered he would rather hear Bethany's voice.

"What kind of business does the bishop own?"

"Our bishop builds and sells storage sheds as well as farming, but he's thinking of branching out into tiny homes."

"Then he is a progressive fellow?"

"In his business, but our church is a conservative one."

"I noticed a propane tank at your home."

"Our Ordnung allows us to use propane to power business machinery, our refrigerators, washing machines and hot water heaters. We also have running water and indoor bathrooms. We aren't that conservative but our cookstoves and furnaces must use wood or coal."

He glanced out over the dense tree-covered hillsides and the snowcapped mountains in the distance. "It doesn't look like you'll run out of fuel anytime soon as long as you have a strong fellow to chop and haul it."

"My brother does that for me." Her voice was strained. Worry marked her brow with frown lines.

"How old is he?"

"Almost fourteen. Our mother died when Jenny was born. Our father was gone soon afterward." The undertone of bitterness in her voice surprised him.

"So you were raised by your grandparents."

"My grandfather took us in. He was a widower."

"It must've been hard to be both mother and sister to your younger siblings." He found it easier to talk to Bethany than anyone he'd spoken to since the attack. Maybe it was because she talked to cows. He smiled at the memory.

"I never saw caring for my siblings as a burden." She turned the horse off the street into the parking lot surrounded by various sizes of storage sheds.

A tall, muscular Amish fellow stepped away from a half-finished shed and slipped his hammer into a tool belt that hung on his hips. He didn't sport a beard, so Michael knew he wasn't married. His clothes were tattered and sweat-stained, but his smile was friendly as he greeted them. "*Guder mariye*, Bethany. Need a new shed, do you?"

Bethany opened her door but didn't step out. "Good morning, Jesse. Is Bishop Schultz about?"

"*Nee*, he isn't. He's gone to Unity. Their bishop is laid up with pneumonia, and Elmer has gone to do the preaching for their service this Sunday and perform a wedding on Tuesday. He won't be back until Wednesday night."

"Have you seen Ivan today?"

"*Nee*, I've not. Who is that with you?"

"Jesse, this is Michael Shetler. He is a newcomer. He came expecting to work for my grandfather. He hadn't heard about Elijah's passing. I thought perhaps the bishop would know of some work and could find a place for him to stay."

Jesse hooked his thumbs under his suspenders. "There is work aplenty here. You're welcome to bunk on my couch until you can find a place, but you'll have to suffer through my cooking. I'm no hand with a skillet."

Michael got out of the buggy and grabbed his duffel bag. He would rather stay somewhere alone, but he didn't have much choice. He forced a smile and a light-hearted reply. "Your cooking can't be worse than mine. You have yourself a boarder until I can find a place of my own. We can work out the rent later."

"No need for that." Jesse moved to take Michael's bag. "Let me get this for you."

Michael handed it over. Jesse nodded toward the building he had been working on. "If you don't mind, I'd like to finish this shed before taking you out to my place."

"I don't mind. I'll give you a hand with it."

Looking at Michael's cane, Jesse raised one eyebrow. "Are you sure?"

"I can still swing a hammer."

"Then your help will be welcome. I'll see you get paid for the work you do."

"Danki."

Michael turned to Bethany. "Looks like your brother has been granted a reprieve if Jedidiah wasn't able to speak to the bishop."

Bethany's eyes brightened. "That's right."

"Oh, Jedidiah was here and spoke to Elmer before he left," Jesse said cheerfully.

Michael watched the hope fade in her eyes and wished there was something he could do to console her.

Chapter Three

Michael watched Bethany drive away with a sharp unexpected sense of loss. She was a lovely woman, but he sensed she was much more than a pretty face. It was obvious that she cared about her family. Anyone who asked a cow for advice had to have a good sense of humor.

He smiled then quickly pushed thoughts of her out of his head. As much as she intrigued him, he was better off not seeing her.

Forming a relationship with Bethany would mean letting her get close. He couldn't risk that. He had jumped at the chance to come to this part of Maine because it was remote and thinly populated but it held an Amish community. He had left his Amish upbringing once with devastating consequences. After the attack he had returned home hopeful that rejoining his faith and family would repair his shattered life. It hadn't worked out that way. He didn't know what more God needed from him.

Michael's plan for his new life was simple. Live and work alone while coming into contact with as few people as possible. He wasn't a loner by nature. He had become a recluse out of necessity. Avoiding people was the only way he felt safe. The only way he could keep his affliction hidden. Staying with Jesse was risky, but he had nowhere else to go. He could only pray he didn't have an episode in front of him.

A doctor in Philadelphia had called it PTSD. Post-traumatic stress disorder, the result of a robbery gone wrong at the jewelry store where he had worked. What it meant was that his life was no longer his own. He lived in near constant fear. When a full-blown flashback hit he relived every detail as his coworkers, his friends, were killed in front of his eyes. The gunshots, the screams, the sirens—he saw it, heard it, felt it all again just as if it were happening to him the first time.

He never knew when a flashback would happen, making it impossible for him to return to work. Even a walk down a city street left him hearing the footsteps of someone following him, waiting to feel the cold, hard barrel of a gun jammed in his back.

He was the one who had let them in. He was the only one who came out alive. Sometimes he felt he should have died with the others, but he couldn't dwell on that thought. God had other plans for him. He just didn't know what they were.

The heavy thudding of his heart and the sweat on his brow warned him that thinking about it was the last thing he should be doing. He took a deep breath. Concentrate on something else. Think about Bethany asking her cow for advice and the shocked look on her face when she realized he'd heard her conversation. He visualized her in detail as his pulse slowed to a more normal speed.

From the corner of his eye he caught sight of the yellow dog trotting along the edge of the highway in his direction. Did she belong to someone or was she a stray surviving as best she could? Her thin ribs proved she wasn't being cared for if someone did own her. Her chances of surviving the rest of the winter on her own didn't look good. She approached as close as the drive leading into the parking lot. After pacing back and forth a few times she sat down and stared at him.

He turned to Jesse. "Do you know who that dog belongs to?"

Jesse glanced at her and shook his head. "I've seen her around. I think she's a stray."

"Would you happen to have anything I can feed her?"

Jesse laughed. "Are you a softhearted fellow?"

"Is there anything wrong with that if I am?"

"*Nee*, I like animals, too. Maybe more than most people, but I think I'm going to like you, Michael Shetler." Jesse clapped him on the back with his massive hand, almost knocking Michael over. "There's a couple of ham sandwiches in the refrigerator inside the office. You are welcome to them. For you or for the dog. Your choice."

"*Danki.*" Michael walked into a small building with Office in a hand-lettered sign over the door. Inside he found a small refrigerator with a coffeepot sitting on top of it. He took out two of the sandwiches, happy to see they contained thick slices of ham and cheese. After taking a couple of bites from one, he walked out with the rest in his hand. The dog was still sitting in the driveway.

He walked to within a few feet of her and laid the sandwich on the ground. As soon as he moved away she jumped up and gulped down the food. Looking up, she wagged her tail, clearly wanting more.

"Sorry, that's all there is. We are two of a kind, it seems. You needed a handout and so did I. We have Jesse over there to thank for sharing his lunch." Michael chuckled. He had teased Bethany about talking to her cow but here he was talking to a dog. It was too bad Bethany wasn't here to share the joke.

What surprised him was how much he wanted to see her again.

Jeffrey Morgan's home was a little more than a mile farther up the road from Bethany's house. As she pulled in she saw Jeffrey's mother getting out of her car. When she caught sight of Bethany she approached the buggy hesitantly.

"Good afternoon, Mrs. Morgan." Bethany stepped down from the buggy unsure of what to say.

"You are Ivan's mother, aren't you?" The woman remained a few feet away.

"I'm his older sister. Our mother passed away some years ago."

"That's right. Jeffrey told me that. I'm sorry about your grandfather. Jeffrey was fond of him."

"Thank you. Is Jeffrey here?"

"No. He's at school."

"I'm afraid he isn't. I just came from the school. Neither he nor my brother showed up for class today."

Mrs. Morgan looked around fearfully and moved closer to Bethany. "Are you saying that the boys played hooky today?"

"I don't know that word."

"*Hooky?* It means they skipped school without permission."

"Then *ja*, they played hooky."

Mrs. Morgan looked toward the house at the sound of the front door opening. Mr. Morgan stepped out. Jeffrey's mother leaned closer. "Don't tell my husband about this. I will speak to Jeffrey."

Puzzled by her fearful reaction, Bethany nodded. "Please send Ivan home if you see him."

"I will."

Bethany waved to Mr. Morgan. He didn't return the gesture. She got in her buggy and left. Where were those boys and what were they up to?

Bethany arrived home just after noon. She parked the buggy by the barn and stabled her horse. She wasn't any closer to finding her brother or figuring out what he was up to. As she came out of the barn, a car horn sounded. She glanced toward the county road that ran past her lane. Frank Pearson's long white passenger van turned off the blacktop and into her drive. Frank was the pastor of a Mennonite congregation a few miles away. He and her grandfather had become good friends. Frank used to visit weekly for a game of chess and to swap fishing stories.

Frank pulled up beside her and rolled down his window. "Good day, Bethany."

"Hello, Frank. Would you like to come in for some coffee?"

"I'm afraid I don't have time today. I have my bereavement support group meeting in twenty minutes. I just stopped in to see how you're getting along and to invite you and your family to attend one of our meetings when you are ready. It doesn't matter what faith you belong to or even if you are a nonbeliever. We all grieve when we lose loved ones."

"*Danki*, Frank. I don't think it's for me."

"If you change your mind, you're always welcome to join us. Please let me know if you need help with anything. I miss Elijah, but I know my grief is nothing compared to yours. I promised him I'd check in on you."

"Our congregation here is small, but we have been well looked after."

"I'm glad to hear it. I'll stop by again in a few days and stay awhile."

Maybe Frank could reach Ivan. "Why don't you come to dinner on Sunday? I know Ivan and Jenny would enjoy seeing you again. Maybe you can interest Ivan in learning to play chess."

"You know, I believe I will. Your cooking is too good to resist. Thanks for the invite."

"You are always welcome here."

After Frank drove away, Bethany headed for her front door. The smell of warm yeasty dough rising greeted her as she entered the house. Gemma was busy kneading dough at the table. Bethany pulled off her coat and straightened her prayer *kapp*. "What are you doing here again so soon? I thought you said tomorrow?"

"What does it look like I'm doing?"

"It looks like you are making a mess in my kitchen."

Gemma giggled as she surveyed the stack of bowls, pans and the flour-covered table. "It does, doesn't it?" She punched down the dough in a second bowl and dumped it onto a floured tabletop.

"Why are you baking bread in my kitchen?"

"Because you didn't have any. I realized on my way

home this morning that the least I could do for a friend was to remedy that."

"I appreciate the gesture but why not bake it at your home and bring the loaves here."

"I didn't want to mess up my kitchen. I just finished washing the floor." Gemma looked at her and winked. "Where have you been, anyway?"

Should she confide in Gemma about Ivan's recent actions and Jedidiah's accusations? Once more Bethany wished her grandfather were still alive. He would know what to do with the boy. She hung her coat on one of the pegs by the kitchen door. "It's a long story."

Gemma looked up. "Oh?"

Bethany went to the far cabinet and pulled out a cup and saucer. She felt the need of some bracing hot tea. "Jedidiah came by earlier. He accused Ivan of stealing two bags of potatoes and a bag of beans from his cellar."

Gemma spun around, outrage written across her face. "He did what?"

"He said Ivan stole those items and he had proof because Ivan sold some of the potatoes to the grocer this morning."

"I don't believe it. I know Ivan has been difficult at times, but he is not a thief."

Bethany filled her cup with hot water from the teakettle on the back of the stove. "That's what I said. I went to the school to hear Ivan's side of the story."

"And?"

"And he wasn't at school. He hasn't been to school all week. He forged a letter from me telling the teacher that he is out sick." Bethany opened a tea bag, added it to her cup and carried it to the kitchen table, where she sat down.

After a long moment of stunned silence, Gemma came to sit across from her. "You poor thing. Still, that doesn't mean he stole from Jedidiah."

"It doesn't prove he didn't. And it certainly doesn't speak well of his character. Jedidiah went straight to Bishop Schultz with the story. I had hoped to speak with the bishop, too, but he is gone to Unity until Wednesday. I don't know how I'll ever convince him to let Ivan remain with us now. What is wrong with my brother? How have I failed him?"

Had Ivan inherited his father's restlessness and his refusal to shoulder his responsibilities? She prayed that wasn't the case.

Gemma reached across the table and laid a comforting hand on Bethany's arm. "I'm so sorry. I had no idea things had progressed to this degree of seriousness. He's always been a little willful, but this is unacceptable behavior and it is his own doing. Bethany, you did not fail him."

"Danki." Bethany appreciated Gemma's attempt to comfort her.

Gemma returned to the other end of the table and began dividing the dough into bread pans. "You'll simply have to talk to the boy and tell him what the bishop has planned. Perhaps that will convince him to mend his ways."

"I hope you are right. Christmas is only five weeks away. I don't know if a change in Ivan's behavior now will be enough to convince Onkel Harvey and the bishop that he should stay with us. Stealing is a serious offense."

Bethany had lost so many people in her family. She couldn't bear the thought of sending her brother away.

She had promised to look after her brother and sister and to keep the family together. It felt like she was breaking that promise and it was tearing her heart to pieces.

"You still have the option to marry. I think Jesse would jump at the chance if you gave him any encouragement."

"I saw him this morning and he didn't appear lovestruck to me."

Gemma laughed. "Did you honestly go see him with marriage in mind?"

"Of course not. I took a stranger to see the bishop at his workplace. The bishop wasn't there but Jesse was."

"What stranger?" Gemma looked intrigued.

"His name is Michael Shetler. He claims my grandfather offered him a job and a place to stay."

"Did he?"

Bethany shrugged. "I never heard Grandfather mention it."

"What's he like? Is he single?"

"He's rude."

"What does that mean? What did he say to you?" Gemma left the bread dough to rise again and returned to her seat, her eyes alight with eagerness. "Tell me."

Bethany blushed at the memory of Michael listening to her conversation with Clarabelle. That was the last time she would speak to any of the farm animals. "He wasn't actually rude. He simply caught me off guard."

"And?"

"When I told him about Elijah's passing he was very upset. I thought the bishop would be the best person to help him find work, so I gave him a ride to the shed factory. Jesse said he would put him to work."

"You took a stranger up in your buggy? Is he old? Is he cute?"

"He walks with a cane."

"So he's old."

"*Nee*. I'd guess he's twenty-five or so. I had the impression it was a recent injury to his leg."

"So he's young. That's *goot*, but is he nice looking?"

Bethany considered the question. "Michael isn't bad looking. He has a rugged attractiveness."

"Michael?" Gemma tipped her head to the side. "He must be single. Is he someone you'd like to know better?"

"I have too much on my mind to spend time thinking about finding a man."

"That's not much of an answer."

"It's the only answer you are going to get. You'll have the chance to see Mr. Shetler for yourself at the church service next Sunday."

"All right. I won't tease you."

Gemma walked over and put on her coat. "Ivan is a good boy at heart. You know that."

Bethany nodded. "I do. Something is wrong, but I don't know what."

"You'll figure it out. You always do. I'm leaving you with a bit of a mess but all you have to do is put the bread in the oven when it's done rising."

"*Danki*, Gemma. I'm blessed to have you as a friend."

"You would do the same for me. Mamm is planning a big Thanksgiving dinner next Thursday. You and the children are invited of course."

"Tell your mother we'd love to come."

"Invite Michael when you see him again."

"I doubt I'll see him before Sunday next and by then it will be too late."

"My *daed* mentioned the other day he needs a bigger garden shed. Maybe I'll go with him to look at the ones the bishop makes. You aren't going to claim you saw Michael first if I decide I like him, are you?"

Bethany shook her head as she smiled at her friend. "He's all yours."

Bethany was waiting at the kitchen table when both children came home. Ivan sniffed the air appreciatively. "Smells good. Can I have a piece of bread with peanut butter? I'm starved."

Bethany clutched her hands together and laid them on the table. "After I have finished speaking to you."

"Told you," Jenny said as she took off her coat and boots.

"Talk about what?" Ivan tried to look innocent. Bethany knew him too well. She wasn't fooled.

"Why don't you start by telling me what you did wrong and why." Bethany was pleased that she sounded calm and in control.

"I don't know what you are talking about." He couldn't meet her gaze.

"You do so," Jenny muttered.

"Stay out of this," Ivan snapped.

"I went to school today. I'm not in trouble," Jenny shot back.

"I'm waiting for an explanation, Ivan." Bethany hoped he would own up to his behavior.

"Okay, I skipped school today. It's no big deal. I can make up the work." His defiant tone made her bristle.

"You will make up the work for today, and Thursday and Wednesday and Tuesday. You will also write a letter of apology to your teacher for your deliberate deception. Is there something else you want to tell me?"

He stared at his shoes. "Like what?"

Bethany shook her head. "Ivan, how could you? Skipping school is bad enough. Forging a letter to your teacher is worse yet, but stealing from our neighbors is terrible. I can't believe you would do such a thing. What has gotten into you?"

"Nothing."

"That is not an answer. Why did you steal beans and potatoes from Jedidiah?"

Ivan shrugged. "He has plenty. The Amish are supposed to share what they have with the less fortunate."

"What makes you less fortunate?"

When he didn't answer Bethany drew a deep breath. "Your behavior has shamed us. Worse than that, your actions have been reported to the bishop."

"So? What does the bishop have to do with this?"

"The bishop is responsible for this community," Bethany said. "Because you have behaved in ways contrary to our teachings, the bishop has decided you need more discipline and guidance than I can give you."

"What does that mean?"

"When Onkel Harvey and his family come to visit for Christmas, you will return to Bird-in-Hand with them."

"What? I don't want to live with Onkel Harvey."

"You should've thought about the consequences before getting into so much trouble."

Jenny, who had been standing quietly beside Ivan, suddenly spoke up. "You're sending him away? Sister, you promised we would all stay together." She looked ready to cry. "You promised."

"This is out of my hands. The bishop and your uncle have decided what Ivan needs. They feel I have insufficient control over you, Ivan. I'm afraid they are right. Bishop Schultz believes you need the firm guidance of a man. If your grandfather was still alive or if I was married, things would be different."

"That's stupid," Ivan said, glaring at Bethany. "I didn't do anything bad enough to be sent away. It isn't fair."

"None of us wants this. You have time before Christmas to change your behavior and convince them to let you stay. You will return the items you've taken from Jedidiah. He knows that you sold one of the bags of potatoes you took. You must give the money you received for them to Jedidiah. You will have to catch up on all your missed schoolwork and behave politely to Jedidiah and to the bishop. We will pray that your improvement is enough to convince Bishop and Onkel Harvey to let you remain with us."

Ivan glared at her. "Jedidiah Zook is a creep. He's never nice to me, so why should I be nice to him?"

Bethany planted her hands on her hips. "That attitude is exactly what got you into this mess."

Jenny wrapped her arms around her brother's waist. "I don't want you to go away. I'll tell the bishop you'll be good."

"They don't care what we think because we're just kids and we don't count."

"That's enough, Ivan. You and I will go now to speak to Jedidiah and return his belongings this evening."

"I can't."

"What do you mean that you can't?"

He shrugged. "I don't have the stuff or the money anymore. I gave it away."

"Who did you give it to?" Bethany asked.

"I don't have to tell you." He pushed Jenny away and rushed through the house and out the back door. Bethany followed, shouting after him, but he ran into the woods at the back of the property and disappeared from her view.

Jenny began crying. Bethany picked her up to console her. Jenny buried her face in the curve of Bethany's neck. "You can't send him away. You can't. Do something, sister."

"I will try, Jenny. I promise I will try."

Ivan returned an hour later. Not knowing what else to do, Bethany sent him to bed without supper. Jenny barely touched her meal. Bethany didn't have an appetite, either. She wrote out a check to Jedidiah for the value of the stolen items and put it in an envelope with a brief letter of apology. She couldn't face him in person.

After both children were in bed, Bethany stood in front of the door to her grandfather's workshop. He wouldn't be in there but she hoped that she could draw comfort from the things he loved. She pushed open the door.

Moonlight reflecting off the snow outside cast a large rectangle of light through the window. It fell across his desk and empty chair. She walked to the chair and laid her hands on the back of it. The wood was cold beneath her fingers. She closed her eyes and drew a deep breath. The smell of the oils he used, the old leather chair and the cleaning rag that was still lying on the desk brought his beloved face into sharp focus. Tears slipped from beneath her closed eyelids and ran down her cheeks. She wiped them away with both hands.

"I miss you, Daadi. We all miss you. I know you are happy with our Lord in heaven and with Mammi and Mamm. That gives me comfort, but I still miss you." Her voice sounded odd in the empty room.

Opening her eyes, she sat in his chair and lit the lamp. The pieces of a watch lay on the white felt-covered board he worked on. His tiny screwdrivers and tools were lined up neatly in their case. Everything was just as it had been the last time he sat in this chair. The cleaning rag was the only thing out of place. She picked it up to return it to the proper drawer and saw an envelope lying beneath it. It was unopened. The name on the return address caught her attention. It was from Michael Shetler of Sugarcreek, Ohio.

Chapter Four

"Why didn't you tell me that you repair watches?"

Michael looked up from Jesse's table saw. Bethany stood in the workshop's doorway he had left open to take advantage of the unusually warm afternoon. She stood with her hands on her hips and a scowl on her pretty face.

The mutt, lying in the rectangle of sunlight, had already alerted him that someone was coming with a soft woof. She shot outside and around the corner of the building. The sight of Bethany made Michael want to smile. She was every bit as appealing as he remembered, even with a slight frown marring her face.

He pushed away his interest. Jesse had filled in a lot of details about the family last night. Bethany was trying to keep her family together. Jesse said without her grandfather and her brother to work the farm she could lose it. A handsome woman in need of help was trouble and Michael had enough trouble. He positioned the two-by-four length of pine board and made the cut. As the saw blade quit spinning he took the board and added it to the stack on his right. He kept his face carefully blank when he met her gaze. "I didn't think it would make a difference."

"It certainly would have."

"How so? Your grandfather is gone. You said you couldn't afford to hire help."

"You neglected to tell me you had sent the first and last months' rent on the cabin."

He picked up another board and settled it in the slot he had created for the correct length so he didn't have to measure and mark each piece of wood. Bishop Schultz used a diesel generator to supply electricity inside his carpentry shop. The smell of fresh sawdust mixed with diesel fumes that drifted through the open door. Michael squeezed the trigger on the saw and lowered the blade. It sliced through the pine board in two seconds, spewing more sawdust on the growing pile beneath the table.

He tossed the cut wood on the stack and reached for another two-by-four. Bethany crossed the room and took hold of the board before he could position it. "Why didn't you tell me you had already paid the rent?"

"I figured you would mention it if you knew about it. Since you didn't say anything and you already had a crisis to deal with, I thought it could wait for a better time."

"That was very considerate of you. A better time is right now. My grandfather never deposited your check. In fact, he never read your last letter. I only found it yesterday evening."

She let go of his board and reached into a small bag she carried over her arm. "I have the check here. I've been unable to bring myself to clean out his workshop.

For that reason, his agreement with you went undiscovered." She held out the check. He didn't take it.

"Do you know the rest of your grandfather's offer?" He kept his gaze averted.

"Your letter said you agreed to work with him for six months. Was there more?"

"If he considered me skillful enough after that time he would make me a fifty-fifty partner in the business." He looked at her. "I can show you his offer in writing if you want to see it."

"There's no need. I believe you. Are you still willing to do that?"

"How can I be a partner now that he is gone?"

"The business belongs to me but I can't repair watches, so it is worthless except for his tools. I had planned to sell them unless Ivan showed an interest in learning the trade."

"Has he?"

"Not yet."

"How is the boy?" he asked softly.

A wry smile lifted the corner of her mouth. "I wish I knew. Right now he seems mad at the world."

"Boys grow up. He'll come around."

"I pray you are right. I have a proposition for you, Mr. Shetler."

"Call me Michael."

She smiled and nodded once. "Michael. It's similar to the one my grandfather offered you. Work for me for six months. You keep two-thirds of everything you earn during that time. I will keep one-third as rent on the shop, for the use of Grandfather's client list and his tools. If at the end of that time I am satisfied with your skill I will sell you the business or we can continue as partners."

"Who is to decide if my skills are adequate?"

"My grandfather did the majority of his work for a man named George Meyers in Philadelphia. He owns a jewelry shop and watch repair business. If Mr. Meyers is satisfied with the quality of work you do, then that is all the assurance I need."

Michael smiled inwardly. One part of the puzzle had finally been solved. George had started this whole thing. It was certainly like George, to go out of his way for someone who didn't deserve the kindness. Michael wondered how much, if anything, George had shared about his condition with Bethany's grandfather. "I wondered how your grandfather got my name. Now I know."

"I'm afraid I don't follow you."

"I used to work for George Meyers." Up until the night he had let two armed criminals into the business George owned.

"Why did you quit? Is that when you got hurt?"

His heart started pounding like a hammer inside his chest as the onset of a panic attack began. In another minute he would be on the ground gasping for air. He wasn't about to recount the horrors he saw that night to Bethany. He had to get outside. "I don't like to talk about it."

He grabbed an armful of cut wood and pushed past Bethany. "Jesse is going to wonder what's keeping me."

She followed him outside. "I'm sorry if it seemed that I was prying. If you don't want to work for me, I understand, but the cabin is still yours for two months."

"I'll think about the job, but I'll take the cabin." He

kept walking. It wasn't that he wanted to be rude but he needed her to leave. His anxiety was rising rapidly.

"The cabin is yours whenever you want."

The yellow dog came around the side of the building and launched herself at him. He sidestepped to keep from being hit with her muddy paws. One of the boards slid out of his arms. "Down."

She dropped to her belly and barked once, then rolled over, inviting him to scratch her muddy stomach.

"I see you still have your friend," Bethany said, humor bubbling beneath her words.

He looked from her to the dog. "I don't have anything to feed you, mutt, unless you eat two-by-fours."

The dog jumped to her feet, picked up the board he had dropped and took off with it in her mouth.

"Hey, bring that back!"

The dog made a sweeping turn and raced back, splashing through puddles of melted snow. She came to a stop and sat in front of him, holding the four-foot length of wood like a prized bone.

"Goot hund." He reached for the board but the dog took off before he touched it. She made a wild run between the sheds lined up at the edge of the property where the snow was still deep.

Bethany burst out laughing. "Good dog, indeed."

He liked the sound of her laughter. The heaviness in his chest dissipated and he grinned. "It seems her previous owner didn't spend much time training her."

"I can see that. She is friendlier since she's had a few meals. She seems to have a lot of puppy in her yet. In a way she reminds me of my brother."

"How so?"

"A lot of potential, but very little focus."

"I'd like to meet this kid."

"I'm sure you will since you'll be living just out our back door."

He frowned. "The cabin is close to your house?"

"Fifty yards, maybe less."

"I assumed it was more secluded."

"It is set back in the woods. We won't bother you if that's what you are worried about."

"I like my privacy." He couldn't very well explain he was worried she'd hear him yelling in the middle of the night.

The dog came trotting back and sat down between them, still holding her trophy. Michael bent to grab the board as Bethany did the same. They smacked heads. His hat flipped off and landed in the snow. The dog dropped the wood, snatched up the hat and took off with it.

Michael held his head and glanced at Bethany. "Are you okay?"

Bethany rubbed her smarting forehead. Maybe it was a sign that she needed some sense knocked into her. She had come to give Michael his money back and had ended up offering him a job instead. The thump on her skull had come too late. "I'm fine."

"Are you sure? Do you want some ice?"

"*Nee*, it won't leave a mark. Will it?" She pulled her hand away.

He bent closer. "I think you're going to have a bump."

"Great."

"I am sorry." He looked down at the dog, now standing a few feet away, still holding his hat. "See what you did to Bethany."

The dog whined and lay down, the picture of dejection. Bethany crouched and offered her hand to the animal. "Don't scold the poor thing. It wasn't her fault. Are you going to keep her?"

"I can't walk away and leave her to fend for herself. Besides, her goofy behavior leaves me smiling more often than not. *Ja*, I will keep her. She seems to have decided she belongs with me."

Bethany knew she should leave but found herself reluctant to go. There was something intriguing about the man. One minute they were discussing his job and the next second he went pale as a sheet and couldn't get away from her fast enough. A few minutes later they were both laughing at the antics of a stray dog. The truth was she liked him. A lot. But she had to find a way to keep her family together. She couldn't allow a distraction to interfere with that.

She took the hat from the dog and handed it to Michael. "I should get going."

"Right." He nodded but didn't move.

She took a few steps toward her buggy but something made her turn around. He was still watching her. "Michael, do you play chess?"

"I enjoy the game. Why?"

"Would you do me a favor?"

"If I can."

"I have a friend of my grandfather coming to supper on Sunday evening. He and Daadi used to play chess every week. I know he misses Daadi and their games. I don't play. If you aren't doing anything, would you like to join us for supper and give Pastor Frank a game or two?"

Hadn't she just decided she didn't need a distraction?

Maybe he would say no. "Don't feel obligated just because I asked."

"I need to get moved in. I'm not sure I'll find the time."

"You have to eat."

"Another time maybe."

"Of course." She turned away, more disappointed than she cared to admit.

"Bethany?"

"Ja?" She spun around hopefully.

"I appreciate the job offer. I'll give it some serious thought. Do I get the key to the cabin from you?"

"It isn't locked. You'll find the key hanging on a nail just inside the door. When you come to my place you'll see a wooded ridge behind the house. The cabin is up there. Just follow the lane. Do you have transportation? I can send Ivan to pick you up."

"Jesse has offered me the loan of a pony and cart until I can send for my horses. Is there someone locally who sells buggies?"

"There's a carriage maker in Unity. I've heard he is reasonable."

"I'll look into it."

"If you change your mind about having supper with us tomorrow night, just show up. There will be plenty to eat."

"Are you a *goot* cook?"

She grinned. "Do you expect a modest Amish woman to brag on herself?"

"I expect a modest Amish woman to tell the truth."

She bobbed her head once. "I could tell you that I'm a very good cook, but I suggest you come to supper and decide for yourself."

After stepping up into her buggy, she looked back and saw he was still watching her. A tingle of pleasure at his interest lifted her spirits. Just as quickly, she dismissed her feeling as foolishness. Her mother's unhappy life spent loving the wrong kind of man had driven home to Bethany just how cruel romantic love could be. She was determined not to suffer the same way. If she married it would be a beneficial arrangement based on sound judgment. Not love. She waved and then drove away. Would Michael come or wouldn't he? She would have to wait an entire day to find out.

Jesse walked past Michael with a load of boards in his arms. "Have you decided to hang on to her or are you going to ignore her and hope she goes away?"

Michael scowled at him. "What does that mean?"

Jesse stopped and gave Michael a funny look. "I was just wondering if you are planning to keep the dog. What did you think I meant?"

Relieved that he wasn't referring to Bethany, Michael decided to share the joke. "Bethany Martin was just here."

Jesse chuckled. "I wouldn't tell a fella to ignore Bethany and hope she goes away, but the same can't be said for some other single women in this community."

Although Jesse hadn't made Bethany's wish list when she had been talking to the cow about walking out with someone, Michael liked the man and thought he would make a decent husband. "Do you have your eye on one maid in particular?"

"Me? *Nee*, I'm not ready to get into harness with any female. They talk too much, and they expect you to talk back to them. I don't have that much to say. I can't imagine a lifetime of staring at a woman who is waiting for me to utter something interesting. If you are looking to go courting, Bethany Martin is a fine woman. You wouldn't be stepping on anyone's toes."

"I'm not interested in courting, but I did wonder why she isn't already married."

"Her grandfather told me that she wants to get her brother and sister raised before she looks to start another family."

"Did you know Elijah well?"

"He was a fine friend. Everyone loved him. He was always laughing, quick with a joke, always ready to lend a helping hand. It didn't matter if you were Amish or not. There are only twenty adult members in this church, six *youngees* and five *kinder*. We know each other well."

Youngees were unmarried teens in their running around time or *rumspringa*. The potential marriage pool in the community was small indeed. Bethany would have to look for a marriage partner farther afield if Jesse or Jedidiah didn't work out.

Michael couldn't seem to curb his curiosity about her and her family. "What's the story with her brother?"

Jesse was silent for a long moment. "I'm not one to speak ill of another."

"I'm sorry. I wasn't looking for gossip. I can form my own opinion of the family. You don't have to say anything."

"It's not that. We are newcomers to this area. Bethany and her family have been here the longest. Two years now. I came sixteen months ago. Jedidiah and the other families came after I did. We get along with the *Englisch* and for the most part they get along with us.

There are a few exceptions. People who would like to see us leave. When something goes wrong, those few are quick to point to the Amish and say it must be our fault. Ivan has been a mischief maker for as long as I've known him, but I don't believe all that is said against him these days."

"You think he is getting blamed for what someone else is doing?"

Jesse stared into the distance for a long minute, and then he looked Michael in the eye. "I think he makes an easy target."

Michael considered Jesse's carefully worded reply. "What does the bishop think?"

"He hasn't confided in me. I should get back to work. I don't want him to think I slack off when he's gone. Oh, and I meant to tell you I've got some extra nylon webbing if you want to fashion a collar for your mutt. What did Bethany want, anyway?"

Michael followed Jesse to the skeleton of the shed he was putting up. "She discovered her grandfather did rent a cabin to me. She found my rent check last night. She came to give me a choice of getting my money back or staying on the property."

"So, am I losing you as a roommate already?"

"You are. I'll leave tomorrow."

"*Goot.* That makes you the best kind of houseguest."

Michael glanced his way. "What kind is that?"

"One who leaves before he has worn out his welcome." Jesse grinned and clapped Michael on the back then pulled his hammer from his tool belt and went to work.

Michael relaxed. He laid down the boards he'd cut and walked back to the workshop. He thought getting a few answers about Bethany would appease his curiosity but he had been mistaken. It seemed it wasn't so easy to put her out of his mind.

Maybe he'd made a mistake telling her he still wanted to rent the cabin. How was he going to stop thinking about her if he lived fifty yards from her home? If he took the job she was going to be his boss.

He would have to discourage her from visiting the workshop. He worked best alone and he liked it that way. That was the reason he had come to Maine. She would just have to learn to accept it.

Bethany opened the oven to check her peach pie and decided it was done. The crust was golden brown and the juices were bubbling up between the lattice strips. She pulled it out and placed it on the cooling rack at the end of the counter. She then lifted the lid on the pot of chili and sniffed the mouthwatering aroma. Using a spoon, she scooped up a sample and blew on it before tasting it. The deep, rich, spicy flavor was delicious but it needed a touch more salt. After adding two shakes, she stirred the pot and replaced the lid. All she needed now was the rest of her company.

Would Michael come? She hoped he would.

"It smells *wunderbar*," Gemma said as she set the plates on the table.

"Let's hope it tastes as good as it smells." Bethany walked to the window that overlooked the path up to the cabin. She had invited Gemma to join them as a defense against her attraction to Michael. Gemma's light-hearted and flirty ways were sure to liven the evening and keep Michael entertained.

"Any sign of him?"

Bethany dropped the window shade. "Any sign of who?"

"The person you're hoping to see. You realize you've been to that window ten times in the last thirty minutes. I can't imagine that you are this anxious to catch sight of Pastor Frank. Therefore, it must be someone else. I'm going to take a wild guess and say it is a man. A newcomer. Someone who walks with a cane." She raised one eyebrow at Bethany. "Am I close?"

"If you must know, I did invite Michael Shetler. He plays chess and I know that Pastor Frank misses the games he used to have with Elijah."

"That was very thoughtful of you. Why am I here? I don't play chess."

"You're here because I didn't want it to look like I had invited Michael for personal reasons. You know what I mean."

"You didn't want him to think you were angling for a return date? Or were you hoping I would catch his interest?"

"Both. When he sees I invited a single woman from our community to join us, he won't think I have designs on him myself."

A sly grin curved Gemma's lips. "What if this backfires and he *does* like me better?"

"Then I will be happy for both of you and you can name your first daughter after me."

Gemma laughed and returned to setting the table. Bethany resisted the urge to look out the window again. It was possible Michael had made his way to the cabin without her seeing him, but she hoped he would at least stop by and let her know he had taken possession.

The rumble of a car announced the arrival of Pastor

Frank. Bethany went to the front door to greet him and saw Michael turning in from the highway in a small cart pulled by a black-and-white pony. To her chagrin, he simply waved and went past the house on the track that led to the cabin. She tried not to let her disappointment show. She stepped aside to allow Frank to enter the house and closed the door against the chilly afternoon. It was clear Michael wasn't eager to see her again.

After seeing Bethany's smile fade when he drove past her home, Michael almost changed his mind and went back. Almost. His best course of action was to see as little of her as possible. Out of sight, out of mind. He hoped. While he found her attractive, he couldn't offer her anything but a business partnership. To encourage anything else would be grossly unfair.

The cabin he had rented was set back in a small grove of trees up the hillside behind her place. As she had promised, the road up to it was well marked and had been plowed recently.

A small weathered barn came with the cabin and he stopped Jesse's pony beside it. A quick tour proved it would be enough for his two buggy horses and his buggy when he got one. The only drawback to the property was the steep hillside behind the barn. With his bum leg he'd never be able to get down to the bottom and lead his horses back up when he turned them out to pasture in the summer. He unharnessed the pony and led him inside to a roomy stall. Jesse had supplied Michael with enough hay and horse chow to last him a week.

He moved the horse feed inside and left the hay in the back of the small wagon. He was thankful to see a water pump stood near the barn. It would make keeping the animals watered easier even in the winter.

As he was heading to the cabin with his duffel bag over his shoulder, he saw the dog come trotting up the road. She had followed him from town as he'd hoped she would. He had tried to coax her into the cart, but she'd refused to have anything to do with it even after he lifted her into the bed. "You're a good girl. I'm glad to see you made it."

She ignored him and went to explore in the barn. Michael put his bag down on the porch and tried to open the door. It was locked. He was sure Bethany had told him it would be unlocked. He tried again to make sure the door wasn't just stuck but it wasn't.

He made his way to the back door with difficulty. The snow was deep enough in places to leave him unsure of his footing. If not for his cane and the wall of the cabin, he would have fallen several times. After all his struggles he found the back door was locked, as well. He could see that it had been opened recently by the arch of snow that had been pushed aside. A trail of footprints led from the stoop up the hill into woods. They were small footprints, those of a woman or a child.

Making his way back to the front porch was easier. The dog was sitting by the door waiting for him. He looked at the house below him on the hillside. It seemed he would have to face Bethany after all to get the key. He made his way down the road and knocked on her front door.

Chapter Five

The moment Bethany opened her door Michael knew he was in trouble. Her bright smile and the eagerness in her eyes pushed at the mental wall he had erected to keep people from getting too close.

He didn't want to shut her out. He wanted to be worthy of the friendliness she seemed so willing to share.

"You have decided to join us, after all. Come in, Michael. Please have a seat." She stepped aside and gestured for him to enter.

He shook his head. "I'm not here to eat."

Disappointment replaced the eagerness in her eyes. "Oh? What can I do for you, then?"

She moved back and he stepped inside. The dog squeezed in to stay at his side. Bethany frowned slightly but didn't say anything.

The house was typical of the Amish houses he'd seen all his life. From the entryway a door to his right led directly into the kitchen. Beautiful pine cabinets lined the walls. The floor was covered with a checkerboard pattern of black-and-white linoleum. The windows had simple white pull-down shades instead of curtains. The delicious aromas of Bethany's home-cooked meal filled the air. His stomach growled.

He resisted the urge to stay and make her smile again. "The cabin is locked. I can't get in."

Bethany cocked her head slightly. "Are you sure? Maybe the door is just stuck."

"I'm sure. The back door is locked, too."

"Why does he need in the cabin?" Ivan demanded, scowling at Michael.

Bethany gave her brother a sharp look. "Michael is going to be living there. Daadi rented the place to him. Do you know anything about the cabin being locked?"

"I don't know why you're asking me," Ivan snapped. "Every time something goes wrong I get blamed." He pushed to his feet and rushed out of the room.

Color blossomed in Bethany's cheeks as she glanced at her guests. "I apologize for Ivan's behavior. I thought he was doing better. Jenny, did you lock the cabin?"

Jenny shook her head, making the ribbons of her *kapp* dance on her shoulders. "I play there sometimes with Ivan and Jeffrey, but I didn't lock the door."

Bethany met Michael's gaze but quickly looked away. "I believe there is a spare key in Grandfather's bedroom. If you'll excuse me, I'll go find it. It may take me a moment or two. I'm not sure where Daadi kept it."

The dog suddenly left Michael's side. He made a grab for her and missed. "Mutt, get back here."

She ignored him and went to investigate the new people in the room. She gave the young Amish woman and the *Englisch* fellow at the table a brief sniff, then rounded the far end. Jenny had her hands out. The dog settled her head in Jenny's lap and looked up with soulful adoring eyes as the girl scratched her behind her ears.

"What a beautiful dog." Jenny stroked her soft fur. "I think she likes me."

Michael walked over and took hold of a length of black nylon webbing Jesse had fashioned into a make-shift collar. "I'm afraid she hasn't learned any manners."

"What's her name?" Jenny asked.

"Mutt." He still wasn't sure he would keep her, although she seemed to have attached herself to him. Maybe she would like Jenny better and stay here.

The slender man in *Englisch* clothing rose to his feet. "Mutt is not much of a name but it's better than Cat. I'm Pastor Frank Pearson. You can call me Frank." He swept a hand toward the young Amish woman seated across from him. "This is Bethany's friend Gemma Lapp and you must be Michael Shetler."

The pastor held out his hand. Meeting new people made Michael uneasy. He rubbed his sweaty palm on his pant leg before taking the man's hand in a firm grip. "I take it you are the chess player."

Frank's expression brightened. "I am. Do you play?"

"Now and again."

"We'll have to arrange a match someday. I'm sorry you didn't get to meet Elijah. He was a true master of the game. He told me quite a bit about you."

Michael grew cold. "Is that so? I don't know what he could have told you. We never met."

The pastor's expression didn't change. "He said you came highly recommended by an old friend of his. I believe it was George Meyers and that you grew up near Sugarcreek in Ohio. My grandmother was from the Sugarcreek area, but she left many years ago. Please, have a seat."

It had been a long day and Michael just wanted to

get settled in a place of his own. He accepted the invitation mainly because his leg was aching.

"Would you like some *kaffi*?" Gemma asked.

He nodded. She rose and brought him a cup and saucer with three pale yellow cookies on the plate. "These are lemon crinkles. My specialty. I hope you like them."

"Danki." The coffee was black and bracing. The cookies were light, tart and delicious.

"You can't call her Mutt," Jenny said from the other end of the table.

"Why don't you name her?" Gemma suggested.

Jenny peered into the dog's eyes. "I'm going to call you Sadie Sue. Do you like that name?"

The dog barked once and everyone laughed.

"That settles it," Michael said. "She is now and forever Sadie Sue."

"How are the cookies?" Gemma gave Michael a smile every bit as sweet as the pastry.

"They're delicious. They remind me of the ones my grandmother used to make." He prayed Bethany would hurry up before he was subjected to more questions. She came back in the room a few seconds later.

"Found it." She held the key aloft.

Michael grimaced as he stood and leaned heavily on the table. He had been sitting just long enough for his leg to stiffen. When the sharp pain subsided he picked up his cane.

"Are you all right?" Bethany asked, reaching a hand toward him.

Her sympathy irritated him. He hated when people treated him as if they expected him to topple over at any second. "I'm fine."

"How were you injured?" Gemma asked softly.

His throat tightened. He couldn't draw a full breath. The walls of the house started to close in. He needed to get outside. "I've got to get going."

He saw the confusion in Bethany's eyes, but nothing mattered except getting enough air. He pushed past her and went out the door. On the porch he stopped to scan the yard and outbuildings for signs of danger. Was someone lurking in the woods beyond the road? He took a step to the side and backed up to the wall of the house so that no one could get behind him. Sadie followed him out and sat at his side, nuzzling his hand. He stroked her head.

After a few deep breaths of the cold air, Michael's panic receded. It was okay. There wasn't any danger. He took one step away from the safety of Bethany's house and then another, glad to escape without having her watch him fall apart.

Gemma propped her elbow on the table with her chin in her hand. "Did that seem odd to anyone else?"

Bethany had to admit Gemma was right. "He acted like he couldn't get out of here fast enough."

"I hope it wasn't my cookies." Gemma sat back and folded her arms across her chest.

Pastor Frank took a sip of his coffee. "I don't think it was anything we said or did. Michael has been through a rough time."

Bethany turned to Frank. "What do you know about him?"

"Only a few things that your grandfather shared with me. I don't feel it's my place to repeat what was said."

Gemma arched one eyebrow. "Okay, now you've made me curious."

Frank smiled but he shook his head. "Many people tell me things in confidence. I take that responsibility seriously. I think it's enough to say that Michael came to New Covenant seeking privacy and a chance to heal in body and mind."

"Is there anything we can do for him?" Bethany asked.

"We can invite him to our Thanksgiving dinner," Gemma suggested. "He shouldn't spend the holiday alone."

Pastor Frank nodded. "Good idea. Treat him like you would anyone else. Be friendly, be kind, be compassionate, don't pry. I suspect he will discover soon enough if he truly belongs here."

Gemma rolled her eyes. "One winter was enough to convince me I didn't belong here. I don't mind snow, but when it gets so deep you can't see the cows standing out in it, that's too much snow."

Bethany chuckled. "And yet here you are facing another winter in northern Maine."

"I can't. What would you do without me?"

"I honestly don't know," Bethany admitted. Gemma was a dear friend and she would miss her terribly if she ever left New Covenant.

"Gemma, will you serve the peach pie and ice cream for me? I must speak with Ivan. His behavior tonight was not acceptable." Bethany braced herself for a verbal battle with Ivan as she climbed the stairs to his bedroom. She knocked softly. He didn't answer.

She opened the door and discovered he wasn't in his room. Her conversation with him would have to wait but it would take place. He wasn't getting out of it this easily. She checked the other rooms and the attic, knowing he sometimes liked to hide in those places, but she didn't find him.

When Bethany came downstairs she joined the others and enjoyed a slice of pie and ice cream. When everyone was finished, Gemma began clearing the table.

Pastor Frank patted his stomach. "That was a very good meal. Invite me more often, Bethany."

She summoned a smile. "Come anytime. I'll feed you."

He laughed as he rose and got ready to leave. She handed him his gloves after he finished buttoning his coat. "I'm glad you came tonight, Frank. We have missed your company."

"I'm glad I came, too. What did Ivan have to say for himself?"

She clasped her hands together. "He wasn't in his room. He must have slipped out the back door. What am I going to do with him?"

"He's a troubled boy. All you can do is show him you care about him, give him the opportunity to confide in you and pray he finds the courage to tell you what's bothering him."

"I know he doesn't want to be sent to live with our uncle. I had hoped learning that he only has until Christmas to mend his ways would be incentive enough."

"Unfortunately, it may only add to the pressure he's under."

"Will you talk to him?"

"As a family friend or in my official capacity as a psychologist? Would your bishop approve of that?"

Bethany squeezed her fingers together tightly. She wasn't sure but she was willing to risk more of the bishop's disapproval. "I think he would allow it but I'm asking as a friend."

"Then I will be happy to see Ivan. Bring him by my home any day after school this week. If he'll come."

"I will do that."

He started out the door but stopped and looked back. "One more thing. Will you give a message to Michael Shetler for me?"

"Of course."

"Tell him my door is always open if he needs someone to talk to. That's all. Good night."

"I'll tell him. Good night, Frank." Bethany closed the door behind him. What did Frank know about Michael's past that he felt he couldn't share with her?

Michael unlocked the front door of the cabin and stepped inside. Instantly he knew someone had been there before him. The back door was open a crack. He was sure it had been locked earlier. He crossed the room and closed the door, uneasy at the thought of someone having access. His anxiety level climbed as he thought about trying to sleep in an unsecured place. He thanked God for the dog at his side. A dead bolt and new locks for the doors were a must first thing in the morning.

The dog stayed by his side as he searched the building. Her calm attitude reassured him that the visitor was long gone. The place was neat and cozy. The cabin was a single room with a tiny kitchen in one corner. A bump out beyond the kitchen contained a modern bathroom with a shower and a propane hot water heater. Two big windows on the south wall let in plenty of evening light. A metal bed frame in the far corner held a bare mattress with a sleeping bag on it. A glance around the room gave him the impression that someone visited often. There were empty food wrappers and several magazines beside the fireplace. Perhaps Ivan and Jenny played here. He walked back to pick up his bag near the front door.

Glass shattered, startling him. Michael saw two boys through the broken window before his leg gave out and he hit the floor. Instantly, he was back in the jewelry store, in the middle of the robbery. He had to get out. He crawled toward the door and pulled it open, expecting another bullet. Someone was screaming. Sirens grew closer. Red lights flashed on the ceiling overhead. The smell of gunpowder choked him.

A dog started barking. There hadn't been a dog there that night. He tried to concentrate on the sound. The dog was real. The rest was a nightmare, so realistic he could hear the robbers' voices, he could see their mask-covered faces, he felt the impact of the bullet and the burning pain in his leg. He kept crawling to get away from them.

"Mister, are you okay?"

The new voice, like the barking dog, wasn't a part of the past. Michael struggled to focus on it. Bethany's brother was kneeling beside him. He didn't want anybody to see him like this. "Go away."

"I'm going to go get help." The boy jumped to his feet and ran toward the house down the hill. Michael crawled after Ivan but couldn't stop him.

Not Bethany. Don't bring Bethany.

It was his last thought before the nightmare sucked him back into the past and made him relive the unbearable. He screamed in pain as a bullet shattered his thigh.

He wept as his coworkers were murdered one by one. The wail of sirens grew louder. He knew he was next.

"Michael, can you hear me?"

Another voice not from the past.

"Don't shoot," Michael begged, but the gunshots came again and again. He jerked each time.

"Can you tell me what's wrong? Are you hurt?" The different voice was insistent. Michael tried to hold on to it. He reached out his hand. Someone took hold of it.

"It's Pastor Frank Pearson. We just met. What's wrong, Michael?"

"He's killing them. He's killing them all. Don't shoot."

"Michael, I want you to listen to me. You're safe. No one is shooting. You're in Bethany's cabin in Maine. No one can hurt you here. You're safe. Michael, you're safe."

"I'm in Maine." Harsh panting filled his ears. He knew he was making that sound but he couldn't stop.

"I want you to listen to my voice. No one is hurting you."

Michael turned his head and tried to focus on the man kneeling beside him. He wanted out of this nightmare, but he didn't know how. "Help."

"I'm here to help you. I think you are having a flashback to something bad that happened before. It's not happening now. It's all in the past. Do you understand? You are safe. No one will hurt you."

Michael had no idea how long he lay on the snowy ground listening to Pastor Frank's voice, but slowly the cold air began penetrating the nightmare. The cold was now. The cold was the present. He took a deep breath and then another. He was looking up at darkening sky. There was a single white cloud drifting overhead. It looked like a catcher's mitt. He heard soft whining.

Turning his head slowly, he focused on Sadie Sue. She lay beside him with her head on his thigh.

Michael's pounding heart began to slow. He laid a hand on her head. *"Goot hund."*

"Are you feeling better?" Pastor Frank was still kneeling at Michael's side.

Embarrassed that anyone had seen him like this, Michael struggled to sit up. "I'm fine."

"I'm glad to hear that. If you would like to tell me about what happened, I will be happy to listen."

"I don't want to talk about it." Michael struggled to get up. Pastor Frank gave him a hand and helped him to his feet.

"That's perfectly understandable."

Michael looked around. "Where is my cane?"

Sadie sat at his side, her wagging tail sweeping the snow from his doorstep. She leaned against him as he patted her head.

Pastor Frank located Michael's cane inside the door and handed it to him. He smiled at the dog. "The Lord provides comfort for us in many amazing ways."

Michael wanted nothing more than to retreat inside the cabin and lock the door. "Thanks for the help. I was fortunate I fell at your feet."

"Actually, you didn't. You fell at Ivan's feet. I had just finished having supper with Gemma and Bethany. I was getting in my van when Ivan raced up and said you needed help."

Ivan was standing a few yards away from them. His pale face and wide eyes revealed how frightened he was. Michael rubbed his hands together to warm them. "I'm sorry I scared you, Ivan."

"You may have done more good than harm," Frank

said softly and beckoned Ivan closer. "He insists he was the one who threw a rock through your window, but I have my doubts."

"I saw two figures," Michael said.

Ivan approached slowly. "I thought you had been hit in the head or something. I thought you were dying."

Michael managed a half smile. "As you can see, I'm not."

"Why did you break the window?" Frank asked.

Ivan stared at the ground and shifted from one foot to the other. "I don't know."

"I think you do," Frank said.

"Jeffrey and I like to hang out here. We were mad that we couldn't use it as a meeting place anymore. I guess we thought you might not stay if the window was broken. We didn't mean to hurt you."

"Actions have consequences," Frank said sternly. "Your wrath served no good purpose. Before you act in anger again, you must think about this day."

"I will. Are you going to tell Bethany about this?"

"No," Michael said emphatically.

Frank placed a hand on Ivan's shoulder. "You'd better go home. Your sister was looking for you."

"To scold me again, right?"

"To talk to you about what's really bothering you. Your sister loves you. You know that."

"Sure, that's why she's sending me away." The boy turned and walked toward the house with lagging steps.

"He's got a chip on his shoulder," Michael said.

"He does, but right now I'm more concerned about you."

Michael grew uncomfortable under Frank's intense scrutiny. "I told you I'm fine."

"How often do you have these flashbacks?"

"I don't know what you're talking about."

"Yes, you do. Why deny it? What's important is that I know exactly what you are going through. I used to be in your shoes. I dealt with PTSD for three years before my symptoms improved. I haven't had a flashback for five years now."

"How?"

"How did I get better? Time and therapy. Why don't we step inside out of the cold?"

Michael limped into the cabin. The dog followed him in and went to lie in front of the fireplace.

"I don't have much in the way of furniture yet. I'm having some stuff shipped from home." There was an overstuffed green leather chair by the fireplace and two straight-backed chairs that came with the cabin. Michael lowered himself into the upholstered chair and glanced at Frank. "What caused your PTSD?"

Frank turned one of the wooden chairs around and straddled it. "I served in the military right out of high school. I saw some brutal fighting and horrible situations at a very young age. I married while I was in the service. I thought I was tough. I thought I was okay but a few months after I got home I started having episodes where I relived the most frightening events I went through. I started having nightmares, panic attacks. I became moody, bitter and depressed. My wife didn't know how to deal with me, and we divorced. Thankfully a fellow veteran recognized what was wrong with me and got me help."

"You stopped having them?" Michael wanted desperately to believe it was possible.

"In time they went away. I found God and He changed

my life. I wanted to do His work, but I also wanted to use modern medicine to help people suffering with mental health issues. I went back to school to become a psychologist and counselor, and then I became a minister. Michael, what triggered your episode today? Do you know?"

Michael shook his head. "It just came out of the blue."

"It may seem that way but there is often a trigger associated with an episode. It can be a sensation that recalls the trauma, such as pain. Strong emotions, feeling helpless, trapped or out of control can bring on a flashback or panic attack. A trigger can be as simple as a smell, a phrase, a sound."

Michael turned to look at the window. "The glass breaking. That's what triggered it today." One of the thieves had broken the glass jewelry case and triggered the alarm.

Michael gazed at Frank. "You said I can get over this."

"Recovery is a process. It takes time and there are often setbacks. It's important to stay positive, but yes, the majority of people with PTSD recover in time. For a few it is a lifelong battle. Therapy can help enormously. Talking about your trauma in a safe environment is a way to lessen the hold it has on you. How often do you have these flashbacks?"

"Three or four times a week. Sometimes every day. This is the first one since I arrived here. That was three days ago."

"And how long do they last?"

"It feels like an eternity but maybe ten minutes." Michael rubbed his thigh. It always ached worse after an episode.

Frank nodded. "And how long does it take for you to recover from one?"

"Twenty minutes or so. Will you have to tell someone about what happened today?"

"I don't but I wish you would let me help. I have a survivors' support group that meets every other week at my church. I invite you to check it out. You aren't the only one dealing with a traumatic past."

Michael shook his head. "I'd rather no one knows about this."

Especially Bethany. It shouldn't matter so much what she thought but it did matter.

Pastor Frank didn't argue. "As you wish. Please let me know if I can be of help in any way. Don't get up. I'll see myself out. I've got some plywood to cover the window. I'll be back with it in half an hour."

"I appreciate that. And for all your help earlier."

After Frank left, Michael set about building a fire in the fireplace. He was surprised that the ashes were still warm. Ivan or his friend had recently had a blaze going here. When Michael had a decent fire burning to drive off the chill, he sat down to wait for Pastor Frank's return. It wasn't long before there was a knock at the door. He got up to answer it.

Ivan stood on his doorstep looking dejected. Bethany stood behind him with her hand clamped on his shoulder.

Michael tried to disguise his rising panic. What had the boy told her?

Chapter Six

Michael didn't look happy to see her. Why should he be?

Bethany kept her chin up in spite of the mortification that weighted her down. Her brother was bent on making it harder for him to remain with her. He should be improving his behavior but he wasn't. Instead he had shown that she couldn't keep him in line. Once again she was forced to apologize for his actions.

She took a deep breath. "Good evening, Michael. I understand that Ivan broke one of the windows here. I'm truly sorry. I will have it replaced as soon as possible. In the meantime, my brother has something he wants to say to you."

"I'm sorry," Ivan mumbled.

It wasn't much of an apology, but she let it pass. "He also told me you were hurt."

"I was startled. I tripped and fell but I wasn't hurt. As you can see."

She couldn't read Michael's reaction. His face was blank. How upset was he? She wanted this awkward episode over as quickly as possible.

"I'm sure that you and I can find a way for Ivan to make amends and decide on a punishment."

"That won't be necessary."

Her brother wasn't getting off the hook so easily this time. "I insist. He needs to take responsibility for what he has done."

"I agree, but Ivan and I will work out the details. He is old enough to decide what's appropriate."

She pressed a hand to her chest. "As the adult in the family, I feel I should have a say in this." Surely he wasn't going to disregard her position as head of the family?

"Ivan and I can reach an agreement that's fair."

Her brother peered up at her. "I am old enough."

Michael nodded and stepped back. "Come in, Ivan, and we will discuss this. I'll send him home after we get the window boarded up. The pastor has gone to get some plywood."

Ivan went inside the cabin and Michael closed the door, leaving Bethany standing on the porch feeling foolish as well as incompetent.

She stomped back to the house but she couldn't stop thinking about Michael's high-handed attitude. *She* was responsible for Ivan. *She* should be a part of any discussion that involved her brother, not dismissed by some stranger as if she were a child.

Inside the house she went to the linen closet and pulled out sheets, pillows and several quilts, knowing there weren't any in the cabin. With her excuse for returning in hand, she headed out of the house. Michael Shetler had a thing or two to learn about dealing with her.

Ivan looked nervous but ready to accept his punishment. Michael walked over to the chair and sat down.

The dog moved to sit beside his knee and leaned against his leg. He waited for the boy to speak first.

Ivan stuffed his hands in his pant pockets. "I'm sorry about the broken window."

"It can be fixed. What sort of punishment do you think you deserve?"

A flash of bitterness crossed Ivan's features. It was gone before Michael could be certain of what he'd seen. He leaned forward. "Why didn't Jeffrey stick around? Why didn't he stay to make sure I was okay? He has been staying here, hasn't he?"

"His dad gets mad real easy. Jeffrey sometimes hangs out here when he does. He took off tonight because he was afraid of getting in trouble at home."

Ivan took a seat beside the dog. "What happened to your leg?"

Michael wasn't prepared to have the tables turned on him but something told him that Ivan could be trusted with at least part of the truth. It might be what the boy needed to hear. "I will tell you on one condition. I don't want this mentioned to your sisters. Okay?"

The boy nodded.

"I was shot during a robbery."

"Are you joking?" Ivan's eyes grew wide.

"No joke."

"Wow. That's—I mean—you are the only person I know who has been shot."

"I would rather you didn't share the story with your sisters or your friends. It's not a pretty memory for me and I don't like pity."

"Sure. I can see you wouldn't want people talking about it. Does it still hurt?"

"All day every day but I was blessed. Other people died."

"People you knew?"

"They were my friends." Michael could feel his anxiety level rising as it did every time he thought about that night. Sadie Sue tried to climb in his lap and lick his face. He stroked her head and grew calmer.

Ivan shook his head in disbelief. "That's awful."

"The man who shot me, what kind of fellow do you think he was?"

"Evil."

"You would think so, but he wasn't much more than a scared boy pretending to be tough. Do you know what his first crime was?"

"What?"

"The first time he was arrested it was for stealing money from a neighbor. He was fourteen."

Ivan pinned his gaze to the floor. "Maybe he didn't have a choice."

Michael pushed Sadie Sue off his lap. She sat quietly beside his chair and watched him intently.

"We all have a choice. Your sister is mighty worried about you, Ivan."

The boy reached out and stroked the dog's head. "What's her name?"

Michael let him skirt around the issue of his sister's concern, knowing the boy would come back to it sooner or later. "I called her Mutt. Your sister, Jenny, named her Sadie Sue."

Ivan chuckled. "Sadie Sue. Only Jenny would think a dog needed a middle name."

"I like your little sister."

"Me, too."

"Bethany has treated me with kindness. She strikes me as a good woman."

"She treats me like I'm a little kid."

"Stop acting like one."

Ivan shot him a sour glare. "I don't. She should treat me like the man of the family."

Michael shrugged. "Being the man of the house isn't about how people treat you. The man of the family takes care of the people in his family. What have you done to take care of Bethany or Jenny lately? Think about it."

Ivan was silent for a few minutes. Finally, he looked up. "I don't have the money to pay for a new window, but I'll split wood for your fireplace for two weeks."

"A month."

"Okay, a month."

"And you are not going to skip school again, not even if Jeffrey asks you to do it."

Ivan tipped his head to the side. "How did you know Jeffrey asked me to skip with him?"

"Because Jeffrey took off tonight and left you to face the consequences alone. Something tells me he is at the bottom of some of your troubles."

Ivan scrambled to his feet. "He's my friend. You don't know anything about him."

"You're right. I don't and I'm sorry. I was wrong to say that."

Ivan relaxed his stance. "My grandfather used to say a wise man is the one who can admit when he is wrong."

"I wish I'd had the chance to meet your grandfather. I owe him a lot."

"You would have liked him."

"I'm sure of it. Ivan, you value your friend Jeffrey

and rightly so, but don't value your sisters less because of that friendship. Do you understand what I'm saying?"

"I think so."

"Catch up on your schoolwork and don't skip."

"Okay."

"You should get on home now. Remember, take care of your sisters. Don't expect them to treat you like you're the man of the family. Be that man. The same way your grandfather was. They will respect you for that."

"I'll try."

Sadie Sue rushed to the door and barked once. Michael got up and went to open it, expecting Frank. Bethany stood on his doorstep, her arms loaded with linens. "I knew you would need sheets and blankets."

"Come in." He glanced at Ivan. Would the boy keep his secret? He hoped his trust wasn't misplaced. "Ivan and I have come to an agreement."

Turning to Ivan, Michael held out his hand. "We have a deal, right?"

"Right." Ivan shook on it. "I have some homework to finish. See ya." The boy went out the door, leaving Michael and Bethany alone.

Suddenly alone with Michael, Bethany stepped past him, determined to show him she wasn't intimidated by his presence. "Where would you like these?"

"On the bed will be fine."

How silly of her. Of course he would want sheets and pillows there. She crossed the room and tossed her burden on the foot of the bed. "I see you have a sleeping bag. You came prepared to rough it."

"It's not mine. I think it belongs to Ivan's friend Jeffrey. Apparently he stays here sometimes when his father is upset with him."

"I wasn't aware of that. Was that the reason the doors were locked?"

"It would be a good guess. What do you know about the boy?"

"Not much. He's been friends with Ivan since we arrived. His family lives over the ridge about a half mile as the crow flies but farther by road. His father drives a delivery truck. I don't think the mother works." She crossed her arms as she faced him. "But I'm not here to talk about Jeffrey."

"You want me to know you are in charge of Ivan, and you don't want me to interfere."

He had practically taken the words out of her mouth. Some of her bluster ebbed away. "That's true. I'm the head of the household."

"I understand and I respect that," he said softly.

His intense gaze left her feeling exposed and vulnerable. Could he tell she doubted her ability to keep her family together? That she felt backed into a corner by the bishop's words? There was no way he could know what was in her mind yet she was sure that he did. She started for the door. "I hope you will be comfortable here."

"I hope so, too. Good night, Bethany."

The gentle way he said her name with such longing brought goose bumps to her arms. She hurried out the door before she could change her mind and stay to learn more about her unusual new neighbor.

Early the next morning the sound of someone chopping wood woke Bethany from a restless sleep. Knowing it would be useless to stay in bed, she got up and dressed for the day. Downstairs she put on a pot of coffee and enjoyed one cup in solitude. As she watched the eastern sky grow lighter, her thoughts turned to Michael. Her annoyance had vanished in the night.

Was he right to exclude her from his talk with Ivan? Last night she didn't think so, but now she was able to look at the situation without embarrassment clouding her thinking. She had been prepared to be a buffer between Ivan and Michael. She wanted her brother to make amends, but she didn't want his punishment to be unjust. Perhaps it was better that she stayed out of it and let Ivan face the consequences of his actions alone.

She glanced at the clock on the wall. Once the children were off to school she still intended to have a talk with Michael. Rising to her feet, she started on breakfast. When the eggs and oatmeal were ready, she called up the stairs. "Ivan, Jenny, time to get ready for school."

She returned to the kitchen and set plates and bowls on the table. It wasn't long before Jenny came down still in her nightgown. She made a beeline to the stove, where she warmed her hands. The upstairs bedrooms weren't heated. Hot flannel-wrapped bricks helped stave off some of the chill, but they didn't last all night. The heavy quilts only helped as long as a person stayed in bed.

When Ivan didn't appear, Bethany went to the staircase again. "Ivan. Time to get ready for school. Did you hear me?"

As she was waiting for a reply, the back door opened and he came in bundled from head to toe in his work clothes. He bent to pull off his boots. "We got four more inches of snow last night. The snowplow just went by on the road and left a huge pile of snow on our side."

She stared at him in amazement. "What were you doing outside?"

"I was chopping wood for Michael, and I shoveled the path to his house. I fed and watered our animals, too, but I didn't gather the eggs. Jenny should do that for you. I'm really hungry. What's for breakfast?"

"Scrambled eggs and oatmeal. It is nice of you to make sure Michael had wood for his fireplace."

"I have to do it for a month." He didn't sound resentful at all. He was actually smiling as he sat down at the table and pulled off his stocking cap.

"How long is he making you do my chores?" Bethany asked.

"He isn't making me do them, and they are my chores now."

Somewhat taken aback, Bethany filled their plates and took her place at the foot of the table. She looked at Ivan. "Would you like to sit at the head of the table and lead the prayers from now on?"

Both his eyebrows rose. "Really?"

It was the responsibility of the male head of an Amish household to signal the beginning and the end of the silent blessing before meals. Their grandfather had always been the one to lead prayers. After his death Bethany took over the task, never once considering that it should have fallen to Ivan. To her, he was still a child, but he wasn't little anymore.

She realized her brother was waiting for her reply. "Of course you may."

He moved his plate and sat down opposite her. Bowing his head, he clasped his hands together. Bethany did the same and silently repeated the blessing. When she was finished she waited with her head bowed for

Ivan's signal. He unfolded his hands and picked up his fork. Jenny had her eyes closed. Ivan cleared his throat.

Jenny peeked at him with one eye. "Are you done?"

He nodded once. "I am."

"Goot." She reached for her glass of milk.

Ivan poured honey and milk on his oatmeal. "Jenny, I want you to gather the eggs for Bethany every day."

Jenny looked puzzled. "I do it when she asks me to."

"It will be your chore every morning before school, starting tomorrow. Bethany has enough to do."

Jenny shrugged. "Okay. Pass me a piece of toast, Ivan."

Bethany couldn't understand this sudden change in Ivan. What had Michael said to him? She wanted to ask but she didn't want to discuss it in front of her little sister. Jenny had a habit of blurting out things she had overheard.

Later, when the children were ready to go meet the bus, Bethany brought out their lunch boxes. "Ivan, did you complete the homework your teacher gave you?"

"Not all of it, but I'll stay in at recess and get the rest of it done."

"I'm pleased to hear you say that." But could she trust that he meant what he said?

"And you won't skip school again. Is that clear?" she said firmly.

"Michael and I talked about it last night. I won't skip." Ivan took his lunch box from her. "He's a *goot* fellow."

"I like him and his dog." Jenny grabbed her lunch box and headed out the door. Ivan followed close behind her, leaving Bethany more curious than ever about what Michael had said to inspire her brother.

After dressing warmly, she hiked up the hill to the cabin and knocked. She waited and knocked again but he didn't answer. She checked the barn and found his pony and cart were gone. Disappointed, she went back down the hill. Her talk with him would just have to wait.

For most of the next day and a half Michael wrestled with the notion of leaving New Covenant. He came here because he hoped the remoteness of the settlement and a change of scenery would put a stop to his anxiety attacks and flashbacks. To have such a profound episode occur within a week of his arrival was deeply disappointing. In the end he decided he had to stay. There was nowhere else to hide. He didn't want his decision to be emotional. As much as he tried to dismiss one important factor, he couldn't. Bethany was here.

If he was going to stay, he needed to work. He had a choice between building sheds with Jesse and the bishop or doing what he loved. The only drawback with repairing timepieces was that he'd be working for Bethany. He liked her. A lot. But there was no future there as long as he could fall apart at any second. His episode Sunday night had driven that fact home.

He would go back to his original plan. Bury himself in his work and remain apart from people as much as possible. He walked down the hill and found Bethany hanging wash on the line at the side of the house. Her clothesline stretched from the back porch to a nearby pine tree. A pulley system allowed her to pin her clothes on the line and move them out without stepping off the porch into the snow.

He nodded to her. "*Guder mariye*, Bethany. May I see your grandfather's workshop?"

She hesitated a fraction of a second then nodded. "Of course. It's this way."

She walked through the house into the kitchen and opened a door. "This was my grandfather's workroom."

His disappointment must have shown on his face. She tipped her head slightly. "Is something wrong?"

He didn't want a workshop attached to the house where family members could come and go as they pleased. He wanted a space all to himself. "I thought the workshop was one of the other buildings on the farm."

She shook her head. "Grandfather liked being close to us. He usually kept the door open, but if you're thinking that we will disturb you, you can keep it closed."

"I don't like interruptions while I'm working."

Her smile was forced. "That's understandable. We will make it a point to not interrupt you. You may add a bolt to the door or a lock if you prefer."

"That will not be necessary. As long as everyone's aware that I'm not to be bothered while I'm working, that should suffice." He stepped through the doorway into a tidy room with a long workbench in front of a large window. The workbench itself was made of oak. It had four shallow drawers across the front.

He opened the first drawer. Numerous screwdrivers were lined up by size in a wooden holder that had obviously been custom-made. The next drawer held a jeweler's loupe and several magnifying lenses all nestled into cotton batting. The third drawer held an assortment of gears and springs Elijah must have scavenged from clocks of all types. The fourth drawer held ledgers, receipt books, stationery and padded envelopes.

Michael looked around the room at the dozen or so clocks hanging on the walls, some in various stages of repair. The running ones ticked softly. "Your grandfather was obviously a man who took great care with his tools." He ran his finger along the top of the workbench. It was satin smooth.

"Daadi believed in a place for everything and everything in its place. He liked to use authentic old tools. He said they simply do the job better than the new ones."

"I have to agree." Along the back of the workbench were several dozen books stacked on top of each other. Michael picked up one and read the title. *"Clocks of the 1800s."*

She picked a book up and ran her fingers over the colorful cover. "Daadi would spend his free time reading about the history of clocks. I would often find him in here late at night poring over antique books on the ancient practice of clock making. I could never understand how he knew what all those little gears and wheels did."

"Repairing a clock can be complicated work, but it can also be simple when the pieces speak for themselves."

"How so?"

"Everything inside of a clock's mechanisms has a purpose. Everything is there for a reason. If you work backward, if you understand what part connects to another part and then another, the clock will tell you what each part does."

She swept her hand through the air, indicating all the timepieces on the walls. "I think you love the art of this the way he did."

"There is something fascinating and beautiful inside each clock I open. I'm happy when I can return it to someone who has treasured it. Often I see them smile when they hear a clock chime again because it brings back good memories."

She smiled softly and swiveled the old leather chair around to face her. "Good memories are important."

She looked at him. "Now that you have had a chance to see the workshop, what do you think? Are you interested in a partnership?"

"I can work in here."

She held out her hand. "Do we have a deal?"

He hesitated a second but then accepted her handshake. "We have a deal."

He held on to her fingers a few seconds longer than he needed to. She blushed as she pulled her hand away.

Bethany couldn't ignore the attraction she felt for Michael. The amazing thing was she had only known him a few days. Maybe letting him work here wasn't a good idea. For some reason she felt off balance when he looked at her with that penetrating gaze of his.

She gave herself a hard mental shake. She was being ridiculous. He needed the work and she needed the income. It wasn't like antique watch repairmen grew on trees. She would have to make sure she kept the relationship strictly business.

"Are you comfortable in the cabin?"

"It's snug. Or it will be when the new window gets in. Pastor Frank took the measurements last night. He's going to order a replacement for me."

She slipped her hands in the pockets of her apron. "Make sure the bill is sent to me. Ivan mentioned that you encouraged him to remain in school. I don't know what else you said to him but he is a changed boy. He's doing chores without being told. He's catching up on his schoolwork. Is he still splitting wood for you?"

"Without fail."

"Good. However, I still think I should have been included in the conversation."

Michael faced her. "Ivan said you treat him like a little child and not like the man of the house. I doubt he would have spoken so plainly about it if you had been in the room. I told him if he'd act like a man he would be treated as such."

"I don't agree with his assessment."

Michael grinned. "I didn't think you would. You have to admit that you don't treat him like a grown fellow."

Of all the nerve. "You haven't been around this family long enough to make an assumption like that."

"It wasn't my assumption. It was Ivan's." He smiled broadly as if inviting her to share the joke. She didn't find it funny.

"And if Ivan's change of heart wears off in a week or two, I imagine I'll be the one to blame." What possessed her to imagine she was attracted to this man? She knew from the first time they met that he was laughing at her. He was still laughing at her.

His smile faded as he seemed to realize she was upset. "I'm sure he will backslide a time or two. That's only natural. No one is looking to assign blame to you."

"That's just it. Men are assigning blame to me. The bishop, my uncle, they assume I can't control a boy Ivan's age. They want to take the problem off my hands. He isn't a problem. He's my brother. I don't know what we will do if the bishop insists on separating us, but I can tell you I won't stand still for it."

"Defying the bishop could get you shunned."

"There are other Amish communities in Maine. As much as I loved my grandfather and shared his vision for New Covenant, I will move lock, stock and barrel before I give up my brother. You don't need to worry about putting a lock on this door. I will not set foot in this room while you are here."

She walked out and slammed the door behind her.

Chapter Seven

"**Y**ou should invite Michael to eat with us," Ivan said at the dinner table three days after Michael had moved into the cabin.

Bethany had spent much of the time regretting her outburst. She owed him an apology. Michael wasn't the cause of her problem. She shouldn't have taken her ill temper out on him. He had been trying to help.

Michael *had* helped although the bishop might not be able to see the improvement in Ivan's attitude. She was also certain he wouldn't simply take her word for it.

"Why can't Sadie Sue eat with us, too?" Jenny asked.

Bethany leveled a don't-be-ridiculous look at Jenny. "Because I won't allow a dog in the house at mealtime. I don't care how much you like her. As for Michael, I haven't asked him because he specifically said that he likes working alone and he likes his privacy. Now that he is going to be working in Grandfather's shop, I want you both to understand that when that door is closed you are not to go in there."

"But what if I need something?" Jenny asked.

Bethany put down her fork to stare at her sister.

"What could you possibly need from Grandfather's workshop?"

"I don't know. I might need to play with Sadie Sue. She likes to fetch sticks."

Bethany tried not to smile at her sister's cajoling tone. "I'm sure there will be plenty of times that you can play with her. Just not while Michael is working."

Ivan helped himself to another dollop of potatoes. "Michael might like to work alone but that doesn't mean he likes to eat alone. You should ask him."

"I'll consider it." That was all she was going to say on the subject. "Are you excited about having Thanksgiving dinner tomorrow at the Lapp farm?"

Jenny held her hand high in the air. "I am. No school for four days."

Bethany looked at her brother. "What about you, Ivan?"

"Jeffrey won't be there. I won't have anyone to hang out with."

"I'm sure that the Miller boys will include you in any games they start." The trio of cousins were in their late teens but they normally included Ivan in their group sports during church get-togethers. There were so few people in New Covenant yet. She wasn't sure that all of those would stay after enduring a Maine winter.

"Is Michael going to be there?" Ivan looked at her hopefully.

Bethany thought back over the times she and Michael had spent together. "I don't believe I mentioned it to him. Jesse may have told him about it."

Ivan pushed back his chair. "I'll go invite him."

"After you finish your supper." Although Bethany hadn't liked hearing that she treated Ivan as a child, she had to admit there were some things their grandfather had done that Ivan could take over.

"I thought perhaps you could read some passages from the Bible for us tonight. I have to work on Jenny's Christmas program costume."

"You really want me to?" He looked amazed.

"Absolutely."

"Sure. I'd be happy to do that. When I'm finished eating can I invite Michael to the Thanksgiving dinner?"

She glanced at the door and then back to her brother. "You'll have to go outside and check if there is a light in the workshop windows. If there is, wait until he is finished working. If there isn't a light, go ahead and go up to the cabin. But first, how was your day at school?"

"I'm caught up on my work." His comment lacked enthusiasm. He wouldn't meet her gaze.

"I'm happy to hear that. What else happened today?"

"Somebody said I stole money from their locker. I didn't but I'm not sure the teacher believed me. She looked through my desk and didn't find anything."

"Oh, Ivan, I'm sorry."

"It's okay."

It wasn't okay but Bethany didn't know how to deal with it. Her brother had built himself a bad reputation. Repairing it would take time. Time he might not have. The bishop would be at the dinner tomorrow. Could she convince him that Ivan had seen the error of his ways after the bishop had heard Jedidiah's tale?

Michael's input might sway the bishop if he could be convinced to attend the dinner. He knew Ivan was chopping wood each day and doing his chores and doing better in school.

She pushed the chicken casserole around on her plate as her appetite vanished. The bishop wouldn't hear Michael's observations if Michael didn't speak to him. She was going to have to apologize to Michael and then ask him to speak on Ivan's behalf as a favor.

Her chicken casserole might as well have been crow. That was what was on the menu for later.

"Ivan, I'll invite Michael to the Thanksgiving dinner at the Lapps' tomorrow. I want you to help your sister practice her lines for the Christmas program."

He looked ready to object but nodded instead. "Okay. I will."

She rose from her chair. "*Danki.* The two of you clear the table. I'm going to speak with Michael."

"Invite Sadie Sue, too," Jenny said.

"*Nee,* I will not invite the dog. If you wish to do something special for her you will have to do it here."

"Can I bake her some cookies?"

"Learn your lines for the Christmas program first."

"All right," Jenny said, but she didn't look happy about it.

Bethany checked the workshop first. The light was off. He must've gone home. She trudged up the hill, bemoaning how quickly it got dark this time of year. As she drew near the cabin she saw Michael was filling a pair of pails at the pump in the yard. His dog sat by his side. She woofed several times, causing him to look around. He caught sight of Bethany and stopped. He watched her with a hint of uncertainty in his eyes. She couldn't blame him.

She forged ahead. "It seems like I am apologizing every time I see you."

He just stared at her.

He wasn't making it easy.

"I wanted to say that I'm sorry for the way I behaved the other day. Although it isn't really an excuse, I am very concerned about my brother. I do not want to send him to live with our uncle. Onkel Harvey is a good man, don't get me wrong. He has a fine family. My reason for wanting to keep Ivan with me is a selfish one. I love my brother. I promised my mother as she lay dying that I would take care of Ivan and Jenny. I don't want to break that promise."

"That's understandable. You are forgiven. There was no need for you to come and apologize."

She pressed a hand to her chest. "I *needed* to apologize."

He picked up one bucket of water and started toward the barn. Bethany picked up the second bucket and followed him. He frowned as he glanced at her. "I can manage this."

"Many hands make light work. Did you find everything you need in my grandfather's workshop today?"

"I did, plus I have many of my own tools."

"I guess that makes sense." In the barn she put the bucket down as he poured the first one into a small tank in the pony's stall. He handed her the empty pail, picked up the full one and poured it into the tank, as well.

He walked out of the barn and Bethany followed him. It appeared that he wasn't in the mood to talk. She followed him anyway.

"I don't know if Jesse mentioned it but our church community is having a Thanksgiving dinner tomorrow. I wanted to make sure you knew you were invited."

"I'll be working."

"It will be a great opportunity to get to know the other Amish families here."

"I'll meet them in time."

"Why wait?" She tried to sound cheerful not desperate.

"Because I'm working tomorrow."

She had hoped she wouldn't have to beg but he left her no choice. "All right, I have a favor to ask of you."

A slight smile curved his lips. "Really? I can't wait to hear this. Has Clarabelle given you the name of a new marriage prospect that you want me to check out?"

"I wish you would forget about the cow."

"I've tried but I can't. It's stuck in my brain."

"Oh, never mind." She turned to go. She'd only taken a few steps when he spoke again.

"Wait. What is it that you need?"

She stayed where she was with her hands pushed deep into the pockets of her coat, so he couldn't see how tightly clenched her fingers were. "The bishop will be there. I need your help convincing him that Ivan has had a change of heart. That he's doing better." She stared at the ground, afraid to see him refuse. "Will you do that? Please?"

Michael groaned inwardly. She had no idea what she was asking. A dinner with dozens of strangers in an unfamiliar house. A crowd. The noise. He grew tense just thinking about it.

Why did she have to look so dejected? So vulnerable? Why was she pinning her hopes on him? It would be amazing if he didn't end the dinner as a babbling ball of fear hiding under the table. He couldn't do it.

She glanced at him from beneath lowered lashes.

How could he not do it?

She wanted to keep her family together. He prayed for strength for the first time in months. Sadie Sue whined as she gazed up at him. "I know, I know. It's a bad idea."

He crossed the few steps between them and stopped inches from Bethany. He lifted her chin so she would look at him. "Okay, I'll do it, but you must understand that my words may not carry much weight. I'm new here. I'm not even a member of your congregation yet."

He would speak to the man and then leave. He didn't have to stay for the meal. He would come home and work in peace.

The joy on Bethany's face was almost worth the discomfort he knew he was going to endure. Beneath his fingers her skin was soft as the silk cloths he used to polish his work. Her beautiful eyes were damp with unshed tears. Her lips were red because she had been biting them. He wanted to soothe them with a kiss.

As sure as the sun would rise again tomorrow, he knew one kiss would not be enough.

He stepped away from her. She blinked rapidly and swiped at her unshed tears with both hands. *"Danki."*

"Please tell me I don't have to cook something and take it to eat."

Her laugh was shaky. "I'll make enough for both of us."

"Where is this party taking place?"

"At the Lapp farm. It's about a half mile from here. You met Gemma the other night. The farm belongs to her parents. We might as well ride together, don't you think? I have to take some tables and chairs for them to use. I'll pick you up at noon. That should give you plenty of time to meet people before they start serving at two o'clock."

A half mile wasn't too far. He could walk that distance home alone.

Bethany grabbed his hand. "Bless you. I mean that from the bottom of my heart. Bless you and the good you are doing for my family."

"I'm doing it for Ivan. The kid deserves a break."

She let go of him and pushed her hands deep into her coat pockets. "Of course. He may not realize it yet, but you are a true friend."

As she hurried away he shook his head. Thanksgiving Day would end in disaster for him. He looked down at Sadie Sue. "I am an idiot. Did you know that? You've adopted an idiot for a master."

Michael waited on the porch with his back against the side of the cabin as Bethany drove up in a large wagon the next morning. The children were sitting beside her. His nerves had been on edge since he woke well before dawn. Sadie Sue was shut inside the cabin. He wished he could take her with him.

"Happy Thanksgiving," Bethany called out. The children echoed her greeting. They were staring at him.

All he had to do was walk down the steps and get in her wagon. His palms were damp; his heart was racing. He counted to three and pushed away from the wall. Bethany had Ivan and Jenny get in the back, giving him more room. Getting up onto the seat was easier said than done. The wagon seat was much higher than a buggy. It wasn't graceful but he finally hauled himself up and onto the padded wooden bench.

"All set," he muttered between his clenched teeth.

"Thank you again for doing this."

"Sure, no problem." He hoped.

"I don't see Sadie," Jenny said.

"I locked her in the house." He couldn't believe how much he'd come to rely on the dog. She alerted him when someone was near. When she was at ease, he was at ease.

Bethany spoke to the team and the wagon lurched forward, jarring his leg. Out on the roadway the going was smoother. He let go of his death grip on the side of the seat.

Bethany glanced his way. "Is your leg paining you?"

"Some. I think there's a change in weather coming."

"The newspaper this morning said we could expect a significant snowstorm over the next three days."

"What is 'significant' to the people of Maine?"

"Two, maybe three, in places."

"Inches?"

"Feet," she said with a smile. "Don't worry. Jesse plows our lanes open with his big team but you should invest in some snowshoes before long."

Snowshoes and a cane. How was that going to work? Maybe moving here had been a mistake.

It didn't take long to reach the Lapp farm. Bethany drew the horse to a stop by the front door. The children jumped off the back of the wagon and ran inside. Bethany turned to him. "Can I help you get down?"

He shook his head. "I don't need help. Besides, if I fall I only want one person to get hurt."

She ignored him, jumped down and came around to his side. "I won't let you fall."

"I should believe a woman who talks to cows? Stand aside." He grimaced as he swung his bad leg over the side.

"Nope. Keep one hand on the seat and put your other hand on my shoulder and lower your weight slowly."

"I'm not getting down until you're out of the way."

"You will get very cold sitting here when the sun goes down."

"Stubborn woman."

"I've been called that before."

"Why am I not surprised." He searched for a way to get down without help. It was a long drop. "Okay, I hate to admit it, but your idea looks like my best option."

He gave her his cane and she leaned it against the wagon wheel. Placing his hand on her shoulder, he scooted over the edge of the seat and started to lower himself to the ground.

One horse took a step forward. The cane fell, clattering against the wheel spokes. The other horse tossed her head and took a step, jerking the wagon. Michael lost his grip on the seat and pulled Bethany off balance.

The second he started to fall Bethany wrapped her arms around him and threw herself over backward, trying to take the brunt of his weight. Her head struck the ground with a painful-sounding thump. She didn't make a sound.

"Are you okay? Bethany, are you okay? Speak to me." Michael was holding himself above her on his forearms. His face was inches from hers. Her lids fluttered up. She looked at him and blinked twice.

"You have pretty eyes." Her voice was a bare whisper.

"What?"

She closed her eyes. "Nothing. I'm okay. Are you hurt?"

At least she was talking. "My pride has a big dent in it, but I don't think anything is broken."

"Then could you get off me? You're very heavy." She winced in pain.

"What is going on here?"

Michael looked up to see an older Amish man with a graying beard glaring at him. Jesse stood at his side.

"Hi, Jesse." Michael rolled off Bethany and lay sprawled beside her. His bad leg was on fire, his shoulders ached, and he had skinned both hands trying to keep his full weight from crashing down on her.

"Michael?" Jesse's eyebrows rose until they touched the brim of his black hat.

"It's me. Happy Thanksgiving."

"What are you doing on the ground?"

Michael laughed even though it hurt. "I put my trust in a woman who has conversations with her cow. Big mistake." He turned his head to gaze at Bethany. "Are you sure you aren't hurt?"

"I'm still checking." She pressed a hand to the back of her head.

Her friend Gemma came out of the house. "What has happened? Bethany, is that you?"

Bethany pushed herself into a sitting position. "Hello, Gemma. Happy Thanksgiving."

Jesse was still frowning at Michael. "I don't understand what you are doing on the ground."

"Bethany kindly gave me a ride here, and when I was trying to get out of her wagon, I fell on her. It was an accident. I think she hit her head pretty hard."

Gemma helped Bethany to her feet. "You poor thing. Are you injured?"

Bethany managed a half-hearted smile. "Only bumps and bruises. I'm afraid Michael is the one who is hurt."

Michael struggled to his feet with Jesse's assistance and leaned against the wagon. "I'm fine. Where's my cane?"

The elderly Amish man beside Jesse picked it up and handed it to Michael with a scowl on his face. "I am Bishop Schultz."

"Just the man I wanted to see. I'm Michael Shetler. I'm a newcomer to the area."

The bishop stroked his beard as he stared at Michael. "Jesse has told me about you."

"I need to unpack the tables and chairs," Bethany said.

"Someone else can take care of that. You need a few minutes' rest to regain your wits," Michael told her in a stern tone.

She scowled at him. "My wits are not scattered."

"That's open to debate. You hit your head pretty hard. You could have a concussion. Gemma, make her go inside and rest."

Michael caught the sidelong glare Bethany shot at him. She wasn't happy to have him telling her what to do. Too bad. In his opinion, she was too pale. He didn't want her keeling over and spoiling the party. That was his job.

Gemma smiled kindly at Michael as she took Bethany's arm. "He is right. Come in. I have some fresh brewed sweet tea and my special lemon cookies, and I'm going to fix an ice pack for your head."

"I would speak with you, Bethany, when you are recovered," Bishop Schultz said. Bethany grew a shade paler.

Inside the house the mouthwatering smells of roasting turkey, fresh baked breads and pumpkin pies filled the air. Michael saw Ivan seated beside two teenage boys looking through a hunting magazine. He beckoned to the boy. "Ivan, can I see you a minute?"

Ivan came over. "What's up?"

"Ask your friends to help you bring in the tables and chairs from the back of the wagon and take care of the horses."

"Sure." He went back to the boys and they all walked outside. A few minutes later they came in carrying the extra seating. Gemma's mother directed them where to set up. Another family arrived with baskets of food, and a festive air began to fill the room as happy chatter and laughter grew in volume.

Michael stayed beside Bethany, who was seated in a wingback chair near the fireplace. She soon had a plate of cookies on her lap and a glass of tea in her hand. Her color was already better when Gemma brought her the ice pack. Michael knew Bethany had taken the brunt of the fall trying to protect him. It should have been the other way around.

His gaze was constantly drawn to her. Her color returned to normal, but the longer he watched her the more flushed she became. Every time he caught her eye she looked away.

After ten minutes, Bethany set her empty glass aside. "I should be helping in the kitchen."

Bethany couldn't take Michael staring at her another minute. Didn't he realize everyone was noticing his attention? She blushed at being the recipient of so many speculative looks. She was about to get up when the bishop approached her with Jedidiah a few steps behind him.

The bishop settled himself in a nearby chair. "Are you feeling recovered, Bethany?"

"I have a headache that I'm sure will get better quickly. Jedidiah, did you get my letter and the check?"

"I did. It was a fair price, though the cost was not the issue. I trust Ivan will repay you?"

She clasped her hands together. "I want you both to know that my brother has improved his attitude one hundred percent since that incident."

"Even if that is true, it is too little too late." The bishop's stern look chilled her.

She gestured to Michael. "This is Michael Shetler. He has taken over Grandfather's watch repair business. He can attest to Ivan's improvements. He has seen it firsthand."

"In what way?" Jedidiah asked.

"The boy broke a window in the cabin I rented from Bethany. I had a talk with him. We settled on his punishment. He has split wood for me every morning, has taken over many of Bethany's outdoor chores, and he has improved his grades at school. I believe his friend has been the instigator of much of the trouble Ivan has been in."

The bishop folded his arms over his chest. "If that is true, the boy has shown bad judgment in his choice of friends."

Jedidiah shifted his weight from one foot to the other. "I spoke with his teacher yesterday evening. We happened to be in the grocery store at the same time. She tells me some of the *Englisch* children have accused Ivan of stealing money."

"One child did. She searched his desk and didn't find anything. It wasn't Ivan," Bethany insisted.

The bishop's face grew somber. "I wish I could give him the benefit of the doubt, but there have been too many instances where he has been involved. Jedidiah has offered to take the boy until his uncle arrives. He feels he can give Ivan the supervision he needs. I have agreed to this."

"*Nee*, you can't take him from me. You can't."

"What if I were to take responsibility for the boy?" Michael offered.

Chapter Eight

Michael was certain that he had lost his mind. The look on Bethany's face told him she thought he was her hero.

The bishop regarded him intently. "Are you sure you understand what this means?"

"I do. I will oversee the boy's discipline. I will stand as substitute for his father. Any person who has difficulties or accusations against the boy can address them with me. If you will allow me, then the boy does not have to leave Bethany's care or his home. Should he go to live with Jedidiah now, he will be unable to complete the bargain he has with me."

The bishop nodded slowly. "I appreciate what Jedidiah has offered. I didn't feel right taking the boy from his sister's care, but I saw no other choice after Jedidiah told me about the theft of his goods. You have given me one. You are new to us but Jesse has vouched for your character, Michael, otherwise I would not agree to this, but I trust his judgment. This arrangement will be only until the boy's uncle arrives at Christmas," the bishop added. "I want to be clear that this isn't a permanent situation, and that you are accepting financial responsibility as well as a moral responsibility to see that Ivan behaves himself."

"I understand that."

Bethany's hopeful gaze was pinned on Michael. "You don't have to do this."

He considered retracting his offer but he wasn't prepared to see the Martin family split up. "I understand that. I want to do it. I'll speak to Ivan about it when we get home today."

"Agreed." The bishop smiled broadly. Even Jedidiah looked relieved. The two men walked away.

"I can't thank you enough," Bethany said with tears in her eyes.

"Let's hope Ivan feels the same way." He was already regretting his rash gesture. His intention was to spend less time with Bethany and her family, not more.

Bethany heard the hesitancy in Michael's voice. "You won't be sorry you did this. It proves that you believe in my brother and that is priceless to me."

Michael rubbed his hands on his pants. "I think I need some fresh air."

He left the room. Once he was out of sight, Gemma hurried over to sit beside Bethany. "What was that all about?"

"Ivan."

"I was afraid that's what the bishop had on his mind when he cornered you. Is he still sending the boy away at Christmas?"

"He wanted to send him to live with Jedidiah until then, but Michael volunteered to be responsible for him."

"How did you manage that?"

"It was his own idea."

Gemma leaned forward eagerly. "Tell me all about your mystery man."

"There isn't much to tell. Apparently, he corresponded with Daadi about working for him. He had already paid the first and last months' rent on the cabin. He likes to keep to himself. And he's from Sugarcreek, Ohio."

"I don't mean the dry details. Does he have a girlfriend back in Ohio? Is he looking to marry? Does he have money?"

"How would I know that?"

Gemma chuckled. "You don't know how to snoop. I could find all that out in ten minutes."

"I'm not so sure. He doesn't like to talk about himself."

"Then he is hiding something. I wonder what it is. How did he know your grandfather?"

"He didn't really. A jeweler by the name of George Meyers recommended Michael to my grandfather and that's all I know. He and Ivan get along. I'm grateful for that."

"You like him, don't you?"

Bethany was wary of the eager look in her friend's eyes. "He's nice enough."

"I'd say he's a lot better than Jesse Crump or Jedidiah. I can't believe he fell into your lap and all you can say is that he's nice enough. He is the answer to your prayers."

"What are you talking about?"

"You need a husband by Christmas and Michael Shetler appears out of the blue. God moves in mysterious ways."

"You're being ridiculous. There is nothing between us."

"I wouldn't say that. I noticed the way he looked at

you when he was sitting beside you. We all noticed. He's interested. The man has potential. With a little effort on your part, you could have him eating out of your hand. I've got to go help Mamm. Can I get you anything else?"

Bethany shook her head and winced. She pressed a hand to the back of her aching head. "I'm gonna sit here with my ice pack for a little longer."

Gemma patted Bethany's knee. "Let me know if you need anything."

Jenny came running to Bethany's side along with Sadie Sue. "Look, sister. I didn't invite her. She came all by herself."

"I wonder how she got out." Bethany stared at the dog. She was sure Michael had locked her in.

Sadie's attention turned to the tables where the food was being set out. She licked her chops. Bethany foresaw a disaster. "*Nee*, Jenny, take her outside."

"But why?"

"Because I asked you to."

"Okay. Come on, Sadie Sue." Jenny headed toward the back door, taking Sadie within a few feet of the table and a steaming plate of sausages. The dog stopped and eyed the dish as Jenny went out the door. No one else was near the dog.

Bethany rose from her chair. "*Nee*, Sadie Sue. Don't do it."

Jenny opened the back door and looked in. "Sadie, come on."

The dog gave the sausages a forlorn glance and trotted out the door. Bethany sank back in her chair with a sigh of relief.

"Was that my dog?" Michael asked as he came in from outside.

"*Ja*, it was Sadie Sue." Remembering Gemma's comments, Bethany found herself tongue-tied. Did he find her attractive? Or was his attentiveness just part of his makeup that had nothing to do with her? Bethany wished she could tell what he was thinking.

He scratched the back of his head. "I wonder how she got out of the house."

Bethany shrugged.

"How are you feeling?" he asked.

"Better." She kept her demeanor cool. Were people watching them and speculating? She caught sight of Gemma smiling widely. Her friend winked.

"I'm glad to hear you are better. I'm going to go take Sadie home and see how she escaped. I hope we don't have to replace another windowpane."

"Will you be coming back?"

"*Nee*, you stay and enjoy your friends. I have work to do."

She didn't want him to go. She was torn by her conflicting feelings. "Don't you even want something to eat?"

"I have plenty back at the cabin. Get someone to drive you home if you aren't feeling better."

"Ivan can drive the wagon."

Michael nodded and walked away. When he opened the door he glanced back at her with such a look of longing that it startled her. Was there something between them and she had been too blind to see it?

Bethany decided the family would walk to the church service on Sunday instead of taking the buggy. The preaching was being held at the home of Nigel and Becca Miller. Their farm was little more than a quarter of a mile beyond the Lapp place. Nigel was a carpenter who made furniture in the off-season.

An unexpectedly warm southern wind was melting the snow, making the sunshine feel even brighter. Rivulets of water trickled along the ditches and flowed out of the snow-covered fields. Amish families—some on foot, most in buggies—were all headed in the same direction. Cheerful greetings and pleasant exchanges filled the crisp air. Everyone was glad to see a break in the weather.

Bethany declined numerous offers of a ride, content to stretch her legs on such a fine morning. The icy grip of winter would return all too soon. Jenny and Ivan trudged along beside her, enjoying the sunshine.

She turned in at the farm lane where a dozen buggies were lined up on the hillside just south of the barn. The horses, still wearing their harnesses, were tied up along a split-rail fence, content to munch on the hay spread in front of them or doze in the sunshine.

The early morning activity was focused around the barn. Men were busy unloading backless seats from the large gray boxlike bench wagon that was used to transport the benches from home to home for the services held every other Sunday. Bishop Schultz was supervising the unloading. When the wagon was empty, he conferred with his minister.

Bethany entered the house. Inside, it was a flurry of activity as the women arranged food on counters and tables. Several small children were being watched over by the Millers' niece. She beckoned Jenny to come help her. The Miller boys were outside playing a game of tag and Ivan went to join them.

Catching sight of Gemma unpacking baskets of food,

Bethany crossed the room toward them and handed over her basket of food for the lunch that would be served after the service. "*Guder mariye*, Gemma."

"Good morning, Bethany. Isn't the weather wonderful?"

"It is." Turning to Becca Miller, Bethany grinned at the baby she held. Little Daniel was six months old with a wide toothless grin and a head of white-blond curls. "Wow, how this little boy is growing. May I hold him?"

"Of course. I hate to admit it but he gets heavy quickly these days." Becca handed the baby over with a timid smile.

Bethany took Daniel and held him to her shoulder, enjoying the feel of a baby in her arms and his wonderful smell. "You're not so heavy."

"He should be. He eats like a little piglet." There was nothing but love in Becca's eyes as she gazed at her son.

Gemma said, "I see the bishop and minister coming. We'd best hurry and join the others in the barn."

As she spoke, Bishop Schultz and Samuel Yoder entered the house and went upstairs, where they would discuss the preaching that was to be done that morning. The three-to-four-hours-long service would be preached without the use of notes. Each man had to speak as God moved him.

Bethany handed the baby back to Becca. The women quickly finished their tasks and left the house.

The barn was already filled with people sitting quietly on rows of backless wooden benches with the women on one side of the aisle and men on the other side. Tarps had been hung over ropes stretched between upright timbers to cordon off an area for the service. Behind them, the sounds of cattle, horses and pigs could be heard. The south-facing doors were open to catch what warmth the sunshine and wind could provide.

Bethany took her place among the unmarried women. Gemma and Jenny sat beside her. In front of them sat the married women, several holding infants. Becca slipped a string of beads and buttons from her pocket. She handed them to her little one. He was then content and played quietly with his toy. Her older boys sat beside their father.

From the men's side of the aisle, the song leader announced the hymn. There was a wave of rustling and activity as people opened their thick black songbooks. The *Ausbund* contained the words of all the hymns but no musical scores. The songs, sung from memory, had been passed down through countless generations. They were sung slowly and in unison by people opening their hearts to receive God's presence without the distraction of musical instruments. The slow cadence allowed everyone to focus on the meaning of each word.

At the end of the first hymn, Bethany took a moment to glance toward the men's side. She spotted Michael sitting behind the married men with Ivan. Her brother squirmed in his seat, looking restless. Michael, on the other hand, held his songbook with a look of intense devotion on his face.

He glanced in her direction and she smiled at him. He immediately looked away and she felt the pinch of his rejection. She hadn't spoken to him since Thanksgiving. Was something wrong? Was he regretting his decision to mentor Ivan? Her brother was thrilled. He didn't object to Michael standing in his father's role.

The song leader announced the second hymn, "O Gott Vater, wir Loben dich" ("Oh God the Father, We Praise You"). It was always the second hymn of an

Amish service. Bethany forgot about Michael and her brother as she joined the entire congregation in singing God's praise, asking that the people present would receive His words and take them into their hearts.

At the end of the second hymn, the minister and Bishop Schultz came in and hung their hats on pegs set in the wall. That was the signal that the preaching would now begin. Bethany tried to listen closely to what was being said, but she found her mind wandering to the subject of Michael. What might he be looking for in a wife?

Michael sat up straight and unobtrusively stretched his bad leg. He was still stiff after his fall on Thursday. The wooden benches were not made for comfort. At least he hadn't fallen asleep the way their host Nigel Miller was doing. A few minutes after the preaching started, the farmer started nodding off in front of Michael. When Nigel began to tip sideways, Michael reached up and caught his arm before he tumbled off his seat.

Nigel jerked awake. *"Danki,"* he whispered as he gave Michael a sheepish grin.

Michael ventured a guess. "Working late?"

Nigel shook his head. "Colicky baby."

He leaned forward to look over at the women. Following his gaze, Michael saw Nigel's wife sitting across the aisle. Becca Miller held the baby sleeping sweetly in her arms. Her face held an expression of pure happiness when she caught her husband's glance. Bethany sat behind her.

What Michael wouldn't give to see Bethany look at him with a similar light in her eyes.

He quickly focused on his hymnal. Such daydreaming was foolishness. He wasn't husband material. He might never be. He tried to push thoughts of Bethany aside but they came back to him at odd times and more often than he cared to admit. He hadn't had another flashback or panic episode since the previous Sunday, but that didn't mean he was well.

Three hours into the service, the bishop stopped speaking and the song leader called out the number of the final hymn. Michael ventured a look in Bethany's direction. She held her songbook open for Jenny seated beside her. She pointed out the words as she sang them.

Bethany should have children of her own. She would make a good mother. He couldn't imagine why God had chosen not to bless her with a husband and children of her own. It didn't seem right.

The song drew to a close. Ivan was up and out the doors the second it ended. Teenage boys were expected to sit at the very back. Michael always assumed it was so their late arrivals and quick getaways didn't disrupt others. He followed more slowly. His eyes were drawn to Bethany as she walked toward the farmhouse with the other women.

How much of his life would he spend like this, watching her from afar, wishing for something that could never happen? Months? Years? What if he never got well?

On Monday afternoon just before the children came home from school, Bethany got out her crafting supplies and spread them on the table. She made a batch of oatmeal cookies and a pot of peppermint hot chocolate and left it simmering on the back of the stove.

She was cutting and folding card stock paper when

Ivan and Jenny came in the door. Jenny's eyes lit up. "Is it time to make our Christmas cards?"

"*Ja*, it is time. Do you have your lists of the people you want to send them to?"

Both children were well prepared and provided a list of more than a dozen people each that they would handcraft a greeting card for. Bethany had her own list that included every family in the New Covenant congregation as well as Pastor Frank, the children's teachers, bus driver and many of the merchants in town that she did business with.

After two mugs each of the hot chocolate and a plate of cookies, they were laughing and sharing ideas for cards. Jenny loved to draw a snow-covered tree branch with a cardinal sitting on it. She added silver glitter to the snow and red glitter to the birds. Ivan liked making construction paper cutouts of a horse and sleigh and gluing them to the card stock. He covered the snowy foreground with glitter. Bethany enjoyed making snowmen out of cotton balls glued together inside the card.

Before long there was glitter on the table, glitter on the floor and glitter on the children, but Bethany didn't care. She had to make this Christmas a special one in case they weren't together next year. "Ivan, you didn't tell me what song you'll be singing at the community Christmas program." Since religious-themed programs could no longer be held in the public schools, the community had decided to keep the Christmas pageant alive and well in the community center. The children and their teachers who wished to participate were eagerly welcomed.

Ivan didn't look up from crafting his card. "I'm going to sing 'O Come, O Come, Emmanuel.'"

"That's one of my favorites. Will you sing it for me now?" she asked with a catch in her throat.

He did and there were tears in her eyes by the time he finished. "That was fine. God has blessed you with a wonderful singing voice."

Jenny laid down her scissors. "I want to sing a song."

Bethany blinked away her tears and smiled. "What song would you like to perform?"

"'Go Tell It on the Mountain.'"

"That's a fine song. Let's all sing it together." Bethany hummed the first note and they all joined in singing at the top of their lungs to the very last verse.

"I don't know how you expect me to get any work done with all the noise and the delicious smell of hot chocolate coming from this room."

Bethany looked up to see Michael standing in the doorway with an indulgent smile lighting his face. Sadie Sue ambled over to Jenny. She got a hug and a pat before settling to the floor beside Jenny's chair with a sprinkling of red glitter across her head.

Bethany pointed at Michael. "That door is to remain closed while you are working."

He held his hands wide. "I'm done for the evening."

"In that case, pull up a chair and start making your Christmas cards. They have to go in the mail by the end of this week if you want them to arrive on time."

"I haven't sent many cards in the last few years, but I will definitely take some of that hot chocolate. Is that peppermint I smell?"

"Help yourself. I will make a list of people for you. Let's start with your mother and father. They will get a card, right?"

He nodded as he filled a white mug from the pot. "I have three brothers and two sisters."

She wrote down the names and addresses that he gave her. She sat poised with a pen. "Grandparents?"

"Gone, I'm afraid."

"Mr. Meyers at the jewelry store where you used to work? Grandfather always sent him one. How about some of the people you worked with? Are you still friends with them?"

He paused with the mug halfway to his mouth. He slowly lowered it. "I don't have friends there anymore."

He put the mug down, walked back into the workroom and closed the door.

Bethany didn't know what to make of his abrupt retreat. She looked at Ivan. "Did I say something wrong?"

Ivan shrugged. "He was shot during a robbery there. He doesn't like to talk about it."

Bethany stared at her brother, unsure she'd heard him correctly. "Michael was shot?"

Ivan nodded. "That's why he limps. I wasn't supposed to tell you. You won't tell him I mentioned it, will you?"

Bethany shook her head. "I won't say anything."

No wonder Michael didn't like to talk about his injury. Someone had robbed him at gunpoint and shot him. Was he the only one? Or were there others, too? She thought back to something her grandfather had mentioned. He told her the man who sent him watches to fix had a store robbed. Somewhere she had her grandfather's correspondences. He kept everything in case he had to prove the work had been done and the timepieces had been returned.

Some things about Michael began to make sense.

The way he was always vigilant. He didn't like crowds. He often stood with his back to the wall. She assumed he was leaning against the wall to rest his leg, but he might just as easily have been doing it to assure himself there was no one behind him.

She looked at Ivan and Jenny. "Let's make Christmas cards for Michael's family. It can be our Christmas gift to him. What do you think?" They both agreed and got to work.

Later that evening, Bethany carried a lantern into her grandfather's room. She put it down on his bedside table and pulled a large box from under his bed. She opened it and began to search for letters from George Meyers. She found the one she was looking for. Holding it in her hand, Bethany was torn by the feeling that she was invading Michael's privacy by snooping into his past. Would it tell her what she needed to know about Michael and what troubled him? Like her brother, she didn't know how to help Michael if she didn't know what was wrong.

She opened the letter and began reading.

Chapter Nine

Michael peered through his jeweler's loupe at a tiny screw he was attempting to insert into the mechanism of an antique gold pocket watch. His concentration was broken by the thump-thump-thump of Sadie Sue's tail against the floor. It was her signal that he wasn't alone but the visitor was someone she knew.

He couldn't believe what a difference having the dog had made on his anxiety level. He was confident in her ability to alert him to strangers. He didn't feel the need to constantly scan his surroundings for danger as often. When he did get agitated, she would distract him by nuzzling him for affection or bringing him the red ball she loved to fetch and dropping it in his lap.

"What are you doing?" Jenny asked as she came up beside him. His workbench was just high enough to allow her to rest her hands and chin on it.

"I'm working. Are you supposed to be in here?"

"I can't come in when the door is closed."

"Is the door closed, Jenny?" He turned the loupe up so that he could see her face. She was the perfect picture of boredom.

"It was closed but then it opened, so I came in."

He tipped his head to the side. "Did it open because you turned the doorknob?"

"Maybe. Are you mad?"

He sighed heavily. "What do you need, Jenny?"

"I want someone to play hide-and-seek with me. Will you, please?"

"I'm working. Ask your sister to play with you."

"She's doing the laundry."

"Then perhaps your brother would enjoy playing with you."

"He says I'm too little and that I'm just a pest. I'm not a pest, am I?"

Michael put down his screwdriver. The tiny screw popped off the magnetized end and went rolling off the workbench onto the floor. He pressed his lips into a hard line. "You are not a pest, but I don't have time to play, Jenny. I have work to do."

Her hopeful expression dissolved into a serious pout.

He got off his stool and awkwardly dropped to one knee to see under the bench. Jenny picked the screw up and handed it to him. "No one wants to play with me."

He paused and thought for a minute. "Why aren't you in school?"

"'Cause the teachers have to go to meetings for two days."

He got back on his work stool. "Play with Sadie."

"Sadie Sue can't play hide-and-seek. She can't count."

He put his loupe back on. "I'm sure Sadie can learn to play hide-and-seek with a little help from you. You go hide, and I will send her to find you." If he was fortunate, he could have ten or twenty minutes of uninterrupted work time before she came looking for the dog.

Bethany opened the door. "Jenny, I thought I told you to stay out of the workroom while Michael is in here."

"He wants me to play with Sadie Sue."

Bethany folded her arms across her chest. "Then bring the dog with you and leave Michael alone."

"We're playing hide-and-seek. I'm going to go hide. Michael, you count for her." Jenny took off at a run.

He waited a long moment, then looked at his dog. "Ten." She wagged her tail.

Bethany grinned at him. She had the most contagious smile. It boosted his spirits every time he saw it. "I'm sorry Jenny bothered you. She has been out of school for the past two days because of teachers' meetings. I think she has a touch of cabin fever."

"I'm ready," Jenny called from somewhere in the house.

Michael looked down at the dog. "Go find Jenny."

Sadie Sue didn't move. He patted her head. *"Goot hund."*

Bethany arched one eyebrow. "I see your plan. Jenny stays hidden and you get some work done?"

"It was the dog's idea." He put his tools down. "What are you baking that smells so good?"

"It's a turkey-and-rice casserole for supper. Is your compliment a sly way of asking if you can join us for supper?"

"You read me like a book."

She tipped her head to study him. "I wish that was true."

He looked away first. He would be in deep trouble if she actually could read his mind. At the moment he was wondering what it would be like to kiss her.

"You are always welcome to eat with us, Michael.

You never need an invitation." She paused, looking as if she wanted to say something else. Her indecision vanished. She smiled softly. "If you'll excuse me, I have to go find Jenny."

She clapped her hands together. "Come on, Sadie. Let's leave Michael to finish his work." Sadie rose and followed Bethany out of the room.

Michael picked up his screwdriver but working had lost its appeal. He laid his equipment aside and went out to the kitchen.

Bethany was diligently checking hiding places for her sister. He was the one who happened to notice that the door to the cellar was open a crack.

He clicked his fingers and Sadie trotted to him. He whispered in her ear and then gave her a small push toward the door. She trotted right past her quarry without seeing her. Jenny would've been safe if she hadn't giggled. Sadie spun around and pushed her nose in behind the door.

"Aw, you found me." Jenny patted the dog's head and looked to Michael. "Keep her here while I go hide again."

"Wait a minute." He turned to the refrigerator and opened it. There were several links of cooked sausage left over from breakfast. He picked up the plate and looked at Bethany. "Is it okay if I give this to the dog?"

"Feed *goot* food to a dog? Are you serious?"

"Please?" he cajoled. He used the same tone on Bethany that Jenny had used on him. To his surprise, it worked.

"Very well, but I don't see why the dog needs sausages. She's filled out fine on dog chow."

He motioned to Jenny. "Come here. We are going to

teach Sadie Sue to find you so you two can play hide-and-seek and leave me alone."

Bethany's eyes brightened. "That might work. Good thinking. Where did you learn how to train dogs?"

"I've never owned a dog before. This will be trial and error." He crumbled the links into pieces and gave them to Jenny. "Put these in your pocket. When I say 'find Jenny,' I want you to hold out a piece in your hand. Got it?"

"Sure."

"Sadie, find Jenny." Sadie cocked her head to the side as she stared at him.

Jenny fished a piece of sausage out of her pocket and held it out to the dog. "Here, girl."

Sadie never needed a second invitation where food was concerned. She ambled over to Jenny and gently took the piece of meat from her hand.

"That was fine," Michael said. "Now I will take her a little farther away. This time, Jenny, don't say anything. Just hold out your hand."

He took Sadie by the collar and led her to the other side of the room but her eyes were still on the little girl. He turned the dog so she was facing the other way. "Sadie, find Jenny."

Sadie spun around and made a beeline for Jenny, gulped down the piece of meat and barked.

Jenny laughed. "I think that means she wants some more."

"She will have to earn another piece." He took the dog by the collar and led her to the other side of the room.

Bethany regarded him with an amused expression. "You have taught a dog to eat sausage. Everyone will be amazed."

"Don't be a doubting Thomas." This time he took Sadie out into the workroom. "Sadie, find Jenny." The dog galloped from the room straight to Jenny and claimed her tidbit.

He was pleased with his experiment so far. "Now comes the real test. Jenny, I want you to go into the other room where Sadie can't see you. I want you to be quiet. Don't call her. Let's see if she will go look for you."

Jenny hurried out of the room. Bethany smothered a giggle. "I think the command should be 'go find sausage.' If I ever lose my breakfast meat I'll know who to call on. Michael and his amazing Sadie Sue."

"Scoff all you want. This is going to work." He looked down at the dog. "Sadie, find Jenny."

Sadie remained at his side watching him intently with her whole back end wagging. Bethany started laughing. She swung her arm out, pointed toward the doorway and yelled, "Find sausage!" Sadie started barking at her.

As much as he enjoyed the sound of Bethany's laughter, he didn't appreciate her lack of confidence. "She is going to get this. Jenny, come back here."

Jenny walked in the room looking confused. "Did I do it wrong?"

He shook his head. "You did fine. It is Sadie who needs a little more work. Why don't you go put on your coat and boots and we will take this outside, where there aren't so many confusing smells for Sadie and fewer people who want to make fun of her."

Jenny put her arms around Sadie's neck. "You'll get it. I know you will. You're the smartest dog in the whole wide world." Sadie licked her face, making her giggle.

Jenny headed for the coatrack. Sadie Sue followed with her nose pressed to Jenny's pocket.

Michael met Bethany's gaze and saw her affection for him in the depths of her eyes. His heart tripped over itself. She cared for him. He knew it as surely as if she spoke the words out loud.

He was falling for this amazing, beautiful, caring woman and he had no idea how to change course.

He had little to offer. He was a broken man. Nothing more than a jumble of pieces like some of the watches that came to him. Sometimes a boxful of gears and a dial couldn't be assembled to work properly no matter how much the owner wanted it repaired.

Bethany tipped her head slightly. "What?"

He shook his head and looked away. "Nothing. I was thinking about a broken watch I received the other day."

"Why does that make you sad?"

"Who said I was sad?"

She leaned closer. "I read you like a book, remember?"

Then she should be able to see how much he had grown to care for her. "It's sad because the watch can't be fixed."

"Why not?"

He turned away, afraid she could see what he was thinking. "An important part is broken. It can't be mended." He was the broken timepiece and could never forget it.

"Do you think another watch repair business might have the part you need?"

"It's not likely."

"If you really want to restore it, you should ask if

someone else can help you. What about asking Mr. Meyers for help?"

Michael heard something in her voice he didn't understand. He looked at her sharply. "What do you know about George Meyers?"

She rubbed her hands together. "He supplied my grandfather with the majority of his work. He also suggested my grandfather write to you and offer you a job here."

Michael tensed. "I told you that."

"I was going through some of Grandfather's things last night and I found the letter George Meyers sent to Grandpa."

Michael swallowed hard. What else was in the letter? "Was it informative?"

"He said you were injured during a robbery at the store."

He shouldn't be surprised. It was newsworthy. "What else did the letter say?"

"That three of his employees were killed by the robbers," she said gently.

He closed his eyes. "That's true."

"I'm so sorry. It must have been terrible for you."

He couldn't speak. Did she pity him now? He couldn't look at her. "What else did George tell your grandfather?"

"Mr. Meyers wanted you to have a chance to start over. I'm glad he asked Grandfather to contact you."

Michael glanced up at her. She meant it. If George had mentioned that Michael was off in the head, Bethany didn't share it. Michael relaxed. George Meyers had given him more than a chance to continue his work. He'd given him a chance at a new life. It had been nearly two weeks since his last PTSD episode. Perhaps he truly was getting better here.

Was his new life one that could include Bethany and the children?

The thought was almost unimaginable. His skin grew clammy. The idea that Bethany might one day love him was terrifyingly wonderful. Was it possible? Did he deserve such a gift? If only he could be sure he would get well.

"I'm ready," Jenny called from the front hall.

"I'll meet you on the back lawn." He was glad of the distraction. He needed to forget about a relationship with Bethany that was anything other than professional. He went out to the workroom, grabbed his coat, pulled on his overshoes and went out the side door with Sadie at his heels. He didn't want Bethany drawn into the darkness that hid inside him, waiting to spring out.

Jenny, dressed in her dark blue coat and bright red mittens, was waiting for him on the snow-covered lawn. She had a red-and-blue knit cap pulled over her white prayer *kapp*. Scooping up some snow, she formed a snowball and tossed it from hand to hand.

"Fetch it, Sadie." Jenny threw the ball, and the dog made a dive for it into a drift, leaving only her back legs and tail visible. She pulled out of the snowbank and shook vigorously, pelting Jenny with clumps of snow. Jenny stumbled and fell. Sadie started licking her face, making Jenny giggle as she tried to fend off the determined pooch. "Stop it, Sadie, stop it."

"She must think you're a sausage," Bethany called from the doorway. She had her arms crossed over her chest and her shoulders hunched against the cold.

Michael packed a snowball and threw it. It smacked against the side of the house above Bethany's head, sending a shower of snow her way. She ducked and brushed the crystals from her clothes. "Hey, that's not fair. I'm not dressed for a snowball fight."

"Then go back inside. Sadie needs to concentrate. You're distracting her." In truth, he was the one distracted by her presence.

"Well, don't expect to get any more sausage from me." She was smiling as she shut the door. A few seconds later he saw her draw the shade aside at the window so she could watch them.

For the next hour he and Jenny worked at teaching Sadie to find the girl. By the time they were both too cold to continue, Sadie was getting it right about half the time. She was still more interested in hunting among the trees than she was in finding Jenny even for a piece of sausage.

"I say we call it quits," Michael said as he sat down on the back porch steps and rubbed his aching thigh.

"She's almost got it." Jenny sat beside him.

"If we work with her a few more days I think she will find you most times, as long as a rabbit doesn't run in front of her."

Jenny tipped her head to smile at him. "Maybe if I had a rabbit in my pocket instead of sausage she would do better."

"You may be onto something. Where can we get a bunch of pocket-size rabbits?"

"You're funny, Michael."

"You are, too, Jenny."

"Are you going to stay with us a long time?"

He shrugged. "That's a hard question to answer."

"Don't you like it here?"

"Truthfully, I don't like the cold."

"Wait till summer. Then you'll really love it here."

He brushed snow from the top of her hat. "I will be here that long, anyway."

"Why don't you have a wife?"

He leaned back to stare at her. "That's kind of a personal question."

"Well? Why don't you?"

"I guess because I've never met someone that I wanted to marry."

"Gemma says my sister needs to be married so Ivan can stay here and not have to go live with our *onkel* Harvey."

"I know your sister loves Ivan just like she loves you. But when people get married it has to be because they love each other and not for any other reason."

"You don't have a wife. You could marry Bethany and you'd sort of be my *daed.*"

"It's not that simple.

"All the kids in my class have *daeds*. Sometimes they feel sorry for me. There is going to be a father-daughter program in the spring. It would be nice if you could come as my *daed.*"

"Jenny, Bethany and I are not going to get married, but I will take you to the father-daughter program anyway. How's that?"

She smiled brightly. "You will?"

"I promise."

"That makes me happy. Can we go in now? My toes are cold."

"Excellent idea. My everything is cold."

She got up and took hold of his hand to pull him to his feet. To his surprise, she hung on to his hand as they walked into the house.

* * *

Bethany was sitting beside the window, mending one of Ivan's shirts, when Jenny and Michael came in. "How goes the training?"

"We've decided that to be one hundred percent effective Jenny must have a rabbit in her pocket when she gets lost. Sadie Sue likes hunting rabbits a little bit more than she likes tracking down Jenny even for a bite of sausage."

The dog, who had been sitting quietly beside Michael, suddenly took off toward the front door. She barked several times when someone knocked.

Bethany got up and went to answer the door. Her *Englisch* neighbor, Greg Janson, tipped his hat. "Good evening, Ms. Martin. I would like a few minutes of your time to discuss something that happened on my farm last night."

A sense of foreboding filled Bethany. "Does this have anything to do with Ivan?"

"In fact it does. I've come to you first. But I'm not opposed to going to the sheriff."

Bethany invited him in. Michael stood in the hallway. Bethany indicated him with one hand. "Michael, this is Greg Janson. He has the farm south of here. Mr. Janson, this is Michael Shetler. He is a business partner."

Mr. Janson nodded. Bethany led the way into the kitchen. "Would you like some coffee, Mr. Janson?"

"No, thank you, ma'am. I'll get right to the point. Last night someone broke into my henhouse and stole three laying hens. The commotion woke my son. He looked out and saw Ivan running down the road with a gunnysack slung over his back."

"If it was nighttime, how was your son able to recognize Ivan?" Michael asked.

"My boy is in the same class as Ivan. He knows him pretty well. They've even been in a scuffle or two together. Plus, the boy was dressed Amish with those flattop black hats you folks prefer."

"I appreciate you coming to me first," Bethany said quietly.

"We have heard a lot of good things about having the Amish for neighbors and for the most part you folks have lived up to your reputation. I don't want to bring the sheriff into this if I don't have to. Things like this can get blown out of proportion. Anybody who has a pig or goat come up missing, they can point a finger at the Amish without any proof. You folks just accept that and forgive the accusers. Nothing gets solved and folks keep on thinking you're guilty. I don't want to see that get started here."

"We appreciate your attitude, Mr. Janson. Would you like to speak to Ivan?" Michael asked.

"I'll leave that up to you."

"I will pay you what the hens are worth." Bethany got up to find her checkbook.

Michael stalled her with a hand to her shoulder. "I'm responsible for Ivan now. I will take care of this."

Mr. Janson held up one hand and shook his head. "I could just as easily have lost them to a lynx or coyote. I don't want to be paid for them. I came here because I want your boy to know that he was seen and that next time he comes on the place I will call the sheriff."

The outside door opened and Ivan came in. He stopped and his eyes grew wide when he saw Mr. Janson. Bethany beckoned to him. "We were just talking about you."

"About me? Why?"

"Because my boy Max saw you stealing our chickens last night," Janson said.

Ivan shook his head. "It wasn't me."

"Max knows you. He was certain."

Ivan looked at Michael. "Honest, I didn't go out last night. Why would I take chickens?"

Michael laid a hand on Ivan's shoulder. "Do you know who might have done it?"

Ivan stared down at his feet. "I only know it wasn't me."

Bethany turned to Mr. Janson. "Thank you for bringing this to our attention."

"Like I said, I don't want it to get out of hand." He tipped his hat to her and left.

Bethany waited until the door closed and then she turned to Ivan. "How could you do something so foolish?"

"I knew you wouldn't believe me."

Michael kept his hand on Ivan's shoulder. "I believe you. Why would someone want to make it look like you are the one who took them?"

"I don't know."

"But you do have an idea who it was, don't you?"

Ivan turned his pleading eyes to Michael. "I can't tell. I promised I wouldn't tell."

Chapter Ten

Bethany was shocked that Michael believed Ivan. Even she doubted her brother's innocence. Yet the crime didn't make any sense. Why would Ivan steal three chickens?

Why would anyone? The vast majority of farms in the area had their own chickens as she did.

"Go on and get ready for supper, Ivan." When her brother left the room, Bethany looked at Michael. "What are we going to do with him?"

"The next time there is a report about something Ivan is suspected of doing, I think it would be best to involve the police."

"The bishop would not agree to that. Our community has taken great pains to avoid any involvement by the *Englisch* law."

"The police can easily rule out Ivan as a suspect by fingerprints or by DNA. Their findings will carry weight with the *Englisch* community."

"You really think someone is deliberately blaming Ivan?"

"I do."

She wished she could be so positive. This setback

was crushing. "I'm not sure I can simply wait for another incident to occur."

"It's the only choice we have unless Ivan can be convinced to break his promise and tells us what he knows."

"Do you know who he's protecting?"

"I think I do but I have no proof. I think you know, too."

"Jeffrey?"

He nodded. She shook her head in bewilderment. "But why? Do you think we should tell the bishop about this?"

Michael took his time answering her. "I'd rather not, but if you feel you should, then I'm okay with it."

"What do we do?"

"We keep to a normal pattern of activity. And we keep a good eye on Ivan. What are your plans for this week?"

"I have a lot of things that need to be done. Christmas is getting closer by the minute. I have a ton of baking to get finished. On Saturday I plan to send the children out to collect fir branches and winterberries for the house and for wreaths. I was hoping that you would go with them."

"I can."

"On Sunday Pastor Frank is coming to supper."

"Why?" He looked at her suspiciously.

"Because he's a friend. We enjoyed his company. He frequently drives us and other Amish people in his van at no charge."

"I see."

She walked to the window and stared out at the low gray clouds scuttling across the sky. A few snowflakes floated down from them. She wound the ribbon of her *kapp* around one finger. "I had asked Frank to speak with Ivan about his behavior but I never took Ivan to see him. He's been doing so much better lately. You have been a good influence on him. But now this."

Michael walked up to stand behind her. She could see their reflection together in the window. She was becoming dependent on him for advice and for comfort. She longed to rest her head against his shoulder and feel she wasn't facing this problem alone.

"I know you're worried," he said quietly.

If she leaned back, would he take her in his arms? It was a foolish thought. "To worry is to doubt God's mercy. I try not to, but it seems to be my best talent."

He chuckled. "I thought speaking Cow was your best talent."

She smiled. "Don't tell Frank I get my advice from Clarabelle. He went to many years of school to become a psychologist and counselor so he could advise folks."

"Jenny thinks you should marry. That way Ivan won't be sent away."

Bethany looked down as her face grew hot. "She's been listening to Gemma. Husbands don't exactly grow on trees in New Covenant."

"Anyone you chose would be getting a fine wife."

She looked up to study his reflection in the glass but it wasn't clear enough to let her see what he was thinking. "Are you making me an offer?"

"You would be getting a very poor bargain if I was."

She turned around so she could look into his eyes. "Why do you say that?"

"Because it's the truth."

There was so much pain in his voice and deep in his eyes that she wanted to hold him and promise to make everything better. She couldn't. She knew that, but it didn't lessen her desire to help him.

The letter from Mr. Meyers hadn't told her why Michael didn't return to work in his store or why he left his family in Ohio to come to Maine. He could have easily fixed watches for Mr. Meyers there the same way he was doing here. "What's wrong, Michael?"

He laid a hand against her cheek. "Nothing that you can fix."

"How do I know that if you can't tell me what troubles you?"

"Trust me. You don't want to know." He turned and walked down the hall and out the back door.

He was so wrong. She wanted to know everything about Michael Shetler. Her mother's voice echoed from the past. *If you don't know a man inside and out, don't marry him. He'll bring you nothing but pain.*

Michael was up early on Saturday because he knew Ivan and Jenny would be over as soon as they could. He hoped that Bethany would accompany them on their trek into the woods to gather winterberries and fir boughs for wreath making but he wasn't sure that she would. It was hard for him to believe that he had only been in New Covenant a little over two weeks. So much had happened. So much had changed. He hadn't had a flashback for thirteen days and not a single panic attack. Maybe his PTSD episodes were behind him for good. He prayed it was true.

Sadie alerted him that the children had arrived by scratching at the door and woofing softly. He opened the door and she shot outside, barking and bounding around Jenny. The girl was pulling a red toboggan. She dropped to her knees and threw her arms around Sadie's neck. The dog responded by licking her face. Jenny's giggle was so much like Bethany's that anyone could tell they were related. Ivan stopped to pet the dog, too.

Bethany came up the hill behind the children. Her bright welcoming smile was like the sun breaking through on a dreary day. He was happy to see her smiling again after the depressing visit with Mr. Janson.

Michael's refusal to talk about his past troubled her, too. He knew that, but his decision would never change.

Bethany pulled a blue toboggan with a bushel basket on it. Like the children, she was bundled for the outdoors with a heavy coat, mittens and snow boots. The red-and-white-striped knit scarf around her neck was identical to the one Jenny was wearing.

Ivan patted Sadie and then hurried to Michael's door. He was pulling a yellow disk sled. "*Guder mariye*, Michael."

"Morning, Ivan. So where are we going?"

The boy pointed up the ridge. "I know the perfect place to get pine boughs. It isn't far."

Michael looked at the pine-covered forest stretching up into the mountains. "I hope that's true. I'm not sure my leg will hold up in all this snow. Besides, don't we have about a million trees to choose from close to home?"

"It has to be balsam fir and we will pull you on the sled if you get tired." Bethany stopped beside Ivan.

"I give up. Why balsam?" Michael returned her smile. The darkness of his past was etched deep in his soul, but just being with her gave him hope that he could be healed. He prayed that God would show him mercy.

Michael couldn't plan any kind of family life until he was sure, but he could dream of the day when he had the right to tell Bethany how he felt about her.

"I want balsam fir because of its wonderful, spicy scent, its lovely color and its short dense needles."

Michael looked at both of their sleds. "Are we planning to bring back a lot of branches? I was thinking we'd have an armful or two."

Bethany began counting on her fingers. "Gemma and her mother want some. We need enough for our house and for your cabin. Plus, I will make some for friends and I also plan to sell a few at the grocer's. Mr. Meriwether lets us set up a display in front of his store. Last year I sold thirty-eight of them and made almost a thousand dollars."

"I didn't know you operated a seasonal business."

"We have to make ends meet any way we can. Are you ready?"

He nodded even though he wasn't looking forward to the hike. Sadie Sue took off after a rabbit.

Ivan put Jenny on her sled and pulled her along as he walked beside Michael. Ivan met Michael's gaze. "The snow might get too deep for her. A man takes care of his family, right?"

Michael smiled. "Right."

When Sadie Sue returned without a bunny, Jenny coaxed her to sit on the sled with her. She and Ivan took turns pulling the dog along. Sadie wasn't sure she liked the ride and kept jumping off and then back on. Their antics had Michael and Bethany laughing as they made their way up into the forest.

Ivan was true to his word. He led them to a small grove of the fir trees less than three hundred yards beyond Michael's cabin. The trees were almost all the same size at about eight feet tall and evenly spaced.

Michael glanced at Bethany. "Someone planted this grove. Do we have permission to harvest these?"

She gave him a reassuring grin. "We do. This land

belongs to Pastor Frank. We are free to use what we like. If we take a whole tree, he asks that we replant one to replace it."

"He's a generous man." Michael hadn't seen him since the night of his flashback. Although he had been tempted to attend the survivors' group meeting, he wasn't ready to have others know about his problem.

Bethany distributed clippers to everyone and they set about filling the sleds with piles of the wonderfully pungent branches. When the children had finished cutting, they went exploring while the adults cinched down the loads with lengths of rope.

Michael tied off the last knot, dusted the snow from a nearby fallen log and sat down to rest. Bethany came over to join him. The view spread out before them was breathtaking. They could see the winding course of the river down below, the silver ribbon of highway that paralleled the river's course and the houses of Fort Craig. In the distance the Appalachian mountain range provided a beautiful backdrop. It was a lovely spot and he had a beautiful woman beside him.

She rubbed her hands up and down on her arms. "It's getting colder."

He slipped his arm around her and she moved closer, making his heart beat faster. Not with fear but with joy.

"How long have you been taking care of your brother and sister?" Michael asked gently. He leaned forward to see her face.

Bethany smiled. "A long time."

"What happened to your parents? Does it bother you to talk about it?"

She shook her head. "My mother passed away shortly after Jenny was born. The doctor had a medical reason but I think she died of a broken heart. My father had left us about a month before that."

"I don't understand."

"Neither did I. If you are thinking that my father died, you are mistaken. My father packed up and moved away. He didn't want to be Amish anymore. It was the third time he had come back into our lives, begged for forgiveness, and was welcomed by our Amish community. I would like to give him credit for trying to shoulder his responsibilities, but I'm not sure he tried very hard."

"He left your mother twice before that? Left her and his children?" Michael could barely believe what he was hearing.

"The first time he went away I was six. I woke up on my sixth birthday to find my mother crying and my father gone. Just gone. He didn't bother to tell me goodbye."

"I'm sorry. That was cruel."

"He came back two years later, said he was sorry and begged Mother to give him another chance. She did. I was overjoyed. Mother was, too, but only for a while. He stayed for three years but even as a child I could see they weren't happy together. He left again. The next time he came back he only stayed a year."

"Did he ever tell you why he couldn't stay or what he did when he was away?"

"Not to me. He refused to talk about his other life. He did come to Mother's funeral. I thought he would take care of us but he said he couldn't. I was sixteen. He left me with a brokenhearted little boy and a newborn babe. We haven't seen or heard from him since."

"It's hard to believe a man could cast aside his responsibilities that way." No wonder she was so committed to keeping the children with her.

"Fortunately, our mother's father, Elijah, stepped up to take us in. My father's brother, Onkel Harvey, was willing to accept us but I wanted to stay with Grandpa. That's how I ended up helping Elijah look for a place to start his new Amish community. Each fall after the farm work was done, we would travel to different locations, looking for a place to settle. When we received a letter from Pastor Frank telling us about New Covenant, we decided to visit during the winter to see just how bad it was going to be. The road leading to our farm was merely a tunnel plowed through four feet of snow."

"I'm sorry about your father."

"Our faith requires a strength of character that he didn't possess. My mother could have gone with him, but she refused to abandon her faith and break her vows to God."

"She must've been a strong woman."

"She was, but each time my father came back and then left again, it was like he took pieces of her strength with him until there was nothing left."

"You have inherited your strength from her."

"I hope so. She wanted Father to come back so badly. She prayed for it. When she knew she was dying, she made me promise I would keep the family together. She didn't say she wanted it for him in case he came back, but I think that's exactly what she hoped for."

"It was a big burden to place on a young girl." He bent and kissed her lips gently.

He felt her sharp intake of breath and he drew back. "Maybe I shouldn't have done that."

"I didn't mind."

He looked away from the comfort she offered. "Did you ever consider leaving the Amish?"

"I think we all question at one time or another if this path to God is the right one for us. I never seriously considered leaving. What about you?"

"I did more than question. I left the Amish life behind and lived in the outside world for five years."

She gave him a funny look. "You did? What made you come back?"

"That is not something I care to talk about." His answer seemed to take her by surprise.

"I'm sorry. I'm just trying to understand. You say you want to live alone but you spend almost as much time with my family as I do."

"Ivan and Jenny can be hard to resist." As was their big sister. He rose to his feet and held out his hand to her. "We should head back."

"Will you remain Amish?"

He could tell it was important to her to know the answer. "I will."

Bethany allowed him to help her up but she pulled her hand away from his quickly. She had shared the most painful part of her life but he was unwilling to speak of his past. Until this moment she considered him someone she could count on. Someone dependable, but was he? He'd left the Amish once. What if he decided to leave again? A seed of doubt had been sown in her mind.

She shouldn't have let him kiss her. There was no promise between them. No plan for the future. That knowledge alone should help keep her emotions from carrying her away where he was concerned.

Ivan came through the trees with a big bundle of winterberry branches in his arms, leaving a thin trail of red berries on the snow behind him. Sadie Sue walked beside him. He laid the branches on top of the blue sled. Bethany looked around. "Where is Jenny?"

"She said she wanted to play hide-and-seek with Sadie Sue. She's gone to hide."

Michael patted the dog's head. "Let's hope she has a bunny in her pocket."

Bethany didn't look amused. "Let's pray we can find her if the dog can't."

"That will be easy. We'll just follow her footsteps in the snow," Ivan said.

Michael took Sadie Sue's head between his hands. "Find Jenny."

Sadie took off into the trees. He looked at Bethany. "Do we follow the dog or just hope she finds Jenny before it gets dark?"

"I'm going to follow the dog." She pointed to the log they had been sitting on. "You don't need to do more hiking than you have already. Rest."

Ivan sat on the log. "I'm going to wait here."

They heard Sadie barking in the distance. Bethany started toward the sound. She hadn't gone far when she saw Jenny and the dog coming toward her. Jenny was covered with snow but she was smiling from ear to ear. "She found me. I buried myself under the snow and she found me. She's the smartest dog in the whole wide world."

Bethany smiled at her sister. "Well, for that she deserves a whole sausage. Are you ready to go home?"

Jenny nodded and they began to walk side by side. She glanced up at Bethany. "Can I ask you something?"

"Sure."

"I've been thinking that you should marry Michael."

Bethany arched one eyebrow. "You've been thinking that, have you?"

Jenny cocked her head to the side as a serious expression settled over her face. "I like him. Ivan wouldn't have to go away and you could have babies."

"I see you have this all figured out. How many babies do you think I should have?"

"Three or four. Mostly girls but you could have one boy if you wanted to."

It hurt Bethany's heart to know her little sister was worrying about Ivan, too. She managed a reassuring smile. "I don't believe the bishop is going to send Ivan away, so I'm not going to marry Michael or anyone else until you and Ivan are grown up. You are my family. I don't need anyone else."

Jenny kicked at the snow. "Ivan said you would say that."

Bethany patted her sister on the head. "Then Ivan is smarter than I gave him credit for."

On Sunday evening Michael was reading Elijah's book on the history of clocks when Sadie perked up and thumped her tail on the floor. She kept her eyes on the front door. A knock followed. Michael knew who was there before he opened the door.

"Good evening, Frank."

"Evening, Michael. I thought I would stop by and see if I could interest you in a game of chess." He had a case under his arm.

"I have a strong suspicion that I'll be outclassed, but sure, come in."

Frank looked at Sadie. "Is this the same dog you had before?"

"It is."

He bent to pat her head. "Living with you certainly agrees with her. I don't see a single rib sticking out anymore. Her coat is gorgeous. Such a pretty golden color." He glanced at Michael. "How have you been?"

Michael led the way to a small table and two chairs set in the corner. He clicked on the floor lamp and took a seat. "Sadie is not the only one improving. I've come a long way."

"Really?" Frank opened his case and lifted out a chessboard and pieces. "Tell me about it."

"I haven't had a flashback or a panic attack since the last time we spoke. I've never gone so long without an episode."

Frank glanced at Michael. "I'm glad to hear it. I've been expecting you to show up at one of my support groups but you keep disappointing me."

"I don't see the need for therapy if I'm getting better on my own. You said some people get over it by themselves."

"I did say that. What do you think has made the difference?"

"Sadie Sue, for one thing. She always alerts me if someone is near. I depend on her sharp nose and ears. If I start getting edgy, she will come over and distract me. She's amazing."

"So instead of being hypervigilant, you rely on the dog to do that for you. I don't want to belittle your progress, but isn't that substituting one kind of crutch for another?"

"Maybe it is but it makes life bearable."

"Bethany tells me Ivan has been in trouble again but that you are sticking up for the boy." Frank began to place the chess pieces on the board.

"I think the saying is 'innocent until proven guilty.'"

"Sadly that is sometimes forgotten in today's society. Have you thought more about your flashback triggers?"

Michael shifted uncomfortably in his chair. "Like I told you, I haven't had one since the night we met."

"I'm glad to see you are improving but I hope you understand that recovery is a slow process. There will be setbacks. They may not be as severe as what you've had in the past but you should be prepared for them. Being prepared ahead of time makes it easier for you and for anyone with you to get through an episode. Black or white?" He held out two chess pieces.

"White. How can I be prepared for one if I never know when they will occur?" Michael positioned his men on the board.

"That's a good question. Since you are working and living close to Bethany, she might benefit from learning about this, too."

Michael glanced up sharply. "I don't want her involved."

"Is that wise? She has a good head on her shoulders. She won't panic."

"No!"

"Okay, but I think you're making a mistake."

"It's mine to make." He was aware of Bethany's withdrawal at the pine branch gathering. Was it because of his kiss or something else? It had been hard for her to relate the story of how her father bounced in and out of her life and then abandoned them. When Michael admitted that he had left the Amish once before, it touched a nerve for her.

Maybe her coolness was for the best. He was better. He knew he was better, but he wasn't sure if it would last.

After beginning the game in silence and playing for a while, Michael realized he wasn't outclassed by Pastor Frank. They were evenly matched and he began to enjoy the game.

"Do you have plans for next Saturday evening?" Frank asked.

"Nope. Why?"

"The city of Presque Isle puts on a holiday parade every year that's worth going to see. I'm getting together a vanload of Amish folks and driving them up to enjoy it. Would you like to join us?"

A big outing, crowds—he wasn't sure he was up to it. "Is it something Ivan and Jenny would enjoy?"

"Absolutely. It's fun for all ages and it's free. I've already asked Bethany and she said she would come."

"I'll consider it. I believe this is checkmate." Michael moved his queen to trap Frank's king.

Frank studied the board and sighed heavily. "I concede. Nice game."

"Another?" Michael asked.

Frank shook his head. "I should get going. I'll save you a seat in the van if you decide to go with us. Think about what I've said. Being prepared to endure a flashback or panic attack can make it easier on everyone involved."

"I'll keep it in mind."

But he wouldn't involve Bethany. Not ever.

Chapter Eleven

Bethany lifted Jenny to stand on a chair. The girl was wearing her Christmas costume and Bethany wanted to make sure the hem was straight. "Hold your arms out," she mumbled around the three straight pins she held between her lips. Two dozen more were stuck into the pincushion shaped like a tomato that she wore on her wrist.

The house smelled of pine and cinnamon. Green boughs graced the window ledges and the fireplace mantel. Christmas cards from faraway friends had started arriving. They were displayed nestled in the pine branches or hung from red yarn stretched across the windows. Christmas was fast approaching, and in spite of her assurance to Jenny, Bethany's last hope of keeping Ivan had crumbled. Her uncle had included a letter in his Christmas card. He strongly believed the bishop was right and Ivan should return with him. It was a bitter blow. It seemed to be God's will to separate her family.

She folded the material of the white gown under and pinned it across the top of Jenny's feet. "Is this how long you want it?"

"I don't know," Jenny said quietly.

"Did the play director tell you if you had to have wings?"

"I can't be an angel without wings."

"But you are the narrator. Should your costume be different than the other angels or the same?"

Jenny put her arms down. "I don't know." Her lower lip trembled.

Bethany took a hold of her sister's hand. "Don't cry. This is for your Christmas pageant. This should be fun. I'll make it long enough to touch the floor and if the director says it should be shorter then I will shorten it. You don't have dress rehearsal for a few days, so I have plenty of time to change it."

"Good thinking." Michael stood in the open doorway to his workroom. "If you cut it too short you won't be able to lengthen it."

She rolled her eyes at him. "Have you had a lot of experience as a seamstress?"

Michael had been joining the conversations more often in the past few days. The workroom door hadn't been closed all week. She welcomed his interactions with her family but she couldn't forget the all-too-brief kiss they'd shared. What did it mean? Did it mean anything to him? During his time in the outside world, had he kissed lots of women?

"As a matter of fact, I have had some sewing experience," he declared. "My brother and I made a camel costume for our Christmas pageant when I was in the sixth grade. We were told it was very lifelike."

Bethany looked around for her fabric marker and realized she had left it in the sewing room. "I'll be right back, Jenny."

She left the room, grabbed the marker from the sewing machine and started back into the kitchen. She was in the hall when she heard Michael say, "Of course you can ask me anything, Jenny. What's wrong?"

Bethany waited in the hall to hear what Jenny had to say. Why was her sister confiding in Michael instead of in her?

"I don't want to be the narrator," Jenny said.

"You don't? Why not? I think you will make a fine narrator."

"Mrs. Whipple says my voice is too small. I didn't know I had a small voice. How do I get a bigger one?"

"I don't think there's anything wrong with your voice, Jenny. Who is Mrs. Whipple?"

"She's one of the ladies helping our director, Miss Carson. I heard her tell Miss Carson that someone else should be the narrator because she couldn't hear me in the back row."

"That made you feel bad, didn't it?"

Bethany didn't hear anything. She assumed Jenny was nodding.

"Jenny, I will be happy to help you make your voice bigger."

"You will?" Jenny sounded thrilled.

"Absolutely. We will practice once your sister is finished with your costume. Just come into the workroom when the two of you are done."

"I'm not supposed to bother you in the workroom."

He chuckled. "That's only when the door is closed. When the door is open you can come in whenever you like."

Bethany walked into the kitchen and saw Jenny had her arms around Michael's neck. He pulled her arms away as a fierce blush stained his cheeks.

"I have to get back to work," he mumbled.

He was so good with children. He should have a dozen of his own.

When she realized where her thoughts were taking her, she pushed them aside. He wasn't the one for her. How could she consider a relationship with someone whose past was so full of secrets, with a man who didn't feel he could confide in her?

Michael closed the cover of a grandmother clock after setting the time. He waited as it ticked its way to the top of the hour. The chimes rang out in clear pure tones. He wiped his fingerprints from the glass. Tomorrow he would pack it up and mail it back to George Meyers. His former boss had been sending a steady stream of work his way, and Michael was grateful.

Jenny appeared in the doorway. "Can I come in?"

"Sure."

She came in and climbed up on his work stool. She opened the drawer and lifted out one of the tools. "Will one of these tools make my voice bigger?"

He smiled and took the pliers from her. "We will save those as a last resort. You stand on a stage, don't you?"

She nodded. He lifted her onto the workbench. "There are a few things you have to do to get a bigger voice. Right now, I want you to close your eyes. And I want you to whisper your first two lines."

Movement caught his eye and he glanced over to see Bethany watching him. He beckoned her to come in. She did but she stayed by the door.

"How was that?" Jenny asked.

"Fine. I want you to keep your eyes closed and pretend you need Ivan to come in from the other room.

He's pretty far away but you can't yell. Want to try it? Talk loud. Say your lines."

"Ivan, a long time ago, in a land far away, there were shepherds tending their flocks in the hills near the little town of Bethlehem. Can you hear me?"

"That's pretty good. Now I want you to try telling him again but this time he is upstairs."

She shook her head. "I don't think he can hear me upstairs."

"Bethany, will you go to the stairwell and see if you can hear Jenny?"

"Of course." She turned and walked out of the room.

Jenny repeated her lines in a loud voice. A few moments later Bethany returned.

"Well?" Michael looked at Bethany for confirmation.

"I heard her, but just barely."

"Hmm. I wonder what will help. Bethany, do you have any suggestions?"

They conferred and with some practice they were able to get Jenny to be heard by someone standing on the stairwell. Jenny was excited that she wouldn't have to give up being the narrator and promised to speak loud enough to be heard on the roof. As she went to change out of her costume, Bethany stayed in the workroom.

She opened one of the drawers. "I've often wondered what all these things are for."

He sensed that she wanted to talk about something else. He would let her work up her courage. "It looks like a lot of stuff but there are just different sizes of the same items. Gears and pins. Pliers and screwdrivers. Tweezers and little magnets to retrieve dropped pieces of metal."

She picked up his jeweler's loupe. "And this is to let

you see things more clearly, isn't it?" She held it to her eye and turned so she was looking at him.

"Is it working?" he asked gently.

"I'm not sure." She pulled it away from her face. "Every time I look I see something different." He knew she was talking about him.

"That is one of the drawbacks of looking too closely."

"I think the problem is I didn't have my subject in focus. What can I do about that?"

"Not much, I'm afraid, if your subject is unwilling to cooperate." He wasn't ready to risk her knowing the whole truth.

"So the loupe is for seeing small pieces in great detail. How do I see the whole picture in greater detail?"

"The trick is to take a step back," he said bluntly. Their relationship had progressed so quickly he wasn't sure of his own feelings or of hers.

She laid the lens down. "I think that's what I need to do."

"I think it would be best if we both did that."

A wry smile curved her lips. "I agree."

She started to walk past him but he caught her arm. "Can we still be friends?"

"I don't see why not," she replied, but he couldn't tell if she meant it.

Bethany expected her next meeting with Michael would be awkward. To prolong the inevitable, she went to visit her friend Gemma after the kids were off to school the following morning.

Gemma welcomed her with a hug and then intense scrutiny. "Okay, out with it. What's troubling you?"

Bethany turned away from her friend's sharp eyes.

"The same thing. Ivan." It was true but it wasn't the whole truth.

"I know you are worried about your brother but something else is on your mind or you wouldn't be here."

Bethany began to remove her bonnet and coat. "You make it sound like I never come to see you unless I'm in some kind of crisis."

Gemma poured two cups of coffee and sat down at the table with them. She pushed one across to Bethany when she sat down. "You visit me without a crisis often, but I know you well enough to see you are deeply troubled. What is it? I'm here to help."

Bethany prided herself on being in control. She didn't believe women were weaker than men, but when she looked up and saw the sympathy in Gemma's eyes, Bethany's pride flew out the window. Tears welled up and spilled down her cheeks. "I'm so confused."

"Oh, you poor dear." Gemma was around the table in a moment and gathered Bethany into her arms. "It's okay. Go ahead and cry."

"I can't abide women who act like watering cans." She sniffled and continued to cry.

Gemma patted Bethany's back. "No one could accuse you of being a watering can. You are one of the strongest women I have ever had the privilege to know."

"Then why do I feel like such a fool?" Bethany wailed.

"Because love makes glorious fools of us all."

"I'm not in love. I can't be in love."

"And yet here you are crying on my shoulder because your mystery man has stolen your heart."

Bethany drew back to stare at Gemma in amazement. "How can you know that?"

"Because I have been in love myself."

"You have? With who?"

"A fellow who is denser than a post. But never mind about me. This is about you. First I have to know how bad it is. Has he kissed you?"

Bethany buried her face in her hands and nodded, unable to speak.

"Did you kiss him back?"

"Maybe just a little," she whispered.

"Do Ivan and Jenny like him?"

"Jenny adores him. Ivan looks up to him and tries to emulate him."

"All right. Has he told you that he loves you?"

"*Nee*, we've not spoken of our feelings."

"So you haven't professed your love. Okay. Things aren't as bad as you are making them out to be."

"How can you say that? I spend my days and nights thinking about him, wondering if he's thinking about me."

"That's normal in any new relationship. I know that you are a wonderful catch for any man. I don't see the problem on this end. Why is he all wrong for you?"

Bethany wiped her face with both hands and drew a ragged breath. "Because I don't know anything about him."

"You know a lot of things about him."

"You don't understand. Something bad happened to him. He has told me in general terms what happened but I know there is something else. Something he won't talk about. He's so secretive. I'm worried that I really may not want to know what he did."

"Bethany, you have to ask yourself what is the one sin that you can't forgive."

She frowned slightly as she looked at Gemma. "There is no sin that cannot be forgiven."

"You believe that with all your heart, don't you?"

"Of course I do. Jesus died on the cross for all men's sins. We are instructed by God to forgive those that have trespassed against us."

"What is the one thing in Michael's past that you could not forgive?"

That made her pause. "I would forgive anything."

"Then why do you have to know what he has done?"

Bethany pulled her coffee mug close and took a sip. It was lukewarm. "It's not that I can't forgive his sins great or small. It's that I believe you can't love someone that you don't trust. How can he love me if he doesn't trust me enough to share his burdens?"

"Has he said that he loves you?"

"*Nee*, he has not."

"But you are in love with him?"

Bethany gave her friend a beseeching glance. "Maybe. I don't know. What would you do in my place?"

"Sell the farm and move to someplace warm."

Bethany managed a half-hearted smile. "You know I'm being serious."

"I do. I trust your judgment, Bethany. Therefore, you should trust your own judgment. You have so many things vying for your attention and that keeps you from thinking straight. You and I both know that you won't marry anyone before Christmas, even if it is the only way to keep Ivan with you. You're much too smart for that. An Amish marriage is forever. Ivan will return to us when he is older. It will be a hard separation, but it won't be forever. If you like Michael Shetler, even if you think you love him, you still need time to get to know one another."

"He asked me if we could be friends."

"Did he mean it?"

Bethany thought back to that moment. "I believe he did."

"That's a good sign. It means he cares about you and he values the relationship the two of you have. What did you say?"

"I said I didn't see why not."

"Well, that should give him some hope. Can you be his friend even if he never confides in you?"

Bethany pondered the question. She liked Michael. More than that, she cared deeply about him. He made her laugh. He understood Ivan better than she ever could. Jenny adored him and looked up to him. Bethany realized her life would be poorer if Michael Shetler wasn't in it. If his friendship was all that she could have, she would gladly hold on to it.

She nodded. "I can be his friend. You, Gemma, are such a wise friend. You give much better advice than Clarabelle."

Gemma looked appalled. "I should hope so. Isn't that your milk cow?"

Bethany chuckled. "Someday I will tell you the story. I will take your advice. I won't rush into anything. I still believe that Ivan is better off with me. I'm not letting him go without a fight."

Gemma took a sip of her coffee and made a bitter face. "That sounds like the Bethany I know and love. How about a fresh cup of hot coffee?"

"And a lemon cookie?"

"Absolutely. They come free with all my advice. How would you like to stay and help me bake cookies for the holidays? I need eight dozen."

"I would be delighted to repay even a small portion of your kindness."

Bethany spent the entire day with Gemma, enjoying her friendship, sampling new cookie recipes and making several dozen of each type to take home. Chocolate chip cookies, oatmeal cookies, gingerbread men, moose munch, sugar cookies and lemon crisps because she knew Michael would enjoy them. With several large plastic containers in her arms, she paused outside Gemma's front door.

"Thank you again."

Gemma waved aside Bethany's gratitude. "Someday I will need your shoulder to cry on."

"It will be available day or night. Are you going with Pastor Frank to see the Christmas parade in town?"

"I am. So are my folks. What about you?"

"The children and I are going for sure. I don't know about Michael."

"We will enjoy it with him or without him, right?"

"Right."

Bethany waved goodbye and headed home. As she approached her lane, she saw the school bus pull away. Four of the local schoolchildren went swarming up the mounds of snow left by the snowplows on her side of the road. She noticed Jeffrey was one of them but she didn't see Ivan.

She stopped to watch them playing king of the mountain. The one who obtained the summit then had to keep others from claiming his throne. There was more pushing and shoving than she liked to see, but all she did was caution them. "Make sure you don't push anyone toward the road. Stay on the outside of those piles."

"We know, Ms. Martin," one of the younger boys replied.

She left them to their fun and walked up her drive. Pastor Frank's van sat parked in front of the house. The sound of laughter and the smell of pizza greeted her as she entered. She stepped into the kitchen to see Pastor Frank, Michael, Ivan and Jenny seated around the table, making Christmas wreaths. All of them wore pine branch crowns around their heads. Michael's held two long branches upright like antlers. Jenny had two small upright branches near the front of her head. Ivan had two bushy branches hanging down. The pastor had red winterberries woven into his.

Bethany shook her head. "What is going on in here?"

"We're making Christmas wreaths to sell at the market," Jenny said.

Bethany set down her containers of cookies. "I see. Who are you supposed to be?" she asked, looking askew at all of them.

"I'm a bunny," Jenny said with a giggle. She got down from the table and hopped around the room.

Ivan slid off his chair. "I'm a hound dog." He started barking and chasing Jenny. Sadie Sue immediately got up from her place under the table and started barking at them as they ran up the stairs with her close on their heels.

Bethany looked at Michael and tried not to laugh. "I assume you are a Christmas reindeer?"

He shook his head, making one of his antlers fall off.

He picked it up and tucked it in again. "I am a Maine moose."

"Of course you are. Pastor Frank?"

"I'm a pastor with a limited imagination wearing a pine branch wreath on my head decorated by Jenny." He gave her a big smile.

She looked at the number of wreaths stacked against the wall. "You have been busy. I know the children just got home a little while ago, so, Michael, did you make these by yourself or did Frank help you?"

"Those were all done by Michael," the pastor said. "I just brought the pizza. It's baking now. You are always feeding me. I thought I'd return the favor."

Michael stretched his neck one way and then the other. "I was tired of fixing clocks and decided to try my hand at wreath making. What do you think?"

She picked up several and checked the construction. "Not bad at all. I'm sure these will sell well with a little more decoration added."

"Did you have a good day?" he asked with a shade of uncertainty in his eyes.

She smiled. "I did. I went to visit Gemma and we baked cookies all day."

"Are there samples?" Pastor Frank's gaze slid to the counter and her plastic containers.

"There are. Pastor Frank, I know you enjoy oatmeal cookies. I have two dozen set aside just for you." She handed him a full plastic baggie.

"These are going straight out to my van so I don't forget them later." He removed his crown before heading out the door.

Bethany held out a container. "I actually made

some moose munch if you want to try that, Michael the Moose."

He got up from his chair. "You don't have to ask me twice."

Opening one of the containers, he took a handful of the mix and turned to face her with his hip leaning against the counter. "How are you today?" he asked.

She cocked her head slightly. "I'm better. I had a wonderful time with Gemma and I've come to realize how truly valuable a great friendship can be."

"Present company excluded?" he asked.

"Present company included," she assured him. His smile warmed her all the way through.

Pastor Frank returned a few minutes later. The children thundered down the stairs when he called out that the pizza was ready. Bethany smiled as they crowded around him eagerly. This was the way it had been before her grandfather died. Friends stopping by. Storytelling, good food and good company. It was comforting to know it didn't have to change.

After supper Bethany and Jenny rehearsed her lines as the men decided to teach Ivan the game of chess. The boy had an aptitude for it and was soon intent on learning more moves. It was almost ten thirty when Bethany called a stop to the game.

"It's a school night and it is way past Ivan's bedtime." She had tucked Jenny in hours ago.

Pastor Frank pulled on his coat. "I apologize for keeping you all up so late. It was like old times and I guess I got carried away. Good night, all."

Bethany and Michael watched him leave from the doorway. When he drove out of sight, she closed the door.

"I'd better leave, too," Michael said. "I had a fine

time tonight, Bethany. I've forgotten how satisfying an ordinary night with friends can be."

"I'm glad you enjoyed yourself. We'll do it again soon."

He put on his hat and coat, but instead of leaving he seemed to come to some decision. "The weather isn't bad and I've been sitting too long. Would you care to take a walk with me?"

"That would be nice." She put on her coat and gloves and walked out the door to stand beside him. "Which way?"

"You have lived here longer than I have. You choose the direction."

"There is a path that leads to an overlook. It's not too steep."

"I'll keep up. Don't worry about me."

She took him at his word. They walked in silence for a time with Sadie Sue ambling alongside Michael. The crunch of their boots in the snow was the only sound. It was cold, but Bethany was warmly dressed and exercise kept her from getting chilled. "What do you think of New Covenant?" It was a safe subject and she was interested in his opinion.

"It's a long way from being a self-supportive community."

"What do you think we need here?"

"You don't have a blacksmith or wheelwright."

"We have a blacksmith coming in the spring. A man with three boys."

"You don't have an Amish school."

"Once we reach ten school-age children in the community, the bishop will allow us to hire a teacher and open a school of our own."

"You need a grocer. Mr. Meriwether's prices are too high."

She chuckled. "Tell me something I don't know. I shop there every week."

"And where is the nearest pizza parlor? What is an Amish settlement without a pizza parlor?"

"There is one in Fort Craig. They even deliver."

"I'll have to get their number. What about you, Bethany? What do you want out of New Covenant?"

"I want to see a happy, healthy, thriving community. We are so few and far between right now. I pray the community survives."

"And if that doesn't happen? What if there is a split in the church? It happens all the time. You won't be immune because of your remoteness."

She shrugged. "I guess we'll just have to face that issue when it comes, if it comes. I like to expect the best that life has to offer."

"Isn't it better to expect the worst and then be pleased when it doesn't show up?"

"I reckon you and I simply look at life differently. Here is the overlook I mentioned. I don't see anyone around now, but it's a popular place with young lovers in the spring and summer."

They came out onto a rock ledge that jutted out between two old pine trees. Below was a stunning view of the Aroostook River. It was a silver ribbon winding its way through the countryside illuminated by a full moon just rising. She pointed east. "See where the farmland stops and the forest starts?"

"I do."

"That is Canada."

"Good to know in case I ever want to leave the country in a hurry."

"It is farther than it looks. Shall we go back?"

"Are you getting cold?"

"A little," she admitted.

They walked back to the house in silence. Bethany was overwhelmed by the smell of pine boughs when she entered the front door. The scent would always remind her of Michael in the future. She turned to face him. "Good night, Michael."

"You take care," he said as he went out into the night with Sadie Sue at his heels. Bethany sighed as she watched him walk up the hill. Being friends was truly the best path for them. Wasn't it?

Only the ache in her heart said it might not be enough.

Chapter Twelve

Bethany rose from bed feeling more rested than she had in weeks. Her first thought was to wonder if Michael shared the same feeling of relief that they were remaining friends, or did he hope for more one day?

She was fixing herself coffee when she heard a truck pull up in front of the house. She looked out the window. Mr. Meriwether got out of his delivery van and started for the house. The sheriff's SUV pulled up behind him. The look on their faces said it wasn't a social visit.

Bethany clutched her chest. "Oh, Ivan, what have you done now?"

Since he wasn't out of bed yet, he couldn't very well answer her question. She opened the door before Mr. Meriwether knocked. He inclined his head. "Good morning, Ms. Martin."

"Good day to you, Mr. Meriwether, Sheriff Lundeen. What can I do for you gentlemen?"

"I'm afraid we are here on an unpleasant errand," the sheriff said.

Mr. Meriwether nodded. "It sure is. Last night a little after midnight someone broke into one of my warehouses. They took several thousand dollars' worth of mechanic's tools, and brand-new toolboxes."

"What does that have to do with me?" she asked, fearing she knew the answer.

The sheriff removed his hat. "Is your brother, Ivan, at home?"

"*Ja*, he is here, though he is still abed."

The sheriff came in, forcing Bethany to step out of his way. "We're going to need to talk to him. The perpetrator was caught on a surveillance camera. It appears to be your brother arriving on foot and then he begins loading the stolen merchandise into a white panel van that pulled up just outside the fence. We didn't get a good look at the driver or the plates."

"It was an Amish boy fitting your brother's description," Mr. Meriwether added as he followed the sheriff inside.

Bethany led them into the living room with her heart pounding so hard she thought they must be able to hear it. This was serious. Thousands of dollars' worth of tools? This wasn't three chickens. She grew sick at heart. "I will go upstairs and get my brother. I'm sure he had nothing to do with this. Please have a seat."

"Thank you for your cooperation, ma'am." The sheriff sat on the edge of her sofa.

She hustled Ivan out of bed with only the briefest of explanations. She went into Jenny's room. "Jenny, get up and go get Michael. Tell him I need him right away."

"But I haven't had any breakfast."

"You can eat later. Now go."

The shock on Ivan's face when he saw the sheriff waiting for him told her he knew nothing about what was going on.

She stood beside Ivan. The sheriff began questioning him. Michael arrived twenty minutes later. "Can you fill me in?" he asked the law officer.

The sheriff looked him up and down. "Are you the boy's parent?"

"I'm not. I'm a friend."

"Then I don't see how this concerns you."

"I gave my word to our bishop that I would assume responsibility for Ivan's action. Anything that concerns him concerns me. If not, we must ask you to leave until the bishop and church elders can join us."

Bethany could see the wheels turning in the sheriff's mind. Did he want one Amish man or a whole roomful of them present for his questioning? Reluctantly he agreed to have Michael present and filled him in on what was known.

Michael was the one who picked up on a discrepancy. "You say the robbery took place a few minutes before eleven. We were here with Pastor Frank Pearson until ten thirty. We all saw Ivan go upstairs."

"But you admit that he could have left the premises after you did," the sheriff pointed out.

"You say a boy arrived on foot and a second perpetrator in a white panel van pulled up a few minutes later. Even if Ivan left here at 10:31, he would have been hard-pressed to run three miles in very cold temperatures and then calmly walk into Mr. Meriwether's warehouse and carry out the tools you claim were stolen."

Bethany could see the sheriff wavering. He said, "It's not outside the realm of possibility. He could have gotten a ride with the person in the van."

"But it is reasonable doubt," Michael insisted. "Were

there fingerprints? Do you have a full view of his face on tape?"

Bethany was grateful for Michael's presence. He seemed to know exactly what to say.

The sheriff leaned forward on the couch and stared at Ivan. "We can't make a positive ID but it appears to be a boy wearing gloves, a dark coat and a black Amish hat."

Michael turned to Ivan. "Did you do it?"

Ivan shook his head. "*Nee.* I did not."

The sheriff sighed as he rose to his feet. "I don't have enough to hold the boy at this point. I have to wait for my forensics team to process the scene. Ivan, you can't leave town. Do you understand?"

Ivan nodded. Michael said, "Believe me, we want you to find this guy as much as you want to find him."

After the sheriff and Meriwether left, Bethany knelt in front of her brother and took his hand. "What do you know about this?"

"I think I can get the tools back, but I'm not going to turn anyone in."

"You can't protect Jeffrey forever," Michael said softly.

"You don't understand. I have to help him."

"Do you know who was driving the van?" Michael asked.

He shook his head. "I'm not sure."

Ivan left the room and Bethany didn't think twice about throwing herself into Michael's arms. She needed him. And he was there for her. "What should I do? I thought sending him to live with my uncle was terrible, but sending him to jail is unthinkable."

"It won't come to that. He's a juvenile. Besides, the evidence they have is circumstantial."

She leaned back to look at his face. "How do you know so much about police proceedings?"

"You know the store where I worked last year was robbed. I answered questions from the police for weeks on end. I can't believe I was able to listen to his interrogation without breaking down. I guess I really am doing better," he mumbled more to himself than to her.

She gazed at his dear face. "Thank you for everything."

He held her away and took a step back. "That's what friends do."

Early the following morning, Bethany heard a car turn into her drive. It was the sheriff again. Had he come to arrest Ivan? He stopped a few feet from her walkway and got out. She opened the door as he reached the porch with her heart in her throat. "Good morning, Sheriff."

"Good morning. Is Ivan here?"

"I hope so. I haven't seen him yet. Has there been another robbery?" She braced herself to hear the answer.

"No. In fact, just the opposite has occurred. Sometime during the night all the tools and equipment stolen from Mr. Meriwether's property were left outside his gate. There doesn't appear to be any damage. Nothing is missing. Mr. Meriwether is dropping all the charges."

Relief made her knees weak. "That's wonderful news." It wouldn't keep Ivan from being sent to live with Uncle Harvey, but it was so much better than having him go to jail that it didn't seem horrible anymore. She couldn't wait to tell Michael.

After the sheriff left, Bethany pulled on her coat and boots, intent on seeing Michael, but a knock on the door stopped her. She opened it and saw Mrs. Morgan, Jeffrey's mother, on the porch. The woman had a large bruise on her face and a split lip.

"Mrs. Morgan, what happened? Come in. Do you need to go to the hospital?" Bethany put her arm around the woman and helped her inside.

"Don't mind me. This is nothing. Is Jeffrey here? He didn't come home last night."

"He's not here. You must be out of your mind with worry. Let me get Ivan. Maybe he knows where Jeffrey is. Come in and sit down." The woman entered the kitchen and sat down as Bethany raced up the stairs to Ivan's room. She sagged with relief when she saw he was still in bed. She shook his shoulder. "Ivan, wake up. Mrs. Morgan is downstairs. She says Jeffrey is missing. Do you know where he is?"

Ivan sat up, rubbing his face. "I thought he was at home."

"When was the last time you saw him?"

"About midnight."

"Midnight? You went out last night?"

"Yeah. I'm sorry. I had to."

Bethany considered sending him to fetch Michael, but she realized there was nothing Michael could do. She went downstairs and found Mrs. Morgan with arms crossed and her head down on the kitchen table, weeping.

Bethany sat down beside her and put her arm around the woman's shoulders. "It's going to be all right. Ivan hasn't seen him since last night."

Michael appeared in the workshop doorway. "What's going on?"

Bethany quickly filled him in. He came and sat down

across from Mrs. Morgan. "I think you should call the police."

Mrs. Morgan looked up and clutched Bethany's arm. "No. I can't do that."

Two nights later, Sadie's low growl brought Michael wide-awake. She left his bedside and trotted to the door. He sat up in bed. "What's wrong, girl?"

Sadie whined, looked back at him and whined again. Michael slipped out of bed, pulling the top quilt over himself against the cold night air. "I'm coming."

He made his way to the window beside the door. He used the corner of the quilt to wipe the frost from the center of the glass. He was expecting to see a lynx or coyote. Instead he watched a human figure approach the back door of Bethany's home and disappear into the shadows. His heart started pounding. Was she in danger?

He tossed the quilt aside, quickly pulling on his clothes and boots. He grabbed his coat from the hook by the door and pulled it on as he stepped outside. Sadie stood by his side but she wasn't growling. She looked at him. He nodded. "Go find him."

She started toward Bethany's house with Michael close behind her. The beam of a flashlight shone from the open back door. Michael couldn't see who was holding it, but he did see the person the light settled on. It was Jeffrey Morgan. The boy entered the house and the light went out. When the kitchen light came on, Michael decided to investigate further. Sadie was already at the back door, scratching and whining to be let in. Michael stood in the shadow of the pine tree off to the side and waited. When the door opened it was Ivan. "Sadie, stop it. You'll wake everybody. Go home."

Michael stepped out of the shadows. "Good evening, Ivan."

The boy's eyes widened in shock. "Michael. What are you doing here?"

"Sadie alerted me to a prowler. You've got some explaining to do."

"I reckon I do. Come into the kitchen." He turned and walked down the hall. Michael followed him.

Jeffrey was at the kitchen table, eating baked beans straight out of the can. As Michael watched Jeffrey tear into his food, it reminded him of the first time he saw Sadie gulp a sandwich down in one bite. Michael looked at Ivan. "What's going on?"

Jeffrey stopped eating to glance at Ivan and shook his head no.

Ivan spread his hands wide. "We can't do it by ourselves. Michael will help."

"He'll make me go back."

Michael took a seat across the table from Jeffrey. Ivan sat beside his friend. "Jeffrey can't go home. He isn't safe there."

Jeffrey had stopped eating and was staring down at the table. "I won't go back."

Michael reached across the table and put two fingers under the boy's chin. Jeffrey flinched but didn't pull away. Michael lifted the child's face until Jeffrey looked at him. "I know a lot about being afraid. I won't make you do anything that you don't want to do. Why don't you tell me about it?"

Jeffrey compressed his lips into a thin line. It was Ivan who spoke. "His dad beats him."

"He hits my mom, too," Jeffrey added in a small voice.

Michael sat back. He had suspected as much after Mrs. Morgan refused to call the police or go to the hospital, but this was beyond his ability to help. He wished Bethany was here.

Jeffrey stuck his fork in the empty can. "That's why I got so mad when I learned you were going to be staying in the cabin. I used to stay there when things are bad at home. I'm sorry I broke your window."

"I thought Ivan threw the rock." Michael glanced between the boys.

Jeffrey looked at Ivan. "He took the blame for me. He sticks up for me a lot."

"The stolen supplies from Jedidiah—was that your doing or Ivan's?"

The boys exchanged guilty glances. Ivan wrinkled his nose. "It was sort of my idea. The bishop preaches that we have to share with those in need. I figured Jedidiah would share if he knew, so I took what I thought he could spare. I didn't know he'd be so upset about it. I was going to leave him a note but I didn't have paper or a pen with me."

"He only did it to help my family. Sometimes my mom and my little brother and sister don't have enough to eat. I helped him carry the stuff," Jeffrey added. "We're sort of both to blame."

Michael sighed. "I see you are equal partners in crime, as it were."

The boys nodded.

Michael shook his head in disbelief. "It's always better to ask first. And the chickens?"

"Mom had to cook our laying hens a few weeks ago.

The little ones missed having eggs in the morning. I only took what we needed to eat."

"How did you boys get the tools returned to Mr. Meriwether?"

Jeffrey looked pleased. "I sort of borrowed my dad's van. I know how to drive it. He hadn't sold the stuff yet." The boy's grin faded. "He got real mean when he found the stuff was missing. I had to get away."

Ivan locked his pleading gaze on Michael. "What are you going to do now? You can't make him go home."

Michael rubbed his aching leg, stalling for time. He didn't know what to do. If Jeffrey was a member of the Amish faith, he would take this to the bishop. This required someone with a level head and a compassionate heart. "Ivan, I think you should go wake your sister."

"I'm up." Bethany came into the room, pulling the belt of her pink robe tight. "I overheard most of this conversation. Jeffrey, do you know your mother is worried sick about you?"

He shrugged one shoulder. "I left her a note tonight. She'll know I'm okay when she reads it."

Michael exchanged a knowing look with Bethany. She sat down beside him. He was glad of her presence. She smiled softly at Jeffrey. "You're a thirteen-year-old boy and it's winter in Maine. How are you surviving? Where are you staying?"

Jeffrey wouldn't look at her. "Here and there."

"And how often in the past two days have you had a decent meal?"

He lifted the empty can. "Tonight."

Michael shared a speaking glance with Bethany.

"What should we do?" she asked, speaking Pennsylvania Dutch. "He isn't Amish. The *Englisch* have many rules about children."

"They do have complicated laws about child custody. I know that much from my time in the outside world. We could be in trouble for not telling the police he is here."

Jeffrey surged to his feet. "I don't know what you're saying but I won't go back."

Michael held up one hand to reassure him. "We are not suggesting that. I think going to Pastor Frank is our best option. He will listen to you, Jeffrey, and he will make the right decision. He will not put you in harm's way."

Jeffrey sank back onto his chair. Ivan laid a hand on his shoulder. "Pastor Frank is a good fellow. You can trust him."

Bethany leaned forward and took Jeffrey's hands in hers. "You have to trust us. We want what is best for both you and your mother. You can't stay out in this weather. You could die."

"That would be better than going back to him."

Michael stood up. "You and I are going to go see Pastor Frank and tell him the situation. I know he will do the right thing. You can try running away again, Jeffrey, but you will be easy to track in the snow. I don't think you'll get far."

Jeffrey put his head down on his folded arms and began to cry.

Bethany waited for Michael to return. She left a lamp on so he would know she was up. It was almost four thirty when he stepped through the door. He looked tired and he was limping heavily. She wanted to throw her arms around him and help him to the sofa but she wasn't sure he would appreciate that gesture. "How did it go?"

He sat down on the sofa beside her with a deep sigh. "Children are complicated creatures. I'm surprised parents choose to have more than one."

"That's a very cynical thing to say. Humans are indeed complicated creatures. Since the good Lord made more than one of us, I assume He sees something wonderful in each of us."

"Even Mr. Morgan?"

"Even him. He deserves forgiveness and our prayers as much if not more than anyone."

Michael sighed. "I know you're right. That is what our faith teaches us. That is what our Lord commands us to do, but sometimes it is hard living by those words. That boy was covered with bruises."

"Pastor Frank didn't make Jeffrey go back to his father, did he?"

"He knew exactly what to do. He notified the police and reported the child abuse. Jeffrey and his brother and sister were taken to a children's home where they will be well cared for until permanent placement can be found. Frank is sure they'll go back to their mother when she is ready. Jeffrey's mother chose to go to a women's shelter."

"And Jeffrey's father?"

"Mr. Morgan was arrested and taken to jail. He is wanted in another state for burglary and arson. Apparently he often made Jeffrey steal stuff for him. It was his idea to dress Jeffrey in Amish clothing in case he was seen. Jeffrey said it was his father who damaged Greg Janson's tractor and let Robert Morris's cattle loose. He felt both men owed him more money for work he'd done for them last summer. It seems they fired him and hired two Amish fellows instead."

"At least everyone will know now that Ivan wasn't to blame for those things. I hope the bishop will reconsider letting him stay with me now. I'll speak to him tomorrow."

"Ivan still made some poor decisions but his heart was in the right place."

She reached out and covered Michael's hand with her own. His fingers were cold. "I was truly glad that you were here to help tonight. I have no idea what I would have done without your guidance."

A small smile lifted one corner of his lips. "You would have figured it out."

She shook her head. "I don't think so. When that little boy started crying at the table, I just wanted to wrap him in a warm blanket and carry him up to a soft bed. He broke my heart."

Michael laced his fingers with hers. "I know just what you mean. It was like finding Sadie all over again. Speaking of which, where is she?"

"Jenny had a nightmare about an hour ago. Sadie is sleeping with her."

He drew back a little. "You let a dog sleep in Jenny's bed? This from a woman who says dogs don't belong in the house?"

"I can admit when I am wrong. Sadie will always be welcome in my house. Provided she has had a bath and that she doesn't have fleas."

"I knew I was forgetting something."

"What?"

"Flea powder for her. Did you notice her scratching a lot?" He began scratching the back of his head.

Bethany popped him on the shoulder. "You are not as funny as you think you are."

He winked. "I'm funny enough to get a smile out of you."

As he gazed at her, his grin slowly faded. She sensed a change come over him. Her heart began beating heavily. He moved closer and she didn't pull away. He cupped her cheek with one hand, sending her pulse pounding and stealing her breath. She waited for his kiss. He caressed her lips with his thumb. "I should go."

She couldn't think clearly, let alone come up with a single objection.

He rose abruptly and left the house.

Chapter Thirteen

Bethany spoke to the bishop the next afternoon at his business. Michael wasn't with her. She relayed her brother's involvement and stressed his innocence. "He believed he was protecting Jeffrey from his father's foul temper. You have to respect him for trying to do good."

"I'm sympathetic to your position, Bethany, but I haven't changed my mind. Ivan followed too eagerly after this *Englisch* boy and he had made poor decisions. You can't deny that. I still feel the boy will benefit from a full-time male role model."

"Michael is providing Ivan with guidance. The two of them get along well and Ivan has improved so much." She held her breath, praying the bishop would see things her way.

"My mind is made up on this. The boy will benefit from his uncle's counsel evermore."

She pressed her hands together. "Please reconsider—"

He cut her off. "Bethany, go home and raise your sister. Your brother will return to you in time if it is God's will."

She had lost. Bethany left the bishop's workplace devoid of hope. If she wanted to keep her family together, the only thing left for her to do was to move away from New Covenant and start over somewhere else, but she had no idea where to go and no money to start over with.

The evening of the community Christmas play was chilly with overcast skies that promised more snow. Ivan insisted they use the sleigh to travel to the community building. He said it was more Amish and it felt more Christmas-like. Both children were excited because there would be a small gift exchange after the program that the bishop had agreed they could participate in.

Michael brought the sleigh to Bethany's front door and spread a thick lap robe over her when she got in. "I don't want you to catch cold."

"Ivan! Come on," Jenny shouted from the back seat, causing the patient horse to toss his head and snort. Ivan came out the door, letting it slam shut behind him. He had been trying to act as if the program was no big deal, but Michael could see he was excited, too. The teenager piled in the back seat with his sister.

After a second or two of getting settled, Ivan said, "Scoot over, Jenny, and give me some room."

"I'm cold and you have more of the blanket."

"I do not."

"You do so."

"Enough," Bethany said, putting an end to the rising family squabble.

Michael lifted his arm and laid it along the back of the seat to give Bethany more room. She moved closer. As much as he wanted to slip his arm around her shoulders, he knew it would be a bad idea. He was already having far too much trouble remembering to treat her as a friend.

"Ready, everyone?" Michael asked. Three confirmations rang out. He slapped the lines and the big horse took off down the snow-covered lane.

Sleigh bells jingled merrily in time to the horse's footfalls. The runners hissed along over the snow as big flakes began to float down. They stuck to Michael's and Ivan's hats, turning their brims white. Jenny tried to catch snowflakes on her tongue between giggles.

Michael leaned down to see Bethany's face. "Are you warm enough?" She nodded, but her cheeks looked rosy and cold. Michael took off his woolen scarf and wrapped it around her head to cover her mouth and nose.

"Danki," she murmured. "Won't you be cold?"

"Nope. It's a perfect evening, isn't it?" The snow obscured the mountains. The fields lay hidden beneath a thick blanket of white. Pine tree branches drooped beneath their icy loads. A hushed stillness filled the air, broken only by the jingle of the harness bells. It was a picture-perfect moment in time and Michael wished it could go on forever.

The community building was only a few miles from the farm in a converted brick factory not far from the city center. For Michael, they reached their destination much too quickly. As they drew closer they saw a dozen buggies and sleighs parked along the south side of the building out of the wind while the parking lot in front of it was full of cars and trucks.

As the kids scrambled out of the sleigh, Michael offered Bethany his hand to help her out. When she took it, he gave her an affectionate squeeze. She graced him with a shy smile in return.

Inside the building, the place was already crowded with people. What had once been the factory floor held rows of folding chairs facing a small stage at the front. Swags of fragrant cedar boughs graced the sills of the tall multipaned windows. A Christmas tree stood in one corner, decorated with colorful paper chains, popcorn and cranberry strands, and handmade ornaments made by the children. A table on the opposite wall bore trays of cookies and candies and a large punch bowl. An atmosphere of joy, goodwill and anticipation permeated the air.

Several *Englisch* people Michael didn't know approached Bethany to tell her how happy they were to learn Ivan had been cleared and how glad they were to have Amish neighbors. Everywhere Michael looked there were welcoming smiles. He had been prepared to feel uneasy in the crowd but he didn't. The Martin children hurried to join their classmates behind the stage. Michael and Bethany found seats out front a few minutes before the curtain rose.

The children performed their assigned roles, singing songs and reciting poetry. Then it came time for Jenny to narrate the Christmas story. She walked out on stage in her white robe with her long hair in two golden braids. Michael glanced at Bethany. Her eyes brimmed with maternal pride. He squeezed her hand and together they watched the community's children bring the story of the first Christmas to life.

When the play was over, Jenny held one hand high. "*Frehlicher Grischtdaag*, everyone. Merry Christmas!"

The curtain fell and Michael clapped until his hands

hurt. The last song of the evening was Ivan's solo. To Michael's surprise, the boy had a beautiful voice. His a cappella rendition of "O Come, O Come, Emmanuel" brought tears to a few eyes, including Bethany's.

Later, when everyone had a plate of treats, Jenny squeezed in between Bethany and Michael. He said, "You did well, Jenny. Your narration was very good."

"Danki."

Bethany slipped her arm around the child and gave her a hug.

Michael rubbed Ivan's head. "Who knew you could sing so well?"

The boy blushed with happiness. Everyone seemed happy, only Bethany's joy appeared forced.

It was full dark by the time the festivities wound down and families began leaving. Michael brushed the accumulated snow from the sleigh's seats and lit the lanterns on the sides. The horse stood quietly, one hip cocked and a dusting of snow across his back. Michael stepped back inside to tell Bethany they were ready.

Scanning the room, he saw her with a group of young Amish women. Two of them held babies on their hips. Bethany raised a hand to smooth the blond curls of a little boy. As she did, her gaze met Michael's across the room.

In that moment, he knew exactly what he wanted. He wanted Bethany to have the life she was meant to live and he wanted to be a part of it. He wanted to spend every Christmas with her for the rest of his life. If only he could be certain his PTSD wouldn't return.

"Is it time to go home? I'm tired." Jenny, sitting on the bottom bleachers, could barely keep her eyes open.

"Yes, it's time to go home." He picked her up and she

draped herself over his shoulder. Bethany joined them a minute later. In the sleigh, Michael let Ivan take the reins while he settled in with Jenny across his lap and Bethany seated beside him. The snow had stopped. A bright three-quarter moon slipped in and out of the clouds as they made their way home.

Snuggled beneath a blanket with Bethany at his side, Michael marveled at the beauty of the winter night in the far north and at the beauty of the woman next to him. When they pulled up in front of her house, Michael carried Jenny inside and up to bed while Ivan took the horse to the barn.

Michael stepped back as Bethany tucked her sister in. "I had a wonderful time. Thank you for inviting me."

"I'm glad." She closed the door to Jenny's room and faced him in the hall.

He stepped closer. She didn't move away. Reaching out, he cupped her cheek. "Good night, Bethany."

"Good night, Michael." Her voice was a soft whisper. Slowly, he lowered his lips to hers and kissed her.

Bethany melted into Michael's embrace. His kiss was gentle and so very sweet. Their mutual decision to take a step back and simply remain friends vanished from her thoughts as she slipped her arms around his neck. He briefly pulled her closer, and then he let her go and took a step away. "I'll see you tomorrow."

She pressed a hand to her lips to hold on to that wondrous moment. Ivan came walking up the stairs and passed them on the way to his room. Embarrassed, Bethany wondered if he had seen her in Michael's arms. He muttered a polite good-night and went in his room. Maybe he hadn't seen anything.

She mumbled a quick goodbye to Michael and fled into her room. She closed the door and leaned against it. There was no way they could go back to being just friends now.

Could she accept him without knowing the secret part of his past he wouldn't share? His kiss seemed to indicate he wanted to be a part of her life, but he hadn't said anything about what kind of future he saw and if she had a place in it.

Christmas was less than two weeks away, and she was going to lose her brother if she failed to convince the bishop to change his mind. Was Gemma right? Was Michael the answer to her prayers?

Chapter Fourteen

Sadie rose from her spot beside the fireplace the next morning and trotted to the front door, wagging her tail. She looked back at Michael and whined. A second later he heard a timid knock. He sprang out of his chair, hoping it was Bethany, and twisted his bad leg in the process. There was so much he wanted to say to her.

He pulled open the door. Jenny, not Bethany, stood on his stoop. She was dressed in a dark blue snowsuit and coat with bright red mittens on her hands. The ribbons of her *kapp* dangled out from beneath her hood. Behind her stood four other bundled-up children. Two boys wore flat-topped black hats, so he knew they were Amish *kinder*. They were all pulling colorful plastic toboggans.

Jenny grinned eagerly. "Can Sadie come out and play with us?"

He glanced down at the dog standing beside him. She wiggled with excitement but she didn't dash out the door. She looked to him for instructions. "I reckon."

He held the door wider and tipped his head toward the outside. "Go on. Have some fun."

Sadie bounded out of the house, jumping in circles around the children and barking.

"*Danki*, Michael," Jenny shouted as they headed toward his barn. He noticed that she was pulling two sleds, one red and one yellow. Why two? Every other child had one. Perhaps they were meeting someone else. They'd only gone a few more feet when he saw Jenny give the rope of one sled to Sadie. She held it in her mouth and trotted along with the group.

They disappeared behind the barn where the ground dropped away sharply, making a perfect hill for sledding. Although he couldn't see them, he could hear them calling encouragement to Sadie. The day was warmer than the past two weeks had been. He glanced back at the business paperwork waiting for him and decided it was time for a break.

He grabbed his hat and coat, put them on and closed the cabin door behind him. A walk in the fresh air was exactly what he needed. Maybe he would walk down and see Bethany. He smiled at the memory of their kiss last night. He was head over heels for her and he believed she felt the same but they hadn't discussed their feelings.

Maybe he was reading more into a kiss than he should. Bethany didn't know about his PTSD. Would that change her feelings toward him? He was better, it had been almost a month since he'd had a flashback, but was he well enough to consider a future with her? How would he know when he was healed?

A freshly shoveled path led from his cabin to Bethany's house. Ivan kept it open for him when he came to chop wood. That was the direction Michael wanted to go but he didn't have an excuse to see Bethany. He didn't want to appear too eager or pushy. The tracks of the children and dog led the other way.

He followed along, trying not to slip and fall in the new snow. When he reached the edge of the barn, he had an excellent view of the children sledding down the hill. Sadie was at the bottom with Jenny. They began to trudge back up, taking care to avoid the others flying down the hill toward them. Jenny was pulling her sled while Sadie pulled the other up the incline. He had never seen a dog do that.

At the top of the hill Jenny positioned her sled, sat down and pushed off with her hands. To his amazement, Sadie jumped on her own sled and went flying down the hill with her ears fluttering backward.

"Michael?"

He turned at the sound of Bethany's voice and saw her walking toward him. She held a package under her arm. He beckoned her closer. "You have to see this."

She smiled as she approached him. "This came for you in the mail. I thought it might be important and you weren't in your workshop."

"I was catching up on some paperwork. You need to see what the children are up to. Jenny stopped by to ask if Sadie could come out and play."

Bethany giggled. He would never tire of hearing her mirth. It always made him smile. He stepped to the side so that she could have his vantage point. He stumbled and would have fallen if she hadn't grabbed his coat to steady him. It was a good reminder that he wasn't fit. Sometimes he forgot how damaged he was when she was around.

She didn't say anything but set his package on a stone by the barn door. She stepped to where he had been standing and looked at the children. "Your dog is sledding all by herself. Did you teach her to do that?"

The wonder and amusement in her voice eased the embarrassment he felt. "*Nee*, this is the first time."

"Oh, she's pulling it back up the hill. I don't believe it. It's like she's one of the children. That is a remarkable animal."

And you are a remarkable woman. For a second he was afraid he had spoken aloud.

"What are you two looking at?" Ivan asked as he walked up beside them. Jeffrey was with him. The boy, his younger siblings and his mother had returned to their home a few days after his father's arrest.

"We are watching Sadie use a sled," Bethany said.

"Are you fooling me?" Ivan walked to the edge of the slope and Jeffrey followed him. They began packing the snow into a ball and rolling it around to make it bigger. When they had one about a foot in diameter they pushed it down the hill toward the group of children.

"Not a good idea." Michael shouted, "Look out below!"

The snowball quickly gained size and speed. Both boys sprinted after it as did Bethany. Michael watched helplessly, knowing he wouldn't be of any use.

Sadie barked and raced up the hill to meet the ball. She leaped to the side and tried to bite it as it rolled past. Her actions changed the direction just enough to let it roll harmlessly past the little girl who fell trying to scramble out of the way.

The snowball came to rest a few feet away from the trees that separated the field from the road. Michael heard Ivan apologizing. "I didn't think it would get so big. I thought it would break apart."

Bethany eyed him sternly.

"Honest, sister. I wasn't trying to hurt anyone. I thought we could make a snowman faster by rolling the balls down the hill to make them bigger."

She looked up at Michael as if seeking his opinion. He didn't think the boys meant any harm, either. He nodded slightly. She turned back to her brother. "Okay. It was almost a good idea. It just shows that you have to consider all parts of a problem before you decide on a solution. The easy way is not often the best way."

The younger children eagerly began creating snowmen of their own.

Jenny beckoned to Michael. "Help me make a tall snowman, Michael."

He wanted to join them. How many happy memories would it take to make him forget the horrible ones? Even if he wanted to, there was no way he could get down the hill without falling and arriving at the bottom inside a massive snowball. He shook his head and held up his cane.

Jenny pulled her sled over to Sadie and whispered something in her ear. Then she gave her the rope. Sadie came charging up the hill, pulling the empty sled. She skidded to a stop in front of Michael, dropped the rope and began barking furiously.

He looked at his dog. "You can't be serious. You want me to sled down the hill." He took another look at the terrain. It actually wasn't a bad idea. He looked at all the people beckoning him to come down. Getting down was the easy part. Getting up the slope would be the real challenge.

Sadie jumped up and put her paws on his chest. He

ruffled her ears. "What kind of Amish man gives in to the whims of children and dogs?"

She barked once and looked downhill.

He followed her gaze and saw Bethany watching him. "Good point. She is down there. I was looking for an excuse to spend some time with her. When an opportunity falls into my lap I shouldn't waste it."

He awkwardly lowered himself into the red plastic sled and used his cane to pull himself to the edge of the incline. He looked at Sadie. "If I break my other leg I'm going to blame you." He pushed off and went flying down the slope.

He remembered how much fun it was to go sledding down a hill when he was a child. As an adult, he was a little more concerned about arriving at his destination in one piece.

Bethany held her breath as Michael shot down the hill with more speed than any of the children had obtained. To her relief, he used his cane as a drag to slow down when he neared the bottom. He came to rest a few feet in front of her. All the children applauded. Ivan jumped forward to help him to his feet. Michael was laughing like one of the *kinder*.

She had never seen him so lighthearted. It seemed that whatever had plagued him when he first came to New Covenant was giving way to a happier man.

She turned around with a snowball in her hand. "I've been wanting to do this for quite some time." She threw the ball and it hit him in the chest.

He brushed at his coat. "I refuse to get in a snowball fight with you. It's not dignified."

"You're right." She scooped up another handful of

snow and packed it together. "I wouldn't want you to do something undignified." She let fly and this one struck him on his shoulder.

He brushed the loose snow away with one hand. "You are asking for trouble."

"I don't think so. I'm pretty sure I can outrun you."

"That was a low blow."

She tossed a newly formed snowball from one hand to the other. "You said you didn't like being treated differently because you need to use a cane."

"I think I will have to make you pay for that remark." He advanced menacingly.

She scuttled backward. "Forgiveness is the foundation of our religion. You don't want me to tell the bishop that you threatened me, do you?"

He kept coming and she kept backing up. "I think he would understand," he growled.

She took another step and tripped over the snowball Jenny had left unfinished. Michael scooped up a handful of snow. Standing over her, he dumped it on her face. She shrieked and rolled away. Surging to her feet, she shook her head to get rid of the snow and then glared at him. "That was just plain mean."

She was adorable. Her cheeks were bright red from the cold. Snow sparkled on her hair and eyelashes. The joy that filled his heart caught him off guard. Meeting her was the best thing that ever happened to him. How had she managed to worm her way so firmly into his heart in such a short amount of time?

"I apologize. I promise no more snow in the face, but I must remind you that you started it."

She looked as if she wanted to argue but gave in.

"Okay, that is true. Now I have had my comeuppance and we are even, right?"

"I'd say so."

The boys had managed a haphazard snowman with a ragged straw hat, but they decided to go on to other adventures, leaving the slightly crooked fellow leaning into the wind.

"He looks lonely," Bethany said.

Michael put his hands on his hips. "I think he just looks homely."

Bethany moved several paces back. "I've been told I need to look at the whole picture."

"And what do you see?"

"A homely, lonely snowman. Let's fancy him up."

They found some winterberry and holly to decorate his straw hat. Bethany used a handful of red berries pressed into the snow to form his mouth. Michael supplied the branches for his arms and he sent one of the children to get a carrot for his nose.

Bethany withdrew a pace to look at him when he was finished. "There's still something missing."

"What?"

"I know." She pulled the red-and-white-striped scarf off and wrapped it around the snowman's neck. "There. He looks great."

Michael chuckled. "He looks like a mighty fancy Amish fellow. Is he one of your suitors?"

"He is and I will accept his offer." It was now or never. She smoothed the snowman's rough cheeks with her mittens, knowing Michael was listening. She'd never been so bold in her life, but she had to try. "The bishop understands why Ivan acted as he did when I explained things to him the other day, but he is still convinced a firmer hand could have prevented much of the trouble Ivan became embroiled in. He won't reconsider sending my brother away. I need an Amish husband before Christmas and the Lord has provided. That is, unless another suitor speaks up and asks me for my hand in marriage." She couldn't look at Michael.

He stepped close to her. "I don't think you should marry this fellow."

She looked into Michael's troubled eyes. "Do you think I'll get a better offer?"

He shook his head and walked away from her. "I wish I could be the man you need, but I'm not, Bethany."

"I think you are."

"You make it so hard to say no."

She moved to stand in front of him. "If it's hard to say no, then maybe you should say yes. I won't make any demands on you. Your time will be your own. You can have one hundred percent of the business. I need your help, Michael."

"I'm sorry."

Jenny came walking back to see what they were up to. She clapped her hands when she saw the snowman. "He's beautiful. He can be Bishop Schultz come to marry Michael and Bethany." Jenny looked at her sister.

Bethany gave Michael a sidelong glance. His face could have been carved from stone. She leaned over and forced a smile for her little sister. "There isn't going to be a wedding. I told you that."

Jenny's face fell. "Okay. I'm going to help Jeffrey and Ivan build a snow cave."

Michael glanced at Bethany and then quickly looked down at his boots. "Are you going to the Christmas parade in the city with Pastor Frank?"

"Yes, we are. What about you?" She avoided meeting his gaze.

"I think I will go." Maybe during the Christmas parade would be a good time to gauge how she felt about them.

Bethany retreated a pace. "I'd better get started on lunch. They're going to be a hungry bunch when they come in."

"I've got some work to do, too."

She regained some of her composure. "That's right. A box came for you. I left it at your barn."

He looked up the slope. "I might work on something that's already in the workshop."

"I'll get the box." She grabbed the empty toboggan that Jenny had left by her snowman's head and trudged up the hill. She picked up his box, got in the sled and pushed off.

When she came to a stop two feet in front of him, he arched one eyebrow. "Show-off."

"I'm just using the gifts God gave me." She handed him the box and walked beside him all the way to his workshop, but the awkwardness between them persisted. Had she ruined their friendship with her desperate attempt to keep Ivan?

A half hour later Bethany was at the kitchen sink, peeling potatoes for French fries, when Jeffrey came in. "I'm hungry. Can I have a sandwich?" Sadie Sue followed him in and plopped down in front of the fireplace with her tongue hanging out.

His cheeks were rosy red from the cold but his lips were tinged with blue. "I think you should stay in for a while. Take off your boots and let me check your feet."

She had learned her first winter here that frostbite was nothing to be trifled with. He did as she instructed. His toes were bright pink but there was a patch of white skin on the back of his left heel. "You are definitely not going back outside. I'm going to get a pan of cool water and I want you to keep your foot in it until I tell you otherwise."

"But we just finished a great snow cave. Ivan is expecting me to come back."

"I'll explain to him why you have to stay in."

Michael had been working in his shop but apparently he had overheard her conversation. "I'll go tell Ivan what's going on."

"Danki," Bethany said and smiled at him. He was always willing to lend a helping hand. In many ways he reminded her of her grandfather. He had the same kind of gentle soul. She fixed a pan of water and had Jeffrey soak his foot.

Michael put on his coat and hat. "Where is your snow cave?"

"Out by the highway. The snowplows have made huge piles there." The snow the previous night had left four more inches on the roadways.

Michael stepped out onto the porch. "I see the piles, but I don't see the kids."

Bethany came out and stood beside him. She shaded her eyes with one hand against the glare of the sun off the white snow. "I don't see them, either."

Mike took a pair of snowshoes off their hooks on the porch. As he did, Bethany heard the grading rumble of the snowplow coming down from the ridge. The truck with a large blade on the front blasted through the new snow, easily making bigger drifts along the side of the road. It was headed down to the intersection where Jeffrey said Ivan and Jenny were playing.

The snowplow driver couldn't see the children for they were on the far side of the high snowbank away from him. She saw a flash of red in the snow and thought it must be Jenny's glove. The snowplow hit the side of the big pile and pushed it farther off the edge of the highway, adding a huge new supply of snow on top of what was already there. The place where she had seen Jenny's glove was completely covered. She started screaming and ran toward her sister.

Michael saw the whole thing happen and was helpless to stop it. How much time did they have? A few minutes? Maybe more if the children were in any kind of air pocket. He turned around and hurried to the house. "Jeffrey, get your shoes back on and run to the neighbors. Jenny and Ivan have been buried by the snowplow. We need everybody who can get here to dig. Go."

Jeffrey rushed to do as he was told. Michael ran to the tower of snow. Bethany was on her knees, digging with her bare hands. Michael grabbed a snow shovel from the porch and rushed to her side. He gave it to her and began using his cane as a probe into the snow, hoping to come in contact with a body. Each time his cane sank all the way in, he prayed harder.

It seemed like hours but it could've only been minutes when he heard the sounds of shouting from up the road. A dozen Amish men came rushing toward them with shovels and rakes. They spread out on either side of Bethany and Michael and began digging. Jeffrey was digging frantically with them. Bethany was crying. She kept saying "no, no, no."

He kept probing inch by inch, knowing Jenny and Ivan were under there somewhere and running out of time. He had never been so scared in his life. Not even when he knew the gunman was going to kill him. Suddenly Sadie Sue was beside him, whining. Bethany stopped digging and looked at the dog and then at Michael.

"It's a long shot," he said. He knelt beside Sadie and said, "Find Jenny." She whined and didn't move. Bethany came to stand beside Michael. "Find Jenny, please."

The dog trotted away from where they were digging and Michael's hopes crashed. He went back to probing and Bethany returned to digging.

Twenty feet away, Sadie Sue started barking and digging at the snow.

Bethany looked at Michael. "I saw her glove here. I know I did." She kept digging and uncovered a red plastic candy wrapper.

Jeffrey had returned. He took Bethany's shovel away and raced over to the dog. He began frantically scooping the snow aside as she dug her way in. Suddenly the dog disappeared completely.

Bethany heard crying and knew at least one of them was alive. Praying as she had never prayed before, she stumbled to where Jeffrey was kneeling. The rest of their neighbors gathered around the hole and began widening it. Sadie came backing out, but she was dragging something. With two strong tugs she emerged from the hole, pulling Jenny out by her coat. Ivan crawled out on his own.

Cheering broke out from everyone. Bethany grabbed up her sister and held her tight and threw her other arm around Ivan. "Thank you, merciful Lord."

She looked at Michael and held out her hand. He came and embraced them all. He never wanted to let them go. As his frantically beating heart slowed, he added Sadie Sue to the group hug. She started licking Jenny's face, making the child giggle.

Ivan looked at Michael. "I knew you'd find us."

Not once during the emergency had Michael thought about the robbery or its aftermath. He had faced a life-and-death challenge without triggering a flashback or a panic attack. He had worked side by side with Bethany to save her family. A family he wanted to be a part of forever.

He caught Bethany's eye. "If you haven't said yes to the snowman, I'd like to reconsider your offer."

"You would?" Hope brightened her face.

"I would."

"Is that a yes?" A grin spread across her face.

"If you'll have me."

"I will." She hugged Ivan and Jenny harder. "I most certainly will."

Chapter Fifteen

On the Saturday evening before Christmas, Bethany, Michael and the children climbed into Pastor Frank's twenty-passenger van with sixteen other members of their Amish community, including the bishop, Jesse, Gemma and her parents.

Bethany kept Jenny close to her. The child had been subdued since the accident and wanted to constantly claim Bethany's attention. Michael didn't seem to mind. Bethany loved him for that. Ivan seemed far less affected.

As the van rolled down the highway Ivan began leading them in song. Michael joined in with his pleasant baritone voice. Christmas hymns new and old filled Bethany's heart with the joy of this most holy season. She knew how blessed she was to have Jenny and Ivan with her and how easily it could have turned out differently. Every time she caught Michael's eye he smiled at her. She hoped it was just a matter of time before he declared his love.

When they reached the city Pastor Frank parked the van on a side street and everyone made their way to the parade route. The streets were lined four deep with bundled-up people all sharing the holiday spirit on a frosty evening. Lavish holiday lights decorated the buildings along Main Street, blinking red and green and ice blue. Lit displays filled every business window.

Jenny, standing at Bethany's side, tugged on her coat. "I can't see."

Jesse leaned down to her. "Would you like to sit on my shoulders? I can see everything and you'll be even taller."

Jenny glanced at Bethany and then took Jesse's hand. "Okay."

He hoisted her to sit piggyback on his shoulders and she laughed. "Ivan, look at me."

"Hey, that's not fair," her brother shot back, but he was smiling.

Bethany reached for Michael's hand and gave it a squeeze. "She's feeling better."

"Kids are resilient and there is nothing like seeing a parade from the back of a giant to perk someone up."

Bethany chuckled and leaned against him. "You can always make me laugh."

Michael knew a depth of joy he never thought he would experience. His PTSD had improved enough for him to believe he was finally over it. The stress of searching for Jenny and Ivan hadn't triggered a flashback. He hadn't even had a nightmare afterward. That horrible part of his life was well and truly over. He smiled at Bethany and took her hand. Although she hadn't said that she loved him, he was sure that love would blossom in time to match his. And he did love her. With all his heart.

A PA system announced the parade was about to

start and the crowd pressed forward. The canon across the park boomed and fireworks lit up the sky. The red streaks in the darkness held his attention. A shiver crawled down his spine. He couldn't shake the sight of red streaks on the floor and red flashes lighting up the night beyond his window.

Sirens sounded. People cheered as the local police and firefighters led the parade in their new machines with lights and sirens. The crowd behind him pressed closer. Michael couldn't breathe. He started hearing a scream and knew it was coming from him. He couldn't shut out the screams. Someone was talking to him, asking him what was wrong. A hand grabbed him and he swatted it. He had to get away.

He felt the impact of the bullet hitting his leg. He fell to the ground and started moaning.

Bethany had no idea what was wrong with Michael. She cried out for help as she knelt beside him. People gathered round, pressing closer, staring, uncertain how to help. Michael gazed wide-eyed into the space, hitting at her when she touched him. Bethany didn't think he knew she was there. Suddenly Pastor Frank was beside her.

"It's okay, Michael. It's Pastor Frank. You're having a flashback. It isn't real. You aren't in any danger. You're safe. Can you hear me? Bethany is here beside me. Is it all right if Bethany holds your hand?"

Michael's hand opened and closed on the sidewalk. Bethany took hold of it. "It's all right, darling. I'm here. I'm with you."

Pastor Frank patted her shoulder. "Keep talking to him. He needs to know that what he is seeing and hearing isn't real. I think we're going to need to get him away from this noise and commotion. I'm going to bring the van up."

Pastor Frank summoned a police officer who went with him.

Bethany held Michael's hand but he kept moaning and muttering people's names. She had no idea how to help him. She'd never felt more useless in her life. She didn't understand what was wrong. Was this what he was afraid of? Jenny was on her knees beside Bethany, crying. "What's the matter with Michael?"

Ivan took his little sister by the shoulders. "He's going to be okay. He'll get over this soon."

Bethany prayed Ivan's words were true.

Michael refused to come out of his cabin the next day. He didn't want to see anyone. He didn't answer the door although he knew both Frank and Bethany were outside. What was the point? Everyone knew now that he was just a shell of a man who looked normal but wasn't. Pastor Frank had been right. He wasn't going to be able to heal himself. He needed help. If he had tried to get help earlier maybe he could've salvaged something of his relationship with Bethany.

When the sun started to set, he went out and harnessed the pony. Pastor Frank's survivors' support group was tonight. Michael wasn't sure he was a survivor, but he definitely needed support.

At the church, he left his horse and cart and walked around the back of the building. A set of steps led to the basement. The door of the room where support group meetings were held stood open. A hand-lettered sign on the wall said Welcome to a Safe Place.

He wasn't sure what a safe place felt like anymore but if he was ever going to find one he had to start somewhere. He stepped inside and stopped in surprise. There were eight *Englisch* men and women seated at a round table with the pastor, but there were a dozen chairs lined up across the back of the room filled with the men and women of his Amish community. Jesse and the bishop. The carpenter Nigel Miller and his wife, Becca. Gemma Lapp and her parents, plus a dozen other Amish people he didn't know by name.

Bethany rose from her seat and came toward him. She held out her hand but he didn't take it. "What are you doing here?"

"I'm here to learn about PTSD and how to help the man I love cope with and overcome this disorder. We all want to be able to help you when you need us."

"The man you love? How can you still say that after what you saw? I was on the pavement, sobbing like a frightened child. I wasn't even aware that you were beside me. How can you love someone who is so damaged? 'The man that you pity' is what you really mean to say. You pity me."

"How can I not love you? In all the world you are the man who opened my heart so that I could clearly see God has chosen you to be my beloved. Are you a perfect man? *Nee*, for only God is perfect. Are you a good man? I believe, I know that you are."

Michael tried to swallow the lump in his throat as tears stung his eyes. "I don't deserve your love."

She smiled at him softly. "I have news for you. God and I believe you do."

Pastor Frank came to stand beside Bethany. "I am delighted that you came tonight, Michael. I wasn't sure that you would, but all of your friends have expressed a sincere interest in learning about PTSD and about how to deal with someone who suffers from it."

Michael started backing away. "I can't do this. Not yet. Not here. I'm sorry, Bethany."

"Michael, please." She held out her hand.

"*Nee*, whatever you thought was between us is over. I'm no good to you." He turned and walked out the door.

Bethany watched helplessly as Michael turned his back on her and left. She didn't understand why he wouldn't even try to accept their help. She looked to Pastor Frank. "What do I do?"

"That's why you're here. To learn about what you can do."

"Should I go after him?"

"No. I'm going to ask everyone to have a seat and I'm going to talk a little about PTSD and what it means to a person suffering from that disorder."

Bethany returned to her seat. Gemma grasped her hand.

Frank smiled at the crowd. "Some of you know exactly what I'm talking about. Others are just learning about the existence of this cruel disorder. Someone with PTSD will experience horrible events over and over again in a way that is so real they believe they are back in that situation."

Bethany listened and tried to learn all she could, but the magnitude of the problem was daunting. After the meeting was over she stayed to talk to Frank alone.

"Tell me how I can help Michael. Why did he push me away? I believe he loves me. I know he does."

"Michael considers himself weak. He is fearful that

others, that you, will see him that way, too. Yet he can't hide from what has happened to him. He has tried to run away from it by moving to this remote settlement, but the change of scenery hasn't changed the disorder. But there is help and there is hope. I believe that shining God's light into the dark recesses of our pain will take away the power the trauma has over us."

"What do I do now?"

"When someone you love suffers from post-traumatic stress disorder, it can be overwhelming. You may feel hurt by your loved one's distance and moodiness. However, it's important to know that you're not a helpless bystander. Your love and support can make all the difference in Michael's recovery. Don't try to pressure him into talking. It may make things worse. Just let him know you're willing to listen when he wants to talk."

"I'm frightened. I'm not sure what I'm walking into but I love him. I have to help."

Michael had to leave. He couldn't stay and see the woman he loved look at him with pity for the rest of his life. He couldn't do it. He didn't own much. Just a few tools, some clothes and a big yellow dog. It should be easy to pick up and go, except it wasn't easy.

He was in the workshop, carefully packing up his tools, when the door opened. He knew who it was without looking. His eyes filled with tears but he refused to let them fall.

She spoke softly. "Please don't leave us."

"You must be out of your mind to want me to stay."

She stepped closer. "I don't think so. I think you're the man I need. You also happen to be the man I love."

His gaze flew to hers. "You don't know what you're saying."

"I know exactly what I'm saying. I am in love with you, Michael Shetler. My heart tells me you are the man I have been waiting for all my life."

He turned away and continued packing his tools. "You want a man who can fall apart in the blink of an eye because some sound or smell triggers a flashback? Is that your idea of an ideal mate? What if I'm driving a team and the children are with me and I don't see the train coming when I cross the tracks?"

"Michael, I know your problem looms large to you, but for me it is only one part of who you are. You are a kind, loving man. You are hardworking. You try to live your faith by caring for those around you. You are great with children and with dogs. You walk with a cane and you have PTSD. I won't pretend to understand what that is like for you. But do you really want to give up a woman who loves you, two children who adore you, and a mangy mutt that thinks you hung the moon?"

He put down his screwdrivers. "Sadie Sue isn't a mangy mutt."

"You're right. She is a very special gift sent by God to help us. She saved Ivan's and Jenny's lives, but I would trade places with that dog in a heartbeat. Do you know why? Because you accept that she loves you regardless of the difficulties you face. I wish you had half that much faith in my love. If you don't, then maybe I am wasting my breath."

Michael wanted to deny his love for Bethany but he couldn't. He knew it took a great deal of courage for her to come to him this way. She was the most remarkable woman he'd ever met.

"Bethany, I don't want to burden you with my weakness. You deserve a strong and stable man."

"I do." She gave him a sly smile. "Unfortunately, Jesse won't have me. That leaves you."

He grinned in spite of himself. "Jesse wouldn't stand a chance against your wit."

"You once told me that you would help me with anything I needed if it was within your power. Did you mean that?"

"I did."

"Then here is what I want. I want to be the person beside you the next time you have a flashback if you ever have one again. I want to know and understand what you are going through, what you are seeing and hearing so I can lead you to a safe place. Tell me what happened to you. Make me understand."

Michael shook his head. "I will never do that to you."

Her eyes filled with disappointment. "Why won't you let me help you?"

"You don't understand."

"Make me."

He stepped close and took her hands in his. "Bethany, if I share with you the pain and guilt and the horrible events that I lived through, then they can become your nightmare, too. You will be haunted by the things I tell you because you love me. I don't want you to know even a small part of the horror I endured."

"I'm a strong woman."

"I know you are."

"Frank told me he suffered with PTSD for many years after he came back from his military service.

It destroyed his marriage and almost took his life. He found a way to deal with it by helping others. He also told me that talking about what happened to you is a way to decrease the power it has over your mind."

"He may be right. I will share my story with him but not with you."

"Don't you trust me?"

"I trust you with my life and all that I have. You must trust me when I say there are some things you are better off not knowing."

"I guess you are asking me for a leap of faith. Okay. I will not ask about it again. Are you going to marry me?"

He shook his head in bewilderment. "You are too bold to be a *goot* Amish maiden."

"I'm an Amish maiden who knows what she wants. You think that marrying me will ruin my life. I'm going to tell you that the only way you can ruin my life is to not marry me. Don't break my heart."

She stepped closer and slid her arms around his neck. "Please, Michael, say that you love me or don't say it— because it doesn't matter. I already know you do. I see it in your eyes. I feel it in your touch. I know it by the way your heart calls to mine."

He groaned and wrapped his arms around her to pull her close. "I can't believe I'm about to give you the opportunity to tell me what to do for the rest of my life."

Michael leaned close. Bethany knew he was going to kiss her. She had never wanted anything more. His lips touched hers with incredible gentleness, a feather-light touch. It wasn't enough.

She cupped his face with her hands. To her delight, he deepened the kiss. Joy clutched her heart and stole her breath. She'd been waiting a lifetime for this moment and never knew it.

He pulled her closer. The sweet softness of his lips moved away from her mouth. He kissed her cheek, her eyelids and her forehead, and then he drew away. Bethany wasn't ready to let him go. She would never be ready to let him go.

"I love you, Bethany," he murmured softly against her temple. "You make me whole. I am broken but you believe I can be mended. You make me believe it. I have lived in despair, ashamed of what I don't understand. I thought I was beyond help. And then you came into my life and I saw hope."

"I love you, too, darling, but it is God that has made us both whole. Will you marry me?"

"To keep Ivan with you?" he asked.

She rose on tiptoe and kissed him. "To keep you by my side always. Will you?"

"Can't you hear my heart shouting the answer?" He kissed her temple and held her close.

Bethany had never felt so cherished. The wonder of his love was almost impossible to comprehend. Emotion choked her. She couldn't speak.

"Did he say yes?" Jenny's whispered question was hushed by Ivan.

Michael choked on a laugh as he realized they weren't alone. He looked up at the ceiling to compose himself. Bethany shook silently in his arms. He knew she was trying not to laugh out loud.

He mustered his most authoritative voice. "Eavesdroppers are likely to be sent to bed without their supper for a week."

Jenny popped up from behind the desk. "I wasn't

eavesdropping. I just came in to ask my sister a question."

Michael kept his arm around Bethany as she turned to face her sister. "Ivan, what is your excuse?" she asked.

Ivan rose more reluctantly. "I came in to keep Jenny from interrupting the two of you."

"And what is the reason the two of you were hiding behind my desk?" he asked.

"I wasn't hiding. I was scratching Sadie's tummy," Jenny announced with a smile at her brilliant excuse. "But I did happen to hear my sister ask you to marry her, Michael. I thought men were supposed to ask first. Did she do it backward?"

Ivan took her hand and started to lead her from the room. "You have a lot to learn, sis. Women like to let men think it was their idea."

Jenny tried to get her hand loose. "Wait. We didn't hear his answer." Ivan didn't let go of her. She grabbed the doorjamb and held on as she looked over her shoulder. "Please, Michael, say you want to marry us."

A tug from her brother propelled her out of the room. He shut the door with a resounding bang.

Bethany turned and leaned against Michael's chest as she shook with laughter. "I'm the one who should tell you to run and get as far away from us as fast as you can."

"I'm afraid that no matter how far I went I wouldn't survive long."

She leaned back to look at his face. "Why is that?"

"Because my heart would remain here in your keeping and a man can't live long without a heart."

"Then you will marry me?" she asked hopefully.

"On one condition."

A faint frown appeared on her face. "What condition?"

"That I also get to ask the question. Bethany Martin, will you do me the honor of becoming my wife?"

"I will."

"Then I promise to love and cherish you all the days of my life," he said and bent to kiss her once more.

The door flew open and Jenny charged in with Sadie at her side. "He said yes and she said yes. We're getting married!" Sadie started barking wildly as she bounced around Jenny. Ivan stood in the doorway with a bright smile on his face.

Bethany gazed up at Michael with all the love in her heart. "Are you sure you want to marry all of us?"

He kissed the tip of her nose. "I want an Amish wife for Christmas, two fine Amish children, a fine house with a workshop and a *goot hund*. What more could a man need?"

"Maybe another kiss from his Amish wife?"

"My darling Bethany, you read me like a book." He leaned in and kissed her again, knowing no matter what trials he faced, he would never face them alone. God and Bethany would be with him always.

Chapter Sixteen

The morning of Second Christmas, December 26, dawned clear and bright in New Covenant, Maine. Bethany and Michael stood in the entryway of her house and greeted their wedding guests. Bethany's aunt and uncle had arrived on Christmas Eve and had helped take over the preparations for the wedding. Ivan and Jesse showed the guests to their seats.

Bethany glanced at her soon-to-be husband. He looked very handsome in his black suit and black string tie. He smiled back at her. "It's not too late to call it off."

She shook her head. "I think it was too late the day I met you."

He snapped his fingers. "That's who we forgot to invite."

"Who?"

"Clarabelle."

Gemma entered with her parents. "A blessed Christmas to you and may you have a blessed life together."

"Thank you for agreeing to be my sidesitter," Bethany said.

"I am honored to be your attendant at your wedding. Michael, who is going to stand up with you?"

"Jesse has agreed to do me the favor."

Gemma made a sour face. "That man is as dense as a post." She went in to take her place on the front bench where Bethany would sit during the ceremony.

"What does she have against Jesse?" Michael asked.

"Nothing, except he hasn't noticed her in all the time she has been trying to catch his attention."

"She likes Jesse? Are you sure?"

"Very sure. Do you think this is everyone?" She glanced into the full living room, where the church benches had been set out in two rows for the men and the women.

"I think so."

"Where are the children?" Bethany looked around. "I hope Jenny is not getting her new dress dirty."

"I think she's trying to figure out some way to smuggle Sadie Sue in."

"As much as I like your dog, I'm not going to have her at my wedding."

He laughed and pointed up the stairwell. "I wouldn't be too sure about that."

Jenny was kneeling at the top of the steps with Sadie Sue lying beside her. The two of them scurried back down the hall when they realized they had been spotted.

"Do you want me to speak to her?" he asked.

"*Nee*, she knows better. She will behave. I hope."

The bishop came up to them. "Are you ready?"

They smiled at each other and nodded. "We're ready," they said in unison.

While the preparations had been rushed, the ceremony itself went off without a hitch. The bishop was short-winded for a change and the preaching lasted only three hours. As Bethany stood beside Michael in front of the bishop, she couldn't help but realize how very blessed she was to have found the perfect man. She couldn't stop smiling.

Afterward, Bethany went upstairs to change her black *kapp* for a white one. In the corner of the room facing the front door, the Eck, or the "corner table," was quickly set up for the wedding party.

When it was ready, Michael took his place with Jesse and Ivan seated to his right. Bethany was ushered back in and took her seat at his left-hand side. It symbolized the place she would occupy in his buggy and in his life. Her cheeks were rosy red and her eyes sparkled with happiness. They clasped hands underneath the table. Michael squeezed her fingers. "You are everything I could have asked for and so much more."

"I promise to try and be a *goot* wife to you," she said with a meekness he distrusted.

"Just be yourself. That will be good enough."

"You realize you get to choose the seating arrangements for the single people this evening, don't you?" Gemma asked.

Michael shrugged. "I haven't given it much thought."

"This might be the first wedding in New Covenant but I'm going to make sure it isn't the last," Bethany said with a wink at her friend.

Jenny sat on the other side of Gemma. "Are you going to pick a husband for me?"

"I may just do that." She smiled at her sister.

Michael leaned back in his seat. "Are you taking up matchmaking now?"

She chuckled. "Clarabelle is my only local competition. I think I can do better than her."

He leaned close to her. "The old cow did right by me."

"I beg to differ. She never once mentioned your name."

"Do you know what?"

"What?" she asked, intrigued by the light in his eyes.

"I can't wait to kiss you again."

Bethany felt the heat rush to her face. "I can't wait for that myself, my husband."

* * * * *

AMISH CHRISTMAS MEMORIES

Vannetta Chapman

This book is dedicated to Vicki Sewell,
who is so much like family that she is family.
I know you know—but I love you.

And be ye kind one to another, tenderhearted,
forgiving one another, even as God
for Christ's sake hath forgiven you.
—*Ephesians* 4:32

He healeth the broken in heart,
and bindeth up their wounds.
—*Psalms* 147:3

Chapter One

Caleb Wittmer glanced up from the fence he was mending. Something had caught his eye—a bright blue against the snow-covered fields that stretched in every direction. There it was again, to the north and west, coming along the dirt road.

He stepped closer to the fence. His horse moved with him, nudged his hand.

"Hold on, Stormy." Caleb squinted his eyes and peered toward the northwest, and then he knew what he was seeing—he just couldn't make sense of it. Why would a woman be walking on a cold December morning with no coat on?

Goose bumps peppered the skin at the back of his neck. As he watched, the woman wandered to the right of the road and then back to the left.

Something wasn't right.

He murmured for the gelding to stay, climbed the fence and strode toward her. He'd covered only half of the distance when he noticed that she was wearing Amish clothing, though not their traditional style or color. She was a stranger, then, from a different community. But what was she doing out in the cold with no coat? More disturbing than that, she wore no covering on her head. All Amish women covered their hair when outside—Swiss, Old Order, New Order. It was one of the many things they had in common. The coverings might be styled differently, but always a woman's head was covered.

He was within thirty feet when he noticed that her long hair was a golden brown, wavy and thick, and unbraided.

At twenty feet he could see the confused look on her face and that she was holding a book.

At ten feet she tumbled to the ground.

Caleb broke into a sprint, covering the last distance in seconds. The mysterious woman was lying in the snow, her eyes closed. Dark brown lashes brushed against skin that still held a slight tan from winter. Freckles dotted the tops of her cheeks and the bridge of her nose. A small book had fallen out of her hands. Her hair was splayed around her head like a cloak she'd thrown on the ground, and a pale blue scarf was wrapped around her neck—but no coat.

Where was the woman's coat?

He shook her gently, but there was no response.

Looking up, he saw Stormy waiting for him at the property line. He'd never be able to take her that way, unless he was willing to dump her over the fence. He couldn't begin to guess why she had fainted, but throwing her over barbed wire and onto the ground wouldn't be helpful.

No, he'd have to go the long way, by the road.

Caleb shook her shoulders one more time, but still there was no response. He clutched her hand. Her fingers were like slivers of ice. How long had she been out-side? Why was she wandering down their road?

Scooping her up, he turned toward the house.

She weighed little more than a large sack of feed, which he'd been lifting since he was a teenager. Carry-ing her was not a problem, but now his heart was rac-ing and his breath came out in quick gasps. What if he was too late? What if she was dying?

He strode toward his parents' house, pulling her body closer to his, willing his heat to warm her, whispering for *Gotte*'s help.

Stormy kept pace on his side of the fence.

The farmhouse seemed to taunt him, as it receded in the distance, but, of course, that was impossible. It was only that he was scared now, worried that he should have seen her sooner, that he might be too late.

Snow began to fall in earnest, but he barely noticed. Tucking his chin to keep the snow out of his eyes, he increased his pace.

"She just collapsed?" His mother had taken the sight of him carrying a nearly frozen woman into their home in stride. She'd told him to place her on the couch as she'd grabbed a blanket.

"*Ya.* She teetered back and forth across the road and then fell into the snow as I was watching."

"No idea who she is?"

"Obviously she's not from here."

Ida nodded. Her dress was of a bright blue fabric, while their community still wore only muted blues and greens, blacks and browns. They were a conservative Amish community, a mixture of Swiss and Pennsylva-nia Dutch, which was why they lived in the southwestern part of Indiana. They weren't a tourist destination like Shipshewana. And unlike some more liberal Amish communities, they didn't abide solar panels and cell phones and *Englisch* clothing. Not that the woman's dress was *Englisch*. It was obviously plain in style, but that color...

He didn't normally notice the color of a girl's dress, but in this case...well, the blue fabric seemed obscenely bright. She remained unconscious, though she seemed to be breathing. Caleb pulled off his knit cap, shrugged out of his coat and tugged off his gloves. Squatting in front of the couch, he watched his mother as she attempted to revive the woman.

She murmured slightly, tossing her head left and right. Almost of its own volition, his hand reached out and touched her face. Her skin felt like satin.

Still she didn't wake.

"She had nothing with her?"

"Nein."

"No purse or coat or—"

Caleb jumped up, snapping his fingers. "A book. She was holding a book when I first saw her."

"You best go and get it. Perhaps her name is written inside. Maybe there's someone we can contact."

Caleb snagged his coat from the floor where he'd dropped it and hurried back outside. Fat snowflakes were still falling. It looked as if the current snowfall was going to be a significant accumulation for only the third of December. Already the front path was completely obscured, any trace of his previous trek across the yard erased. At this rate they would have a Christmas to remember. It was unusual, as most of their snow usually came in January.

He jogged back the half mile, passing the place where he had been mending the fence. His tools were still there. He'd need to return them to the barn, but that wasn't an emergency. The woman? She was. He slowed when he reached the tall pine tree and scanned the ground. Nothing, not even his footprints from earlier.

He'd forgotten his hat and the snow was cold and heavy on his head. He shook the snow off his head, wiped his eyes and walked up and down the fence line—a hundred feet in both directions. There was nothing, but he was sure that she had been holding a book of some sort. He closed his eyes, saw it fall from her hand as she dropped to the ground. She'd wandered off the east side of the road, closer to the fence.

This was not the way his Monday was supposed to go. He didn't mind helping a neighbor, or a stranger, but he'd had an entire list of chores to complete. Farm life, his life, worked better when he stayed focused on the things he'd committed to doing. *When women entered his life, trouble often followed.* He pushed that thought away as soon as it formed. This wasn't about him. He needed to find the book. He hadn't opened his eyes that morning knowing he would save a stranger from freezing to death, but now that he had there was nothing left to do but see this thing through.

They'd find out who she was and where she belonged.

They'd return her, and he could get on with his life.

But first he needed to find the book.

He turned east, walked back and forth between the road and the fence, making a zigzag type of pattern. Then just when he was beginning to think he'd imagined the entire thing, that he'd return home and find there was no mysterious woman on their couch, he spied it—a lump of snow where there should have been flat ground.

He dropped to his knees and brushed the snow away.

The book had a green-and-gold cover with a photograph of a snowy path going through the woods, and beneath that the words *The Road Not Taken and Other Poems*. Had he read something like that in school? He was twenty-five now and that had been many years ago. He shook his head, picked up the book and hurried back home.

When he walked back into the living room, his father was there, and his mother was placing a cup of hot tea into the woman's hands. She was sitting up now, looking around with a dazed sort of expression.

"I think this is yours." Caleb placed the book on the couch beside her.

"Danki."

That one word confirmed what he'd suspected earlier. She wasn't from their part of the state. The Daviess County Amish had a distinctive Southern twang. This woman didn't.

Caleb's father sat in the reading chair. His mother perched on the edge of the rocker. Caleb folded his arms and stood behind them both. Across from them, the woman stared at the tea, then raised her eyes first to his *mamm*, then his *dat*, and finally settled her gaze on him.

"What happened? Where am I?"

"You don't know?" Caleb glanced at his parents, who seemed content to let him carry the conversation. "You were walking down the road, and then you collapsed."

"Why would I do such a thing?"

Caleb shrugged. "What's your name?"

The woman's eyes widened and her hand shook so that she could barely hold the mug of tea without spilling it. She set it carefully on the coffee table. "I don't— I don't know my name."

"My name is John Wittmer," Caleb's father said. "This my *fraa*, Ida, and you've met Caleb."

"How can you not know your own name?" Caleb asked. "Do you know where you live?"

"Nein."

"What were you doing out there?"

"Out where?"

"Where's your coat and your *kapp*?"

"Caleb, now's not the time to interrogate the poor girl." Ida stood and moved beside her on the couch. She picked up the small book of poetry. "You were carrying this, when Caleb found you. Do you remember it?"

"I don't. This was mine?"

"Found it in the snow," Caleb said. "Right beside where you collapsed."

"So it must be mine."

"Perhaps there's something written on the inside." Ida tapped the cover. "Maybe you should look."

Caleb noticed that the woman's hands trembled as she opened the cover and stared down at the first page. With one finger, she traced the handwriting there.

"Rachel. I think my name is Rachel."

Rachel let her fingers brush over the word again and again. *Rachel*. Yes, that was her name. She was sure of it. She remembered writing it in the front of the book—she'd used a pen that her *mamm* had given her.

She could almost picture herself, somewhere else. She could almost see her mother.

"My *mamm* gave me the pen and the book...for my birthday, I think. I wrote my name—wrote it right here."

"Your *mamm*. So you remember her?"

"Praise be to *Gotte*," John said, a smile spreading across his face.

"Is there someone we can call? If you remember the name of your bishop..." Caleb had sat down in the rocker his mother had vacated and was staring at her intensely.

They all were.

She closed her eyes, hoping to feel the memory again. She tried to see the room or the house or the people, but the image had receded as quickly as it had come, leaving her with a pulsing headache.

She struggled to keep the feelings of panic at bay. Her heart was hammering, and her hands were shaking, and she could barely make sense of the questions they were pelting at her.

Who were these people?

Where was she?

Who was she?

She needed to remember what had happened.

She needed to go home.

Instead she dropped the book into Ida's lap and covered her face with her hands. "I think—I think I'm going to be sick."

She bounded off the couch and dashed to the kitchen, making it to the sink just in time to lose whatever she'd eaten. Unfortunately, the sink had been full of breakfast dishes. She turned on the tap and attempted to rinse off a plate, but her hands were shaking so badly that she kept knocking it against the side of the sink.

"I'll take care of that." Ida's hands slid over hers, taking the plate and setting it back into the sink. She pulled a clean dish towel from a drawer and handed it to her. "Come and sit down."

She sank into a chair at the table and pressed her fingertips to her forehead. If only the pounding would stop, she could think.

"We best take her to town," John said.

"I'll get the buggy." Caleb brushed past her.

She remembered being in his arms, the way he'd pulled her close to his body, the way he'd petitioned *Gotte* to help them. Or had she dreamed that? But then he turned, and his blue eyes met hers, and she knew she hadn't imagined it. She could smell the snow on his coat, remember the rough texture of the fabric, hear the concern in his voice.

"We best wrap her in a blanket," Ida said. "And bring the book. There might be other clues in it."

And then they were bundling her up and helping her into the buggy. The ride passed in a blur of un-recognizable farms and stores and hillsides. The only thing familiar was the clip-clop of the horse's hooves and the feel of the small heater blowing from the front of the buggy.

Had she been in a buggy just like it before?

Caleb directed the horse under a covered drop-off area, next to a door marked Emergency.

"I don't think—"

"That it's an emergency? *Ya*, it is." He helped her from the buggy. Ida had rushed in ahead of them, and John said he'd park the buggy and meet them inside.

The next few hours passed in a flurry of hospital forms and medical personnel and tests. Finally, the doctor who had first examined her walked into the room, computer tablet in hand. She was a young woman, probably in her thirties, with dark black hair, glasses and a quick smile. Something about her manner put Rachel at ease, though another part of her dreaded hearing what the woman was about to say.

John had left to find them coffee and a snack, but Ida and Caleb both stood when the doctor walked into the room.

"Thank you all for your patience." She motioned for them to sit back down. "I know the barrage of tests we put a patient through can be trying, but trust me when I say that it's important for us to collect as much information as we can."

She turned toward Rachel.

"Hi, Rachel. Do you remember me?"

"*Ya.* You're Dr. Gold."

"Great. Can you tell me what day it is?"

Her eyes darted to the whiteboard that listed the name of her nurse and orderly. "December third."

"Very good." Dr. Gold laughed. "We know you can read."

The doctor placed her tablet on the table next to Rachel's bed. "Mind if I check that bump on your head one more time?"

Rachel leaned forward and jerked only slightly when the doctor gently probed the back of her head.

"Still tender."

"*Ya.*"

"Still no memory of what happened before Caleb found you?"

"Nein."

"And you can't remember how you got this bump?"

"The first thing I remember is…is Caleb carrying me to his house."

The doctor plumped the pillows behind her, waited until Rachel had sat back and then shone the penlight in her eyes again.

"I'm sorry. I know this is uncomfortable."

"It's just the headache…"

Dr. Gold nodded in sympathy and then clicked off the light. "Rachel, you have a slight concussion, which is why you're experiencing a sensitivity to light, a blinding headache and nausea."

She remembered vomiting in Ida's sink and grimaced.

"How long will that last?"

"In most cases, symptoms improve in seven to ten days."

"That's *gut.*"

"But the actual healing of your brain could take months."

"I don't understand."

"Most often a concussion occurs when you've sustained a blow to the head. In this case, you have a sizable knot at the back of your head and toward the top. Can you remember anything at all that led up to your accident?"

Rachel shook her head and spikes of pain brought tears to her eyes.

"I'm not surprised. You have what we call retrograde amnesia caused by a concussion. Often in such a situation, patients have problems remembering events leading up to an accident."

"I still don't understand."

"Retrograde amnesia or a concussion?"

"Both."

Dr. Gold smiled and patted her hand. "Concussions happen all too often. The brain itself is rather like Jell-O. When a concussion occurs, your brain slides back and forth and bumps up against the walls of your skull. Basically the brain is bruised, and like all bruises it takes time to heal."

"What would cause such a thing?" Caleb asked. His expression had turned rather fierce. "Does it mean that someone hit her?"

"Not necessarily." Dr. Gold cocked her head, studying both Ida and Caleb for a few seconds. Then she turned her attention back to Rachel. "You could have been in a car accident, or fallen off a bicycle or simply tripped, and hit your head against the ground."

"And that would cause a concussion?" Ida asked. "Just falling?"

Caleb sank back into the chair and leaned forward, elbows on his knees, fingers interlaced. "Did it happen when she fell in the snow?"

"Not likely," Dr. Gold said. "I suspect that Rachel sustained her injury before you ever saw her. It's why she was meandering back and forth across the road. Concussions often result in vertigo."

"Can you tell how long it's been?" Ida asked.

"I can't. There was no bleeding from the wound, so I rather doubt that someone hit her. More likely it was a simple accident."

"What about my memory?" Rachel asked. "When will it return?"

"Memories are tricky things. You remembered my name, and you know who these people are. Correct?"

"Caleb." She met his gaze, remembered again being in his arms. "And Ida, his *mamm*."

"Which is a good sign. This tells us your brain is still working the way it should."

"But I wouldn't have remembered my name if it hadn't been written in that book, and I still don't know where I live or who I am."

"In most cases those memories will return in time."

"How much time?"

"Remember what I said earlier? You don't just have a concussion. You also have retrograde amnesia."

"And what does that mean?"

"That it may be a few days or weeks or even months before you regain your memories."

Rachel felt as if she was falling into a long, dark tunnel. She stared down at the cotton blanket covering her and grasped it between both of her hands. "That long?"

"I'm afraid so, but the good news is that your memory is working now, and it will continue to work. You may not be able to remember what happened before the accident, but you can create new memories. Plus you're healthy in every other way."

"But what am I to do? Where will I live?"

"If you'd like, we have a social worker here at the hospital that can meet with you and find temporary housing for you. We'll also put you in contact with a liaison with the Daviess County Sheriff's Office. Perhaps your family has reported you missing. It could be that they're looking for you even now."

"What do I do until they find me?"

"Be patient. Give your brain time to heal. Live your life."

"I don't have any money, though."

"There are charities that provide funds for those in need. You don't need to worry about money right now."

"She doesn't need to worry about where to live, either." Ida stood and moved to the side of the bed. She was about Rachel's height but looked a bit shorter, owing to her weight. She wasn't big exactly, but rounded, like a grandmother should be. She was probably close to fifty with gray and brown strands of hair peeking out from under her prayer *kapp*. "Rachel, we would be happy to have you stay with us. We have an extra room. It's only Caleb and John and myself, so it's a fairly quiet environment. You can rest and heal."

Rachel didn't know if that was a good idea. Ida and John seemed like a nice couple, and Caleb had saved her, but she wasn't sure they wanted a brain-injured person living with them. Then again, what choice did she have?

She didn't want to go to a police station.

She didn't want to wait on a social worker.

"Stay with us," Ida repeated.

"Ya." Rachel nodded, wiping away the tears that had begun to slide down her cheeks. "Okay. *Danki.*"

Dr. Gold was pleased with the arrangement, and Ida was grinning as if Christmas had come early, but when Rachel glanced at Caleb, she wasn't sure if she saw relief or regret in his eyes.

Chapter Two

They returned to Ida and John's house. The snow had stopped, but it sat in heaps on the side of the road. The clouds had cleared, the sun was shining and Rachel suspected the snow would melt completely by the next day. The *Englisch* homes they passed already had Christmas decorations out on the lawn. Rachel wasn't sure what Amish homes did to celebrate for the season. She wasn't sure what her family had done in the past.

The rest of the day passed in a blur.

She met with the local bishop, Amos Hilty, a kind, elderly man as round as he was tall with tufts of white hair that reminded her of a cotton ball.

She learned that the local community was a blend of Swiss Amish and Pennsylvania Dutch Amish, but she couldn't tell them which she had been. From the style and color of her dress, they guessed that she came from one of the more progressive districts. Amos assured her that he'd contact the local districts to see if anyone had reported a young woman missing.

"We'll find your family, Rachel. Try not to worry. Trust that *Gotte* has a plan and a purpose for your life."

She wasn't sure how *Gotte* could use her accident, her loss of memory, for His good, but she smiled and thanked the bishop for helping her.

Several times that afternoon she had to excuse herself and lie down because of the vertigo and nausea, and bone-deep exhaustion. Ida's cooking smelled wonderful—it was a meat loaf she'd thrown together and served with mashed potatoes, canned squash, gravy and fresh bread. Rachel thought she could eat three plates, but when she'd taken her first bite, the nausea had returned, and she'd fled to the bathroom.

Now it was ten thirty in the evening and everyone was asleep, but she was starving. Pulling on the robe Ida had loaned her, she padded down the hall to the kitchen. She pulled a pitcher of milk from the icebox and found a tin of cookies when Caleb walked in.

"If you'd eaten your dinner, you wouldn't be so hungry late at night." When she didn't answer and just stood there frozen, as if she'd been caught stealing, he'd walked closer, bumped his shoulder against hers and said, "I'm kidding. Pour me a glass?"

So she did, and they sat down at the table together. She could just make out his outline from the light of the full moon slanting through the window. Oddly, the darkness comforted her, knowing he couldn't see her well, either. She felt less exposed, less vulnerable.

"I can't remember if I thanked you…for finding me in the snow. For bringing me here."

"You didn't."

"Danki."

"Gem Gschehne."

The words slipped effortlessly between them and

brought her a small measure of comfort. At least she remembered how to be polite. Surely that was something.

"You owe me, you know."

Her head snapped up, and she peered at him through the darkness.

"You scared at least a year off my life when I saw you out there."

"Lucky for me you did."

"I'm not sure luck had anything to do with it. *Gotte* was watching over you, for sure and certain."

"If He was watching over me, why did this happen? Why can't I remember anything? What am I supposed to do next?"

"I'm not going to pretend I have the answers to any of those questions."

"Might be a good time to lie to me and say you do."

Caleb's laugh was soft and low and genuine. "We both would regret that later."

"I suppose." She sipped the cold milk. At least her stomach didn't reject it. Maybe she would feel better if she could keep some food down. She hesitantly reached for an oatmeal cranberry cookie.

"Your *mamm*'s a *gut* cook."

"*Ya*, she is."

"So it's just you? You're an only child?"

"*Ya*, though my *mamm* wanted to have more children."

"Why didn't she?"

"Something went wrong when she had me, and the doctors said she wouldn't be able to conceive again."

"Gotte's wille."

"She always wanted a girl, too, so I suppose you're

an answer to that prayer, even if you're a temporary answer."

"When you marry, she'll have a daughter-in-law."

"So they keep reminding me." He laughed again, but there was something sad and bitter at the same time in it. His next words had a serious, let's-get-down-to-business tone. "How are you feeling? I know you keep telling my parents that you're fine, but it's obvious you aren't."

"Lost. Confused. Sick to my stomach."

"Food should help settle your stomach."

She bit into the cookie, which was delicious but could use a little nutmeg. "I just remembered something."

"You did?"

"Cookies need nutmeg."

Caleb reached for another. "It's a beginning."

"Not much of one."

"The doctor told you this could take a while."

"I know…but can you imagine what it's like for me? I don't know who I am."

"You know your name is Rachel."

"Only because you found my book."

"Not many Amish girls read Robert Frost. That narrows the prospective field of candidates down a little."

"Perhaps we could advertise somewhere…"

"The Budget." Caleb nodded and ran a thumb under his suspenders. "Actually that's not a bad idea. If you write something up in the morning—"

"What would I write? I don't remember anything."

"Okay. *Gut* point, but perhaps your family will post there. We'll watch the paper closely."

"Danki."

"Gem Gschehne."

And there it was again—an odd familiarity that bound them together.

"Are you always this nice?"

"*Nein.* I'm on my best behavior with you because you've had a brain injury."

"Oh, is that so?"

"My normal personality is bullheaded and old-fashioned, which are both apparently bad things. And that's a direct quote."

"From?"

"My last girlfriend."

"Oh. Well, I can't remember my last boyfriend, so you're still a step ahead of me."

Caleb cleared his throat, returned the pitcher of milk to the refrigerator and then sat down across from her again. When he clasped his hands together, she knew she wasn't going to like what he was about to say. She suddenly felt defensive and bristly, like a cat rubbed the wrong way.

"My parents wanted to give you a few days to adjust, but I think there are some things you should know."

"There are?"

"Our community is quite conservative—we're a branch of the Swiss Amish, as Bishop Amos explained."

"He's a nice man."

"As long as you're staying…well, this is awkward, but…"

"Just spit it out, Caleb." She'd had this sort of conversation before, though she couldn't remember the details. Somewhere in her injured brain was the memory of someone else trying to set her straight. Why did people always think they knew what was best for her?

"Our women always keep their heads covered—always."

"Oh." Rachel's hand went to her hair, which was unbraided and not covered. "Even in the house?"

Caleb glanced at her and then away. Finally, he shrugged and said, "Depends, but my point is that for some reason you weren't wearing a *kapp* when I found you."

"Maybe I lost it."

"And your hair was down—you know, unbraided, like it is now."

She pulled her hair over her right shoulder, nervously running her fingers through it. "Anything else?"

"Your clothes are all wrong."

"Excuse me?"

"Wrong color, wrong...pattern or whatever you call it."

"The color is wrong?"

"We only wear muted colors—no bright greens or blues."

"Because?"

"Because it draws attention and we're called to a life of humility and selflessness."

Rachel jumped up, walked to the sink and rinsed out her cup. When she had her temper under control, or thought she did, she turned back to him. "Any other words of wisdom?"

Caleb was now standing, too, but near the table with his arms crossed in front, as if he was afraid she'd come too close. "Not that I know of...not now..."

"But?"

"Look, Rachel. I'm not being rude or mean. These

are things I think you'd be better hearing from me than having people say behind your back."

"Is that what type of community you have? One that talks behind people's backs?"

"Every community does that, and it's more from curiosity and boredom than meanness."

"All right, then, tell me. What else do I need to know? So I won't incite gossip and all."

"It's only that you're obviously from a more progressive district."

"Oh, it's obvious, is it?"

"And so you might want to question your first instinct for things, stop and watch what other people do, be sensitive to offending others."

"You are kidding me. That's what you're worried about?"

"I'm worried about a lot of things."

"I've lost my entire world, everyone I knew, and you're concerned I'll *offend* someone?"

"I've hurt your feelings, and I didn't mean to do that."

"That's something, I suppose."

"But you'll thank me tomorrow or the next day or a week from now."

"I'm not so sure about that, Caleb, but there is one thing I do know." She stepped closer and looked down at her hair, which was still pulled forward and reached well past her waist. When she glanced back up at him, she saw that he was staring at it. She waited for him to raise his eyes to hers.

He swallowed and shifted from one foot to the other. "There was one thing you wanted to say?"

"*Ya.* Your old girlfriend?"

"Emily?"

"The one who told you that you were stubborn and old-fashioned."

"That would be Emily." He reached up and rubbed at the back of his neck. When he did, she smelled the soap he'd used earlier, noticed the muscles in his arm flex. His blond hair flopped forward, and it occurred to her that he was a nice-looking guy—nice-looking but with a terrible attitude and zero people skills.

"Between you and me—she was right. You are stubborn. You are old-fashioned, and you should keep your helpful hints to yourself."

And with that, she turned and fled down the hall, feeling better than she had since Caleb had rescued her from the snow.

The next morning, Caleb took as long with his chores as he dared. There was really no point in avoiding Rachel. She lived in their house now, and he would have to get used to her being around.

His mind darted back to her long hair. It wasn't brown exactly, or chestnut—more the warm color of honey. It had reminded him of kitten fur. As she'd stood next to him in the kitchen, he'd had the irrational urge to reach out and comb his fingers through it. The moonlight had softened her expression, and for a moment the look of vulnerability had vanished. Sure, it had vanished and been replaced with anger.

He remembered her parting words and almost laughed. He'd only been trying to help, but he'd never been particularly tactful. The fact that she'd called him on it...well, it showed that she had spunk and hopefully that she was healing. He decided to take it for a good sign rather than be offended.

When he walked into the kitchen, he noticed that her hair was properly braided, and she'd apparently borrowed one of his mother's *kapps*. Unfortunately, she wore the same dress as the day before. She gave him a pointed look, as if daring him to say something about it, but what could he say? It really wasn't his business. He'd done his duty by warning her. The rest was out of his hands.

Everyone sat at the table, waiting on him, so he washed his hands quickly and joined them. After a silent prayer, he began to fill his plate. He heaped on portions of scrambled eggs, sizzling sausage, homemade biscuits and breakfast potatoes, which were chopped and fried with onions and bell pepper.

"Someone's hungry this morning," Ida said.

"*Ya*. Mucking out stalls can do that to a man." He noticed that Rachel was eating, and she looked rested. "How are you feeling this morning, Rachel?"

"Better. Thank you, Caleb." Her tone was rather formal, and the look she gave him could freeze birds to a tree branch.

He nodded and focused on his plate of food. When he was nearly finished, he began to discuss the day's work with his father. They had a small enough farm—only seventy acres—but there was always work to do.

"Guess I'll finish mending that fence this morning."

"*Ya, gut* idea."

His mother jumped up and fetched the coffeepot from the stove burner. She refilled everyone's mugs, starting with Rachel's. Usually his mother threw in her opinion on their work, but she'd been deep in conversation with Rachel the entire meal. They'd been thick as thieves talking about who knew what—girl stuff, he supposed.

"Have you thought any more about the alpacas?" Caleb asked.

His father added creamer to his coffee. "I'm a little hesitant, to tell you the truth. I know nothing about the animals."

"They're a good investment," Caleb insisted. "Mr. Vann has decided he's too old to manage such a big farm."

Ida looked up in surprise. "It's hardly bigger than ours, and Mr. Vann is only—"

"Nearly seventy."

"Not so old, then." His father shared a smile with his mom. Must have been an old-people's joke, though his parents were only forty-eight.

"He has no children close enough to help on a daily basis," Caleb explained. "He's gifting the farm to his children and grandchildren, who will only use it for a weekend place. Obviously they can't keep the alpacas."

"I'm wondering if it's the best time of year to get into a new business."

"Better than planting season or harvesting, and he's letting them go cheap. I'm telling you, if we don't get them today, they'll probably be gone."

"Even a bargain costs money," John said.

"*Ya*, I'm aware of that, but we have plenty put back."

"What good are they, Caleb?" His mother held up a hand. "I'm not arguing with you. It's only that I know nothing about them."

"The yarn is quite popular," Rachel said.

Everyone turned to stare at her. She blushed the color

of a pretty rose and added, "I don't know how I knew that."

"Did you maybe have alpacas before? At your parents' farm?"

"I don't—I don't think so, but I can remember the yarn. Spinners and knitters and even weavers use it."

"Any chance you recall how much trouble they are to raise?" His father laughed at his own joke, and then he reached across the table and patted her hand. "I don't expect you to answer that. I was only teasing because my son seems set on bringing strange animals onto our farm."

"I thought you were a traditionalist," Rachel said, then immediately pressed her fingers to her lips as if she wanted to pull back the words.

But if Caleb was worried he might have to answer that, might have to explain in front of his parents their conversation the night before, he was pleasantly mistaken.

Ida was up and clearing dishes, and she answered for him. "Oh, *ya*. In nearly every way that's true. Caleb is quite traditional."

"Unless it comes to animals," his father said. "We've tried camels."

"How was I to know they'd be so hard to milk?"

"And goats."

"We learned a lot that time."

"*Ya*, we learned if water can go through a fence, then so can a goat."

"We're a little off topic here." Caleb tried to ignore the fact that Rachel was now grinning at him as if she'd discovered the most amusing thing that she might insult him with later. "Let's just go look at the alpacas together. We could go this morning, and I'll fix the fence this afternoon."

"How about we do it the other way around?"

"Deal."

He was up and out of his chair, already glancing at the clock. If he worked quickly, they could be there before noon—surely before anyone else came along and bought the alpacas out from under their noses.

"Caleb, would you mind making sure that the front porch and steps are free of ice?"

"The front porch?"

"We're going to have visitors, and I don't want anyone slipping."

Visitors? On a Tuesday morning? "I was headed out to work on the fence line."

"And then look at alpacas. I heard."

He tugged on his ear. His mother was acting so strangely. Since when did she have weekday visitors? When had she ever asked him to clean off the front-porch steps?

"Shouldn't take but a few minutes," his father said. "Your mother wouldn't ask if she didn't need it."

The rebuke was mild, but still he felt his cheeks flushing.

"*Ya*, of course. Anything else?"

"You could move your muddy boots off the front porch, as well as that sanding project you've never finished."

"Did I miss something? Are we having Sunday service here on a Tuesday?" He meant it as a joke, but it came out as a whine.

Rachel jumped up to help his mother, not even attempting to hide her smile.

"Some ladies are stopping by." His mother reached up and patted his shoulder. "I just don't want them tripping over your things."

He rolled his eyes but assured her that he'd take care of it right away.

When he stepped out onto the front porch, his dad clapped him on the back. "Give them a little space. Your *mamm*, she's happy to have another girl around the place."

"*Ya*, that makes sense, but—"

"She's convinced that *Gotte* brought Rachel into our lives for a reason."

"To give me more work?"

"And, of course, we all want to make the transition easier for Rachel. This is bound to be a difficult time."

From the grin on Rachel's face, he didn't think it was as difficult as his father imagined, but instead of arguing with him, he found the stiff outdoor broom and began sweeping the steps to make sure there was no ice or water or snow there. *Woman's work*, he thought, but that wasn't what was bothering him. Change was in the air, and Caleb had never been one to embrace change—unless it was regarding farm animals.

In every other way, stubborn and old-fashioned was more his style.

Ida had shared with Rachel that a few ladies would be stopping by. "They heard about your situation and want to help."

She wasn't sure what that meant, but she'd nodded politely, and then Caleb had brought up alpacas, and the conversation had twisted and turned from there.

Now it was nearly noon, and she plopped onto the couch and stared at the items stacked on the coffee table.

Ida sat across from her, holding a steaming mug of coffee. "Seems everyone from our community pitched in. It's *gut, ya*?"

"Of course. I'm a bit stunned. How did they even know that I'd need these things? How did they know I was here?"

"Word travels fast in an Amish community. Certainly you remember that."

"We used to call it the Amish grapevine."

Ida laughed. "I've heard that before, too, but 'grapevine' has a gossipy sound to it. This is really just neighbors helping neighbors."

Rachel picked the top dress off the pile of clothes. The color was midnight blue—Caleb would be happy about that—and the fabric was a good cotton that would last. It was also soft to the touch. She ran her hand across it, humbled by all that these women, who were strangers to her, had given.

"We'll need to take those in, of course. You're shorter and smaller than Rebekah's girls."

"Won't they need these?"

"Not likely, both have put on a good bit of weight since marrying, and that was before they were expecting her first grandchildren. No, I don't think they'll be needing them back."

There were underclothes, *kapps*, two outdoor bonnets and a coat. All except the underclothes were used, but in good condition. Someone had brought a Bible and a journal for writing in. She thought those might come in handy. Dr. Gold had mentioned that writing a little every day might help her memories return. There was also a new scarf and gloves, knitted in a dark gray that had a touch of shimmer to it. "This is beautiful work."

"Melinda can do wonders with a knitting needle. I've always been more of a crochet person myself."

Rachel stood up, went to the room she was staying in and returned with the blue scarf she'd apparently been wearing when Caleb had found her. No coat, but a scarf—strange indeed. "I think—I think I might be a knitter."

"That's why you knew about the alpaca yarn."

"Maybe. I think so. I know this is called a stockinette pattern—you alternate rows of knitting with rows of purling." She closed her eyes, could almost see herself adjusting the tension in her yarn, squinting at a pattern, knitting needles flying. She could be imagining, or she could be remembering. There was no way to know.

"Are you remembering anything else?"

"Only that this—" She ran her fingers over the scarf, then draped it around her neck. "It seems very familiar."

"That's a beginning."

"If only I could remember more, but when I try, the headaches return."

Ida walked over to the bookcase and brought back the packet of information from the doctor at the hospital. Rachel had already rifled through it twice. There were instructions, what to expect, warning signs, as well as two cards—one for her next appointment with Dr. Gold and another card with the name and contact information for a Dr. Michie. She'd spoken with the doctor a few minutes before leaving the hospital. She was a counselor of some sort and had told Rachel to call her if she'd like to make an appointment.

Ida sat beside Rachel on the couch and they both stared down at the top page.

Ida read aloud from the sheet. "'Symptoms of a concussion include brief loss of consciousness.'"

"Check."

"'Memory problems.'"

"We all know I have that."

"'Confusion.'"

Rachel leaned forward, propped her elbows on her knees and pressed her fingertips to her forehead. "Sometimes, when I can't remember how I know something, I feel terribly confused."

Ida nodded and continued with the list. "'Drowsiness or feeling sluggish.'"

"Twice this morning I went back and laid down on the bed for a few minutes."

"Only because I insisted. You need to recognize when things are overwhelming you. It's important for a woman to learn to take care of herself. You're no use to your family—"

"I don't have one."

"Or anyone else if you allow yourself to become ill or exhausted."

Rachel heard the concern in Ida's voice, but she couldn't bring herself to meet her gaze. "I'm batting a thousand, as my *bruder* would say…"

She slapped her hand over her mouth.

Ida reached over and clutched her hand. "That's *gut*, Rachel. You're starting to remember. That's a *gut* sign."

"I suppose."

"Can you remember his name?"

"Nein."

"Older or younger?"

She closed her eyes and tried to picture her family, tried to recall anything from her past, but to no avail.

Her heart was racing and her mind was spinning off in a dozen directions, but she couldn't quite grasp even one solid piece of information about her former life—other than she had a brother. Was he worried? Was he looking for her?

Finally, she motioned for Ida to continue with the list of symptoms. They knew she had a concussion, the doctor had confirmed as much, but it helped to know that the things she was feeling and experiencing weren't unusual.

"'Dizziness or blurred vision.'"

"A little yesterday, when I first woke up in the hospital."

"'Headache.'"

"*Ya*, especially when I try to remember."

"'Nausea or vomiting.'"

"Not since I started eating."

"'Sensitivity to light.'"

"That's on there?" She scooted closer and peered at the sheet. "I tried going outside for a few moments earlier, but the sunshine felt like a pitchfork in my brain. I found myself wishing I had my sunglasses."

"Another puzzle piece. You have a *bruder* and you wore sunglasses."

"Doesn't everyone?"

"Perhaps." Ida tapped the last item on the list. "What about balance problems? Any trouble there?"

"I'm not sure. Let's check." Rachel jumped up and pretended to walk a straight line, holding her hands out to the side. She pivoted and started back toward Ida, touching her nose with first her right and then left index finger as she walked. Ida began to laugh, and then Rachel began to laugh, and soon they were giggling like schoolgirls.

And, of course, that was the moment that Caleb walked inside, a frown pulling down the corners of his mouth. Why did he always seem to be disapproving of her? She pitied the woman that did decide to marry him or even date him. Caleb Wittmer might be a good man, but he wasn't much fun to be around, and life should include some fun. Shouldn't it?

"We're about to head over to see the alpacas."

"Oh, well, I hope it goes well, dear."

"Actually I was wondering…"

"About?"

"Lunch."

Ida started laughing again, and then she spread her arms to encompass the pile of goods their neighbors had brought. "We've been pretty busy in here."

"I see that."

"Our neighbors brought all of these things for Rachel."

"Wunderbaar."

"Honestly I forgot about making lunch, but I'll throw some sandwiches together."

Caleb nodded as if that made sense. His mother brushed past him, humming as she went into the kitchen.

"Let me guess." Rachel couldn't have stopped the smile spreading across her face if she'd tried, which she didn't. "You're not used to eating sandwiches."

"Actually I can't remember the last time *Mamm* didn't have lunch waiting on the table."

Rachel attempted to make sympathetic noises, but

it probably came out like she'd managed to choke on something. She knew she should keep her mouth shut. Instead she said, "Men can make a sandwich, too, Caleb. Maybe you should give your *mamm* a little bit of a break here. Having me around? It's a lot of extra work."

He narrowed his eyes and pulled in a deep breath.

Rachel immediately regretted baiting him.

"Your community has been very nice. They even brought me some appropriate clothing." Oops. She'd done it again.

Instead of aggravating Caleb, he seemed to relax. Perhaps poking at one another felt like safe ground to him. "That is a *gut* thing. I see you even have several *kapps* and bonnets there."

He picked one up. Unfortunately, it happened to be on top of the pile of underclothes. When he glanced down and saw the stack of underthings, he dropped the bonnet, turned a bright shade of red and then pivoted and fled from the room.

Rachel grabbed a pillow and buried her face in it so that he couldn't hear her laughter. Which felt so much better than worrying about what Caleb thought of her— that question was behind the laughter. She didn't want to think about that, though, or about why it mattered.

She needed to remember who she was. Borrowed clothes, a guest room in someone else's house and Caleb looking over her shoulder to see if she was following the rules were not how she wanted to live the rest of her life.

Chapter Three

Caleb bought the seven alpacas that afternoon.

His father had finally said, "You saved the money yourself. If it's what you want, then give it a try."

"Strangest animal I've ever seen" was his mother's only comment.

Caleb spent the rest of the week making sure the alpacas had adequate space in the barn, reinforcing fencing where he would pasture them and generally getting to know the strange beasts.

His parents came out once a day to check on the animals and his best friend, Gabriel, had been by twice. Mostly he'd laughed at Caleb's feeble attempts to interact with them.

As for Rachel, she hadn't stepped outside of the house at all. If anything, she'd seemed physically worse on Wednesday and Thursday. At one point, his *mamm* had walked down to the phone shack and contacted the doctor, who had called in a prescription for nausea and told her to be patient. "These things take time" were the doctor's exact words.

So Caleb was surprised when he was in the field

with the alpacas on Friday morning and looked up to see Rachel leaning against the fence. She wore a proper dress and coat, plus one of the outer bonnets she'd been given, though there was little wind and the sun had melted away every last trace of snow. She also sported sunglasses, an old pair of his mother's if he remembered correctly. In the crook of her arm she was carrying a bowl that his mother used to dump scraps into.

"Nice to see you outside."

"If I sit in the house one more day, I might go crazy. One can only read so much or do so many crossword puzzles."

"I wouldn't know."

"What's that supposed to mean?"

"Only that I work every day from sunrise until dark."

"Life of a farmer, I guess."

"Amish women work hard, too. At least most of them do."

"Kind of hard to find a job if you can't remember anything more than your first name."

Caleb shrugged. Rachel could find work if she wanted it. They both knew it. Instead of defending herself further, she changed the subject.

"Have you named them?"

"*Nein.* We don't name our cows."

"I don't see any cows."

"We only have three—all dairy cows. They're in the east pasture."

"Oh. I guess I haven't been in that direction yet." She reached out her hand and one of the alpacas moseyed over to sniff at her palm.

"I'd call you Mocha."

The alpaca stood completely still and allowed her to rub its top notch of hair.

"How'd you do that? They won't let me within five feet of them."

When the male alpaca began to crunch on something, one of the females bounded over to join him. Soon he could barely see Rachel because the entire herd of alpacas had congregated near the fence. Caleb walked over to see what she was giving him.

"Apple slices?"

"*Ya.* Your *mamm* is making an apple pie, but she didn't want to include the skins. It seems like I always did when I baked a pie…" She shook her head back and forth, as if she could rattle the memory free.

Caleb scratched at his jaw. "I didn't think of giving them scraps."

"Makes sense, though. Most animals enjoy apple slices. We had a dog once that loved them."

Her head jerked up and she met Caleb's gaze, surprise coloring her features.

"You're remembering more every day."

"Small inconsequential things. It's frustrating."

"Not to my alpacas."

She smiled at that, and Caleb felt inexplicably better. He didn't pretend to understand Rachel, but he somehow thought of himself as responsible for her. Perhaps that was normal considering he'd found her in the snow only a few days before.

"Did you get a good deal on the animals?"

"I think so. Less than three thousand dollars for all seven, and there are two females."

"Hopefully you'll have baby alpacas running around by spring."

"That's the plan."

"Do you expect they'll be much work?"

"Not according to Mr. Vann. They mainly eat hay and grass, though some mineral supplements are good, too."

"So you won't be spending much money to maintain them."

"*Nein.* Also, they don't bite or butt or spit. I tried raising a llama once, but that didn't go so well."

Rachel crossed her arms on the fence and rested her head on top of them, watching the group of alpacas dart away and then flop and roll in a patch of dirt. He'd seen them do that before, but watching Rachel watching them, seeing the smile grow on her face, he realized for the first time what funny animals they were.

"They're herd animals, so it's a good thing I was able to buy seven."

"I think you made a good business decision, Caleb. You'll know for sure once you shear them, but my guess is that you'll make a nice return on your investment."

"Mr. Vann said to watch the top notch. If the hair grows to cover their eyes, I'm supposed to have it cut, which will mean learning to do it myself because I'm not about to pay someone else to do it."

Rachel covered her mouth to hide a giggle, which Caleb heard nonetheless.

"What's so funny?"

"Explain that to me," she said.

"Explain what?"

"You're so old-fashioned about other things." She held up a hand when he began to protest. "You admitted it yourself, the first night I was here. The night that you told me about your last girlfriend."

"She wasn't right about everything."

"But you said…what was it? 'My normal personality is bullheaded and old-fashioned.'"

"*Ya.* I suppose it's true."

"Not exactly unusual among the Amish."

"Oh, you remember that, do you?"

"So why are you such a risk taker as far as animals?"

"Crops, too," he admitted. He'd been watching the animals, but now he turned to study Rachel. "I'll answer your question, but first tell me why you want to know."

"Curious, I guess. Sort of like your alpacas."

The horses were grazing in the adjacent pasture. The gelding had wandered close to the fence separating it from the alpacas. The horse was focused on the winter grass, but one of the tan alpacas had zeroed in on the horse. It stuck its nose through the fence, then jumped back, jumped almost vertically. Which caused the other alpacas to trot over, and then they were all gawking at the horse and making a high-pitched noise that sounded like a cat with its tail caught in a door.

"So you're not asking merely to give me grief?"

"Not at all." With her fingers, she crossed her heart. "Promise."

He leaned against the fence, studying the animals but thinking of the woman standing beside him. Rachel was a jumbled mix of paradoxes. One moment she seemed vulnerable, the next fiercely independent, and then sometimes she was quietly curious.

Glancing at her, he realized—not for the first time—what a beautiful woman she was. Probably back in her own community she had a boyfriend who was wondering what had happened to her. The thought made him uncomfortable, as if they should be doing more to return her to her home. But what could they do?

Nothing, so far as he knew, so instead he settled for being honest and answering her question.

"I like the Plain life. I've seen my fair share of folks leave our faith—about half of them came back, tails tucked between their legs. The other half? They either never visit their family at all—"

"Is it allowed?"

"Oh, *ya*. Our bishop encourages families to support one another, even when a member chooses a different path."

Rachel nodded, as if that made sense.

"These people I'm thinking of, they have a standing invitation to come home and see their loved ones."

"But they don't?"

"Most don't. The ones that do, they seem put out that they have to leave their cell phone in the car."

"Are you speaking from personal experience?"

"You're asking if anyone in my family has gone over to the *Englisch* side?" Caleb ran his hand along the top rail of the metal fence—it was smooth and cold to the touch. "Two cousins, on my mother's side."

"So that makes you conservative…as far as people are concerned."

"I think being Plain means we stand for something. We stand for a different lifestyle. Once we start making compromises, there's no difference between us and the *Englisch*—in that case, who wouldn't leave?"

Rachel was shaking her head, her bonnet strings swaying back and forth, but she smiled and said, "All right. I've never heard it expressed that way before, but—"

"You might have. Maybe you don't remember."

"Good point. So you're conservative because you think it's good for families and believers."

"Right."

"But the farming? And animals?"

"In business you want to be conservative—for sure and certain you do."

"But?"

"It's exciting to try something new. *Ya?* Look at those animals. They seem like giant poodles to me. Who figured out that their wool would be a good crop?"

"Caleb, you surprise me."

"Ya?" He reached forward and brushed some grass off her coat sleeve, no doubt left by one of his alpacas that had been nosing closer for apple peels. "Is that *gut* or bad?"

"Both. The alpacas will be entertaining."

They'd returned to flopping down in the dirt.

"Your herd looks like they will produce a variety of coffee colors."

"Coffee, huh?"

"Something *Englischers* love—lots of browns and tans and mochas and cappuccinos. Maybe even a cinnamon hue on that far one."

"Cappuccino?" He could feel the frown forming on his lips. No doubt she loved visiting a coffee shop and wasting her money.

"Plus their fiber is hypoallergenic, which is what makes it very popular."

"Funny that you know that."

She simply shrugged.

"I know nothing about shearing, but I can learn."

"Do you have a local library?"

"Sure."

"You can search how to do that on their computers."

He felt something freeze inside of him. This happened every time he began to feel comfortable with Rachel. She said or did something that reminded him she didn't belong here and probably wouldn't be staying. He stepped away from the fence, so now they were facing each other, though Rachel was a good head shorter than he was.

"We don't use the computers."

"Why?" She cocked her head and looked genuinely puzzled.

"Because we choose not to. We're *Plain*…" He couldn't help emphasizing the last word, though he realized it sounded patronizing.

"Uh-huh. Well, I can tell you're getting aggravated, so I suppose I should go back inside."

"We just talked about what it means to be Plain, and then you throw out a comment about using computers."

"There's nothing wrong with a computer, Caleb." She stepped closer, right up into his personal space, and stared up at him.

He took a step back.

"Computers aren't evil."

"Never said they were, but they're not Plain."

"A computer isn't going to cause anyone to leave the faith."

"It could. The things you can see on one…well, it's like bait to our *youngies*…"

"Of which you are one."

He laughed at that. "Turned twenty-five last year."

"Me, too."

They both froze, the argument suddenly forgotten.

"Another piece of the puzzle of Rachel," he said softly.

She glanced at him uncertainly, a range of emotions playing across her face, and then she turned and wandered back into the house, pausing now and again to look back at the alpacas.

* * *

Rachel spent the rest of Friday morning helping Ida, but honestly there wasn't much to do for a family of three—four if she counted herself. Was she a part of Ida's family? Was this her home now? When would she remember her past?

And beneath those questions were Caleb's words, mocking her.

Amish women work hard, too. At least most of them do.

Did he think she liked not being able to remember her own last name or where she was from? Did he think she enjoyed being ill?

"The headaches are better, *ya*?" Ida was crocheting a gray-and-black winter scarf for Caleb. She only brought it out during the day, not wanting him to see it until Christmas morning.

Rachel was sitting and staring at the crochet needle that Ida had given her. She'd even shown her how to use it, but the rhythm and stitch pattern seemed completely foreign. If she'd crocheted in her other life, she certainly couldn't remember doing so.

"Some."

"That's *gut*. You're a little better every day. You could be entirely well by Christmas."

"Does your community celebrate on December twenty-fifth or on January sixth?"

"Both. The older generation—older than me even, they prefer Old Christmas."

"Probably includes Caleb."

"Caleb likes both holidays—mainly because I cook his favorite dishes."

"I wish I could remember how to use this." Rachel

stared at the crochet needle. "I wish I remembered something useful."

"That seems to happen when you're not thinking about it." She pointed to the journal that contained the list that Rachel had made. The list was pitifully short, in her opinion. She opened the journal and stared down at the first page.

My name is Rachel.
I have a brother.
I know about alpaca wool.
Used to wear sunglasses?
I'm 25 years old.

"Those things could describe a lot of women."

"And yet they describe you, and *Gotte* made you special and unique."

"Now you're trying to cheer me up."

"Indeed." Ida peered at her over the reading glasses she wore while crocheting. The frames were a pretty blue, which probably irked Caleb to no end. A blue dress was out of the question—blue frames couldn't be far behind.

"Do you know what I think is wrong with you?"

Rachel nearly choked on the water she'd been sipping. She'd known Ida for only less than a week, and yet already she knew the woman had a gentle spirit—one that wasn't critical.

"What's wrong with me?"

Now Ida was smiling. "Uh-huh."

"Tell me, Ida. Because it may just be that my brain is bruised, but I feel all out of sorts."

"You have cabin fever."

"Pardon me?"

"Cabin fever. I used to suffer from it something terrible when Caleb was a babe. That was a hard winter, and we were inside—in this very house—too much. Finally, his father came into the kitchen one morning and told me that he had finished all of his work in the barn."

"A farmer's work is never done…"

"Exactly. When John came in that morning, he claimed he'd finished the work that *had* to be done, took the babe from my arms and told me to go to town."

"And did it help?"

"Immensely. After that, one day a week he'd come in and take care of Caleb for a few hours while I went on little errands."

"So I need to go on little errands?"

"Wouldn't hurt." Ida dropped her crochet work in her lap and pulled a scrap of paper from her apron pocket. "Here's some things I need from the general store. It's on the main road. You won't have any trouble finding it. While you're out, maybe you can find something whimsical to do."

"Whimsical?"

"Impulsive. Something you hadn't planned on. Life on a farm can be awfully predictable. A surprise, even a little one, can brighten the spirit."

"How am I supposed to get there?"

"John told me he'd bring around the buggy after lunch."

"What if I don't remember how to drive a buggy?"

"We won't know that until you try. If you don't remember, then I'll ask Caleb to go with you."

The rest of the morning sped by and suddenly lunch was over and the buggy and horse were waiting near the front porch.

Maybe it was the thought of a little freedom, or perhaps it was fear that Caleb would be saddled with her for an afternoon when he'd rather be with his alpacas—he'd frowned fiercely when Ida shared their plan during lunch—but whatever the cause, Rachel was determined to drive the buggy herself. She needn't have worried. As soon as she climbed up into the buggy, something deep inside of her brain took over.

Her hands picked up the reins.

She clucked to the horse.

Her spirit soared, and she pulled away.

Ida had given her an envelope with cash in it and drawn a crude map on the back of the list. The way to the general store was simple and consisted of driving down the lane to the main road, making a right and heading into town. Rachel suspected the map was in case she forgot how to get home, but her confidence had surged as soon as she'd begun driving the buggy. She didn't think she'd be getting lost.

The dark cloud that had been hovering over her mood lifted by the time she hit the main road. Farms dotted the way into town, and many had Christmas displays in the yards. *Englisch* homes had lights strung across shrubs and trees. She wondered what they'd look like at night.

Other houses sported giant inflatable yard decorations. There were large white polar bears wearing red neckties, yellow cartoon characters with blue pants and round eyeglasses that she had seen on *Englisch* coloring books, and even reindeer pulling a sleigh. A few Amish homes had wooden nativities, and their porches were decorated with green cedar wrapped around the porch railing.

As she neared town, she passed a sign that read Welcome to Montgomery, Indiana. The name didn't ring any bells. But then, she already knew she wasn't from here.

So how had she happened on the road that led to Caleb's home?

Where was she from?

In town, the main road was filled with other buggies as well as cars. She saw even more decorations, including festive window displays, city banners wishing everyone "Happy Holidays" and churches reminding people when their Christmas services would be held. It was only December seventh, but it seemed that everyone was getting ready for the holiday early.

She was waiting at a signal light when a car of *Englischers* pulled up beside her, and a young child waved. She waved back as they pulled away. If it hadn't been for the child, she wouldn't have been looking in that direction, but she was…and so she saw the sign that said Montgomery Public Library.

She was in the wrong lane. She had to drive another block before turning, but the entire time she could hear Caleb's words in her ears.

Amish women work hard, too. At least most of them do.

He might not want to use the *Englisch* computers to learn about his new alpaca herd, but she was more than willing to look for a job on them. Something told her that if she wanted to move forward, the internet would be the place to start.

Find a job. Earn some money. Remember who she was.

It was a short list, and suddenly Rachel was sure it was one she could conquer.

Chapter Four

Rachel's library search was not fruitful.

First of all, the library was small—smaller than she had imagined. The room was about the size of Ida's sitting room. The walls were lined with bookcases that were filled to capacity with books, but there wasn't exactly a large variety of material and much of it looked quite dated. Worse, there were only two computers. Both were being used when she walked in, so she had to wait. While she did, she perused the bookshelves. There was a single shelf with books labeled Christian Fiction. She thought to check one out, then realized she didn't have any identification.

The librarian had been watching her—she was an older lady with shoulder-length silver hair and was wearing a bright red sweater that said Ho Ho Ho across the front. She stood about only five feet tall, and Rachel couldn't help envisioning one of the elves she'd seen as part of a lawn display on her drive into town.

"Problem, dear?"

"Only that I don't...well, I don't have any identification. I'm staying with John and Ida Wittmer."

"You must be the girl Caleb found in the snow."

"*Ya.* Unless he found two, and I haven't met the other one yet."

"I'm pretty sure it was you—Amish, young, pretty and with freckles." She walked over to Rachel, patted her on the arm and smiled. "I mean no offense, dear. You're quite the topic of conversation around our little township—a real Christmas mystery."

"I never thought of it that way." Rachel turned back to the books, allowed her fingertips to caress the spines. Had she always liked to read? What were her favorite types of books?

"You can pick out up to three items."

"But I don't have an identification card."

"So you mentioned."

"I don't even remember my own last name, and… and I don't have a home address."

"For now, your home address is Ida and John's place, which I know because they both have a card here."

"They do? I thought Caleb said…"

"I'm well aware of Caleb's opinion on the matter, but I suspect one day he will marry and perhaps his wife will be able to soften that stubborn spirit."

Rachel didn't know how to answer that. From what she'd seen of Caleb Wittmer it would take more than a wife to change his attitudes—it would take divine intervention.

"As far as your last name, we'll just put Rachel for now. I make up the entire library staff—well, me and one part-time girl who works a few hours in the afternoon. So there's no one to tell me what I can and can't do. I'm Mary Agnes Putnam, by the way, but most people just call me Mary Agnes."

The woman was as good as her word. While Rachel picked out one novel and a slim volume of poems by William Blake, Mary Agnes printed her a library card on an old printer, which sounded as if it was in distress. Rachel looked over a few cooking books, several historical tomes and some children's titles. As she was walking toward the checkout desk, she spied a pile of books with the word *Self-help* neatly printed and taped to the wall beside it. She dug through the stack and came up with *Crocheting for Dummies*. Maybe she'd feel useful if she could at least use Ida's crochet needle properly.

Mary Agnes checked out her material, and Rachel confessed, "I came in to use the computer."

"Indeed? We get that a lot around here."

"Maybe I should come back." She glanced over at the two old gentlemen who were still at their monitors.

"I'll take care of those two for you. They're playing chess—with one another—on the computer!" She leaned forward and lowered her voice. "We have a chessboard on the game shelf, and even a table where they can play, but both Albert and Wayne say they need to learn to travel the *information highway*. That's what they call it. So they play chess every day on the monitors. Fancy the things that people do."

Mary Agnes ran off the two men, who claimed it was time for their lunch, anyway. She showed Rachel how to log on and directed her to Montgomery's virtual job-search board.

But thirty minutes on the computer only increased Rachel's frustration. She couldn't fill in any applications with no last name. She didn't know what her educational level was. Ida had mentioned that most Amish students attended school through eighth grade. Had she?

Who knew? Maybe she'd lived in a district that went to school through twelfth grade like the *Englischers*. Did any Amish do that? She certainly couldn't recall her employment history, though if she was twenty-five she must have worked somewhere.

Sighing in frustration, she logged off, picked up her three books and thanked Mary Agnes for her help. She stepped out into a day that felt more like fall than winter. She should go on to the store and pick up the items on Ida's list, but then she remembered Ida telling her to take her time. What was it she had said?

Do something whimsical.

She couldn't imagine what that might be, so she walked over to the parking area and checked on the buggy horse, who was contentedly cropping grass.

Whimsical?

There was a park bench in the middle of the grassy area on the north side of the library. No one else was around, so she made her way across the small area and sat down, eventually putting her head back and closing her eyes. The sun felt good on her face, and some of the tension in her shoulders eased—as long as she didn't think about her predicament.

Instead of worrying, she focused on the word *predicament*. She could practically see the definition printed on a page. *An unpleasantly difficult, perplexing or dangerous situation.* Now, why could she remember that and not her own name? She was puzzling over that enormous question when someone cleared his throat.

She opened her eyes to find Bishop Amos standing beside her.

"Oh. I didn't hear you walk up." She jumped up, but

Amos waved her back onto the bench and sat down beside her.

"This is one of my favorite places in Montgomery."

"It is?"

"I can see and hear what's going on, but I'm away from the sidewalk or street. Sometimes I bring birdseed and scatter it out in front of me."

"The sunshine feels *gut*."

"*Ya?* And how do you feel?"

Rachel could have lied and said she was fine, but something about the way Amos asked the question and waited for an answer told her he was really interested. So she found herself confessing to her frustration at not being able to remember things, her guilt that Ida and John had done so much for her, and her conversation with Caleb over how she needed to get a job.

"He said that, did he? That you should go to work... today?"

"Not in so many words, but it's what he meant."

Amos was maybe the oldest bishop that Rachel had ever known. His skin looked like fine tissue paper, and the only hair on his head were wispy strands at the very top. He had giant white bushy eyebrows that wiggled up and down when he smiled, which he did a lot. Rachel had met him only twice, and already she knew that he was *that* kind of bishop—the kind, fatherly, compassionate type.

"Caleb's a good boy," he finally said, folding both hands on top of his walking cane and leaning forward to stare down at the ground.

Rachel glanced down to see what he was looking at and spied a trail of ants marching beneath their feet. Funny how she hadn't noticed them before.

"Can't be easy, I imagine." Amos paused, as if he was waiting for her to agree.

"What can't be easy?"

"Being an only child in an Amish family. It's unusual. You're the odd man out. Might make a person keep to himself. Might make him more stubborn." Amos glanced sideways at her and the bushy eyebrows arched up and down again.

"Yes, I can understand that. What I don't understand is why does he have to take it out on me? Why be so insulting? I'm not a lazy person."

"Of course you're not."

"And I'd get a job if I could."

"Having something to do does add value to our days."

"But no one will hire me. I was just inside looking on the computers, and I can't get past the first page of the application. It keeps reminding me to fill in all the boxes, when I don't know what to put in them. You know things like 'last name' and 'address' and 'place of birth.'"

"A computer can be good for some things," Amos admitted. "I myself like to check the weather on it."

He straightened up, popping his back in the process, and smiled at Rachel as if he'd answered all of her questions when, in fact, he hadn't.

"You use the computers?"

"*Ya.* We're not so backward here in Montgomery. Personally, I hope the day never comes when I see one in an Amish home, but many things are useful in small doses—automobiles, telephones, computers. They're useful for certain things and certain times."

"What do you mean, exactly?"

"Only that in some instances it's best to do a thing face-to-face."

"You think I should go knocking on business doors and ask them to hire me? Why would they when I'm a complete stranger to them and have no references?"

"I'll be your reference."

"Thank you, Amos, but I don't think—"

"There's a quilt shop here in town, owned by a nice Mennonite woman."

"I can't remember if I know how to quilt."

"And there's Gasthof Amish Village."

"What is that? I saw a sign for it as I came into town."

Instead of answering, he said, "I know the owner there as well as the person who manages the auction house."

"We have an auction house?"

"Yes, I think one of those might be a good answer for your dilemma, Rachel."

"You mean for Caleb's dilemma."

"Oh, you can't do this because Caleb wants you to— or because you think it will please Ida or John or even me."

"I suppose I could use the money."

"More than that, you need to listen to your heart." Amos tapped his chest. "Your heart is asking something of you, Rachel. Your job is to listen and pray—then and only then should you decide what you will do."

"And in the meantime?"

"In the meantime, I'll check around. We'll talk on Sunday and see if what your heart is saying matches up with any opportunities I've found."

He tapped his walking stick against the ground, bounded off the bench with the energy of a man twenty years younger and settled his hat onto his head. "*Gotte* be with you, Rachel."

"And with you." The words slipped off her tongue, unbidden, remembered.

Caleb was in the back pasture, mending yet another section of fence that the alpacas had managed to push through.

"Worse than goats?" Gabriel asked.

"Maybe not worse, but as bad..." Caleb wiped the back of his arm across his brow. Sweating in December was probably a bad sign. His mother would say it meant a blue norther was waiting around the corner.

Gabriel moved next to him and held the fence post in place while he twisted the strands of wire. When they'd finished, they sat on top of a stack of small hay squares, watching the alpacas.

"Strange animals," Gabriel said.

"Indeed."

"Are they growing on you?"

"I haven't asked to get my money back yet, if that's what you're asking."

"Is that an option?"

"Probably not."

Gabriel pulled a piece of hay from the bale and stuck it in his mouth. They'd been friends as long as Caleb could remember. Gabriel was the brother Caleb had never had.

"Ida stopped by to see my *fraa*, told her that Rachel had taken a real liking to the animals. Even named them all."

"And what did Beth think about that?"

"That it was a *gut* sign. That maybe it meant she wouldn't run away."

Caleb snorted. "Why would she run? She's living a pretty sweet life here."

"Is that a problem?"

"Nein."

"Only—"

"I suggested she get a job."

"Huh-oh."

"And she took offense."

"I wonder why."

"Come on, Gabriel. We are Plain and we work. It's what we do. It's not like we can sit around all day and watch television or play on our cell phones."

"Saw my cousin with one of those the other day. I've no idea how he affords it."

"My point is that my comment wasn't out of line. I was trying to be helpful."

"Ah."

"What does 'ah' mean?"

"It's what Amish men do, according to Beth. We give our opinion, even when no one has asked for it, and then say that we're trying to help."

"Only Amish men?"

Gabriel laughed, and the easiness of it, the way it went all the way to his eyes, stirred an unfamiliar sense of envy in Caleb. Between the two of them Caleb had always been the first to do things. He was the first to shave, the first to ask a girl on a date and the first to be dumped by a girl. He'd joined the church a year before Gabriel. He was two inches taller than his best friend and twenty pounds heavier—muscle, not extra poundage. He was smarter in school, faster in sports and a better farmer.

None of that mattered.

They were best friends in every sense of the word.

Maybe he'd considered himself special in some way because he was an only child. It could, after all, be both a blessing and a curse.

Gabriel was the middle child in a family of seven. He'd always worn well-patched hand-me-down clothes. He didn't purchase his own buggy until he'd married, and he'd never had his own bedroom. None of that seemed to bother Gabriel, though.

Things didn't matter to Gabriel. People did.

He'd met Beth and they'd courted and married and had a child. In one year, he'd achieved everything Caleb had dreamed of, everything that had slipped through his fingers when Emily had walked away after proclaiming him stubborn and strong-willed and impossible to be with. He hadn't shared that last part with Rachel. The memory of those words still stung, and perhaps that was why he had stopped courting. Finding someone to share his life with hadn't happened, and he was beginning to doubt it ever would.

"Beth has another theory." An alpaca had wandered closer to them. Gabriel reached out to touch it, but the animal jumped, screeched its cat sound and bounded away.

"Why am I worried?"

"It's about Rachel."

"Beth has only met her once. How can she have a theory?"

"I suppose it's actually about you."

"Worse still." Caleb crossed his arms, fighting off

the urge to be offended. "Well, let's have it. Beth has proved her wisdom by marrying you. Perhaps I should listen to her."

"Compliments won't make this any better." Gabriel sat up, propped his elbows on his knees and interlaced his fingers. "Her first theory is that you were used to being an only."

"An only?"

"Only child. And we both know your *mamm* has always wanted a daughter around the house."

"Remember the year she set me up on dates once a month? Talk about a nightmare."

"But now she has a girl in the house…one that *Gotte* practically brought to your doorstep."

"She wandered here. Remember? If I hadn't seen her when I did, she probably would have kept on walking."

"If you hadn't seen her, hadn't rescued her, she might have died there in the snow. Remember it reached into the twenties that night, and you said yourself she had no coat."

Caleb didn't pretend to understand the how or why of Rachel's appearance, so instead he motioned for Gabriel to continue.

"So now your *mamm* has a daughter, your *dat* has someone to dote on and suddenly you're not the center of their attention."

"A welcome relief, I can tell you."

"Uh-huh, and yet your mood hasn't exactly improved."

"So I'm what…jealous?"

Gabriel shrugged. "It's only a theory—Beth's theory, not mine."

"Ridiculous."

"If you say so."

"And her second theory?"

Gabriel stood and brushed hay from his pants. When he glanced up, there was a twinkle in his eye and a smile tugging at his lips. "Easy. That you're falling for Rachel."

"Falling for her?"

"Romantically speaking."

"Rachel?"

"Love does strange things to a man. Trust me, I know. Muddles your thoughts, changes your appetite, feels like the flu at times. It can certainly put you in a foul mood."

Instead of answering that, because it was too preposterous to merit a reply, Caleb stood as well and began gathering up his tools.

"Told you…it's Beth's theory, not mine."

Caleb grunted.

"Though it does make some sense. You said yourself she's beautiful."

How he wished he'd never shared that opinion with his best friend.

"No one would blame you."

Once Caleb had everything in the wooden toolbox with the handy carrying handle, he turned and walked toward the barn.

"Where are you going?" Gabriel called after him.

But Caleb only offered a backhanded wave.

As if it wasn't bad enough that his life had been disrupted by a mysterious Amish woman, now he had people gossiping that he was in love. Well, he had an answer for that. One way or another he would find where Rachel belonged and he'd take her there, and then his life would return to normal.

At least that was his plan.

It didn't actually improve his mood, but it gave him something else to focus on.

Chapter Five

If Rachel had hoped to spend Saturday inside with Ida, teaching herself to crochet and writing in her journal, she was sadly mistaken.

"A cold front is blowing through tonight. I need you to help Caleb with this list of to-dos while the weather is good."

This was presented to her as they were eating breakfast, and she'd made the mistake of glancing over at Caleb, who had rolled his eyes. So he wasn't any happier about the day's agenda than she was.

John didn't seem to notice the tension in the air. "I'd help if I could, but I promised Big Atlee that I'd help him mend his barn's south wall."

"I could do that," Caleb said.

"*Nein.* Help your mother. You know how she loves Christmas."

"Big Atlee?" Rachel asked.

"Oh, *ya.* We have a Big Atlee—he's bigger than Caleb even, and Little Atlee…"

"Who isn't really little," Ida pointed out.

"But smaller than Big Atlee, and then there's Limping Atlee."

"You actually call him Limping Atlee?"

"He doesn't mind. Thinks it's clever." John smiled at her and drained his coffee cup. "You know how it is with the Amish—no need for new fancy names when old ones will do, even if it means having two or three in the same family."

Rachel watched as Ida followed her husband into the mudroom. They spoke softy as he donned his jacket and hat, and then Ida stood on tiptoe to kiss him lightly on the lips. For a moment, his arms tightened around her waist, and a smile spread across her lips, and Ida looked like the young woman she must have once been.

"They're romantic fools," Caleb said, nodding toward his parents.

"I think it's sweet."

"*Ya*, until they forget and hold hands in public."

Rachel might have thought that Caleb was being harsh, but his ears had turned red. Was he actually embarrassed that his parents sometimes showed their affection for one another? "What's wrong with holding hands?"

"It's just not what we do."

"Is that so?"

"I love my parents, but they sometimes forget that others are watching. They also have a tendency to butt into other people's business."

She didn't know how to answer that, so she stood to begin clearing the dishes.

"Meet me in the barn when you're done," he said, and then Caleb, too, was gone.

Rachel took her time with the washing and drying.

By the time Ida came back in, she had the kitchen looking positively sparkly.

"Oh, dear, I didn't mean for you to do all the work. I just wanted to walk John out to his buggy."

"How long have you been married?"

"Twenty-eight years, and it's been a journey, let me tell you. We've had our ups and downs, good years and bad." Ida was looking out the window, watching John drive down the lane. When she turned back toward Rachel, her expression had become more serious. "Caleb gets his stubborn streak honestly, and it's not from me. They are both good men, though. And I've never once doubted that John loved me. What more could a woman ask for?"

To remember her own name?

To go home for Christmas?

To know where home was?

But all those things sounded whiny in her head, so Rachel didn't say them. Instead she scooped the to-do list off the table, stuck it in her apron pocket and snagged her borrowed coat from the hook in the mudroom.

"That's going to be too hot, Rachel…though no doubt it will be perfect tomorrow." Ida hurried back to her room and returned with a tattered jacket. "This old jacket will be better. I use it when I'm working outside sometimes."

The sleeves were too long, the garment nearly reached to her knees and she could have wrapped it around herself twice. Instead of pointing out those things, Rachel thanked her, glanced in the small mirror in the bathroom to be sure her *kapp* was on straight and hurried out to the barn.

Caleb's eyes widened when he saw her. "She gave you that to wear?"

"It's a little big."

"It belonged to my *grossdaddi*. It's one of the few things of his that she kept."

"Oh."

Caleb shook his head, as if he didn't stand a chance of ever understanding the ways of women. He'd already hooked the smaller buggy horse up to an open wagon, and he motioned for her to climb aboard.

Once she was settled beside him, he took off for the far southeast side of the property.

"The list says we're to bring back cedar limbs, pinecones if we can find any, fall leaves, cattails and a small bale of hay."

"*Ya*. It cheers her to make a holiday display that she leaves by the door."

"I thought you Montgomery Amish were conservative." She didn't mean to needle him, but somehow the words popped out of her mouth before she fully considered how they would sound.

"Oh, you won't be finding a Christmas tree in our homes, that's for certain."

"Presents?"

"Simple, homemade things." He glanced at her curiously. "You don't remember any of this?"

"Not really. It's as if…as if there's simply a hole where my memories used to be. When I try hard to remember, when I actively focus on it, the headaches return."

Caleb nodded as if that made sense. "Best not focus on it, then."

"Easier said than done."

But Caleb apparently didn't hear that. He'd pulled the wagon to a stop at the edge of a stand of trees, and now spoke to the horse, set the brake and climbed out of the wagon. As an afterthought he reached into the back of the wagon and pulled out a handsaw and a basket.

He handed Rachel the basket and motioned toward the stand of trees.

She didn't speak for a moment, then simply followed him, though she wondered where they were going. When they reached the middle of the grove, she understood. It was as if someone had carved out a spot— a secret garden of sorts. The area was cleared of trees, though she could only just see the bright blue sky above if she stood exactly in the middle. The trees surrounding them—cedar and pine and oak and birch—created a canopy that allowed the light to sift through.

"This is beautiful," she said.

"One of *Mamm*'s favorite places. Toward the back are a couple of pine trees. If you'll look for the pine-cones, I'll saw off a few cedar branches."

Rachel's anxiety slipped away under that umbrella of trees. She stopped worrying about finding a job and trying to remember her past. She breathed in deeply the scent of the pines and enjoyed the unseasonal warmness of the day. She sifted through the brown and red and copper-colored leaves, filling her basket with pinecones for Ida. She was thinking of that, of a holiday display by the front door in this Plain conservative home, when something shifted.

She saw only a flash of tan, then a copper color, and suddenly Caleb's hands were on her arms, pulling her back and urging her to be silent.

She dropped the basket. Pinecones spilled across the

leaves. She reached for them instinctively as she might have reached for a glass of water that was tipped off a table, but it was too late. Caleb's voice in her ear again urged her to move back, and she was thinking of that— of how his voice caused goose bumps to cascade down her arms—when she saw the copperhead. It slithered through the leaves, its hourglass pattern blending nearly perfectly with the foliage around it.

Her breath caught in her throat, her heartbeat accelerated and adrenaline surged through her system.

"Are you okay?"

"Ya."

"You're sure?"

"How did you...?"

"I was reaching over you to get a pine bough for *Mamm*."

"My mind was wandering, I guess...thinking of Christmas."

"I saw it slither and..." Caleb seemed to suddenly realize that his hands were still on her arms. He took a step back. "I should have warned you."

"Nein. I may have forgotten a few things..."

"Nearly everything."

"...but I'm not stupid. I know that snakes sometimes come out on winter days—especially warm winter days and if their den is close to a sunny spot."

Rachel shivered, realizing how close she'd been to it. Surely it wouldn't have struck her, but it might have...if it had felt threatened, and she had been rooting around in its winter home.

She stepped closer to Caleb. *"Danki."*

"For what?"

"For saving me...again."

And there it was, that thing that had been between them since they'd first met, since five days earlier when Caleb had found her collapsed in the middle of the road. Gratitude swelled in her heart that he had saved her, and she realized the source for some of the friction between them.

She'd always considered herself to be someone who didn't need saving.

She'd always been fiercely independent.

She wasn't sure how she knew that about herself when she didn't even know her own last name, but it felt right. Her stubbornness, her unwillingness to accept help, was all tied up in how she had ended up in this small community in southwest Indiana.

Two terrible, life-changing situations. She could have died the first time, been injured the second. She hadn't been because Caleb had been there—both times.

A pained expression crossed Caleb's face.

"You're uncomfortable with that, aren't you?"

"With what?" He picked up a stick, squatted and pushed it around the area where she'd been collecting pinecones, apparently checking for any additional snakes.

"You're uncomfortable with saving me, that's what." She laughed out loud—part nervousness and part relief. It wasn't that Caleb hated her, it was that he was what the romance books would call a reluctant hero. "You're not responsible for me, you know."

"What's that supposed to mean?"

"Some cultures believe that if you save someone's life, then you're responsible for them from that point on."

"I've never heard that before."

"It makes a certain sense. If you'd saved a horse or a dog, then you'd take it home and care for it. Right?"

"Maybe."

She kneeled beside him in the leaves, certain that he'd scared any other snakes away. "But I'm not a horse or a dog."

He purposely scooted a little to the left, away from her.

"I'm a woman."

"Uh-huh."

"But that doesn't mean you're responsible for me, Caleb." She reached out and pushed him, catching him unaware. Losing his balance, he plopped into the leaves and looked at her as if she'd lost what was left of her mind.

And yet that felt right, too—the teasing and the laughter.

Instead of explaining the thoughts that were tumbling through her mind, she resumed picking up the pinecones, this time humming as she did so.

Caleb didn't know what had come over Rachel.

He'd nearly had a heart attack when he'd seen the copperhead slithering inches from her hand, and then he'd reacted on instinct, pulling her away and urging her to be quiet.

Which she had, at first, but when she had realized what had happened, she'd looked up at him with such gratitude that Caleb had felt like he was drowning in her warm brown eyes. And then she'd begun talking about saving people and responsibility. While he was still trying to follow her train of thought, she'd begun to laugh.

He didn't have a clue as to why women acted the

way they did, and he vowed—not for the first time—
to give up trying.

"Do we have enough items?" Rachel had shed the
jacket that was his *grossdaddi*'s and set it across the
seat of the wagon.

"Items?"

"For your *mamm*, for her decorations."

"Oh. *Ya.* I guess so." But there was one more thing on
the list that he was holding, so he helped Rachel climb
up into the wagon, jogged around to the other side and
joined her, then called out to the mare.

"Where are we going?"

"You'll see."

"Does it include snakes?"

"Nein."

"Bears?"

"No bears here that I know of."

"Maybe a hive of Africanized bees?"

He glanced over at her and found her smiling mis-
chievously.

"You're a strange person, did you know that?"

"Caleb Wittmer, what would make you say such a
thing?"

"You were nearly bitten by a venomous snake less
than ten minutes ago, and now you're making jokes?"

Rachel pulled her *kapp* strings forward and ran her
fingers up and down the length of the fabric. "I wasn't,
though, just like I didn't perish in the snow. I guess
Gotte isn't through with me yet."

"I suppose not."

Caleb had fallen into the habit of thinking of Rachel
as young and immature, but he realized now that nothing was further from the truth. It was only that some-

times she would get that faraway expression, and he would assume she was lost in childish daydreams. In other words he'd judged her and done so too harshly. That was something he'd be needing to pray about, something he'd need to ask forgiveness for.

"No time like the present," he muttered.

"What's that?"

"I was just thinking that I needed to apologize to you, and there's no time like the present." He pulled off his hat and resettled it on his head. "Not something I much enjoy doing."

"And what do you have to apologize for? Saving me?"

"*Nein*. Judging you."

Rachel waited. She didn't jump in. She didn't make it any easier for him.

"I shouldn't have offered you my advice about getting a job. I should have known that you would already be thinking about that."

She studied him a minute, and then she began to laugh.

"Something funny about that?"

"Only that I did need a little push. It's not that I wasn't going to look, but I thought I'd wake up the day after you found me or the day after that and remember everything. What was the use in looking for a job when I wouldn't be staying? Why look for employment when I'd soon have my old life back?"

"It has only been a week."

"And yet, I don't remember much more with each passing day. It doesn't look as if I'll be traipsing home anytime soon."

"I'm sorry it didn't work out that way."

"You helped me see that I need to accept my situation, as it is, until it changes."

Caleb nodded as if he agreed, but in truth he was simply relieved that she wasn't still angry with him.

Her forehead wrinkled and she stared out across him, at the field they were passing. "I did speak to the bishop."

"Ya?"

"While I was in town yesterday. He's going to help me find a job."

"That's *gut*."

"I think so, since it's true that 'Amish women work hard...at least most of them do.'"

Caleb winced to hear his own words quoted back to him, but at least she'd been listening. It was important for every member of a household to contribute to the well-being of that household. Maybe she was realizing that. He certainly didn't want to bring it up—it would only seem like he was lecturing her again. Fortunately, they were at the pond, and he could change the subject.

"This is a *gut* fishing spot in the summer." He called out to the horse to stop and set the brake on the wagon.

"I didn't know you had a pond."

"Sometimes *Mamm* packs a picnic and brings it down here on warm days." It struck him that Rachel wouldn't care about that. She almost certainly wouldn't still be here by the time summer rolled around.

"So what are we here to find? I can't remember what else is on there." She tried to snag his *mamm*'s list out of his hand, but he held it out of her reach, causing her to laugh more and nearly fall into his lap. He had no idea why he was acting like a *youngie*, but it felt nice to relax and enjoy the afternoon. He hopped out of the wagon, pulled a rake and a pair of garden shears from the back of the wagon, and began walking along the edge of the pond.

"We need cattails," he said.

"Not real cattails."

"*Nein.* The kind that grow around a pond, like those." He pointed to a tall stand of bulrushes. As they moved closer to the edge of the pond, he said, "Watch where you put your feet. You wouldn't want to sink in that mud."

"Native Americans used cattails to make mats and baskets."

"Is that so?"

"*Ya*, and the head can be dipped in oil and used as a torch."

Caleb turned to stare at her quizzically.

"I have no idea how I knew that." Instead of becoming gloomy over that realization, she smiled and gestured toward the tall weeds with brown cigar-shaped heads. "How are we supposed to reach them?"

Caleb held up the rake.

"Ah."

Rachel was happy to point out the tallest, prettiest cattails, as she continued to regale him with trivia.

The lower parts of the leaves could be used in salads.

Young cattails could be roasted.

Pollen of the cattail could be added to pancakes.

"Maybe you were a botanist before."

"*Ya*, because there are a lot of female Amish botanists."

The banter between them felt light and comfortable. The afternoon was warm, and it was hard for Caleb to wrap his mind around the fact that earlier that week she might have perished in the snow, but it was true. Indiana weather was like that—fickle.

What if he hadn't been mending that particular section of fence on Monday as she walked down the road?

What if she'd arrived at that spot an hour later, after he'd already gone?

For the first time since that fateful morning, Caleb was grateful that he had found her, that *Gotte* had brought Rachel into their lives. She might not be there for long. Regardless of what his friends Gabriel and Beth thought, he was neither jealous of her presence nor interested in her in a romantic way.

But perhaps they could be friends, for as long as she was there. A month or a year from now, he'd look back and laugh at the strange woman who had plopped into their lives.

As they finished pulling the cattails from around the pond, he kept thinking of the way her arms had felt under his hands, of the look in her eyes as she'd gazed up at him, then at the snake, and then back at him. It was as if the defensive Rachel, the one that made him feel like a cat rubbed the wrong way, had vanished, and instead he'd found himself staring at a woman he hadn't met yet.

He continued to steal glances at her as they loaded their items on the wagon, then he directed the horse back toward the house.

"You can quit looking at me that way."

"Which way?"

"As if I might disappear before your eyes."

"You gave me a scare, I won't deny it."

"My brother was bitten by a copperhead once." She didn't seem to realize she was remembering. A smile wreathed her face, and she held her head back, basking in the warmth of the sun. "He said it hurt worse than the time that he broke his leg. He didn't want to go to the doctor, but *Mamm* insisted. The doctor said it was probably a juvenile snake, considering the bite marks. Ethan said if that was a juvenile he never wanted to cross a full-grown adult. Did you know that the length of their fangs is directly proportional to the length of the snake? So the longer—"

"Rachel."

"Ya?"

"You just said your *bruder*'s name."

"I did?"

"Ethan." They repeated it together.

They rode in silence, until Caleb pulled the mare to a stop beside the front porch. "Another piece of the puzzle."

"Lots of folks named Ethan," she said, staring up at him again, looking at him as if he'd hung the moon.

He pulled on the collar of his work shirt, which felt suddenly tight. They were one step closer to finding Rachel's family. One step closer to his life returning to normal. He couldn't fathom why that didn't feel as good as he had imagined it would.

Rachel wasn't too surprised when Caleb hurried away, claiming he'd remembered work to do in the barn. She helped Ida to unload the hay bales, cedar branches, pinecones and cattails.

"My son ran off like a beagle chasing a jackrabbit. Any idea what that's about?"

So Rachel described their encounter with the snake and recounted how Caleb had saved her…again. She didn't mention how it had felt to have his arms around her. It was an awkward thing to say to a guy's mother, and besides, she didn't know what it meant. She didn't understand the myriad of emotions still clouding her thoughts!

Ida had plopped down into one of the rockers and was staring at her with her mouth hanging open.

"What? Did my *kapp* fall off?" Rachel reached up and checked her head. Everything seemed all right.

"I should have told you."

"About?"

"The snakes."

"Oh. That."

"Yes, that. I just sent you out there, traipsing through the woods."

"I'm not a child, Ida."

"I didn't even think to tell you to watch out for snakes. It's unseasonably warm today, and with the cold front due tonight…all of the animals are acting crazy. I saw one of the alpacas standing in the water trough."

"It's not your fault, and I wasn't hurt."

"Because of Caleb's quick thinking. I guess the Lord was watching over you, child…both times that Caleb saved you."

Rachel didn't know what to say to that, so she helped Ida set the small bales of hay in a haphazard pile beside the door and cover them with cedar branches, pinecones and leaves. The cattails propped up behind it all in old milking cans added a nice touch. It did look festive. More of an autumn display than Christmas, but at least it cheered up the place.

They'd finished with the decorations and gone inside

to work on dinner when Rachel remembered to tell Ida about her brother.

"And his name is Ethan?"

"*Ya*, I guess so."

"That's *gut*, Rachel. It's *gut* that you're starting to remember."

"But it's taking so long. I'd hoped that I would be home by Christmas." She glanced up from the potato casserole she was mixing in time to see a look of regret pass over Ida's face.

The dear woman plastered on a smile and said, "If that's your heart's desire, that is what we'll pray for—that you can be home by Christmas."

"Ida, I didn't mean to sound ungrateful."

"And you're not, only homesick I suspect."

Rachel wiped her hands on a dish towel, then walked over to Ida, stood in front of her and waited for her to raise her eyes.

"I will never forget what you've done for me. How you've taken me in and given me a home. Treated me like family."

Ida leaned forward and kissed her on the cheek, then, claiming that her allergies were bothering her, she hurried from the room. Rachel couldn't remember Ida ever mentioning allergies. She had a feeling that the tears in her eyes were caused by something else entirely, and she realized in that moment that wanting something and getting it were two entirely different things.

She wanted to be reunited with her family.

Caleb wanted her gone, or at least she'd thought that he did. Didn't he? Certainly his life had been simpler before he'd found her on the road.

But receiving what they wanted would hurt Ida. For

whatever reason, she enjoyed having Rachel around. Perhaps her life had been rather lonely, with only the one son. Perhaps she was enjoying the idea of having a daughter.

That thought caused Rachel's hands to freeze over the sliced potatoes that she was dotting with paprika. Did Ida consider her a daughter? Was that possible in less than a week?

The more she thought of it, the more certain she was. She only had to look at the jacket hung over the back of the kitchen chair, the jacket Ida had insisted she wear outside, the jacket that belonged to her father.

Rachel added pats of butter to the potatoes, sprinkled Parmesan cheese across the top and popped the dish into the oven. She would find her family, but she wouldn't forget Ida or her kindness. She vowed then and there that they would be friends for life.

Chapter Six

The cold front that had threatened Saturday arrived in the middle of the night with a foot of snow and winds strong enough to cause the shingles on the roof to rattle. Rachel woke to the smell of fresh-brewed coffee, but one look outside sent her scurrying back under the covers like a child. That was the phrase that pulled her out of bed. She wasn't a child. She was a woman and should act like one, but what she'd give for a day where she could burrow beneath the quilts, forget any chores and make the world go away.

Her mood didn't improve as she pulled on her Sunday dress and braided her hair.

What was she doing here?

When would she remember who she was?

Why wasn't her family looking for her?

By the time she made it to the kitchen, she felt as if the day had already knocked her down. It didn't help that the morning had dawned cloudy and dreary. The landscape outside the window was colorless—snow on empty fields, a gray sky, a vast horizon.

None of it looked familiar to her.

Why should that still surprise her? She'd known she didn't belong here from the moment she'd opened her eyes on Ida's couch. The fun she'd had yesterday had been a distraction from her situation, nothing more.

"This will help." Ida pushed a mug of steaming coffee into her hands, but she didn't ask any questions.

That was one thing Rachel appreciated about Ida—she didn't push.

Caleb, on the other hand, had no trouble sticking his nose into her business as they all sat down to eat.

"You're awfully quiet, Rachel."

"I've nothing to say."

"Did you sleep badly?"

She didn't bother answering him. Why admit that she'd tossed and turned most of the night? She knew that the circles under her eyes were testament to her sleeplessness. So why did he have to ask?

John focused on his meal, and Ida sent her the occasional sympathetic look.

Rachel pushed the food around on her plate and sipped her coffee.

When Ida stood up to clear off the breakfast dishes, Rachel jumped up to help her, but Ida placed a hand on her shoulder and said, "Take some time for yourself, Rachel. There are only a few dishes. I can take care of them."

So she went to the living room and sat in the rocker closest to the banked fire. Though she was facing away from the kitchen, she still heard every whispered word. Unfortunately, she had excellent hearing. She had always been able to make out the slightest whisper. There! Another thing she knew about herself. Maybe she could advertise for a lost daughter with exceptional hearing.

"What's with her this morning?"

"Perhaps she's simply sad."

"Because she can't remember?"

"Of course because she can't remember."

Rachel couldn't make out the next statement as Ida was running water in the sink, but when she turned off the faucet, the last of her and Caleb's conversation came in loud and clear.

"Seems to me she needs to move on."

"Easy for you to say, son. You know who you are."

"Rachel knows who she is, she simply doesn't know who she was."

"Our past figures into who we become."

"I suppose."

"Perhaps you could go a little easy on her."

"What did I do?"

"I'm just saying that a little compassion goes a long way."

"The women in this house are awfully sensitive if I'm in trouble for asking how she slept."

"Why don't you go and help your *dat* with the buggy?"

"Great idea."

Another moment passed before the back door slammed, and she knew Caleb had left the kitchen. She should go in there now and thank Ida for standing up for her. She couldn't find the energy, though, so instead she sat there, staring at the coals of the fire and wondering how she was going to endure the day of worship and fellowship.

Perhaps that was what she was dreading—church. Sundays had always been a bright spot for her. She loved the hymns, seeing her friends and resting for the day. She loved being with her family. Tears slipped down her cheeks, but she quickly brushed them away. She shouldn't wallow in this. She'd decided yesterday that she would be more positive.

But deciding on an attitude and actually maintaining that attitude were two different things entirely.

Their service was held in Amos's barn, but Rachel's mood only worsened throughout the morning. She didn't remember any of the names of the ladies she had met earlier in the week. The songs were familiar, but she stumbled over the words. The preaching might have been what she needed to hear, but she seemed to hear it from a great distance. The text was something from the Book of Numbers, something about Balaam and a donkey and *Gotte*'s messenger. She heard the words from the sermon but couldn't connect them to anything, and she couldn't remember when they were supposed to stand or sit or kneel.

She was always just a fraction of a second behind everyone else.

Her every move seemed to scream that she didn't belong here.

By the time the service ended, she was pressing her fingertips into her temples trying to still the pounding in her head, and Ida insisted that she rest while the other women set out the luncheon. They were meeting in Bishop Amos's barn, and Ida suggested that she go to the house and find a dark room for a few minutes. Instead Rachel walked out of the barn's main room, down an adjacent section of the building, and ended up stopping in front of the last stall, where she found a half-dozen goats curled up around one another. She went into the stall, latched the door and sat down in the hay.

Which was where Bishop Amos found her, one goat in her lap, another leaning against her shoulder and a third chewing on her *kapp* strings.

"Tough morning." He said it as a fact instead of a question. Perhaps that was why she didn't take offense as she had with Caleb.

Amos shooed a goat out of a crate, turned it over and sat on it. The young goat settled at his feet, and Amos reached forward to rub it gently between the ears.

"Many folks don't understand goats."

Rachel glanced at him in surprise. She'd expected him to want to talk about her situation. She'd dreaded it actually. But goats...now, there was a safe topic.

"I love how soft their ears are." The little guy she was holding looked up at her. She reached for its ear and rubbed it between her thumb and forefinger. The goat butted her hand as if to tell her not to stop. The goats all had long white ears, and black marks high on their foreheads. Their coats were a chocolate brown. "They're such sweet animals."

"Indeed. Did you know that one doe can produce ninety quarts of fresh milk a month?"

"That's a lot of milk."

"It is, but here's the thing—a farmer can't have just one doe."

"Why's that?"

"It would get lonely."

"Would it stop producing milk?"

"Most likely it would. You see, goats are social animals. They need each other."

Rachel had been tracing the pattern of brown and white on the goat nearest her.

"A goat will die if it's left alone. It'll quit eating and just—" he snapped his fingers "—lose its will to live."

"I'm not a goat."

"And you're not alone." Amos smiled at her as he gently pulled the hem of his pants leg out of a kid's mouth.

She remembered that now—a young goat was called a kid. The kid scampered to the other side of the stall and began head-butting another kid approximately the same size.

"But it can feel as if you're alone sometimes, and loneliness is a heavy burden. I understand that firsthand."

Something about his tone of voice convinced Rachel that he was speaking from personal experience. Instead of explaining, he changed the subject.

"I found a couple of jobs for you."

"A couple?"

He pulled a folded sheet of paper from his pocket and handed it to her. "Often what we first try doesn't succeed, so I wanted you to have more than one choice."

She opened the sheet and stared down at it. "Thank you so much."

He waved away her thanks. "At the bottom is the name of the counselor your doctor recommended— the same one you spoke with briefly at the hospital."

"Oh, I don't know if I can…"

"Afford it? Surely you remember that we take care of such things." His smile grew, and he stood and brushed hay from his pants, then stuck his thumbs under his suspenders. "*Ya.* The cost is already taken care of. I'm not saying that you have to go or even that you should go, only that you can if you'd like to."

Without pausing to think if it was proper, Rachel jumped up and threw herself into his arms. *"Danki."*

Amos smelled of soap and hay and some blend of tobacco. She'd seen him tap a pipe against the palm of his hand a time or two, but she'd never seen him actually light it. She stood there in his arms, remembering the scent and feel of her own grandfather.

Amos patted her on the back, but he didn't say anything. She wondered if she'd overstepped her bounds, if she'd done something inappropriate, but then she pulled back and saw the twinkle in his eyes.

"You remind me of my granddaughter—same sweet spirit." He walked to the half door of the stall, stepped to the other side and latched it. "You know, Rachel, *Gotte* made everything for a reason. Donkeys, goats, even people each have a special purpose. You'll find the reason that *Gotte* made you. You'll find where you belong."

She sat back down and stared at the stall's door for a long time. How had he known to say the words that she needed to hear? *You'll find where you belong.*

If she was to be honest, that was her biggest fear—never finding her place.

Could she remember if she tried harder?

Was it possible to force memories to the front of your mind?

Or was her brain permanently damaged?

All she knew for certain was that it was the most important thing she had to do—more important than finding a job or learning to crochet again. She needed to know where she belonged. Regardless what the doctor had said, she wasn't sure she ever would regain her memories. She glanced again at the paper, at the name of the counselor she'd spoken with briefly at the hospital. Amish generally didn't see a physician unless something of a serious nature was wrong, and she didn't know anyone who had ever been to a counselor. Why would they pay someone to listen to them talk? They had big families and neighbors and community.

But Rachel didn't have any of those things—not really. So maybe for her, a counselor would be a good idea. There was always a possibility that it wouldn't do a bit of good at all, but, oh, how she wanted to believe that it might.

Caleb had tried not to stare at Rachel during the service, but she was seated two rows ahead of him and to the left—on the women's side, of course. He hadn't been staring at her so much as looking in her direction. She'd kept her head down through most of the service. She'd thumbed away tears several times. She'd seemed lost when they'd stood to sing or kneeled to pray.

He did not understand her moods at all.

Yesterday, when they'd been out gathering things for his mother, her mood had been quite chipper. Then when he'd pulled her away from the snake, she'd looked at him with pure gratitude. He'd thought she was going to throw her arms around his neck. That idea caused his palms to sweat as if he'd been chopping wood for an hour. In many ways, she scared him more than a copperhead snake did. Now, why was that?

She hadn't been in the serving line with the other women, and he didn't see her eating, but toward the end of the meal he saw Bishop Amos walk back into the main room from the stall area. A few minutes after that, several children dashed back where he had been, and then almost immediately after that, Rachel came out.

Instead of eating, she grabbed a cup of water and sat down at a far table.

"Go and talk to her," Gabriel said.

"*Ya.* Go and invite her to sit with us." Beth was cradling their sleeping baby in her left arm and eating with her right.

"Who?"

"You know who," they both said.

"Who said I want to talk to her?"

"Your face." Gabriel grinned at him as he picked up another chicken leg from his plate. "Now go over there."

When Gabriel and Beth started laughing, Caleb stood up in disgust. "You two are acting *narrisch*. Maybe you need to go for a walk or something."

But he wasn't actually angry with his best friend or his best friend's wife. He just felt...out of sorts. Their laughter actually eased the knot of tension in his stomach. His friends helped to remind him that life wasn't so serious.

Why did he constantly forget that?

He'd stood up and was walking toward the dessert table, but he was thinking of that, of how he should attempt to be more lighthearted, when he practically collided with Rachel.

She let out a startled "oh." He put up his hands to try to stop his momentum, and the cup of water sloshed over the front of both of them.

"There should be some dish towels behind the table."

He didn't ask how she knew that. It seemed that Rachel remembered things best when she wasn't trying to remember them. He followed her over to the now empty serving line. She pawed around in a box behind the table and finally came up with two dish towels.

"I'm glad it was water and not milk or coffee," she said.

"I'm glad it was only half-full."

His statement caused her to laugh and that caused him to laugh, and suddenly he was reminded of Gabriel and Beth.

"Say, would you like to come over and sit with me and my friends?"

She shrugged as if it didn't matter to her where she sat, but she followed him back to the table. On the way, he snagged two different desserts and sat them down in front of them, and said, "Take your pick."

Rachel stared at the desserts as if she couldn't decide, and Caleb was afraid he'd ushered in another emotional moment, but then a smile pulled at the corner of her lips and she said, "Give me a choice, and I'll always pick chocolate. I may not know my name, but I remember that."

"Smart woman," Gabriel proclaimed.

Beth started talking about the merits of dark chocolate over regular chocolate. Rachel told them about the goats in the back stall.

"So you're that kind of girl, huh?" Caleb wiggled his eyebrows. "You know, the kind that goes and sits with the goats during a party."

"*Ya.* I'm shy all right. At least I think I am."

Gabriel was about to respond to that when the baby began to fuss, and Beth claimed she needed to go and feed him.

"Want to come with me? If you haven't been in Amos's house, you should. He makes cuckoo clocks and has them everywhere. It's amazing."

The girls bundled up in their coats and then walked out into the wintry day, leaving Caleb staring at the dessert that Rachel hadn't eaten and his own empty plate.

"You've got it bad, buddy."

"Got what?" He pulled her plate toward him and

stabbed his fork into the chocolate pie. Not that he was hungry, but it was chocolate pie. It would be a shame to see it tossed because Rachel forgot to eat it. *Who forgets to eat a piece of pie?*

"See, that's what I'm talking about. You ask a question, but then your mind wanders before I can answer it."

"How do you know that?"

"Because I know you."

"*Ya*, okay. Maybe. I've been a little distracted lately."

"A little? You practically bowled Rachel over when you went up to the dessert table."

"I was trying to think how to approach her."

"Approach her?"

"*Ya.*"

"She's not a wild horse, buddy."

"Good analogy."

"I wasn't making an analogy, and I haven't heard that word since we were in eighth-grade English class."

"She resembles a wild horse in a lot of ways—"

"Who does?"

"Rachel." Caleb pointed his fork at him. "Now whose mind is wandering?"

Gabriel raised his hands in surrender. "So this wild-horse thing. What did you mean by that?"

"Think of it. A wild horse doesn't initially know who to trust."

"Do you think Rachel doesn't trust you?"

"I think she's still scared, skittish even."

"Go on."

"Wild horses are unpredictable."

"Because they're scared, and they're wild."

"Exactly. So we need to prove ourselves trustworthy."

"We?"

"Then she'll relax, and then she'll remember who she is."

"Is that what the doctor said?"

"After that, she can go home." Caleb scraped up the last bit of chocolate crumbs into a pile, but he didn't bother eating them. Instead he stared at them, as if the answers he sought were there, amid the pile of dough and chocolate and cream.

"Is that what you want?"

"I have no idea, Gabriel." He stood and gathered up the plates. "But when I do, I'll let you know."

As he walked toward the buckets where he needed to put his dishes, he paused to look out the barn's window. Beth and Rachel were stepping up onto Amos's porch, walking close together, bundled against the cold. She didn't look skittish, not around Beth, but she certainly acted that way around him.

Why was that?

Why did he make her nervous?

And what could he do to help her feel at home and safe?

"Do you like babies?" Beth asked. Simon had fallen asleep after eating and was making little baby sounds. His mouth formed a small o, and his long eyelashes lay softly against his skin.

"Who doesn't like babies?"

"My little *schweschder*." Beth smiled and set the chair to rocking. "She says they only eat, poop and sleep."

"She might have a point." Rachel glanced around the bishop's guest room. The living room had been full of cuckoo clocks, but the room they were in had only one—a clock shaped like a schoolhouse, with a small owl that popped out on the quarter hour. "I like them—at least I think I do. Babies are small and sweet and easy to please."

"Indeed."

"Tell me about you and Gabriel."

"Not much to tell. We grew up together, stepped out together when we were old enough and then married."

"So you always knew he was the one?"

"Actually that took a little convincing. Gabriel was a perfect boyfriend—always bringing me flowers or chocolate or taking me to a movie."

"Sounds like he was intent on wooing you."

Beth shrugged. She was about the same age as Rachel, but plump, with a round face and a ready smile. "I guess. Truth is, Gabriel liked to play, and he liked having me around to go with him. When it was time to settle down? He wasn't so sure about that."

"What changed his mind?"

"I told him that I wanted to marry and start a family. I said if he didn't, that was fine, but it might be time for me to step out with someone else."

"You said that to him?"

Beth grinned, her head bobbing up and down.

"Would you have…stepped out with someone else?"

"*Ya.* I wasn't going to wait until I was an old maid. Gabriel would have been happy betting his extra money on buggy races…"

"And buying you flowers."

"That, too. He might have carried on that way for years. My point is that he saw no need to stop being a boy, but I was bored with those things. I wanted a home and a baby." She kissed the top of Simon's head, and the baby popped the corner of his fist into his mouth and began sucking on it.

"I don't know what I want," Rachel admitted. "I feel...restless, I suppose."

"Of course you do. You're still trying to figure out who you are. Probably Gabriel was, too—before we decided to marry."

"But the difference is he had his friends and family to help him figure that out. He had you."

"You have *frienden* here, Rachel. Whether you realize it or not."

Rachel noticed that Beth didn't say this flippantly, and waited for Rachel to look up at her, to see how serious she was, to nod in agreement.

"Now, tell me about Caleb." Rachel raised the baby to settle against her breast and rubbed his back in soft, slow circles.

"What about him?"

"He seems smitten."

"With whom?" She'd never even heard Caleb mention a girl, other than the one who had dumped him for being old-fashioned.

"With you, silly. Tell me you haven't noticed."

At first, she stared at Beth, her mouth open and heat rising in her cheeks, but then she began to laugh. The owl poked out of the cuckoo clock, chiming the quarter hour and causing her to laugh even harder, which caused Beth to join her.

"I don't know what we're laughing about." Beth dabbed at tears that were leaking out of her eyes. "But it feels *gut* to do so."

"We're laughing at the thought of Caleb being interested in me...in, you know, that way."

"So you don't think he is?" Now Beth was wrapping a blanket around Simon, tucking it up under his legs and resettling him in the crook of her arm.

"*Nein.* I think he can't wait to be rid of me."

"Really?"

"I aggravate him all the time."

"You do?"

"He corrects everything about me—my hair, my clothes, even the fact that I haven't found a job yet."

"You've only been here a week."

"Exactly."

"Do you want a job?"

"I don't know. Maybe. It might help with this restless feeling if I was doing something useful. It might help me remember who I am...or was."

"How do you plan to find one?"

Rachel reached into her pocket and pulled out the sheet of paper Amos had handed her. She stared down at it a moment and then passed it to Beth.

"Bishop Amos wrote this?"

"*Ya.* How'd you know?"

"He has a funny way of making his *t*'s. Always has." She tapped the sheet of paper. "This is a *gut* list."

"A quilt shop, a bakery, a restaurant and a school."

"Which would you like to work at?"

"I've no idea."

"Of the four, I personally would pick the quilt shop. Katherine, she's demanding but fair."

Rachel chewed on her bottom lip a minute. Finally, she said, "I suppose I could give it a try."

"Have you given any thought to seeing this doctor?"

"*Nein.* I mean, I have thought about it, but I haven't made up my mind. Seems a little…drastic."

"Could help, though. Several of the people I went to school with have been to see her—you wouldn't be her first Amish patient."

"Did they have memory problems, too?"

"*Nein.* One of the girls was an older teenager and she struggled with eating too little, another miscarried a baby the first year she was married—had real trouble moving on from that, which is understandable. The man who went to her, he blamed himself for his parents' dying in a buggy accident."

"My problems seem kind of small compared to those."

"They're not small when you're the one dealing with them every day."

"That's true, though I imagine Caleb will think it's a waste of the church's money."

"Caleb isn't as harsh as you make him sound. Maybe he comes across that way because he's intimidated by you."

"Me?" Rachel's voice rose in a squeak.

"I think that Caleb is somewhat afraid of women, but he must like you. After all, he saved you—twice."

"Anyone would have done that, I think. It's not like he could have left me lying in the snow."

"I heard that when he saved you from the snake, that he was quite shook up."

"That only happened yesterday. How did you—"

"Everyone's talking about it. You know how it is with the Amish grapevine. Or maybe you don't remember that part." Beth glanced up at the clock, which was about to cuckoo again. She stood and began gathering her things. "Here's something you should remember about Caleb…"

Rachel was pulling on her coat, but she stopped, her arm midway into the sleeve, at the seriousness in Beth's voice.

"It's not my place to share the details, but Caleb was hurt by the two girls he tried to date."

"He told me a little about that."

Beth's eyebrows rose in surprise, but she didn't comment on that. "Since then, well, it's been almost a year…"

"That long?"

"Caleb hasn't appeared interested in putting his heart on the line again. I think, that at our age, if you're hurt from something once, you shy away from it. But if you're hurt twice? It can spoil your outlook for a long time."

"He's rather young to be deciding he wants to be a confirmed bachelor."

"Except maybe it's not something you decide. Maybe it's just something that kind of becomes a habit."

"I guess."

"Anyway. Trust me—he's interested."

"In…"

"In you, silly."

"But he doesn't even know me, not really. I don't even know me."

They were walking to the door of the guest room, and Beth stopped, reached out and put a hand on Rachel's arm. "Maybe who you are isn't just your memories. I know they're important, and I know that you want yours back. I don't blame you."

She brushed at the sleeve of Rachel's coat, knocking off some imaginary lint. "But who you really are? That's your heart and how you perceive things and how you treat people. It's not just your experiences."

"So what am I to do? Forget about remembering?"

"Nein." Beth's voice softened, and she glanced down at the babe in her arms. "But maybe you're not just trying to remember for yourself. Maybe the real reason to remember is that people love and miss you—the people back home, wherever home is. I'm sure they're very worried."

"And Caleb?"

"I'd say sit back and enjoy your time together. Who knows. Maybe he'll start bringing you chocolate and taking you to *Englisch* movies."

Which was such a ludicrous thought that Rachel began to laugh as they walked back out into the snowy Sunday afternoon.

Chapter Seven

By the time they made it back home after the Sunday afternoon meal, Caleb had resolved in his mind to be kinder to Rachel. He didn't really think he'd been unkind, but perhaps he had been harsh. It certainly wasn't his place to judge her clothing or how soon she found a job. He couldn't begin to imagine what she was going through, and although he thought she should *get over it*, he couldn't honestly say that it would be easy for him if he'd forgotten everyone and everything.

The talk with Gabriel had helped.

Rachel needed to feel safe, to trust them, and then she'd remember. Once she remembered, they could return her to her home, like a lost puppy that people put up posters for in town. Had Rachel's family put up posters for her? Were they even looking for her?

He and his *dat* completed a few chores that had to be done, even on a Sunday, and then his *mamm* served a simple dinner. Afterward they all sat in the house's main room, the fire throwing out heat and a soft glow, lanterns lit against the winter darkness outside, a north wind rattling the windows. Caleb was staring at *The*

Budget, which he'd already read and so provided very little entertainment, when he saw a posting that read:

> Lost donkey, gray-colored with one white ear and one black, northwest side of Shipshewana, last seen on County Road 265. Bruno was like a pet to our family. Please call the phone shack if you've seen him.

The article ended with a phone number. He read it again, and suddenly it felt like a light bulb had gone off over his head. Of course Rachel's family was looking for her. Only, they didn't know where to look. How did you look for an Amish person that was lost? Caleb could think of only a few ways.

You could drive around, which no doubt they had done.

You could ask your neighbors, but news traveled fast in any Amish community, and if they'd known anything, her family would have been told about it within the first twenty-four hours.

You could notify the police, but most Amish families—even the more liberal ones—were hesitant to involve local authorities unless they were sure something terrible had happened. Bishops usually coordinated any communication between families and local police, and Amos was already in contact with law enforcement, as well as area bishops.

He glanced over at Rachel, who had her Bible open on her lap but was staring out the window. What if she'd been having problems at home? Maybe they didn't think she was hurt or in danger. Maybe they were trying to give her time and space. If that was the case, then eventually, like the family who missed their donkey, they would put out an appeal for information.

They might even put a notice in *The Budget*.

Scribes submitted letters for each community, and the paper was published once a week. It contained national as well as local news. It contained letters from Mennonite and Amish communities. This was how he could help Rachel. He could pore over the letters every week, looking for any mention of a beautiful young woman with a slight smattering of freckles.

He nearly slapped his forehead. He'd had this very conversation with Rachel once before. He'd promised her they'd scour the paper looking for anything that might reference a lost woman, but somehow in the business of the day-to-day workings of a farm, he'd forgotten about that promise.

He stared down at the paper he was holding. It couldn't possibly have news of Rachel's disappearance. Scribes would have penned the letters two weeks ago and mailed them to the national office, then they would have been typeset and printed. The next edition was the earliest he could expect to find anything about a girl that had gone missing a week ago.

He slapped the newspaper shut, causing his *dat* to glance up from the *Farmers' Almanac*, and his *mamm* to look up from her crochet work. Some communities frowned upon needlework on Sundays, but his *mamm* long ago insisted that if it was enjoyable and relaxing, then it wasn't work. If it wasn't work, it was permitted.

"It's been a long time since I won a game of checkers."

"Because your *mamm* and I won't play anymore. You

always win." John stretched and said, "I'm too tired to get throttled on a checkerboard."

His *mamm* shook her head. "You won't talk me into it, either. I'm enjoying what I'm doing, *danki* very much."

Rachel must have been listening, because she finally turned to look at him when the room grew quiet.

"Me? I don't even know if I know how to play."

"One way to find out." Caleb wiggled his eyebrows. "If you dare."

She started laughing then, which was something he hadn't heard from her very often.

Forty-five minutes later, she'd won her third game and Caleb's *mamm* had decided they all needed coffee and dessert. Throughout the game he'd caught Rachel studying him, as if she was trying to figure something out. When he called her on it, she shrugged and turned her attention back to the checkerboard. It wasn't until they were seated around the table, enjoying apple-crumb cake and sipping decaffeinated coffee, that she admitted what was on her mind.

"I'd like to go into town tomorrow, to try working at the quilt shop. If that's okay with everyone."

"Of course," Caleb's *dat* said.

"I think you'll love working for Katherine." His mom stood to refill their coffee cups. "And maybe it will help you remember something."

"I wasn't sure how I would get there, though. You only have the two buggies and—"

"Don't worry about that," Caleb's *dat* said. "You can take the older mare and leave us with Stormy. I don't have any reason to go to town tomorrow."

Which might have aggravated Caleb the day before—his *dat* just handing off the buggy and mare to Rachel—but not tonight. Tonight he was optimistic. He was still picturing Rachel as a wild horse that needed settling, a lost donkey that needed to be found. Look at her now. She was smiling and thanking his parents, and then looking at him questioningly.

So he plopped a large forkful of apple-crumb cake into his mouth, sat back and smiled at her. She smiled back, though there was some hesitancy there.

She would learn to trust him. He was certain of it.

Then she'd begin to remember, and then she'd go home.

Wild horse or not, she belonged back with her people. The least he could do would be to help make that happen.

Rachel's morning wasn't going so well. The owner of the quilt shop, Katherine, had been kind enough. Amos had spoken with her the Friday before, and she seemed pleased when Rachel showed up at her shop thirty minutes before opening on Monday morning. No, the problem wasn't her new boss. The problem was that she couldn't remember a thing about fabric, quilting or running a cash register.

"Let me help you with that," Katherine said. Her boss was older, gray-haired and plump. She was also Mennonite, which usually worked out well for Amish employees. She understood their ways and was patient when they needed a day off to help a family member.

Katherine ran the customer's credit card through, handed the woman a special ten-percent-off card that she kept on the shelf under the register and said, "Sorry for the trouble."

When the *Englisch* woman had walked out the door, Katherine turned to Rachel and said, "It's okay. You can't expect to remember everything right away. I shouldn't have left you on the register."

She was kind enough not to point out that they'd already tried allowing Rachel to cut fabric and that hadn't gone well at all. How hard could it be to measure and cut a yard of fabric? But it seemed the process was beyond her.

"I don't even remember if I used to work in a quilt shop."

"It's a pretty standard register, so if you worked in any shop, you probably used something similar. There are a lot of different types of transactions, though, and it takes most employees a while to master all of them."

It didn't seem to Rachel that there were so many things to master in checking out a customer—cash, credit or debit? But her mind went blank when she tried to remember which buttons to push on the cash register.

She reached up and rubbed her right temple.

"Headache?"

"A little."

"Go to the break room and have a cup of tea. After that, you can work on putting together some of the quilting kits. We're selling a lot of those to *Englischers* for Christmas gifts."

Rachel nodded, but the last thing she wanted to do was work on quilting kits. Katherine had shown her how to assemble them earlier in the morning, but she had trouble reading the pattern instructions and many of the pieces were quite small.

She wanted this job to work, though, so instead of questioning her next assignment, she went to the break room, made herself a cup of herbal tea and was staring at the employee bulletin board when her co-worker, Melinda, walked up. She was thin and beautiful and impossibly young, probably under twenty.

"Planning to go on a skiing trip?"

"Huh?"

"You're staring a hole in that poster." Melinda tapped the Swiss Valley Ski poster.

"Something about it looks familiar, but I don't know why."

"Want to go up there this weekend?"

"All the way in Michigan?"

"Six hours by bus. We leave early in the morning, get there by noon and ski all day. Sometimes we hire a driver and share the cost."

"I don't think I know how to ski."

"You'd enjoy it," Melinda assured her. "And when you get on the skis, it might all come back, just like riding a bicycle."

Which was a spectacularly bad example, as Rachel had no idea if she could even ride a bicycle.

Why couldn't she remember anything?

Why did life have to be so hard at every turn?

She blinked away tears and said, "I'll think about it."

After she rinsed her mug out in the sink, she walked into the back workroom. It was a cheery area with windows along one wall and felt design boards on the other three.

She walked to the quilt kit bin and picked up a Happy New Year pattern and large Ziploc bag. Then she walked over to the fabric stack, pulled out the bolts of fabric she'd need, carried them to the cutting center and began to measure and cut.

Twenty minutes later, Katherine came in to check on her.

"How are you doing?"

"*Gut.* I've finished one and am starting another."

Katherine picked up the Ziploc full of fabric and frowned. "You're working on the New Year kit?"

"Ya."

"But you've used Christmas fabric."

"Oh."

Katherine sighed as she pulled out the fabric. "We'll have to put this in our scraps bin now."

"I'm—I'm sorry."

Her boss looked at her with eyes filled with sympathy, which only made Rachel feel worse. "Maybe you're pushing too hard. Maybe you need to give this some time."

"I like working, though."

"I know you do, and we like having you here, but, Rachel... I can't afford to lose customers because you take ten minutes to check them out. And this fabric? It's very expensive, and now it's wasted."

"It's only that I couldn't remember what batik meant and—"

Katherine smiled at her and patted her arm. "Why don't you go on home today? Talk to Ida and John. I think it would be better if we wait, maybe another month or so, and then try again."

"You mean I'm fired?"

"Not fired." Katherine shook her head so that her gray bob of hair swung back and forth. "Let's call it an extended leave of absence."

But Rachel didn't want a leave of absence. She wanted things to be normal again. She retrieved her purse from her locker and walked toward the front of the shop. Katherine stopped her at the door and pushed an envelope into her hands. "Your payment for working this morning—and don't even try to give it back to me."

Rachel nodded, muttered *"danki"* and stuck the envelope into her purse. This was bad. She wanted to be useful. She wanted to earn money to help Ida and John. She wanted to help pay for her food and any future medical bills. She couldn't just mooch off their family forever.

Caleb had been studying *The Budget* and then staring at her for over an hour the night before. She could see in his eyes that he was trying to think of how to return her to where she belonged. She was like a lost envelope with Return to Sender stamped across the front—only, no one knew who her sender was. Everyone was waiting for her to fully recover from the accident, but she wasn't getting any better.

Her mood plunged even lower as she climbed into the buggy and pulled out onto the road. At least she remembered how to drive a buggy. She stopped at the light and looked left and that was when she saw the sign for Dr. Jan Michie, Psychologist. Dr. Michie was the person Amos had recommended, the woman she'd spoken to briefly at the hospital. Even Beth had said the woman was a good doctor. Rachel had been clinging to the hope that she would improve on her own.

She wasn't improving, though.

So she tugged on the mare's reins and pulled into the doctor's parking lot, set the brake on the buggy and picked up her purse.

She wasn't helpless. There were things she could do to hurry her recovery along, and seeing a doctor was one of them. She'd do whatever Dr. Michie suggested, because she would find her lost memories. Then she'd be whole again, she would find her family and life would be exactly as it had been before.

Caleb saw Rachel turn into the doctor's parking lot. He pulled up beside her as she was getting out of her buggy. Reaching over and opening the passenger door of his buggy, he called out, "Going to the doctor?"

"Maybe. I mean, *ya*. I am."

"Do you have a minute?"

"I suppose."

"Then come in out of the cold. Tell me about your morning."

Rachel glanced toward the front door of the doctor's office, turned back to Caleb and finally smiled. "All right. It's not like I have an appointment."

She stepped up into the buggy and shut the door.

He only had a small heater in the front of the buggy, but it had been running full blast and the interior was reasonably warm.

"So why are you going to the doctor…if you don't have an appointment?"

Rachel cornered herself in the buggy and looked directly at him. Caleb suddenly realized that she was quite different from the two women he had stepped out with. They'd been young girls, unsure of their heart or mind. It had hurt his pride when they'd dropped him for someone else. In truth, it had devastated him and sent his self-confidence into a tailspin, but he could see now that those relationships weren't meant to be. When he was ready to step out again, and he wasn't interested at all at the moment, but when he was, it would be with someone like Rachel. Someone more mature, more serious, but still able to laugh at the ups and downs of life.

She took her time, weighed her words and listened. Had she been this way before her accident, or was it because she was out of her environment?

Finally, she sighed and glanced back toward the quilt shop. "You know I worked at Katherine's this morning."

"And it made you ill?"

"Nein." She smiled at his joke. "It didn't go very well. I couldn't quite catch on…"

"Catch on?"

"Remember how to do things."

"What kind of things?"

"Run the register, cut fabric, sew."

"You've forgotten all of those things?"

"Apparently."

"I'm sorry, Rachel. This must be very hard for you."

"It is." She squeezed her eyes shut and pulled in a deep breath. When she looked at him again, she seemed to have found some inner calm. "I don't mind not remembering how to sew. I don't even mind being a terrible employee at the quilting shop. It's only frustrating to know that I must have been good at something before, but I have no idea what that thing was."

He nodded, remembering the time he'd tried working in a nearby furniture factory. They'd been in the middle of a long drought, and his parents had needed the money. It was a terrible idea, and he hadn't been good at it at all. That—not being good at something— had taught him to appreciate the work that he was able to do well.

"You'll find what you're good at. The quilt shop wasn't the only place on Bishop Amos's list."

"I would like to find a job that would help me to pay my way." She scrubbed a hand over her face. "Whatever happened to me—whether it was an accident or something else—has made me realize some things."

"Such as?"

"It's important to be useful each day, to be able to contribute in some way. I have a feeling that before... that maybe I was dissatisfied a lot, that I wanted more out of life." She shook her head, allowing her gaze to slide back toward him. "I guess that might be hard for you to understand. You seem very satisfied living with your parents and working on the farm."

"Oh, *ya*. I am now, but I wasn't always." Instead of explaining, he added, "And there are times when I'm restless to try something new. Remember how much I wanted the alpacas?"

"Seems like you've had them longer than a week."

"Seems like you've been here longer than a week." In fact, he'd found her in the snow exactly seven days ago. Looking back, that seemed like a different season in his life completely.

Rachel nodded, her eyes scanning the scene outside the buggy window, across the parking lot to the fields beyond, and then going back to him. "Those first few days, I had the feeling that you wanted to be rid of me."

Caleb pulled off his hat and stared at it. Finally, he replaced it on his head and said, "Could be I saw you as an outsider, an intruder of sorts."

"Intruder, huh?" She smiled at the thought. "Sounds like a burglar or something."

"But I see now how much my *mamm* and *dat* like having you around."

"And what of you?" She pressed her fingers to her

lips, as if she could snatch back the question. "That was inappropriate. I'm sorry."

"It wasn't, not really. I'm glad you're here, Rachel. I've never had a *schweschder*—obviously…"

"Is that how you think of me? As a *schweschder*?"

"Not exactly." He frowned and tapped his thumb against the buggy seat. "Maybe we could try being friends."

"I'd like that."

"And when I'm being bullheaded or nosing into your business, you could just tell me."

"And when I'm being lazy, you could tell me."

"Sounds like a plan, as long as you don't storm off mad, and I don't grow moody."

She ducked her chin, leaned forward and gave him a look that caused him to squirm. Out of the blue, she said, "I wonder if I had a boyfriend before. I can't even remember that."

"I imagine you did."

"You can't know for sure, though. You barely know me."

"I know you better than…better than you think."

"Maybe so." She flopped back against the seat. "I feel so torn. It's hard to move forward when you're trying to recover your past. The doctor in the hospital said my memories would probably return."

"But they're not."

"So I need to take the next step. I need to go and see the doctor, especially since both the doctor at the emergency room and Bishop Amos recommended that I do so."

"But it's an *Englisch* doctor."

"Yup." She smiled at him, but it wavered and slipped

into a frown. "That's the only kind we have around here—no Amish docs that I'm aware of."

"It seems so drastic."

"Why would you say that?"

"Because you're not in danger of dying. What will people think?"

"I don't care what people think."

"Maybe you should." How could she not consider their community before making a decision of this magnitude? Their *Ordnung* plainly said they should remain separate, that they shouldn't take up *Englisch* ways. It seemed to him that running to a doctor when you wanted to talk was doing just that. Unfortunately, from the expression on Rachel's face he could tell that he'd offended her again. "Maybe you should give it a little more time."

Her chin came up, and her eyes widened as if she couldn't quite believe he'd criticized her—again.

"This recovery isn't happening on its own, so it's time that I did something proactive. If I don't, this could take years, and I don't want to wait that long." Her defensiveness dissolved as suddenly as it had appeared. She reached across and patted his arm. "I'm glad you happened by."

"You are?"

"*Ya.* Talking to you helps, Caleb."

"Helps how?"

"Helps to clear my thinking. Saying it out loud stops the loop of thoughts going on in my mind." She opened the door, hopped out of the buggy and then leaned back inside. "I enjoyed beating you at checkers last night."

"I'd rather win now and then."

"See you around."

"I guess you will." He'd meant it as a joke, something to lighten her mood, but Rachel cocked her head as if it was one more puzzle she had to figure out.

Finally, she smiled, waved and strode off to the front door of the doctor's office.

The *Englisch* doctor.

The one that was going to help her recover her memories.

Rachel walked into the doctor's office. It was pleasantly decorated—the walls were painted a soft warm yellow and decorated with pictures of pastures, fields and sunrises. She gave her name to the receptionist and explained that she didn't have an appointment.

"Should I come back? I don't know what I was thinking just stopping by."

"Let me check with Dr. Michie first."

She turned back toward the waiting area and sat in one of the comfy chairs. The table in front of her had a few magazines, and to the right of her was a built-in cabinet with a coffee machine and all sorts of coffee and tea. Soft music played in the background. A small Christmas tree sat in a corner on the far side of the room. It was decorated with ornaments made by children—that was obvious from the overabundance of glue used on them and the fact that glitter had fallen onto the tree skirt.

Overall, not a bad place to wait.

She made herself a cup of herbal tea and picked up a magazine. Five minutes later, Dr. Michie poked her head through the door into the waiting room.

"Rachel? Would you like to come on back? You can bring your drink with you."

"Danki."

She followed the doctor back to her office. She'd met her only once, in the hospital. Jan Michie was slightly taller than her, not thin but not overweight, either, and had brown hair cut in a short shag. She wore glasses from a chain and was dressed as she had been before— neutral-covered slacks and a knit top. The most calming feature about her was her demeanor. She always seemed relaxed and unhurried.

"Thank you for seeing me, Dr. Michie."

"Call me Jan, please. I was hoping I'd hear from you. How are you doing?"

"Okay, but not great. Obviously. If I was great, I wouldn't be here."

"Tell me about that."

"Are you sure you have time?"

"Yes. I had a few open hours, and I was catching up on paperwork."

"But if you need to…"

Jan shook her head and sat back in her chair, sipping from a blue coffee mug. When she saw Rachel staring at the mug, she turned it so she could read the logo better. It said, I'm a Psychiatrist. What's Your Superpower?

"Cute," Rachel said.

"From my nephew."

The doctor didn't rush her or ask more questions, which was exactly what Rachel needed. She glanced around the office, which was also nicely decorated, and then stared out the window. Someone had filled up a bird feeder, and a variety of winter birds she couldn't name were hopping around enjoying the buffet.

Had she enjoyed bird-watching before?

What kind of person had she been?

Was her family looking for her?

Instead of asking any of those questions, Rachel blurted out, "Caleb doesn't think I should be here."

"Is that why you came to see me? To talk about Caleb?"

"Yes and no. I'm tired of not remembering. I want my life back. I want me back."

"We talked about this in the hospital. Do you remember that conversation?"

"I do. You said sometimes it takes weeks or months or even years."

"How's your memory of more recent events?"

"Gut."

"And you've kept your follow-up doctor appointments?"

"The first is later this week, but I feel as fit as a horse." She tapped her head. "The thing is that I don't want to wait any longer—not months and certainly not years. I want to do whatever I need to do to regain my memories."

Jan sat back, folded her arms and studied her for a moment. Then she opened a file that had been sitting on her desk and read through a few pages of notes—probably from when they'd visited in the hospital. Finally, she shut the file and said, "Okay. Then let's talk about what you can do to hurry this process along."

"Wunderbaar."

"I'm not guaranteeing anything."

"Of course not."

"But at this point, I'm pretty sure anything we do won't hurt your recovery."

"And it might help."

"Exactly." Jan paused, steepled her fingers and finally asked, "And you're sure that you want to remember? Because sometimes when we delve into our past, we find things weren't as rosy as we'd have liked them to be."

"I don't understand."

"Sometimes not remembering is a way of protecting yourself. Perhaps you had an incident that was painful physically or emotionally, and so your mind doesn't want to remember because it's traumatic to do so. Sometimes what we uncover isn't what we would have hoped to find."

"I hadn't really thought of that. I guess it's possible, though unlikely."

"Abuse happens in all types of families. I'm sure you realize the Amish aren't exempt."

"But I don't feel abused."

Jan waited.

"I appreciate you warning me, but I think not knowing is worse than anything we might discover—*gut* or bad makes no difference. I just want to know. I want to know who I was before."

They spent a few minutes talking about what might help her recover her memories—spending thirty minutes each morning and each evening just sitting, resting, allowing her mind to relax.

"Pretend you're floating in the ocean."

"Don't know if I've ever done that."

"What I mean is just relax. Don't try to remember. Don't do anything. Some people have trouble being still and quiet, but it can be a very healing thing. Find a special place where you can go and do this."

"Will a stall in a barn do?"

"Perfectly, as long as there are no distractions."

"Okay."

"And remember to write in a journal. Would you like me to give you one or can you purchase one?"

"I have one that I've been writing in." Rachel shared with her the short list of things she'd remembered thus far—her name, that she had a brother named Ethan, wearing sunglasses, knowing about alpaca wool and that she was twenty-five.

"Great. Be sure and continue adding to that list. Nothing is too small to include. In fact, it would be good to make daily entries, and bring it with you for your next appointment."

"What do I write about…if I don't have anything to add to my memory list?"

"Absolutely anything. Don't try to force your thoughts in any one direction. If it comes into your mind during your journaling time, jot it down."

"Sounds easy enough."

"You had a poetry book with you when Caleb found you, correct?"

"Ya."

"Read through it, not forcefully, not intent on making yourself remember. Putting more pressure on your mind will only cause it to skitter in another direction."

"Like when you're trying to remember the words to a hymn and just can't."

"Exactly, but when you quit thinking about it…"

"Usually when I'm doing laundry."

"Then the words come." Jan tapped her pen against her desk. "The poetry book is one of the only physical clues we have to your past, and I think it's an important one. I'd like you to spend a few minutes each day reading it, but do so as if it were a letter from an old friend—something you enjoy revisiting again."

Rachel began to feel optimistic. Dr. Michie made her sound less like a freak and more like a person with a treatable condition.

"If you have time and a buggy, drive around a little. Just pick a direction and drive. We can't really guess what will stir your memories."

"I can do that."

"Be sure and make a note in the journal if anything looks familiar or causes you to experience a strong reaction."

"I will."

"Also if you have any dreams that leave you with intense feelings, jot those down, too."

Rachel nodded and stood when Jan glanced at her watch.

The doctor plucked a business card from her desk drawer and handed it to her. "If you need to talk, call me." Then she stood and walked her into the reception area. She asked her receptionist to make Rachel an appointment for the next week.

"One more thing." She put a hand on Rachel's shoulder. "If there's anything that you find you enjoy doing— then do that thing. If you like it, then your mind is signaling to you that it's a safe activity, and the opposite is true, too. If something seems terribly hard—"

"Like cutting fabric." She'd shared her attempt at working across the street.

"Yes, like cutting fabric—if it seems hard, if it brings on the headaches, simply stop. Don't push. If it seems like something you'd enjoy, though, allow yourself to do it without understanding why."

"I can't imagine what that will be."

"You'll know when you see it."

Rachel walked back out into the weak afternoon sun. The day was as dreary as it had been before. The shop that she wouldn't be working at still sat across the street, its parking lot now half-full of customers. Nothing had really changed, but for a reason she couldn't put her thumb on, and for the first time since she'd woken in Montgomery, Indiana, Rachel felt hopeful.

There was a small general store on the way back to the Wittmer farm. She stopped and went inside, unsure what she was looking for or why she was bothering to shop when she had such a small amount of money to her name. Then she remembered what Jan had said, about doing something she enjoyed. She'd been surprised to find thirty dollars in the envelope from the quilt shop. She didn't think she'd earned that much, but apparently she had. While she could give the money to Ida to help pay for her food, she had a feeling Ida would rather she follow the doctor's directions.

So she walked up and down the aisles, pausing in front of the paperback novels, the cookbooks, even the coloring books. None looked particularly interesting to her. She turned down the next aisle and saw a large display of yarn. Beside that was a variety of crochet needles, books and knitting needles. She reached forward, ran her fingers down a pair of 5.5-m knitting needles and almost laughed. She picked the package up, turned it over and over, and finally slipped it into her basket. Next she chose a package of variegated yarn—beautiful blues melding into one another, from sky blue to navy. It would make a lovely scarf for Ida, and she knew just the pattern to use. She could almost see the directions in her mind—a stockinette stitch that produced a nice woven look.

She checked the items in her basket to be sure she had what she needed, added another skein of the yarn and then walked to the register to pay for everything. She couldn't have said if she really knew how to knit, but it felt like she knew, and after all…the doctor had told her to follow her instincts. For now, her instincts were leading her toward a hot mug of tea and a knitting session.

Chapter Eight

Caleb had been studying Rachel all through dinner and even afterward as she set to work with her new knitting needles and yarn. She'd apparently begun the project earlier in the afternoon—after losing her job, visiting the doctor and going by the general store. She'd been busy. Whatever she was knitting already stretched across her lap. How much of the yarn had she bought? It was a medley of blues—quite appropriate. He couldn't fault her there, not that he was looking for a reason to find fault. He just didn't understand her moods, and he was worried about this doctor situation.

He'd tried to catch her eye a few times, but she'd been completely focused on counting her stitches. Twice now she'd shushed him.

His *mamm* had laughed and said, "That's why I was never very good at knitting—you have to count."

Rachel had nodded in agreement as she continued mumbling, "Thirty-seven, thirty-eight, thirty-nine…"

He waited for her to reach the end of a row and tug again on the ball of yarn, and then he jumped in with the first thing that came to mind. "I could use some help in the barn brushing down the horses."

She stopped, midstitch, and stared at him. "Now?"

"Sure. Now's a *gut* time."

She bent forward to peer out the window at the pitch-black night. The cloud cover was so heavy that no stars or moonlight shone through, but she shrugged and said, "*Ya*. I could help with that, I guess."

Caleb noticed his parents exchange a glance, but he chose to ignore that. The year before, his *mamm* had spent many an hour trying her best at matchmaking and dropping none-too-subtle hints about *grandkinner*. She'd finally given up sometime in the last six months, but he knew that sparkle in her eye meant she was considering meddling. He shook his head once, definitively. She only smiled and raised her eyebrows as if to say "I have no idea what you mean."

"*Gut* to see you *youngies* taking responsibility for our animals." His *dat* peered at them over the top of *The Budget*. "Those alpacas—I'm not exactly sure what to do with them."

"Mostly they enjoy attention," Rachel said, as if she'd been raising alpacas all of her life.

For all Caleb knew, she had been.

"I'll put a kettle of water on to boil, and we can have tea and some of those leftover cinnamon rolls when you all are done." His *mamm* added, with a distinctive twinkle in her eye, "But don't hurry on our account."

Caleb rubbed at the muscle just over his left shoulder and waited for Rachel to shrug into her coat.

They walked out to the barn in silence, the wind at their back causing them to walk closer together—shoulder to shoulder—as a barricade against the cold.

When they stepped into the barn, the smells of hay and animals and wood surrounded him. He watched Rachel as she walked around the main room, studying the tools and projects and sacks of feed. Finally, she turned to him and said, "You and your *dat* keep a clean barn."

"Of course."

"Not all Amish do."

"You remember that?"

She shrugged, unprovoked by his intrusiveness. She'd been quieter, calmer, since going to the *Englisch* doctor…or maybe it was the knitting that had settled her nerves. "I'm not sure what I remember, but I do know this is especially clean. Can't say I'm surprised, since you're so…"

"So what?" He didn't want to care what Rachel thought about him, but he braced himself for her criticism as if it was a dart she was about to hurl his way.

"Industrious. That's the word I'm looking for."

"Never been called that before. Thick-headed, stubborn—"

"Old-fashioned. *Ya*, I know. But what I mean is that you seem to like what you do out here, and it shows. It's not about doing things the old way…though plainly you do." She picked up a handheld seed broadcaster, studied it a minute and placed it back in its cubby. "People can be old-fashioned and messy. This place looks as clean as a veterinarian's hospital."

Had she worked for a veterinarian?

Everything she said, he wondered if it was a piece of the puzzle of Rachel, but maybe he was reading too much into things. Maybe he was afraid it was all going to come together at once, and she'd be whisked away. That was what he wanted, for her to be returned home, but he hoped it would happen slowly so that he could get used to the idea. He should already be used to it, since he spent an inordinate amount of time thinking about it—about her.

"So why did you want me to come out here?"

"I told you—"

"To brush down the horses at seven thirty in the evening. *Ya*, I heard you."

"Could be a guy just likes a little help with the work. Plus I get a little restless, especially on winter nights. We've been sitting in that house since five o'clock."

She only smiled wider, and he knew that he wasn't fooling her. She didn't call him on it, but plainly she knew that he'd brought her out here to talk about the doctor. She'd said nothing about it at dinner, which meant she'd talked to his *mamm* earlier. While he tried to figure out how to broach the subject, they might as well brush down the animals.

The alpacas usually stayed outside, even in the evening. They had a lean-to with a roof and a wall against the northern wind. They could also come into the barn through the southern stalls, where he left the outer doors open. He'd been doing that the last three nights, and each morning he'd arrived to find them bedded down inside. Apparently they knew a good deal when they saw one, and since his *dat* had only the two buggy horses, they had several unused stalls.

He handed her a brush and pointed to the nearest stall, and together they walked in and began brushing down Ginger, their older mare. Rachel didn't ask any questions about how to use the brush or where to begin on the animal. She talked to it softly and then began stroking it from the top of its head and down its neck. The animal apparently liked what she was doing. When she stopped to move her *kapp* strings out of the way, the mare nudged her hand to encourage her to keep brushing.

He thought Rachel looked especially pretty in the glow of the lantern. He was suddenly glad that she had fallen into their lives. He was already starting to think of events in terms of "before Rachel" or "after Rachel," as if she was some sort of dividing line in his life. She was certainly unlike any of the girls he had stepped out with. Rachel had a mind of her own, even if she couldn't remember her name. She had strong opinions, but she was willing to listen to others—that was rare in a person. And though she seemed to struggle with her moods, he couldn't know if that was because of the frustration of her situation or something more. She seemed to always push through. She seemed to always end up with that same small knowing smile she was wearing now.

A bead of sweat broke out along his hairline, and he felt as if he could hear the rush of ocean waves in his ears. What did that mean?

Was he falling for her?

Did he have…romantic feelings for Rachel?

That would be ridiculous. Why would he even entertain pursuing a relationship with her? It wasn't like she was staying here. It wasn't like they had a chance to build a life together. Then again, how much control did one have over whom they fell in love with?

He dropped the brush, bent to pick it up and stumbled as he was standing back up.

She looked at him quizzically but didn't say anything.

He couldn't be in love with Rachel. He just couldn't. He liked things done the old way, while she was eager to embrace change. He was quiet and steady—his mood was the same nearly every day. She was smiling and chatty one moment, quiet and droopy the next. He lived in Montgomery, Indiana, and they had no idea where she lived. He couldn't even speak to her *dat* about courting her because they didn't know who her father was.

It was with those thoughts whirling in his head that he swallowed, began brushing the other side of the mare and broached the subject he'd wanted to talk about since she had come home earlier that afternoon.

Rachel thought Caleb was acting a bit strangely—staring at her one moment, then dropping things, then stumbling, and then blushing when he saw she'd noticed. If she didn't know better, she'd ask him if he'd been sipping the wine that many Amish households kept for special occasions.

She didn't, though.

The thought of Caleb Wittmer drinking a glass of wine almost caused her to laugh out loud. So instead of quizzing him about his odd behavior, she waited for him to begin the interrogation that she knew was coming. She certainly wasn't going to make it any easier for him, but she did feel a bit sympathetic that he was grappling with it so.

Finally, he began brushing the mare with strong sure strokes and jumped in.

"I don't understand why you have to see an *Englisch* doctor."

"We already talked about this in the buggy."

"I know we did, but explain it to me. I really do want to understand."

"And I want to understand why you're so dead set against it."

"Good, let's have a conversation. You start."

"All right. I want to see Dr. Michie, who is an *Englisch* doctor, because I want to get well. And we don't have any Amish doctors."

"We may not have doctors, but we have people in our community who can help you."

"Like who?" Rachel crossed her arms, her aggravation building. She should have known that he would have a better idea. Caleb always thought he knew the answer to things. Though she'd promised herself that she would be more patient with him after all Beth had told her, that was proving more difficult than she'd thought it would be.

They'd had that nice moment in the buggy earlier in the day—he'd seemed almost kind then. No doubt he was a kind person, but sometimes his certainty that he knew the best answer for every question got in the way.

If only he wasn't so aggravating and pushy, she might actually enjoy being around him.

He was studying her now as if she was a child and he needed to think how to persuade her without causing a tantrum. She did not have tantrums! She might have strong opinions, but there was nothing wrong with that.

"You were about to suggest people in your community who could help me find my memories."

"Let me think," he said.

"Uh-huh. I'm waiting."

They both continued brushing down the mare. It had been a long day for Rachel with too many ups and downs. She was embarrassed that she'd lost her job at the quilt shop on the first day she'd shown up, but she was also optimistic after seeing Dr. Michie. Now Caleb was ruining even that.

Ginger moved closer, so she continued brushing her mane. It was amazing how much animals enjoyed human attention.

"Many people in our community see a chiropractor," Caleb pointed out.

"I don't have a sore back!"

"I'm just saying that there are…" He paused, his eyes going up and to the right as he tried to think of another word.

"More traditional?"

"That's it. There are more traditional ways to address, uh, health issues."

"This is a *mental* health issue."

"Maybe it is. Maybe it isn't. Your brain was apparently bruised—sounds physical to me."

She shook her head in exasperation.

"We have midwives."

"Not having a baby."

"And we have an herbalist." He snapped his fingers. "That's it. You could go see Doreen."

"An herbalist?"

"*Ya.* She's very *gut.* Lots of people say so."

"Have you ever seen her yourself?"

"*Nein.*"

"Have your parents?"

"Not that I can remember."

"But you want me to go and see her."

"*Ya.*"

"I thought herbalists helped people who had digestive

issues or maybe trouble sleeping." She started to add "people who were depressed," but she wasn't ready to admit she had that problem. Maybe she did, but maybe her feelings were a natural reaction to what had happened. If her moods were a side effect of her amnesia, would that still be considered depression? She'd have to ask Dr. Michie the next time she saw her.

"I have another appointment with Dr. Michie next week."

"Oh."

She could practically hear him snap his mouth shut, as he no doubt tried to stop the suggestion that was about to come out. Maybe he did realize how irritating he was—points in his favor. She felt her aggravation with him soften.

She felt her resolve wobble.

"If you think it's a *gut* idea to see this Doreen, I suppose I could give it a try." She didn't want to see an herbalist, but it might be worth it to please Caleb. He suddenly looked so relieved, almost as if it was already Christmas morning. "No idea where she is or what I'll say to her."

"I'll take you."

Caleb glanced away when she stared up at him.

"Now, why would you do that?"

"Just trying to help."

Ginger again nudged her hand, encouraging her to keep brushing, and Rachel laughed—whether at herself, Caleb or the mare, she couldn't have said.

"I don't have anything to do tomorrow, since I lost my job. The manager at the restaurant didn't want to see me until Wednesday."

"Tomorrow afternoon, then. I'll take you over to Doreen's."

"It's a date!" Rachel wanted to take back the word as soon as she said it, but Caleb was looking at her as if she'd just told him there was an alien standing behind him. It really was comical.

Did he think she wanted a date with him? He looked seriously stumped, so she shook her head, patted the mare one last time and moved over to Stormy's stall. There was no point in trying to clear up misunderstandings as far as Caleb Wittmer was concerned. She'd tried that before, and she usually ended up digging a deeper hole.

She started working on Stormy, who really was a beautiful animal. His coat was a deep black, and he was delighted to receive the attention. After twenty minutes, Caleb admitted they should go back inside, that his *mamm* probably had the tea ready. They both knew that brushing the horses had been an excuse for them to have a little privacy.

As they walked back toward the house, staying close together against the north wind that seemed to cut right through her coat, Rachel felt her mood plummet again. She'd felt almost content for a few moments, working on the scarf for Ida. The yarn and knitting needles had seemed to move effortlessly between her fingers. But now her emotions were churning again. She'd agreed to see this Doreen, but she didn't hold much hope that any herb would help her to remember. It was quite possible that Dr. Michie's suggestions wouldn't, either.

All she knew was that she wanted to go home, to be where she belonged, and she was willing to try just about anything to achieve that.

* * *

Caleb barely said a word through their evening snack and as he made his way to bed. Did Rachel think they were going on a date?

How did he get himself into these messes?

And why, as Gabriel had pointed out, was he so skittish around her? He should be happy that she'd agreed to see the herbalist, though why he'd suggested Doreen he couldn't have said. All he knew was that Rachel didn't need to see that *Englisch* doctor. Amish folks did see doctors—sure they did—for things like broken legs or deep cuts or rotten teeth. They didn't see a doctor for their feelings, and this Michie woman… It wasn't as if she was a specialist in memories. There was no such thing. Was there?

He went to sleep Monday night feeling like he'd done a good thing steering Rachel back toward the Amish way. He wanted her to get well, wanted it as much as she did, but he didn't think paying a woman to talk to her for an hour was the answer. If she needed to talk to someone, she could talk to him. He wouldn't charge her a thing!

The next morning again dawned dark and gray. They were certainly having a string of gloomy days. Saturday's sunshine and the episode with the snake seemed like it had happened weeks or months ago. Unfortunately Rachel's mood seemed to mirror the weather. He was learning that mornings were the hardest for her. She seemed to perk up by afternoon. And cloudy days? They were the worst.

His *mamm* and *dat* seemed a little surprised that Caleb had suggested Doreen, but they didn't offer an opinion. Instead they shared a look. He'd seen unspo-

ken words pass between them as long as he could remember, and he still didn't understand how they did
that. His *mamm* sipped her coffee and said, "I wish
I could tag along, but I promised to go over and help
Rebekah finish up a quilt for the new grandbaby she's
expecting. Both her girls are due with their first about
the same time, and she's in quite a tizzy over getting
ready for them."

So it was that after lunch he found himself pulling
the buggy up to the front door and waiting for Rachel.
He didn't have to wait long, and when she did come out,
she at least looked perkier than she had that morning.

"Feeling better?" he asked.

"Who said I was feeling bad?"

"Doesn't take a genius to see."

"I guess."

"Want to talk about it?"

"Nein."

"Fair enough."

They traveled in an uncomfortable silence. Caleb
didn't remember where Doreen lived, but his *mamm*
had written down instructions on the back of an envelope. Fortunately, it was only a few miles away, so he
wouldn't have to endure Rachel's silence for very long.

He needn't have worried.

By the time they were on the main road, she was
chatting about red birds and Beth's baby and the knitting she'd started the evening before.

"Going better than the crochet work, huh?"

"You noticed that?"

"Looked like a cat had taken hold of your yarn ball."

"Think you could do better?"

"Nein. I wasn't saying that at all." He couldn't help

smiling, though. The world felt right when Rachel teased him. When she was quiet and sad, he felt as if he had a stone in the pit of his stomach.

"Tell me about this Doreen," she said.

"Not much to tell."

"Really?"

"She's older." He thought she might have celebrated her ninetieth birthday, but he decided not to bring that up.

"Amish?"

"*Nein.* She's Mennonite." Some folks thought she was struggling with dementia, but he was sure that was an exaggeration. Though he had heard that she wore a knitted cap with pom-poms even during the heat of summer.

They pulled up to a tiny little home that was probably surrounded by gardens, but snow covered the entire property now. No one had shoveled the walk. He supposed she didn't get out much, being as old as she was. There was no sign near the lawn advertising her herbs, but the name Penner was stenciled on the mailbox.

"Her name is Doreen Penner," he explained as he pulled the buggy to a stop.

"I wonder where she keeps her plants in the winter."

But they didn't have to wonder for long. Doreen answered the door, with a striped cat in her arms and a rather large parrot sitting on her shoulder. "I don't know you, so I guess you're here to see me about some herbs. Come in. Come in."

"Come in," squawked the bird.

As Caleb had feared, she was wearing a knitted cap done in a striped purple pattern with a large pom-pom on the top, but her clothing was even stranger than her headwear. She wore a denim dress embroidered with cats chasing yarn, cats chasing butterflies, even cats chasing children. The dress reached to the floor, and her outfit was rounded out with pink bunny slippers and a pink sweater that was unraveling. The cat stared at them briefly, yawned and then began to lick Doreen's hand.

Rachel shot Caleb a look that told him there would be a reckoning coming as soon as they left the house. She thanked Doreen politely and stepped inside.

The home looked to be four rooms—a living room with windows that faced the street, a dining room to the left of that. Beyond, Caleb could just make out a kitchen, and the bedroom must have been to the right of the back room.

Every conceivable surface was covered with plants. They were crowded onto tabletops and windowsills, lined along the floor beneath windows and even crowded on top of stacks of books. Doreen placed the cat on the floor, and it immediately disappeared between a large aloe vera plant and a cactus.

Who grew cactuses in Indiana?

"Come into the kitchen and tell me what type of treatment you're needing."

"Actually we just wanted to talk with you," Rachel said.

A calico cat had replaced the striped one at Doreen's feet. It walked over to Rachel and began to rub against her legs. She stooped to pet it, and Caleb could hear the beast purring from where he stood. This was a nightmare—instead of a physician's office, he'd brought Rachel to a house with an undetermined number of cats, one large bird and an old woman wearing a purple knitted cap on her head.

Caleb fought the urge to turn around and head back out to the buggy, but Rachel was already walking toward the kitchen, explaining that she'd suffered a slight concussion and amnesia.

"Is that so?"

"*Ya.* It happened a little over a week ago, as near as we can tell."

"So you're not from around here. That would explain why I don't recognize you, though I've seen your beau at barn raisings and such."

Caleb wished he could melt into the yellow linoleum floor. Rachel's beau? Had the old woman actually said that?

"Sit. Both of you, sit and talk to Doreen."

The chairs were filled with more books, some newspapers and seed packets. Caleb cleared off a place for Rachel to sit and then another for himself.

"Caleb, he found me in the snow out near his parents' farm. They took me to the hospital." Rachel put a hand at the back of her head. "I had a lump, but no other injuries."

"And you can't remember any details of your past?"

"Not at first. A few things have returned since then—the name of my *bruder*, that I wore sunglasses, a couple of childhood memories."

"How interesting." Doreen sounded delighted to be presented with such a challenge. She hobbled over to the stove and set a kettle on the burner.

Caleb glanced at Rachel in alarm. "I'm not sure we can stay long enough—"

"Nonsense. It's rude to not offer guests a cup of tea. Isn't that right, Peaches?" The bird's head and back were adorned with turquoise blue feathers, but its breast was a bright orange.

It squawked, "Tea," and then flew away to perch in the boxed windowsill amid a sea of plants.

"Macaws aren't the smartest parrots…"

"Smart bird." Peaches's head bobbed up and down when he spoke.

"African gray parrots are better at understanding and mimicking human speech, but Peaches is good company."

"Good company." The bird began to groom himself, and Caleb didn't know whether to laugh or hang his head in his hands. Who let a bird fly around their home? There wasn't a cage in sight. Doreen made a cooing sound, pulled a baby carrot from her sweater pocket and offered it to the bird, who squawked, "Carrot," and snatched it from her hand.

"Do you think you can help me?" Rachel asked.

Doreen's back was to them as she fiddled with the teakettle. Rachel glanced at Caleb, then pressed her fingers over her lips in an attempt to hold in her laughter.

"A cheerful heart is good medicine," Doreen said, pulling three cups and saucers from her cabinet. There was no place to put them on the counter, so Caleb jumped up and took them, carrying them over to the table. Doreen followed with a metal tin. Her hands shaking, she slowly opened it, dug around among the contents, pulled out three bags and placed them in the mugs. "The Good Book says that."

"Proverbs," Rachel said.

"Proverbs," squawked Peaches, though his attention had switched to a solid yellow cat. He dropped to the floor, strutted across the room to the cat, who was lying near the back door, and began to preen it.

"Yes. Now, some people think herbs are just weeds, but we know better—Peaches and I do. *Gotte* gives us everything we need. People have been using plants for medicine since Adam and Eve stepped out of the garden—after all, there were no pharmacies then."

"What kinds of things do you treat?" Rachel asked.

"Mistletoe can help with a nervous disposition or high blood pressure."

"I don't have either of those things."

"Peppermint helps with sleeplessness."

"She doesn't have trouble sleeping," Caleb said. If they didn't move this along, they'd be here all afternoon. They hadn't come for a botany lesson. In fact, he couldn't quite remember now why he'd thought this would be a good idea.

If Doreen heard him, she chose not to respond.

"Rhubarb is useful for eczema or arthritis." Her hands shook as she reached for Rachel's and covered them with her own. "Now, your situation is unusual. I would normally use ginkgo leaves for someone who is confused, but you seem mentally alert."

"*Ya*, I think I am."

"What you need, what I've put in your cup, is rosemary."

"Rosemary?" Rachel asked.

"Rosemary," Peaches squawked, flying across the room and landing on the table.

Caleb jumped backward, causing his chair to scrape against the floor. He couldn't believe he was seeing a large blue-and-orange bird on a kitchen table. Certainly, that couldn't be healthy.

At the same moment, the kettle whistled. Caleb jumped up. "I'll fetch that." He did not want to drink anything Doreen gave him. What if the parrot had been in her cabinets? What type of disease could they catch from the bird? Or the cats? He might as well eat off the barn floor.

Rachel seemed nowhere near as tense as he was. In fact, she actually seemed to be considering drinking the rosemary tea.

He filled their cups, then stood behind Doreen, telling Rachel with hand motions not to drink or eat anything. Rachel, being more than a little mischievous, smiled at him, raised the cup to her lips and nearly drained the contents in one swallow.

"That's a girl." Doreen dunked her own tea bag up and down. "I think your beau will enjoy it, as well. What was your name, young man?"

"Caleb." He shrugged back into his coat. "I just remembered somewhere we need to be."

"Need to be," the bird squawked and jumped to Doreen's shoulder, where it began to poke its beak in the woman's purple cap.

"One of the reasons I wear the cap in the house." Doreen smiled as if she'd said the most clever thing. "It's better than having my hair preened. Peaches is very affectionate."

Caleb wanted to leave—immediately.

Rachel was in much less of a hurry. She wouldn't meet his gaze, and he couldn't quite tell if she found this situation humorous, or if she was simply hiding the anger she was going to unleash on him once they were back in the buggy. Not that he would blame her.

"*Danki* for the tea, Doreen. Do we owe you anything?"

"For a cup of tea?"

Caleb had walked around the table and was pulling Rachel to her feet. She continued trying to thank Doreen. Peaches was squawking about seeds and carrots. Yet another cat had jumped into Caleb's vacated seat. He felt as if he was caught in a bad dream.

Rachel's life had been topsy-turvy since she'd opened her eyes with no memories the week before. It had been dramatic and terrible and frightening and difficult. Today was like the cherry on someone's ice-cream sundae. She honestly didn't know whether to laugh or cry.

Caleb practically pulled her out of Doreen's house— the bird was still squawking and one of the cats tried to follow them outside, but Doreen scooped it up in her arms. Rachel glanced back to see Doreen standing in the doorway, Peaches on her shoulder, one cat in her arms and another rubbing against her legs. The dear old woman waved at them and hollered, "Come back anytime."

Which didn't seem likely.

Caleb seemed intent to get her into the buggy as quickly as possible. Even the gelding, Stormy, seemed surprised to see them back so soon. How long had they been inside Doreen's house? Fifteen minutes? Twenty at the most.

She climbed up into the buggy and pulled the buggy blanket over her lap. Caleb jumped in, called out to Stormy and took off at a speed that had the gelding tossing his head and threatening to break into a gallop.

And then it happened. All of the tension and worry

and anxiety of the last week caught up with her. She sat forward and covered her face with her hands.

"I'm sorry, Rachel. I really am."

She took two deep breaths—she knew what was coming, but was powerless to stop it.

"That was one of my worst ideas ever. I'd heard that Doreen had gone a little strange, but I had no idea…" Caleb touched her shoulder. "Are you okay?"

He called to Stormy and pulled the horse over into a parking area. "Are you—are you crying? Wait…you're laughing?"

Her shoulders shook and her laughter came from a place deep inside. She laughed until she had to clasp her stomach from the ache. Tears sprang from her eyes, and every time she thought she had control of herself, she'd glance at Caleb—Caleb, who was staring at her with eyes wide and a look of disbelief on his face—and she'd dissolve into laughter again.

He waited her out and handed her a handkerchief when she seemed to be finished.

"Oh, my. I haven't laughed that hard since my sister fell in our pond trying to pull in a fish." Another puzzle piece, and she knew then, she was convinced, that there would be more until her life resembled something that she recognized. "The look on your face when Peaches jumped on the table made me wish I had an *Englisch* camera."

"Never seen anything like it." He crossed his arms as if he was still perturbed about the whole thing.

"And your pantomiming not to drink." Laughter spilled out of her again and she wiped at her eyes.

"So why did you drink it?"

"I thought that was the reason you took me there— to receive Doreen's cure."

"You did it to spite me."

"Actually it simply seemed polite, and I didn't think a little rosemary could hurt me. Seems my *mamm* used to add some to our tea when we had a headache."

"Cats all over the place, plants everywhere, that bird... It was a nightmare."

"Carrot," Rachel squawked, and then she was laughing again, only this time Caleb joined her.

She was rearranging the blanket on her lap, trying to get control of her emotions, when he reached across and placed his hand under her chin, turning her face toward him. His touch caused her stomach to do funny things, or maybe that was the burst of laughter or even the rosemary tea.

"You're something else, Rachel. You're a special woman. Did you know?"

"Because I can laugh at an old woman's attempts to lighten other people's loads?"

"Because you can find the humor even in an extremely uncomfortable situation." She had the bizarre thought that he was going to kiss her then, but instead he pulled back his hand and picked up the horse's reins.

They continued toward home, and though the clouds still pressed down, Rachel's heart felt lighter. "Parrots are known for their problem-solving abilities, and the African gray she mentioned? It's said they have the intelligence of a five-year-old but the temperament of a two-year-old."

"A two-year-old that never grows up."

"Indeed, but I suspect Peaches is a good companion for Doreen."

Caleb shifted in his seat. "Are you going to the restaurant tomorrow...to work?"

"I suppose. I really should find a job. Sitting around all day isn't helping me, though the knitting...it makes me feel calmer."

"Wasn't the schoolhouse on Amos's list?"

"*Ya.* I thought I would try it if the restaurant doesn't work out."

"Maybe you should try the schoolhouse first."

"Why? I'm not sure they really need me. Most schools have only one teacher. Amos said the teacher in your community could use an extra hand during the holidays, preparing for the school play and all. I had the feeling it was a charity position if nothing else worked out for me."

"I know Martha. She's a *gut* teacher, but she definitely has her hands full. Our schoolhouse is brimming with children. Plans are to build another and divide in the summer."

"Why do you think I should work there?"

"Because you know things."

"I know things?"

"*Ya.* Like about the parrots."

"Oh, that was just...something I remembered."

"And the snake. Remember all the things you told me about snakes?"

"Why did I know that?"

"I think maybe you were a teacher before. That would even explain the book of poetry you were carrying with you."

Rachel stared out the window at the snowy fields. Could she see herself teaching? She supposed she could. She wasn't sure she had the temperament for it—her moods were too up and down, but perhaps it had been something that she was good at.

She turned toward Caleb and studied his profile. He was a nice-looking man, and he was trying to help her. "Your last idea was terrible."

"True."

"I want to continue seeing Dr. Michie."

"Can't blame you. She probably doesn't have cats or parrots in her office."

"But I think you might be right."

"You do?"

"*Ya.* I'll go to the schoolhouse tomorrow. We'll see what Martha says."

Chapter Nine

The next week flew by for Rachel.

She saw Dr. Michie two more times. Though she was still remembering very little of her past, she was learning to cope with her current situation. She didn't mention her moods to the doctor. Frankly, she was embarrassed that she woke each day feeling as if she couldn't crawl out of bed. Once up, after she'd had coffee and eaten, her mood usually improved. If the weather was sunny, she walked to the little one-room school. If it was snowing or if the wind was blowing, Caleb or John drove her there. As far as the evenings went, some were good and some were bad. Wasn't that true for everyone?

She kept her appointment with the medical doctor who had treated her at the hospital. Dr. Gold assured her that she was healing, and reminded her that "these things take time."

Martha was easy to work with. She was a few years younger than Rachel, and she planned to marry as soon as school was out. There would be openings for two new teachers, since the board had decided to proceed with

plans to build an additional schoolhouse on the far side
of the district. Rachel sometimes wondered if she should
apply for the job, but as Dr. Michie had told her, "Don't
worry about making tomorrow's decisions today."

So she'd focused on the children and the upcoming
Christmas play, and in her spare time she did those
things that Dr. Michie had suggested. On the afternoons
Caleb picked her up from the school, they drove in a
random direction to help her look for anything familiar. A comfortable friendship developed between them
and maybe something more.

Sometimes when she thought of how much she owed
the good man sitting next to her in the buggy, how *Gotte*
had blessed her life with the presence of him, she was
certain that their friendship would develop into love.
Each night she'd allow her mind to play back the events
of the day—and more often than not, her thoughts focused on something Caleb had said, or the casual touch
of his hand as he helped her into or out of the buggy, or
the way her heart raced when she looked up from her
knitting and caught him studying her. Was that love?
Did she care for Caleb the way a wife cared for a husband? And did he return her feelings?

The knitting was the only thing that completely relaxed her. Because she had to focus on counting her
stitches and following a pattern that she somehow remembered, she wasn't able to worry or question or
think. She found that creating something that would
be useful to someone else gave her a sense of satisfaction. Perhaps she had been a skilled knitter in her other
life. She might never know. More and more she was
coming to terms with that.

One night she'd stayed up past everyone else. The

house smelled of fresh cedar and pinecones and baked desserts. Candles adorned every windowsill, and three wrapped presents in plain brown paper with midnight blue bows were arranged on the top shelf of the bookcase. Ida was in full holiday mode.

It was hard for Rachel to fathom that it was the week before Christmas. Her dreams of being home for the holidays seemed foolish now. She still didn't know where home was. She was alone in the sitting room when Caleb's *dat* wandered in claiming he was suddenly hungry and needed a small snack.

He brought back the pitcher of milk, two glasses and the coconut-cream pie that Ida had made for dinner.

"Actually I'm full, but *danki*."

"You're very welcome. Since you don't want any, maybe I'll just finish it." He smiled at her and wiggled his eyebrows, as if this would be their little secret.

Rachel continued knitting. Christmas would arrive before she knew it, and she still didn't have all the projects done she'd hoped to finish.

John ate his pie in silence, and then he sat back and stared at the fire in the potbelly stove.

"When I met Ida, I knew she was the one, but Ida... she wasn't so sure."

Rachel glanced up in surprise. John smiled weakly and then turned his attention back toward the fire.

"She wasn't being unkind, but she wanted to be sure—*absolutely sure* was the way she put it."

"That's a rare thing, to be absolutely sure of something, to be beyond-a-doubt sure."

"Indeed it is. I was persistent, and eventually she agreed to marry me."

"So it was love."

"Maybe...or maybe it became love sometime down the road." He stood and returned his dishes to the kitchen. She heard the water running as he rinsed his plate and cup. When he walked back into the sitting room, he picked up where he'd left off—or maybe he simply said what he'd meant to say all along. "We've had a *gut* life, me and Ida. I'm glad she gave me a chance. Sometimes that is all it takes, you know—giving love a chance to grow."

He walked over and kissed her on top of the head, something that surprised Rachel as much as his words. She stayed up another hour, the knitting sitting in her lap unfinished, her eyes on the fire and her heart wondering if she was brave enough to give Caleb a chance.

Caleb was supposed to pick Rachel up the next day. He made the mistake of arriving a few minutes early. There was a literal traffic jam of buggies in the schoolyard. He should have come later, but he hadn't wanted her to start walking home. It was snowing and nearly dark outside, though the time was only four in the afternoon. A line of buggies waited to pick up children, which was quite unusual. Amish students were made of hardy stuff. They were used to walking to and from school. Next thing he knew they'd be whipping out cell phones to call their parents to come and get them.

That was a ridiculous thought, and he knew it.

Still, he didn't like change—any hint of change caused his anxiousness to rise like cream in a pail of fresh milk.

Then he walked into the classroom and saw the decorations and the children, and he knew—absolutely knew—that he should turn around and walk back out.

Too late for that, though. Rachel had spied him and was walking toward him with a strained smile on her face.

"What's wrong?" she asked.

"Who said anything was wrong?"

"The look on your face."

"What's that supposed to mean?"

"You're scowling."

"Am not." He plastered on a smile, but it seemed to take the strength of a giant to hold it in place, so he returned to studying the chaos in front of him.

"What are they doing?"

"Practicing for the play."

"What kind of play?"

"The Christmas play, of course."

"Doesn't look like it."

"See, that's the fun part. We took the traditional Christmas play…you know the one, Christmas Bees."

"A *gut* play, but they don't look as if they're dressed up as bees."

"They're not, that's what I was explaining. I changed it a little, and we're calling it the Christmas Cats."

She pointed at the decorations—instead of snowflakes connected one to another, there was a string of cats, paws linking them together. Some wore glasses, some were short and fat, others were tall and lanky. Each wore a sweater that bore the name of a student.

"Why did you have to change it?"

"Because the children didn't want to be bees this year," she said.

"Cats? That makes no sense. What do cats have to do with Christmas?"

"It's funny. You'll see."

"But why would you change it?"

"So the children would be interested."

"Why couldn't they be interested in bees?"

Before Rachel could answer, one of the students ran up and said, "I don't want to say this." He thrust a sheet of paper into her hands. "I want to make up my own words."

"Let's see how that works." She threw a is-the-day-over-yet gaze at Caleb, but it did nothing to ease the ache in his jaw. Why would he think it was a *gut* idea for Rachel to work at the schoolhouse? Sure, Martha had been eager to receive help during the holiday season, but he should have known that Rachel would try to change things, to encourage the children to be different, to make them less Amish.

Bishop Amos had walked in the back door. As Rachel hurried away, he approached Caleb and motioned toward two chairs, where they could sit.

"She's doing a *gut* job, *ya*?" Amos slipped a thumb under his right suspender and smiled at the children.

"I'm not so sure."

"How's that?"

"She's using cats—changing the Christmas Bees to Christmas Cats. Why would she do that?" Caleb was sure that the bishop would be as shocked as he was, and possibly even insist that she change everything back. He didn't know how they could do that before the play the next evening, but maybe if everyone pitched in.

"*Ya*, we talked about that. Very cute idea."

"Cute?"

Amos looked at him, quizzically, then broke into a smile. "Sometimes I forget how much you hate change, Caleb."

"We're Amish. Change is what we work against."

"I can see how you'd feel that way." Amos combed

his fingers through his beard. "That's not completely accurate, though. All things change. Think of how early Christians often had to worship hidden away in back rooms. We no longer need to do that. We are free to worship as we please."

"What does that have to do with the children's school play?"

"I'm only making the point that all change isn't bad. It's unfettered change that we avoid. Rachel came to me and asked about the changes in the script before she presented them to the children."

"She did? Why would you approve it?"

"It's a small change, Caleb. You'll see. Instead of being a bee holding up a shield with a word on it, they're cats and they hold up slate boards with their words chalked on it. The entire thing is quite clever."

Caleb allowed his head to sink into his hands.

This was a nightmare. The bishop might not see it yet—no one ever said that bishops were perfect—but when the parents found out what their children were doing, Amos would understand that Rachel had made a huge mistake.

At that moment, the group of smaller cats began to recite their lines:

Cats follow, oh, this is true.
But cats can make good things, too.
And that, today, is what we have for you.

At which point, one cat fell into another, knocking each other over and creating a domino effect down the line. All of the children, or rather cats, were laughing and meowing as they clamored to their feet. The falling down was a clever ruse to pick up their slates.

Caleb stared around the room as the children recited, "Be reverent, in spirit low, at the manger lowly. Be generous, be thoughtful." One cat tapped another on the head when he said "thoughtful."

"See?" Amos said. "Same words, same meaning and celebration, only presented a little differently."

Different ought to be Rachel's middle name.

For all he knew, it was.

Rachel's head was pounding as she pulled on her coat and followed the last child out of the schoolhouse. Caleb was waiting in the buggy. He had at least turned the heater on so that she wasn't chilled quite to the bone, but he still had his customary grimace in place. Hadn't he been laughing this morning at breakfast? How was she able to irritate him so thoroughly and so completely in such a short amount of time?

The clouds seemed to press in around them and the snow fell relentlessly. She tried to remember what spring felt like, but then remembering wasn't exactly her strong suit lately.

They'd driven the short distance down the road and pulled into the lane to home. Suddenly she couldn't abide his sulky silence any longer.

"What have I done now?"

"I have no idea what you're talking about."

"Of course you do. You're glaring, and if you pull that hat down any harder over your head, you're going to bruise your scalp."

"All right. Since you asked…"

"I did."

"Why do you have to change everything?"

"Excuse me?"

"Why are Christmas Bees not good enough for you? Why couldn't the children cut out snowflakes for decorations? Why did you have to change it to cats?"

"Oh, Caleb…"

"Not an answer." They'd made it to the barn. He still held the reins, and Stormy waited patiently for him to jump down and open the barn door. Instead Caleb turned to look at her. "I honestly want to know."

"The children were dragging their feet, giving Martha a hard time, not wanting to participate. I don't know why. Some years… I think some years are like that."

"Which is why they're paying you to help her."

"And I did. So I changed up a few things. Now the children are excited, in case you didn't notice, and participating happily."

"Why can't they be happy with the old ways?"

"They are. They're not asking to sit on Santa's lap or put a Christmas tree in the schoolhouse."

"There is that to be thankful for."

Rachel tied the strings of her outer bonnet, picked up her school bag and purse, and reached for the door handle of the buggy. "You know, Caleb, I did check with Amos before I made any changes. I didn't know that I had to run everything by you, as well."

And then she fled into the house.

Inside was warm and cozy, and Ida met her with a hug and a smile, pushing a hot mug of tea into her hands. But for once tea didn't work. Rachel admitted to having a headache and fled to her room, where she spent the next ten minutes having a good cry. Not a very mature thing to do, but it certainly helped her to feel better.

She avoided speaking to Caleb the rest of the evening. The next morning she left early, insisting that she could walk the short distance to school. She came home only long enough to make a sandwich for dinner and change clothes. Then she returned to the schoolhouse, promising Ida that she'd see her there.

For some reason she wasn't a bit nervous about the play or the children or even the parents' reactions. But if she was honest, she longed for Caleb to approve of the work she'd done with the children.

She caught sight of him coming in the back door twenty minutes before the play was set to begin. The room was crowded with parents and older siblings and even a few *Englisch* neighbors. Generally everyone in an Amish community came to a schoolhouse Christmas celebration—whether they had children attending the school or not.

The Christmas program included stories, songs and, of course, the play. It was all a smashing success. The audience joined in singing a final carol, and then the students presented Martha with a gift box holding new pens, beautiful stationery, hand lotion and candles. It was obvious that every child there had a hand in contributing.

Nothing unexpected happened until Martha called up Rachel, and one of the youngest—a lad named Nathan—handed her a gift-wrapped book. "It's more poetry, because we know you like it," he said. The entire audience laughed at that as young Nathan screwed up his face when he said the word *poetry*. Rachel laughed along with them and thanked both the children and Martha for allowing her to help.

Bishop Amos had mentioned to her that Martha would like her to continue helping after the short Christmas break—like most Amish communities they took off only the day before, the day of and the day after Christmas. She supposed she would continue doing the job. The work was exhausting, but looking at the children she knew it was worth it.

Ida and John both gave her a hug and then said they were riding home with a neighbor, which seemed a bit odd to her. It also felt awkward. The last thing she wanted was to be alone with Caleb. She was surprised when he turned left out of the schoolhouse parking area instead of right.

"Have you bumped your head? Home is the other way."

"Thought maybe we'd celebrate."

"Celebrate?"

"Your play. It was very *gut*."

He glanced her way, grimaced and resettled his hat on his head. "Don't look at me so. I can admit to being wrong."

"You can?"

Now he laughed, and the sound caused the tension she'd been carrying since the day before to dissipate. "Rachel, I am sorry that I criticized your handling of the school play. Obviously you know more about children—and parents—than I do. Will you forgive me?"

A dozen memories passed through her mind then.

Caleb staring at her when she woke on Ida's couch.

Caleb standing in the door to the hospital room, looking at her as if she might perish before his eyes.

Caleb pulling her away from the snake.

Caleb attempting to protect her from a parrot and one very sweet old woman.

Those memories softened her heart and ministered to the hurting places from when he had criticized her rather harshly. But it was John's words that echoed in her mind and convinced her to accept his apology.

What was it he had said? *Sometimes that is all it takes...giving love a chance to grow.*

"That was a very nice apology."

"It was?"

"Indeed, and I do forgive you, Caleb."

"That's it?" He was smiling at her now. "I don't have to write sentences or read extra chapters?"

"Hmm... I hadn't thought about that. Maybe it would be a *gut* idea..."

He claimed her hand, pulled it toward him across the buggy seat. "I shouldn't be putting ideas in your head."

She tried to act as if it was normal for Caleb to be holding her hand. "Where are we going?"

"To celebrate your play—I said that already."

"And what is your idea of celebration?"

But she should have known he'd pick the ice-cream shop, which was open late on Fridays. Caleb loved ice cream. Of course, he chose vanilla, while she went for cherry pistachio. Their choices reflected their personalities, and maybe that was okay. Maybe it was fine that they didn't view life the same way. Maybe it took different points of view to make things work.

On the drive home, he pulled her across the seat and tucked the blanket around both of their laps. "Cold in here," he said gruffly, but his eyes said something more.

And when they'd pulled into the barn, instead of jumping out of the buggy, he turned toward her, placed his hands on both sides of her face and asked if it would be all right if he kissed her.

She nodded, unable to speak, unable to even think clearly, as she melted into the kiss.

Chapter Ten

Gabriel went into town with Caleb the next day. They were standing in line waiting to order food when he slapped Caleb on the shoulder. "Don't look so glum. So you love her?"

"I do. I love her. Don't ask me how I know that after only one kiss, but, well… I've been fighting these feelings for a while."

"It's a *gut* thing."

"It is?"

"Indeed. Trust me on this, I know."

"But what…?" Caleb's mind was spinning. He was in love with Rachel. When had that happened? How had it happened? And the worst fear of all—what would he do if she didn't feel the same?

They placed their orders and found a table.

"You know what the old folks say." Gabriel leaned forward as if he was about to share a priceless nugget of wisdom. "No dream comes true until you wake up and go to work."

"I don't think that proverb is referring to love and marriage."

"Could be, though."

"I don't see how."

"Ask her. Then you'll know how she feels."

The girl at the counter called their names, indicating their orders were ready. "I'll get that," Gabriel said.

Caleb nodded and sat there, staring at a copy of *The Budget* that had been left on the table. He pulled it toward him, barely seeing the printed words, and turned the page more out of habit than any real need to read.

He loved Rachel.

How could he not have realized that before?

How could he have been so blind?

He turned the page again and glanced up at Gabriel, who was thanking the woman at the counter and carrying the tray of coffee and sweets toward their table. He looked down at the newspaper again, seeing but not seeing it, and then his vision cleared. Words danced across his vision. *Young woman missing, age twenty-five, brown hair and freckles.*

With his pulse thrumming so loudly that it felt as if his ears were clogged, he pulled the paper closer and began to read.

It had become a habit to read *The Budget* and check for news of Rachel. At first he'd done it in the hopes that she could be returned home, like a parcel that had been left at the wrong house. Then he'd done it because he knew how much it meant to her—to find her family again. And now? Now he read the words with fear coursing through his heart.

Deborah and Clarence Yoder of Goshen, Indiana, have asked for help in locating their daughter, Rachel, who has been missing since Friday,

November 30. Rachel was last seen walking home
from the neighborhood schoolhouse, where she
has been an apprentice teacher for the past several months.

The Yoders explained that they did not file a miss-
ing-persons report, believing that Rachel might have
traveled to a neighboring community to see extended
family. As the weeks had passed, and Rachel had not
been in contact, they'd become more concerned.

Rachel was described as five foot six inches, with
brown hair, brown eyes, a smattering of freckles and a
slender build. She recently celebrated her twenty-fifth
birthday. Anyone with information was told to contact
the Yoders at the phone-shack number listed at the end
of the article.

"Anything interesting in there?" Gabriel set the tray
down on the table and plopped into the booth across
from him. "Say, you look like you've read your own
obituary."

Caleb stared down at the article in *The Budget*. He
couldn't believe what he was seeing. Why now? What
were the odds that today of all days he would find the
one thing he'd spent weeks looking for? Printed in
black-and-white were the words that he'd both longed
for and dreaded seeing.

Ignoring Gabriel, he pulled the paper closer and read
the piece again, then he pushed it toward his best friend.

Gabriel let out a long, low whistle as he crammed a
sticky bun into his mouth. He read the article between
gulps of coffee and finally tossed the paper back toward Caleb. Hoping he had misread or imagined the
entire thing, Caleb read the words a third time. When

he noticed his hands shaking, he dropped the paper onto the table.

Gabriel sat staring at him, waiting. Finally, he crossed his arms on the table and leaned forward. Lowering his voice, he asked, "Do you think it's her?"

"Sounds like it."

"Can't be sure."

"Until we call the number."

"Or let Rachel call the number." Gabriel nudged Caleb's blueberry muffin and coffee toward him. "Eat. You look like you're going to be sick."

Could this be his Rachel? It had to be. Didn't it?

"Maybe it's not her."

"It's her." Caleb was clutching his coffee mug so hard that his knuckles had turned white. He took a swallow, hoping the caffeine would wake him up, prove that this was all just a bad dream. "The article says that this girl—this Rachel—went missing on Friday."

"And you found our Rachel on Monday."

"So where would she have been from Friday to Monday?"

Glancing around the coffee shop, he realized the answer to that question didn't matter. None of his questions were important. The only question that mattered was whether the Rachel that belonged to the Yoders and the one living in his parents' home were the same.

But then he noticed the fourth paragraph, which he'd overlooked before.

Rachel was believed to have been wearing a dark gray coat, a blue scarf, and she might have been carrying a small book of poetry.

His heart sank. He tore the article out of the paper, folded it, stuffed it into his pocket and then took another sip of the coffee. It tasted bitter, and he pushed the mug away. "I have to tell her."

"Technically you don't have to…"

Caleb pierced him with a glare.

"But you should."

"Of course I should. I love her, as you so astutely pointed out, and love doesn't keep secrets." Already he'd accepted his feelings for Rachel. After fighting them for the past three weeks, it seemed ridiculous to continue doing so. If he didn't care about her, this news wouldn't hurt so badly.

"Listen, Caleb…" Gabriel waited until Caleb met his gaze. "This doesn't mean it's the end. It only means that you're turning a corner, beginning a new chapter, walking into a fresh start."

It was with those apt analogies ringing in his ears that Caleb stood, tossed his uneaten muffin in the trash, set the coffee cup in the to-be-washed tray and headed out into a cold and blustery December afternoon.

Rachel was hard at work finishing Caleb's sweater. Since she'd discovered that she could knit—in fact, had a real talent for it—she'd moved at lightning speed making mittens and a scarf for Ida and a hat for John. All that was left was to complete Caleb's sweater. She'd fussed over which yarn to buy but settled for a variegated gray—something conservative enough that he should approve of it.

Unlike the dress she'd been wearing when he'd first found her.

That thought brought a smile to her lips.

She'd considered him to be so arrogant and stuffy—more traditional than the old men who sat in the back on Sundays and gave pointed looks to the *youngies*. Caleb wasn't like that, though. It was only that he cared deeply and worried about the future of his community—she'd learned those things for certain when he'd confronted her at the schoolhouse. The memory sent a river of warmth through her. Had he actually kissed her? What did it mean, if anything? And when were they going to talk about it, or was he going to pretend it had never happened?

But it had happened, and she understood that he'd crept around her defenses and was laying claim to her heart. At least that was how it felt. But how could she ever fall in love when she didn't even know who she was? Correction, she knew who she was now, but she didn't know who she had been. There was a difference.

"Your needles are a blur over there." Ida plopped down across from her at the table and pulled out her crochet work.

"Remember when I tried crocheting?"

"You worked that yarn into the biggest knot I had seen in quite some time."

"I couldn't get the stitches right, couldn't figure out how to hold the needle. It all felt so...wrong."

"Obviously you were a knitter before."

"And still am."

"Indeed."

A comfortable silence fell between them. It occurred to Rachel that although she'd longed to be home by Christmas, to at least know where home was, she was grateful to have this place with people who cared about her until the Lord saw fit to restore her memory.

Thinking of the Wittmer family caused her mind to drift back again to Caleb and the way he'd looked at her the night before and the kiss. It was only a kiss. She was acting like a *youngie*. She was acting starstruck and moony, when in fact she was a grown woman.

She was about to bring up the subject of beaus and kisses and love—Ida seemed to have a pretty level head regarding just about any subject—when Caleb burst through the back door.

Rachel was facing him, so she saw him skid to a stop, his mouth open as if he was about to speak. But then he snapped it shut again after he'd glanced at his *mamm*.

Ida looked over her shoulder. "Caleb. You're home."

"*Ya.* I'm home." He moved toward the coffeepot, which happened to be on the portion of kitchen counter directly behind Ida. Eyebrows arched, mouthing something Rachel couldn't understand, he motioned with his arms. He looked for all the world as if he was playing some bizarre game of charades, but she had no idea what he was trying to say. She shook her head and started to laugh.

"Am I missing something?" Ida asked, not bothering to look up from her project—which, if Rachel wasn't mistaken, was a pair of blue mittens that would match her own scarf very well.

"Only Caleb trying to tell me some secret apparently."

Caleb shook his head from side to side and held a finger up to his lips to silence her.

"Oops."

"Oops?" Ida was smiling now.

"I think it must be a Christmas secret."

"*Ya*, that's exactly what it is." Caleb clomped around the table, took the knitting from Rachel's hands and pulled her to her feet. "Maybe you could get your coat and walk with me to the barn."

"The barn, huh? Must be a pretty big secret."

"*Mamm*, we need to go on a Christmas errand. We might be gone for an hour."

"You two have fun. I have a few Christmas surprises of my own to tend to."

But Rachel's smile faded as Caleb pulled her across the yard and to the still-harnessed horse.

"Get in."

"The buggy?"

"*Ya.*"

"This isn't about Christmas?"

"*Nein.*"

Suddenly her feet wouldn't move. She felt as if cold fingers had gripped her neck. Caleb opened the door and put his hand on her elbow. His expression was somber, pained almost. What had happened in the last few hours? What could it be that he wouldn't share with his own mother?

The frigid December wind seemed to whip right through her coat, but being warm wasn't her biggest concern.

"Tell me," she whispered as she climbed up into the buggy.

He leaned forward and kissed her once—briefly, softly, and then he shut the door, jogged around the buggy and hopped in. His eyes met hers and Rachel felt as if she was falling, as if Caleb was all that stood between her and some giant wave about to sweep over them.

He pulled a page torn from *The Budget* out of his pocket. It had been folded several times, and he set it gently in her lap, pointing to an article midway down the page. As she picked up the paper, he fidgeted with the small heater in the buggy, cranking it all the way up.

"I don't understand." She stared down at the paper, trying to focus on a single line of print.

"It's your family—your real family. I think I found them."

She read the article once and then again. By the time she'd finished it the second time, tears stung her eyes and her throat felt as if it had closed up completely. She shook her head, noticed that Caleb had directed the horse away from the barn and they were moving down the lane.

"How did you find this?"

"I've been looking."

She closed her eyes and tried to settle her emotions. Caleb's hand on hers brought her back into the moment.

"At first I studied *The Budget* every night."

"You were that eager to be rid of me?"

"I thought it was what you wanted—to go home."

"It was what I wanted, and I've been watching, too..." She glanced back down at the article, noted the date at the top of the page. "This is today's paper—I haven't seen it yet."

"Then later, I suppose I continued looking in spite of how I felt."

"How you felt?"

"I was convinced that you couldn't be happy here, and that the single thing that would bring you happiness was to know where you came from, to find your old life. And who could blame you? Of course you want to be reunited with your family."

She nodded, trying to find words to express the conflicting emotions weighing on her heart—trying and failing.

He pulled into the small parking area next to the phone shack, but instead of getting out, he turned toward her and covered both of her hands with his.

"You're shaking."

"Am I?"

"Rachel, whether this is your family or not, you know you have a place here."

She didn't know what to say to that, so she leaned forward and kissed his cheek. He offered to wait in the buggy. "*Nein.* Come with me, please. I'd like you…to be with me."

It was a typical phone shack, three feet by three feet, with a counter running along one wall. On top of that counter was a push-button phone, a recording machine, a pad of paper, a pen and, of course, a jar to put your money in. A hand-printed sign read Calls Now Fifty Cents.

Caleb fetched the coins from his pocket and deposited them in the jar.

Rachel's hands were shaking too badly to punch in the number listed in the article, so Caleb did it for her. He again offered to step outside, to give her some privacy, but she pulled him back next to her and clutched his hand as the line on the other end began to ring.

A man answered on the fifth ring, and Rachel began to cry, tears running down her face like raindrops against a windowpane. "Ethan? Ethan, is that you?"

"Rachel?"

"*Ya. Ya*, it's me."

And then she collapsed onto the stool, the phone slipping to the counter as she covered her face with her hands and began to weep.

She was aware of Caleb picking up the phone, speaking to her brother, and then he said, "*Ya.* We'll call back in ten minutes. Go and get them. *Nein.* We'll wait. We'll wait right here."

It was perhaps the longest ten minutes of her life.

Caleb put his arms around her, held her until her shivering stopped, then thumbed the tears from her cheeks.

"It's really them?" His voice was grave, and Rachel realized for the first time the effect this turn of events must be having on him.

"*Ya.* It is. That was—that was Ethan."

"Your *bruder* who was bit by the snake."

She nodded. "He's my older *bruder.* Always acted as if he had to look out for me."

"So you're remembering?"

"Some. Not everything." But suddenly she did remember… Ethan as well as her sisters—Clara and Becca and Miriam. She remembered, and she missed them so much that it felt as if her heart would burst.

"It's been ten minutes. Are you ready?"

"*Ya.* As ready as I can be."

She clutched Caleb's left hand as he punched the number in with his right, and then she was hearing her mother and father on the line and all of the fear and loss and grief melted into nothing, like snow disappearing on a sunny day.

She'd found her family.

She was going home.

Caleb felt drained as they walked out of the phone shack and toward the buggy. The day had been saturated in emotion—disbelief, realization, love and now gratefulness and joy, and beneath all of that a little fear. Only hours before, he had realized that he loved Rachel, but he couldn't ask her to stay. He understood then that he'd made up a story in his head—something along the lines of Rachel not wanting to go home, of her amnesia being the result of an unhappy home life there.

But what he'd just witnessed was the opposite of that.

He knew, without a doubt, that Rachel loved her family and that they loved her.

He knew that she was going home.

"They wanted to come and get me, to hire a driver to bring them down here and then carry us all back."

"Nearly five hours, if I remember correctly. I've only been through Goshen a time or two."

"I couldn't let them do that." She hugged her arms around herself, pulling her coat more tightly. "And tomorrow is Sunday. We don't travel on Sunday unless it's an emergency."

"Rachel—"

"It's okay. Really. Just knowing that they're there, waiting for me, that's what matters. I can take a bus on Monday."

"Christmas Eve."

"Ya."

The snow had begun to fall again, leaving a fine layer on the top of her shoulders, on the borrowed coat. Night was coming, and in the remaining light he could just make out her expression—relief and joy and wistfulness.

He wanted to remember her this way, standing in the light snow, standing as if she was inside an *Englisch* snow globe. The snow falling, her cheeks rosy, her eyes studying him. It would have been a beautiful December evening, except for the breaking of his heart in two.

"Do you think I can get a bus ride on Christmas Eve? I told them I would, but do you think that will be possible? Tomorrow is the beginning of the holiday for most businesses. Do you think they'll be running?"

"Sure and certain." He attempted a confident smile as he helped her into the buggy. Once he joined her, he picked up the conversation where they'd left it. "Lots of folks going home for Christmas. The bus will leave at six o'clock Monday morning, like it always does. We should be able to—"

"We?" Her eyes widened and her mouth gaped open.

"You don't think I'm just going to put you on a bus, send you on your way and leave you in the hands of a bunch of strangers."

"I'm a grown woman, Caleb Wittmer."

"That you are," he mumbled. Forcing a smile, he said, "Rachel—"

"Yoder. My name is Rachel Yoder." It was as if she'd discovered the cure for the common cold. She clasped her hands over her mouth in what seemed like disbelief. "No wonder the bishop couldn't find who I was. Must be hundreds of Yoders in Indiana."

"Thousands."

"Tens of thousands." They both smiled at the exaggeration, but it helped to ease the tension between them.

"What I meant to say was, Rachel Yoder, if you would allow me, I'd be happy to accompany you to Goshen."

She was shaking her head before he finished. "I can't let you do that."

"Let me?"

"If you went with me on Monday, you wouldn't get back home until Christmas Day or possibly the day after. I can't let you leave your family. You're—you're all they have."

"You know my *mamm* and *dat* pretty well by now. Do you really think they'd want me to send you off on the bus all alone? You don't even have all of your memories back yet."

"My memories are returning, though. Slowly they are returning."

Caleb almost told her then—how he felt, how they should be together, that he wanted to spend the rest of his life with her. But the smile on her lips as she said those words—*slowly they are returning*—told him what he needed to know. Rachel wanted to be with her family. It would be wrong for him to stand in the way of that.

He was happy before he met Rachel, surely he could find that contentment again. Couldn't he?

Caleb plastered on a smile, called out to Stormy and set them trotting toward home. He'd do the right thing. He'd see her home, and then he'd bury any feelings that he had for her.

He was a little concerned about how he would break the news to his *mamm* and *dat*, but he needn't have worried. Rachel walked in the front door and practically flew into Ida's arms, tears running down her face as she told her about the news article and the phone call and her family. Ida assured her that everything would be fine, and John patted her on the shoulder.

For a moment everyone was talking and saying things like "*Gotte* is *gut*" and "we knew they'd find you" and "just in time for Christmas."

They all sat, and Caleb explained how he'd seen the

article while he was with Gabriel, how he didn't want
to raise anyone's hopes, so he'd made up the story about
a Christmas errand.

"It was a Christmas errand of sorts," his *dat* pointed
out.

Ida pulled Rachel into the kitchen, set her at the table
and put on a kettle to boil.

"Your *mamm*, she thinks a mug of hot tea can solve
just about everything." His father had been sitting by
the giant potbelly stove that warmed the sitting room
and kitchen. Now he stood, fed the fire another log and
turned to study his son.

"Answered prayers can be difficult things."

"I suppose."

"Have you told her?"

"Told her what?"

"That you care for her."

"Why does it seem that everyone knew how I felt
before I did?"

"It was pretty plain to those of us who love you."
John sat down and picked up the object he'd been whittling on.

"Is that an alpaca?"

"It is."

"We have the real thing just outside the door."

"Ah, but Rachel doesn't, and she seems to have taken
a liking to them."

"So you were preparing for her to leave, before we
even saw the news article."

"She was never ours to have." His *dat* peered over
the reading glasses he wore whenever he worked on his
small wood projects.

Caleb sank onto the couch, his eyes focused on the

blazing fire, his heart somewhere else entirely. "I have no idea what to do."

"If you want good advice, consult an old man."

"Things were different for you, when you were courting *Mamm*. It was a simpler time."

"You think so?"

"Wasn't it?"

"Your mother, her people are over in Ohio…"

"I'm aware."

"I'd gone to work on a mission project in the area, after a tornado had passed through."

Caleb sat up straighter. "You never told me that."

"You never asked."

"How could I have when I didn't know—"

"Your *mamm*, she was, she is the baby of the family. Everyone else had moved off. I didn't think she'd want to leave her parents. She felt…responsible for them, I guess."

"But you asked her."

"I did. I was afraid to, like you're afraid now. I told myself it would be better if she didn't know how I felt, but your *mamm* already knew. She only needed to hear it from me."

"And she agreed to come here—to Indiana."

"*Ya*—eventually she did."

"What of her parents?"

"They moved to Maine, where one of her *bruders* had settled with his family."

"I don't remember any of this."

"They died somewhat young, at least it seems that way to me now. Funny how our idea of old age changes the more years we tack on. But they were happy there. And your *mamm*? I believe she's been happy here."

Caleb could lean forward and just see Rachel and his *mamm* sitting at the table. Both were cradling mugs of tea, the steam rising. Rachel seemed calmer. Perhaps his *mamm* was right. Maybe a mug of hot tea could cure many things—including homesickness and regret.

"I know the proper thing is to take her home, and I think it's best if I don't tell her how I feel. She's been through so much already. It would be wrong for me to add one more thing…"

"So you'd make her decision for her." His *dat* had stopped whittling and was watching him now, waiting.

"You think I should tell her."

"I've already said as much. Rachel's a grown woman, with a *gut* head on her shoulders and a big heart. Trust her, and while you're at it give *Gotte* a little credit, that He didn't lead you down this road for no reason. Believe that He has a purpose and a plan."

The evening passed quickly—what Caleb thought of as their last night together. It wasn't. They still had Sunday, but he couldn't help thinking that he wouldn't see her again, that he'd miss her. They exchanged gifts with Rachel. Her cheeks were flushed, and she continually glanced his way. When she handed him a half-finished sweater, he acted as if he was going to slip it on over his clothes.

"*Nein.* You can't wear it until it's done."

"You mean it's not?" He held it up and studied it with one eye closed. "I thought maybe my arm went here," he said, pointing to a hole.

"Give it back." She attempted to pull it away from him as she laughed and blushed.

"So you're going to finish it?"

"I am."

He rubbed his chin and said, "I suppose you could mail it to me."

Suddenly the levity between them vanished, as they all remembered anew that this was their last weekend together.

His *mamm* jumped up to pull a freshly baked peach pie from the oven. His *dat* pretended he needed to add wood to the blazing fire.

"How about a game of checkers?" Caleb asked gruffly.

"I beat you the last three times."

"Which doesn't mean you'll do so again."

He told himself to treasure the memories they were making, but in his heart he kept hearing the echoes of his father's words.

Rachel's a grown woman, with a gut *head on her shoulders and a big heart.*

Trust her.

Give Gotte *a little credit.*

Believe that He has a purpose and a plan.

His *dat* was spot on, as was usually the case. The question was what he planned to do about it.

Chapter Eleven

Rachel had thought the next day would be difficult. They had a quick breakfast and then bundled up to ride together to church—the second service she'd attended with Caleb and his family. This time was completely different. It seemed the Amish grapevine had been hard at work. Everyone had heard the good news about Rachel. The women hugged her or gave her a pat on the arm. The men nodded and smiled as if their own daughter had been found. It seemed natural at lunch to sit with Beth and Gabriel and baby Simon and Caleb.

"I'm going to miss you all," she admitted.

Gabriel darted a glance at Caleb and then he said, "There won't be anyone here to give Caleb a hard time with Christmas plays or inappropriately blue dresses."

"He told you about that?"

Gabriel laughed when Caleb tried to hit him with a roll. He caught it and stuffed half of it in his mouth.

Beth seemed to understand the feelings Rachel was wrestling with. "You can come back in the spring, for the shearing of the alpacas."

She glanced at Caleb, who looked as if he was holding his breath.

"*Ya.* I'd like that."

He reached for her hand under the table, interlaced his fingers with hers. And for a moment she believed that everything was going to be all right. The day passed in a blur of moments that she vowed to hold on to, memories that she hoped would last her until spring.

The next morning, she was worried that goodbyes would be difficult, but it seemed that Rachel had cried herself dry the evening before. All that was left was a dull ache as she realized how much she would miss Ida and John and even the alpacas.

She promised to write.

Ida blinked back her tears, and John continually cleared his throat. By the time Rachel and Caleb boarded the bus, the snow had begun to fall again.

"The bus driver assured me the weather won't slow us down," Caleb said. "In case you were worried."

"I wasn't."

"At least we have plenty of room."

There were only about ten passengers on the bus, but still they'd chosen to sit next to each other. What good was having your own row to stretch out in? Rachel didn't want extra space. She wanted to be with Caleb. But how could she be with him and still be reunited with her family? And what if…what if he didn't even care for her as she did for him?

Did she love Caleb Wittmer?

Could a person fall in love in such a short time?

But then their time together hadn't been ordinary in any way. From the moment she'd opened her eyes in his home and looked up into his face, she'd felt as if she'd been living a fairy tale that was both terrible and wonderful beyond her wildest dreams.

"Nervous about seeing your family?"

"*Nein.* I'm… The thing is that I'm remembering more."

"That's *gut*, right?"

"It is." As the bus pulled out of Montgomery, she told Caleb about her older brother, how they had all doted on him, since he was the only boy in a home with four young girls.

"I suppose he's married."

"He's not, actually. There was an incident with a girl—she left our Amish community to attend an *Englisch* college. It broke Ethan's heart, and he wasn't ready to try again."

"Sounds as if you care for him."

"Very much. He's a hard worker, and a *gut* man. A real blessing to my parents."

"And your *schweschdern*?"

"Miriam is the oldest." She stared out the window, wondering what all she had missed in the last three weeks. Was that how long it had been? Seemed longer. Seemed like a lifetime. "She's expecting, in the spring, I think."

"You'll be an *aenti*."

Rachel smiled at that thought. She could see her sister now, the way her pregnancy had just started to show. Why was it that her memories that had stayed locked away for so long were now washing over her like waves?

"You'll like Clara and Becca. They're younger, but *gut* girls. Clara is the baby of the family—she's nine. She loves to work outside with the animals, especially the goats. One time…" Rachel realized that Caleb had pulled away from her, was rubbing at the middle of his forehead. "Are you feeling ill?"

"Nein."

"Wishing you hadn't—"

"It's nothing like that." He pulled in a deep breath and then slowly released it. "This is where I want to be, Rachel—with you. When you started talking about your family, I realized I hadn't really thought about meeting them."

"You weren't going to simply leave me at the bus station, were you?"

"Your parents said they'd be there to meet you."

"So we wave goodbye and then you start right back home?"

"Not exactly."

"Do they even have another bus going south later today?"

"I don't know." He reached for her hand, intertwined their fingers. "I simply hadn't thought it through."

"You'll be staying the night, Caleb Wittmer, with my family. You can sleep in Ethan's room. There's an extra bed."

"Are you sure I won't be a burden?"

"There's always room for one more in an Amish home."

"I suppose."

"You can go home tomorrow, and be back in time to have Christmas dinner with your parents."

He nodded as if what she said made sense. Rachel sensed a wariness in his eyes, though. Perhaps he was ready to be rid of her, but then she looked down at her hand clasped in his and knew that wasn't true. So why was Caleb nervous about meeting her family? And what could she do to put his mind at ease?

She never expected to fall asleep, but the next thing she knew she was dreaming about playing in a creek—splashing water and throwing a ball as a large dog swam after it.

"We have a Labrador."

"What?" Caleb had been reading the book on alpacas that he'd borrowed from the library. He snapped it shut and adjusted his back against the window so that he could study her.

"A Labrador. She's white and loves to swim." Rachel shook her head, trying to rid herself of the cobwebs. "I think her name is Biscuit."

"Anything else? Anything about...what happened to you?"

"*Nein.* Nothing." She pulled out her knitting to continue working on Caleb's sweater. But she couldn't focus, couldn't remember if she was supposed to knit or purl. Afraid she would mess it up, she set aside the project and began rooting around in the bag that Ida had sent. She pulled out the thermos and a Tupperware container full of peanut-butter squares. As she was passing the snack to Caleb, she looked out the window and saw a large truck pass.

"I rode in one of those."

"That? An eighteen-wheeler?"

"*Ya.* I—I..." Suddenly her throat was dry and her heart was racing. She tried to focus on her breathing, as the counselor had told her. *Don't force the memories, Rachel. Breath and relax, and eventually you will remember the things you've forgotten.*

"Are you okay?"

Caleb's voice sounded as if it was coming to her down a long tunnel. She pushed the container of sweets into his lap and ducked her head between her knees.

"Uh-oh. Are you going to be sick? Should I ask the driver to pull over?"

She shook her head, realized he couldn't see that and forced herself to sit back up. "*Nein.* I was just a little…*narrisch.*"

"Maybe you need to eat." He handed her a peanut-butter bar and unscrewed the cap on the thermos.

She didn't think eating would help, but the worried look on his face was more than she could bear, so she nibbled at the cookie and took a sip of the coffee, then watched another large truck trundle by.

"I remember climbing up into it."

"The truck?"

"*Ya.* I was walking down…down a road, and it was very dark. There was a lot of traffic, and I didn't know…didn't know what to do." The nausea threatened to overwhelm her again, but she breathed deeply and pushed through the memory. What she was remembering wasn't happening to her now. It couldn't hurt her. "I had ridden in a car before that, but then…they were nearly to their destination and so they let me out."

"On the side of the road?"

"*Nein.* A station—a gas station, I guess. It was late, and I didn't want to admit that I was lost." The fear had been nearly paralyzing. She remembered that clearly. How her legs had been shaking, and she'd hopped from the passenger van, assuring the man and woman that she would be fine. "I didn't know what to do, didn't know where I was, and no other cars came, so I started walking…down the highway."

"That must have been terrifying."

"The trucker pulled over on the side of the road, and at first I thought to run, but it had begun to snow, and I was shivering…"

"Do you remember anything about him?"

"Only that he was an older man, a *grossdaddi*. He had pictures of his *grandkinner* tucked up on the dash. I remember thinking he couldn't be bad because of those pictures."

Caleb placed another peanut-butter bar in her hands. She looked down, surprised to find she'd eaten the first. And the nausea? It seemed to be receding.

"Did you maybe leave your coat in the truck?"

"The bathroom." Rachel shook her head, surprised that she could see the truck and the van and the bathroom so clearly. "I took it off in the gas station's bathroom so I could wash my hands. Even took off my *kapp* and bonnet so I could attempt to rebraid my hair. I left them both there, across the top of the stall door."

"And walked out into the cold."

"Didn't even realize it until I was down the road, and then it seemed too far to go back. I remember thinking that if I just kept walking I'd see something I recognized."

"But you didn't."

"We went through a large city… I remember the maze of freeways."

"Indianapolis."

"And then we crossed some farmland, and I looked out and saw… I must have seen an Amish barn, or something that looked familiar. I remember telling the old guy that he could just let me out there. He didn't want to. He kept asking me if I was sure."

"You were in Montgomery then."

"*Ya.* I think so."

They sat silently, Rachel marveling at all that had happened, how she had ended up on Caleb's road—lost and confused. He must have been thinking the same thing, because he leaned forward and rested his forehead against the back of the seat in front of them.

"What are you thinking?" she asked.

"Something that has occurred to me before—that if I hadn't been fixing that portion of fence at the exact moment you stumbled by, that you might have died that night."

"But you were, Caleb." She waited until he glanced over at her. "I don't know what happened, why I was wandering around lost, but I do know—beyond a shadow of a doubt—that *Gotte* was watching out for me, and that His plan for me? It was you."

His plan for me? It was you.

Rachel's words echoed through Caleb's mind as they continued their ride northeast. She knitted as they navigated the freeways of Indianapolis, and then she asked to trade seats as they entered the farming country of northern Indiana. Her nose pressed to the window, she looked like a small child, watching for home.

But Caleb knew she was watching for more clues to her past.

When they entered Nappanee, she began pointing out things to him—Amish Acres and Burkholder Country Store and the Dutch Village Market. The town looked like something out of a postcard, with a light dusting of snow covering the cars and people scurrying about tending to their final Christmas errands—Amish and

Englisch alike, both preparing to celebrate the birth of Christ.

Something inside of Caleb relaxed in that moment. Something changed.

Watching an *Englisch* family pass an Amish one on the sidewalk, he realized that the differences were quite superficial—the way they dressed, the *Englisch* man pausing in front of a car while the Amish man continued two spaces down to a horse and buggy. Both were men spending a few hours in town with their families on a cold Christmas Eve day.

Who was he to say that the Amish folks were better than *Englisch*?

Or that conservative Amish was better than those communities that were a tad more progressive? He noticed the woman was wearing a bright blue dress, nearly the color of the one Rachel had been wearing that first day, the color he had found so inappropriate. Why had that mattered to him so much? Now that he knew Rachel, and he did believe that he knew her well, he understood that she was a *gut* woman. But he might have missed knowing that, or anything else about her, simply because he dismissed her out of hand over the color of the fabric of her dress.

Perhaps he had spent too much of his life determined to emphasize the differences between his community and others.

He'd done it for good reasons.

Fear that the Amish lifestyle might fade away.

Worry that if he had a family, it wouldn't be possible to raise children as he'd been raised.

Anxiety that their faith might become less important, and their ambition more so.

The answer to those concerns was prayer, not stubbornness. He could see that now as clearly as he could see the color that had blossomed in Rachel's cheeks. *Gotte* had prepared a path for her, and that path had included Caleb.

If his Heavenly Father could be trusted with this dear woman sitting beside him, with her care and welfare even at her most vulnerable moment, then Caleb could trust that He was looking out for their faith and community, as well.

"Why are you looking at me that way?" Rachel placed her hand on the top of her head. "My *kapp* falling off?"

"Nein."

"Color of my dress is okay, right?"

"Now you're giving me a hard time."

"I want to make sure I'm presentable." Her smile practically sparkled. "Am I?"

Caleb's heart filled with gratitude. He didn't know what their future held, but he did know that Rachel was going to be okay. "What did you ask me?"

"If I look presentable. If my dress is okay." She bumped her shoulder against his.

"It's fine—quite pretty."

"Why, thank you, Caleb Wittmer."

"You're welcome, Rachel Yoder."

Then they were pulling into the Goshen bus stop, where only one family stood waiting—one family, but three buggies. He could tell they were together because they were huddled in a group—men, women and *youngies*. It would seem that the entire family had come to welcome Rachel home.

The next few hours passed in a blur.

Caleb was introduced to Deborah and Clarence, Rachel's parents. Clarence was a tall man, tall and thin. He pumped Caleb's hand, thanking him repeatedly for bringing Rachel home. Deborah looked like an older version of Rachel, right down to the freckles. She pulled him into a hug and whispered, "*Gotte* bless you, Caleb. *Gotte* bless you for your kindness."

He said hello to Clara and Becca, but they looked so much alike that he couldn't remember who was who. Miriam was easy enough to pick out because of the fact that she was in at least her second trimester of pregnancy. Her husband, Clyde, stood holding his wife's hand and beaming at Rachel. It was obvious they had all been very worried, and now on Christmas Eve of all days, that worry had been taken away.

Ethan nodded toward the newest buggy and said, "Care to ride with me? I have to stop by a friend's and pick up one last Christmas gift. Unless you're too tired…"

"*Nein.* That sounds *gut.*" He suspected that as the eldest child Ethan had some questions for him, but instead he started their conversation by explaining what had occurred on their end.

Ethan told him how they'd first thought Rachel had simply left for the weekend, and then everyone became increasingly more worried when she didn't call or write.

"But we knew she carried that book of poetry everywhere, so I thought…"

"You're the one who wrote the article in *The Budget.*"

Ethan was a few years older than Caleb. He scratched at his clean-shaven jaw and shrugged. "I wrote something like it, gave it to our scribe. She cleaned it up and submitted it to the paper."

"Your parents never called the police?"

"*Nein.* They talked to them, but our local sheriff has been here a long time. He's aware that Amish *youngies* sometimes leave town with no word—there's less conflict that way."

"Does that happen a lot?" Caleb's old worries of the Amish way of life disintegrating popped back into his mind, but he refused to dwell on them. *Youngies* came and went. It was true in every community. He'd heard it was true among the *Englisch*, as well. It was a time of transition, and when faced with such a decision, some chose a different path.

"Not a lot, but some. Enough that our sheriff wouldn't take the case seriously until we had something else to suggest there had been foul play."

"When I found Rachel, she didn't remember anything—not her name or where she was from. She still struggles with some of the effects of the amnesia. Her memories—they're not all back yet."

"And your family took her in."

"If your *mamm* is anything like mine, you know that wasn't even a question. Of course we took her in."

Ethan pulled off his hat and resettled it on his head. The buggy was tolerably warm with a small heater in the front, and snow continued to fall lightly. But Ethan's mind obviously wasn't on the weather or even where he was going. Caleb could practically see him trying to piece together the time line of what had happened.

"You found her? In the snow? Was she hurt at all? Did she really not know where she was?"

Caleb couldn't blame him for questioning his story. What had that been like, to have your sister simply vanish?

"Yes, yes, not at all and no—she didn't even know her name, let alone where she was."

Ethan grunted, "It's what *Mamm* told us, what Rachel told her. Just so hard to believe."

"Trust me. It's something I won't forget no matter if I live to be a very old man—the sight of her weaving down the road, wearing no coat or *kapp* and then collapsing in the snow."

"You took her to the doctor?"

"We have a small hospital, really more of a medical clinic. The doctors there looked her over, made sure she wasn't hurt in any way."

"Other than losing her memory and nearly freezing."

"She also had a bump on the back of her head."

"What?"

"Maybe she forgot to mention that to your *mamm*. She had a big bump on the back of her head. She still doesn't remember how it happened, but that's what caused her memory loss."

"How did she end up so far from here?"

"She remembered a little of that on the way here." Caleb told him what Rachel had shared with him on the bus.

"You've been a *gut* friend to her."

Caleb almost corrected him, almost confessed his feelings for Rachel there and then, but they were pulling into an Amish home with a small sign out front that read Rugs For Sale. When they'd picked up the Christmas present Ethan had ordered, they turned back toward the Yoder home, stopping at the local grocer to buy three gallons of ice cream.

"I'd almost forgotten it's Christmas Eve," Caleb admitted.

"*Ya.* It is, but this…" Ethan patted the grocery bag on the seat. "This is a homecoming present. Rachel might not remember, but peppermint is her favorite ice cream."

They rode in silence the rest of the way home.

The house they pulled up to was much larger than the one Caleb had been raised in, but then the Yoders had five children, plus Miriam's husband and soon their child. Plainly, they were prepared for the family to keep expanding.

Ethan pulled the horse and buggy into the barn.

It was while they were removing the harness and stabling the horse that Caleb thought to ask Ethan something. "Did she have a beau?"

"Rachel?"

"*Ya.*" It occurred to him that there had been only family members waiting for them at the bus drop-off.

"*Nein.* Rachel was trying to find her way. She was struggling a bit. That's why, at first, we thought she'd simply needed some time to clear her head."

"Would that have been like her? To just…walk away? To tell no one?" It certainly didn't sound like the Rachel that he knew. But then, maybe she'd been a different person before.

"It wasn't like her at all. Look…" Ethan paused at the door to the barn before pushing out into the gathering dusk. "The week before? It had been hard on Rachel. I don't know how much she remembers, or if she'd even want me sharing the details with you, but we are grateful that she's home, that you and your family cared for her."

And then they were walking toward the house on a snowy Christmas Eve, Caleb shouldering more questions than ever.

* * *

Rachel's heart was so full of emotion that she felt like a balloon that had been overfilled and was about to burst.

That described exactly how she felt.

About to burst with happiness.

Her younger sisters sat on each side of her, as if they were afraid she might disappear again. Miriam kept smiling at her, one hand placed on her stomach, the other holding Clyde's hand. Her mother sat by her father, as he prepared to read the Christmas story. Ethan and Caleb rounded out their group. Each time she glanced around the room, one of them was watching her.

A conversation that she'd had with Ethan came back to her then. It had been the night before her accident, or whatever she'd had. They'd been in the barn together, and she'd been aggravated with everyone—her parents, her older sister, even the younger girls. They'd all grated on her nerves and she'd felt so suffocated, so out of place, that she'd said something to Ethan about it. His response had surprised her.

"Home is where you belong. It may not be where you always stay, but it's the place that fits—like an old shoe. It's why we keep returning to it over and again, no matter how old we become or how far away we move."

His words had only served to frustrate her more. He'd said them as if things were so clear, so simple, and she didn't think they were. He'd been right, though. She knew that now, knew it with a certainty that she couldn't have imagined then.

She cleared her throat and sat up straighter. "I know *Dat*'s about to read the story of the Baby Jesus. I know that's our tradition—what we've always done. I remember that much, even though a few days ago I didn't know my own last name."

Light laughter filtered through the group.

"We're glad you're here now."

"*Gotte* is *gut*."

"We thought you simply wanted to get out of chores for a few days."

She waited until they'd quieted down again, until she had their attention, because this was important, and she thought she could only get through it once.

"I still don't remember everything, don't remember how I lost my memory, though I remember being lost."

Now there were murmurs of sympathy and Becca on her right and Clara on her left reached for her hands.

"I do remember the night before." She waited for Ethan to look up, to nod slightly. "I was feeling out of sorts, as if everyone had a purpose in their life and understood what it was—everyone except me."

She stopped, her throat clogged with the tears she didn't want to shed.

Her *mamm* leaned forward and waited for her to meet her gaze. "We've all felt that way at times, dear."

"I understand that now, that what I was feeling was probably normal. At the time, I didn't, though. I went outside, hoping to clear my head, and made my way to the barn."

"Where you found me," Ethan said.

"And I asked you—I can remember this as clearly as if it were this afternoon—I asked you…"

"What if I never find where I belong." They said the words together and their eyes locked, as an understanding of that night and all that had transpired since passed between them.

Rachel glanced at Caleb, who was sitting forward now, listening intently.

"Ethan said, 'Home is where you belong.'" She swiped at the tears slipping down her face. "He said it as if it was a simple fact, like it's going to snow tomorrow or daylight will arrive at six thirty. He said it as if there was no doubt. But me? I had plenty of doubts."

Her *dat* stared down at the open Bible in his lap. When he looked up, a gentle smile eased the worry lines around his eyes. "We're so glad you're home, so grateful to Caleb and his family, and mostly thankful to *Gotte* that He watched over you."

"I know that now, *Dat*. I know that home, that here with you all, is exactly where I belong." She wanted to add "until *Gotte* has other plans," but suddenly everyone was talking at once, everyone except for Caleb, who was watching her as if she'd just said the one thing that could break his heart.

Chapter Twelve

Rachel woke Christmas morning to the smells that she'd known all her life—a fire in the stove downstairs, cedar sprigs placed throughout the house, cinnamon rolls in the oven, coffee percolating on the stove. She made her way downstairs and found her *mamm* sitting at the table.

"Gudemariye, Mamm."

"And to you, Rachel." She waited until Rachel had poured a mug of coffee and sat down across from her. "I want to explain to you why we didn't call the police…"

"You don't have to do that."

"I do, for me." She traced the rim of her mug with her thumb. "I was terrified, when you didn't come home that first night. I hope you never know that sort of fear, wondering where your child had gone, wondering what you could have done differently."

"I'm sorry that I put you through that."

"You remember nothing of the fight we had?"

"Nein." The word was a whisper, nothing more than a breath carried over an aching heart.

"You wanted to quit your job, your apprenticeship at the school."

"I was teaching?"

Her mother studied her a moment and finally nodded. "You had tried several jobs, but none of them suited you. Oh, they were fine jobs, as far as jobs go, but you weren't satisfied."

"I wanted more."

"You kept saying that it wasn't what you were meant to do, as if you had some destiny beyond being a *gut* wife and mother. I didn't understand that. Just as I didn't understand why you broke up with Samuel."

Rachel covered her mouth with her hand. "Samuel King. He was two years younger than me, and I thought… I thought he was a child."

Her *mamm* leaned forward, pulled Rachel's hands across the table and covered them with her own. "Sweetheart, I've had a lot of time to think since you've been gone, a lot of time to pray. I want to say I'm so sorry…"

"This wasn't your fault."

"I'm so sorry that I didn't attempt to understand what you were going through more."

"How could you?"

Her *mamm* stared into her eyes a moment, as if she was searching for something. Finally, she patted Rachel's hand, sat back and took another sip from her coffee. "Our life is simple—Plain. Our choices are few, and we like it that way. Only three dresses to choose from, only a few jobs, only a handful of beaus."

"I don't think a dozen beaus or job choices would have satisfied me at that point. I was…lost."

"And that's okay. *Gotte* had a plan for you, whether

we understood it or not. I'm just so grateful you're home."

Rachel didn't think her heart could hurt any more than it already did, but seeing her mother cry opened a whole new chasm inside of her. She hopped up, stumbled around the table and threw herself into her mother's arms.

That was how her *dat* and Ethan and Caleb found them as they stamped their feet in the mudroom and then plodded into the kitchen with Christmas greetings on their lips. Deborah and Rachel jumped up and began pulling together things for the family breakfast. It was traditional to keep it rather simple—some sweet rolls, milk for the youngsters, coffee for those who were older.

They'd have a family devotional, spend time considering the miracle of Christ's birth, and then later they'd have a big lunch with extended family. In the evening they would exchange gifts. But as her large family tumbled into the room and around the table, Rachel realized that the most precious moment of the holiday was occurring right then. She'd been reunited with her family. The rift that had existed between her and her mother—a rift that she hadn't been able to remember but knew in her heart was there—had been healed. The only thing to mar the near perfect morning was the fact that Caleb would be leaving before lunch, and she didn't know if she'd ever see him again.

Caleb rode in the back seat of the buggy, with Rachel on his left and both of her younger sisters on his right. Ethan was driving the buggy, and Miriam's husband, Clyde, was sitting next to him in the front seat. The entire family had wanted to see him off, but they'd decided to limit it to one buggy.

Caleb had wanted a moment alone with Rachel. He had to satisfy himself with being jostled against her as Clara and Becca prattled on about seeing their cousins, and how much snow they'd had, and presents that would be opened later that evening.

He'd about given up on the hope of speaking privately with Rachel, when they pulled up to the bus stop and Ethan said, "Rachel, we'll wait here if you'd like to walk with Caleb to get his ticket."

The girls fell into a chorus of "not fair" and "we want to go," but Clyde distracted them with a game of I Spy.

Rachel and Caleb walked to the store where tickets were usually sold, but taped on the window was a sign that read:

Closed for Christmas. If you're waiting for a bus, purchase your ticket from the driver.

"You don't have to wait," Caleb said.

"I want to."

"I bought you a Christmas present."

"You already gave me one."

"A skein of yarn? That wasn't your real gift."

"I love yarn."

"I have another for you, but I left it at home." Why had he done that? He'd known this would be goodbye.

"Your sweater...it's not finished yet."

"A fine pair we are." He reached for her hand, instantly feeling better when their fingers were laced together.

They huddled under the overhang of the building's roof, waiting on the bus that should arrive in the next ten minutes. Ten minutes. How was he supposed to tell her what was on his heart in so short a time? But then his watch ticked off another two minutes, and he knew that he had to try.

Rachel was talking about her family, apologizing for the chaos and her sisters and the fact that they weren't as traditional as he was used to.

"I don't care about any of that."

"Excuse me?"

"I need to tell you something, Rachel."

"You do?"

"But I don't want… I don't want you to answer me, not now." He reached out, tucked a wayward lock of hair into her *kapp* and allowed his fingers to linger on her cheek.

"I'm so fortunate that you found me."

"*Nein.* I'm the fortunate one. I love you, Rachel Yoder."

"You do?"

"I know our lives are very different."

"Not so different."

"And I live a long way from here."

"Only five hours."

"I know that you need time with your family, time to be home."

"I do?"

"You need time to remember, time to understand who you are and what you want in life."

"I want you." She seemed as surprised as he was at that confession.

Three of the sweetest words Caleb had ever heard, but he knew with complete certainty that now wasn't their time to make any big decisions. He heard the bus pulling into the parking area. Leaning closer, he kissed her once and then again. He pressed his forehead to hers, and then he said, "I'll write."

"You will?"

"And call."

"I'm going to miss you."

"I love you," he said again, aware that she hadn't said those words yet, that she wasn't ready yet. It confirmed that he was doing the right thing leaving her there, leaving her with her family. He kissed her once more, then pushed his hat down on his head and jogged toward the bus.

Rachel watched Caleb jog away and she wanted to sit down, put her head on her arms and weep. When her life was finally coming together, when things were finally starting to make sense, why did he have to leave?

Had he really said he loved her?

She walked back to the buggy in a daze.

Her little sisters had moved on from I Spy to playing finger games with pieces of yarn they both kept in their pockets. Clyde was looking out the window and saying that by this time next year he would be a father. But Ethan's gaze met hers, and she knew he knew.

Had Caleb spoken to him?

Or did she simply have a love-dazed look about her? Because she was in love with Caleb Wittmer. For the life of her, she couldn't think of why she hadn't told him, but she would. In time, she would.

The day passed in a flurry of family and celebration and gift giving. Though their holidays were dramatically scaled back as compared to *Englischers'* celebration, the fact that they had over twenty people in the house with her *aentis* and *onkels* and grandparents and cousins meant that there wasn't a quiet moment. And though she felt terrible that she had no gifts for anyone—she hadn't known she'd be back home and, in fact, she still had Caleb's sweater in her bag waiting to be finished—that didn't stop everyone from stacking gifts around her.

She received a new coat, gloves, mittens, an outdoor bonnet, a scarf and a small book of poetry. Her *mamm* gave her a basket overflowing with writing supplies— stationery, a new pen, envelopes and stamps. She kissed Rachel's cheek and whispered, "Maybe you can write to Caleb," which was what she thought about doing for the next hour. But she fell into bed without uncapping the pen, a whirlwind of emotions clouding her thoughts. She was exhausted, heartsick that Caleb was gone and tremendously happy to finally be home.

New Year's Day arrived with a blizzard that kept everyone inside. Rachel finally began writing Caleb. She had tried several times before that. Each night she'd sat in front of her little desk, pulled the paper toward her and stared at it.

What could she say to him that he didn't already know about her?

How could she describe her feelings?

When could she expect to see him again?

The questions swirled and collided in her mind until she would invariably push the paper away, climb into bed and huddle under the covers. She was still grateful to be home, but a malaise had settled over her feelings until it felt as if she was viewing everything from a distance. She constantly berated herself for feeling blue. She should feel grateful! Had she learned nothing from her time away from home? Yet no matter how much she told herself that she should feel happy, she often found herself on the verge of tears.

After she cleared the breakfast dishes, her *mamm* suggested she spend some time on the sun porch.

"It's still snowing."

"Not on the porch."

"I'll freeze."

"We put windows in years ago and a small butane heater. Remember?"

Rachel nodded, but in truth she didn't remember at all. There was much she still couldn't recall, though each day brought at least one new revelation about her past—she couldn't abide peas, she was the family's designated baker, she visited the local library at least once a week, she had a kitten named Stripes that slept in the office in the barn.

"There's a rocker and even a small desk there," her *mamm* continued. Rachel's younger sisters were playing jacks in the barn, Miriam had gone to her mother-in-law's for the week and Ethan and her *dat* were in the barn working on a table that they planned to sell at the next auction. Only Rachel and her *mamm* remained in the house. It was quiet and forced Rachel's thoughts to address questions she didn't have answers to. The entire thing made her want to go back upstairs, back to bed.

"You know, your *dat* built the porch for me because I sometimes suffer from winter blues, or seasonal depression, as the *Englisch* doctor calls it."

"I thought he built the porch for us kids."

"It was a *wunderbaar* place for you all to get a bit of sunshine when the weather kept us in for days on end, but *nein*, he built it for me."

"And did it help?"

"*Ya.* As a matter of fact it did."

"Do you think I'm depressed, *Mamm*?"

"I don't know. What do you think?"

"Maybe."

"How's your energy level?"

"Low to nonexistent. It's as if I have the flu, but I don't."

"Moody?"

"You know I am. You caught me crying when I spilled the flour on the floor yesterday."

"Problems sleeping?"

"I toss and turn a lot."

"Perhaps we should make an appointment with the doctor."

Rachel shrugged. "I'm still a little confused, a little lost, and I miss Caleb." She hesitated, not sure if she was ready to share her deepest fears yet.

Instead of pushing her to say more, her *mamm* went to the kitchen, brewed two mugs of hot tea and brought them back. That kindness reminded her of Ida and gave her the courage to speak her fears. "What if Caleb doesn't really care about me?"

"So you think he doesn't know his own mind?"

"What if those feelings arose out of the oddness of our situation? He saved a coatless girl who might have died in the snow. Maybe that's not love he feels. Maybe it's relief or surprise or merely affection."

"Have you written him yet? Have you asked Caleb these things?"

"*Nein.* I want to. I mean to, but then when I sit down… I don't know what to say."

"Say what's in your heart, dear."

So with her *mamm* claiming that it would be a lovely place to write a letter, Rachel found herself alone on the sun porch. The new pen and paper waited before her as snow billowed outside the window. She noticed the calendar on the wall, stood up and pulled it off the hook.

Scanning back through the months, she marveled at all that had happened. If she had known what she would endure, she might have hidden upstairs the entire year. But those trials had brought her Caleb, and she would never wish away the times they had shared. She carried the old calendar to the desk, opened the drawer and pulled out the new one that her father always picked up at the hardware store. Opening it, she saw a beautiful sunrise over fields laden with snow. Across the bottom was printed:

Hope smiles from the threshold of the year to come,
Whispering, "It will be happier."
Alfred Lord Tennyson

Did she believe that? Could she trust *Gotte* that this New Year would be happier, would be better than the last?

She stared out the window, glanced back at the calendar. She prayed, she doodled and finally the words began to flow.

January 1
Dear Caleb,
You must think terribly of me, since I've yet to write. I received your postcard and your letter. Thank you so much. I've wanted to write to you, but when I try, my thoughts and feelings become

tangled. Do you think that what we feel for each other could be situational? Do you worry that when I regain all of my memories, and life finally returns to normal, when spring comes and you are busy with your alpacas and farming…do you think we will feel the same?

Please give my best to your parents.

Sincerely,

Rachel

She sealed the envelope, carried it out to the mailbox and tried to fill the rest of the day with useful activities. The hours seemed hollow, though. She felt as if she was walking in a dream that she couldn't quite wake from.

Caleb's reply arrived so quickly that she marveled at the efficiency of the postal service. Her mother handed her the letter and nodded toward the sunroom. She settled at the desk and tore it open with shaking hands.

January 6

Dear Rachel,

I check the mailbox each day, sure that I will find a letter from you, and today that dream came true.

I am pleased to hear that you do have feelings for me, and I am sure that the love I feel for you is genuine and lasting. It may have begun when I picked you up out of the snow, but remember I didn't even like you very much then. I hope that line made you laugh or at least smile.

The alpacas don't seem to mind the snow. Their coats have become quite thick. I'm looking forward to the first shearing.

My regards to your family and my deepest feelings for you,
Caleb

A week later, she received a nice fat envelope from Montgomery, Indiana. In it was a circle letter from Ida to Deborah. Ida spoke of her crochet work, updated Rachel on the families she'd met in the area and asked what types of flowers they planted in the spring. John wrote a half a page below that, the comments directed more to Rachel's father, although one line assured Rachel that they continued to pray for her each day.

And below both of those messages were two pages from Caleb. He spoke to Ethan about the alpacas. Rachel hadn't realized Ethan was interested in the animals. Her *mamm* paused in reading the letter as Rachel told them how she'd named each one, and how they acted when they were spooked, and how gentle they could be if you fed them carrots.

"Can we get one?" Becca asked.

"We'll help. We promise we will," Clara chimed in.

At the bottom of Caleb's writing, he wrote a personal line to each person in the family. The letter surprised Rachel. Though his tone was informal, it reminded her of the letters her friends had received, years ago when she was first out of school. They would hear of a boy in another community, or perhaps the boy had visited a relative in their area, and the boy would begin to write—not merely to the girl, but to the family. It was a sort of long-distance courting, this getting to know one another.

Was Caleb courting her?

Is that what his letter meant?

Her *mamm* was holding up another envelope, but Rachel had missed whatever she'd said.

"What?"

"There's another letter here."

"It's for me?"

"Seems to be. It's a smaller envelope that was inside this large one, and your name is on the outside."

Her younger sisters began making kissing sounds, Ethan asked to see the portion about the alpacas and her father picked up *The Budget* after winking at her.

As if she was in a dream, Rachel stood, walked across the room and accepted the small envelope. Her fingers traced her name on the outside. She glanced up at her *mamm*.

"Perhaps you'd like to read it in the sunroom."

"*Ya*. I would."

Which caused Clara and Becca to fall into a fit of giggles.

Rachel paid them no mind. Caleb had written to her before. She'd lived with his family for nearly a month. Why did this seem different? Why was her heart hammering and her pulse racing?

She hurried to the sunroom and sat in the rocker, near the small heater, which she cranked to high.

The room was cheery even on a dark winter evening. Her *mamm* had used yellow and green and blue fabric to sew several lap throws that were scattered around the room. An afghan made from variegated purple yarn was folded and placed in a basket near her feet. She pulled the afghan across her lap and opened the envelope.

Dearest Rachel,

I hope you enjoyed my letter to your family. I

suppose it might appear quite old-fashioned, to write to a girl's family, but as you know I'm an old-fashioned sort of guy. Your letter caused me to realize that perhaps I haven't made my intentions clear. Oh, I blurted out my feelings casually enough, no doubt flabbergasting you as you stood under the overhang of the store on a snowy Christmas morning. I meant what I said then, and I'll say it again here—I love you, Rachel Yoder, and I'd like to court you. I realize long-distance relationships are difficult, and I know that you are still recovering from your accident. I'd like to hear more about the things you are remembering, the things you worry about and how well you are settling in. I want to know everything about you, Rachel.

It occurs to me that we barely know one another, and yet I remain affectionately yours,
Caleb

She read the letter twice more, and then she moved to the table in the corner of the room, pulled her stationery toward her and began to write. She poured out her heart in a way that she hadn't in the first letter. She found herself filling page after page, telling him about her mother's seasonal depression, that she might suffer from the same, and describing the sunroom to him. She held nothing back, and why would she? If he cared about her, then he wouldn't run from such revelations. And if he did run, then he wasn't the man she thought he was.

Chapter Thirteen

Caleb had never thought of himself as an impatient man, but waiting for spring, waiting for an opportunity to go and visit Rachel—that took all the patience he could muster. They continued exchanging letters through January and February, and finally, in March, the last of the snow melted.

"Give her our love," his *mamm* said, pushing a lunch sack into his hands as the bus pulled into the parking area.

"And tell her *dat* that I hope to meet him someday." Caleb's father winked. They'd talked about his relationship with Rachel on several occasions. He knew how Caleb felt, and he was the one who had suggested that Caleb write to the whole family. "Show her you want to be a part of her entire life, not just make her a part of yours."

The ride to Goshen was more familiar this time. He passed through Indianapolis without gawking at the skyscrapers, and he breathed a sigh of relief when they navigated the highway interchange and popped out the other side. Caleb knew he was getting close once he saw the signs for Nappanee.

The plan was to stay for a week, attend the auction in Shipshewana and speak to both Rachel's parents and her bishop about his intentions—if she still felt the same way. Their letters had been filled with everyday tidbits, but they rarely wrote about their feelings. He didn't want to push her. He certainly didn't want to rush her, and he could tell from her letters that the time at home was doing exactly what it should—it was healing both her heart and her mind.

Ethan and Rachel were waiting for him when the bus pulled into Goshen. He gazed out at the blustery spring day, at the woman that he had thought of and dreamed of and prayed for, and he felt as if his heart was taking flight like a child's kite.

Rachel waited at the buggy, one hand patting the buggy horse as the other held her *kapp* on her head. Ethan jogged up to see if he needed help with his bags.

Caleb stood staring at her, his suitcase in one hand, his hat in the other, until Ethan slapped him on the back and said, "She's doing better—*our Rachel is.*"

And those two words—*our Rachel*—helped him to start moving toward her again.

Her color was better, the dark circles under her eyes were gone and a ready smile played on her lips. She'd gained some needed weight. She looked more like a woman and less like a lost girl. Her dress was a pale green, freshly laundered and covered with a white apron.

She looked more beautiful than he remembered.

He wasn't sure how to greet her.

Ethan must have sensed their awkwardness because

he muttered, "I think there's something I was supposed to pick up in the store," and gave them a few minutes alone.

Rachel cocked her head, her smile widened and she looked directly into his eyes. "How are you, Caleb?"

"*Gut*, and you…you look fabulous."

And then his heart won over any thoughts of impropriety.

He dropped his bag on the ground, crammed his hat on his head and closed the gap between them. Rachel stepped into his arms, and he was content for the first time since Christmas Day.

On the ride to the Yoder farm, Ethan continued to pepper him with questions about the alpacas. He planned to go with Caleb to the auction, and he hoped to purchase a few of his own. He asked about shearing and mating and feeding and bedding.

Caleb tried to answer intelligently, but his mind was on the woman in the front seat of the buggy.

If he'd thought they'd have time alone when he reached the house, he was mistaken. Rachel's little sisters were home, and they insisted he follow them to the barn, peek in on the new foal and pet the newest litter of kittens. He thought the time spent with Ethan and Clarence would be pure torture, but he finally relaxed, realized Rachel wasn't going anywhere and enjoyed the time with her *bruder* and *dat*. After all, her family would be his family if this trip was the success he'd prayed for.

Dinner was a busy, raucous affair, especially with Miriam's new infant, a boy that they had named Stephen.

"We all call him baby Stevie," Clara explained. "Stephen sounds old, and he's not going to be old for years and years yet."

"He won't let you call him that when he goes to school," Becca reminded her.

"That won't be for a long time."

"Time flies."

"I wish this dinnertime would fly so I wouldn't have to listen to you."

"That's enough, girls." Deborah gave her youngest daughters a serious look. They waited until she'd turned her back to make faces at each other.

Later that evening, Rachel asked him, "Is my family too much?"

"What do you mean?"

"Too loud, boisterous, nosy... I almost died when Becca asked if you'd kissed me yet."

They were sitting in two rockers in the sunroom he'd barely noticed during his first visit—the sunroom that Rachel had told him so much about.

"I want to kiss you again right now."

"You do?"

"*Ya*, but I believe your parents can see us from the sitting room."

"I'm sure they can."

So he reached over and snagged her hand instead, laced his fingers with hers and said, "Tell me about this porch. What you've done, it's amazing."

"I told you about my *mamm*'s seasonal depression. She says she doesn't suffer from it as much as she once did, and the doctor we visited, he said it's related to our hormones and that's why hers is better."

"So you only have, what...twenty or thirty more years to deal with it."

She laughed when he said that, and another part of Caleb relaxed.

"The doctor offered medicine, which I will take if I need to, but so far things are better, and I guess... I guess it's because I've finally found what I feel satisfied doing."

"This room has Rachel written all over it."

"*Mamm* said to think of it as my room, my shop."

A display of finished knitted projects adorned an open cabinet with small handwritten prices affixed to each item. Another part of the room was dedicated to turning the lamb's wool she'd purchased into yarn. It included a basket with several sizes of carding paddles. There were also spools and cardboard spindles, a spinning wheel and what looked like several jars of dye.

"How did you learn to do all of this?"

"There's an older woman in our church who taught me some of it. The rest, I checked out books from the library and searched for information on the computer."

They both laughed at the mention of a library computer, remembering that long-ago argument about what was and wasn't proper.

Colorful skeins of yarn hung from hooks along one wall. Rachel stood and pulled him over to them. "These are the color of the sheep's wool, and these I dyed myself."

"What did you use?"

"All natural things because people who purchase the yarn or the finished items, many of them are *Englischers*, and they want to know that no harsh chemicals are used."

"What sort of natural things?"

"Berries mostly, evergreen for those and roots for the browns."

She showed him some of her finished things—sweaters and blankets and scarves and baby blankets.

"It's hard to believe that you've done all this since Christmas."

"I've had a lot of time on my hands, and *Mamm* was right when she says it's best to keep busy."

"You sound better. You have sounded better for many weeks now."

Rachel nodded, her *kapp* strings bouncing, and he was reminded of her lying in the snow, her hair fanned out around her and her complexion frighteningly pale.

Pulling him back over to the rocking chairs, she lowered her voice—not so her family wouldn't hear. They had to already know what she was telling him, but perhaps it was simply difficult for her to discuss.

"At first, I thought my depression was a result of the accident."

"You wrote that your doctor said that was possible."

"It's so embarrassing, to admit to having these feelings…"

"Please don't be embarrassed with me. I care about you."

She squeezed his hand, then leaned back and set her rocker into motion. "I'm learning that many people care about me. Only, I couldn't see that before. Apparently, this has been a problem since I first left school, and my parents wanted me to speak to the bishop or see a doctor, but I refused."

"Because you were ashamed?"

"I suppose, or maybe I thought it wouldn't do any good."

Caleb rubbed his thumb over the grain of the rocking chair's arm. No doubt Ethan had made the chair. He was a fine carpenter.

"When my *mamm* finally told me how she suffered with the same thing, I didn't feel like such a freak anymore."

"You're not a freak. You're a beautiful, kind woman."

"Some of it is seasonal, we think. It's called SAD—seasonal affective disorder."

"And you said that you're not taking any medicine for it."

"Not at this time—perhaps I will next winter, if I need it. But this room…the sunshine helps. Doing something I love."

"The knitting."

"*Ya*, it helps, too."

Which left Caleb with quite the predicament, because he wanted to ask Rachel to marry him. He had come here to do that very thing, but how could he take her from a place where she was flourishing? How could he ask her to move away from the family that cared so much for her?

Yet he couldn't move away from his parents.

He was their only child.

He simply could not leave them alone.

"Do you have a headache?" Rachel jumped up. "*Mamm* has some over-the-counter medicine."

"It's okay. I'm just tired, I think."

It was later that evening, when he was tossing and turning in the extra bed in Ethan's room, that Rachel's brother finally said, "Maybe if you talk about it, you'll stop keeping me awake."

So they did, and that turned out to be a very good thing.

Because suddenly, without any doubt, Caleb knew exactly what he needed to do.

Rachel barely had any time alone with Caleb.

On Friday they visited the auction. Ethan purchased a half dozen alpacas. Caleb and Ethan went back on Saturday to see to their delivery.

Sunday dawned sunny and beautiful.

Though they could still often have winter weather in March in northern Indiana, for the day at least, spring had arrived.

Rachel put on her Sunday dress, fussed over her hair, which she then covered with a *kapp*, and made her way downstairs.

"Caleb is out in the barn with Ethan and your *dat*."

"I thought he might be."

"He's a nice young man, Rachel. I think *Gotte* brought you two together at the exact time when you needed each other most."

Rachel didn't answer that because she didn't know how.

She had thought for a moment the night before that Caleb was going to ask her to marry him—but then his mood had suddenly changed, and he'd gone to bed. Was he having second thoughts? She'd been completely honest with him about her moods, about her condition, and she wouldn't blame him if he decided that she was too much to take on. At the same time, she was no longer ashamed of her condition, or of the feelings she struggled with.

She understood that everyone she met was dealing

with something. It was only that some people's struggles were more visible than others.

Rachel felt good now, stronger, but she knew there would still be dark days ahead.

Now that she knew why, that thought didn't frighten her as much as it once had.

The Sunday service was one of the finest that she remembered—the preaching was particularly moving, the singing beautiful and the luncheon delicious. Caleb spent some of the time with her, but he also went off with her *bruder* to join a game of baseball, and once she saw him speaking with their bishop. It was a *wunderbaar* day, but she'd barely spent any time alone with him. The next week would fly by, and then he'd be returning home.

What had she expected to happen?

Her life wasn't a romance novel, where the beau dropped to one knee and pulled out a sparkling diamond ring. They didn't even wear rings. And yet, a part of her had thought that something would be settled between them.

They had nothing scheduled for Monday, and her *bruder* and *dat* had committed to helping a neighbor repair his barn. Caleb offered to go with them, but Ethan shook his head, her *dat* said, "Not necessary, but *danki*," and her *mamm* pushed another cup of coffee into his hands.

"Perhaps Rachel could take you to see the schoolhouse, where she used to teach. It's a pleasant walk."

Caleb had grown up attending a one-room schoolhouse, same as she had, same as nearly every Amish child did. She didn't think there would be much for him to see there, but then again they had nothing else planned. The day had turned slightly cooler and rain was expected before the end of the week. Clouds scudded across the sky, occasionally blocking the sun.

She supposed her life was like the sky. Some days would be sunny and others filled with rain. The thought caused her to think of blue, and she wondered whether blueberries could be used as a dye. Her thoughts often turned to her knitting, and with it a keen sense of satisfaction.

The schoolteacher had the children sing a few songs for their visitors. Afterward she let them go to recess early and told Caleb how much help Rachel had been when she had apprenticed there. Rachel still had very little recollection of those days.

It was when they were walking home, Caleb holding her hand, the March wind blowing the last remnants of winter away, that she saw the curve in the road, and she remembered.

She stopped suddenly, pulling Caleb to a halt, since he was still holding her hand.

"What is it? Are you okay? What's wrong?"

"This is where it happened."

He didn't ask what she meant—instead he waited. He understood that this was a pivotal moment.

"I was walking home, a bit vexed that the school day hadn't gone well. I remember thinking I wasn't very *gut* at being a teacher, that I might never find what I was *gut* at."

She moved forward slowly, looked left and right, and then knelt down and touched a place on the ground where rocks were poking up through the soil.

"The car came around the corner so fast. One minute I was lost in thought, and the next I realized he was going to hit me. It was…blue—not a truck. I jumped out of the way at the same moment that he swerved, and I lost my balance. I remember thinking that I was going to stain my dress, and then nothing—nothing until I woke up in the family's van, unable to remember who I was or what I was doing there."

Her arms had begun to tremble. The memory was so strong that her heart raced as she recalled her fear and the throbbing in her head when she was in the van, and how nauseous she'd felt—how alone.

Caleb knelt beside her, put his arms around her and waited.

When she'd composed herself, she said, "It's a weight off me, to know…to have at least that memory back."

She didn't realize that she was crying until he reached forward and wiped away her tears.

"I'm not glad it happened to you, Rachel, but I am so very thankful that *Gotte* used it to bring us together."

They walked the rest of the way home in silence. When she turned toward the front porch, Caleb tugged on her hand and nodded toward the garden. So they went there, found her mother's bench and sat and watched the birds hop from bush to bush, searching for seeds.

"I need to tell you something." He waited until she turned her attention completely to him. "I love you, Rachel Yoder, and I want to marry you."

"You do?"

"I do. I've told you of my feelings many times, on Christmas Day, and in our letters."

"I was afraid you were having second thoughts."

"*Nein.* I'm sure of my feelings. It's only that…"

"Are you worried about my moods? About my condition?"

"I am not. You are perfect exactly as you are. Everyone struggles with something, Rachel. At least you are dealing with your situation."

"Am I not conservative enough for you?" Perhaps she shouldn't have gone on and on about her knitting business, about the yarns and dyes, about her hopes to sell in *Englisch* shops.

"You are perfect. Conservative or liberal doesn't matter so long as we share the same faith. We can work out our differences."

"Then what is it? I hear a *but* in your voice."

"I can't leave my parents. I can't leave them alone."

"And I wouldn't ask you to."

"This is what I am struggling with. I see how much better you are here. How can I take you from this place? Your family…"

"Is loud and complicated and exhausting, and I love them, but, Caleb, my family is my roots. They always will be." She looked down at their hands. It felt so natural for her hand to be cradled in his. "You? You are my future."

"Your *bruder* said as much."

"He did?"

"Ya." He shook his head. "At times it seems like my thinking is muddled. I'm unable to move forward or see a solution until someone points out the obvious."

"Ethan pointed out the obvious?"

"He told me if I was so worried about taking you from here, to go home and build you a sunroom."

"And you would do that for me?"

"Ya. That and so much more."

He pulled her into his arms then, held her in the warm afternoon sun. She breathed in the scent of him, the comfort of his presence, and she prayed that he would never let her go.

"You're so precious to me, Rachel. You brought color into my life."

"And you brought hope into mine."

"You made me look at things honestly, things I'd been too stubborn to see, but now...now I can see that our life is *gut*—our Plain life is *gut*, in all its variations."

"The future might not always be as bright and hopeful as today," she whispered. The old fear pushed against her hopes and dreams of happiness, but Caleb only laughed.

"We're both old enough to know that every life has its share of trouble, but we can face those days together. *Gotte* will see us through."

"He's certainly guided us through to this point, and who would have ever imagined the course our lives took."

Caleb kissed her again, pressed his forehead to hers and whispered, "And He can be trusted with our future, as well."

Which was a truth that Rachel understood better every day—she could feel it, ringing through her heart.

Epilogue

The wedding took place a short eight weeks later. Rachel had feared those eight weeks would drag by, but in fact they flew. There was so much to do, and she felt a lightness in her heart that she'd never known before.

They married in her parents' yard, under the tall oak tree. She wore a lavender dress with a matching lavender apron. Her *kapp* was brand-new. Family and friends and church members filled the benches that had been set up across the grass. Caleb's parents sat in the front row with her parents. The event would last all day and include lunch, dinner and games for the *youngies*. A long table on the front porch held the gifts that those attending had brought—dishes and sheets and towels and more than one quilt. They would be living with Caleb's parents at first, but Rachel knew the items would come in handy.

Although many Amish couples did not take honeymoons, they had opted to travel to Niagara Falls, a place she'd always longed to see. It helped that there was a large alpaca farm in the vicinity that they both had an interest in visiting.

Rachel was looking forward to the trip, but even more than that she was looking forward to returning to the quaint house in Montgomery, Indiana. Caleb had already begun work on a sunroom, for when the days turned dark. "Plus you'll need a place for your shop," he noted.

She planned to offer not only her sheep yarn and finished projects, but also alpaca yarn and Ida's crocheted items. Their days would be full and, hopefully, *Gotte* would bless them with many children.

Morning sunshine fell through the trees as she and Caleb stood in front of the bishop. Caleb looked terribly handsome in his black suit—a traditional Amish suit that appeared to be brand-new. It wasn't what he was wearing that pierced her heart, but the way he looked at her.

"Do you, Caleb Wittmer, and you, Rachel Yoder, vow to remain together until death?" Bishop Joel studied them both over his reading glasses. He wasn't old as bishops went—not nearly as old as Bishop Amos—and yet there was a quiet wisdom about him. He had been a calming, guiding presence in her life, especially since she'd returned home. She was suddenly grateful for him, and so glad that he was presiding over her wedding.

"We do."

"And will you both be loyal and care for each other during adversity?"

"We will."

"And during affliction?"

"Yes."

"And during sickness?"

Caleb squeezed her hands.

"We will."

Joel tucked his Bible under his arm and covered their hands with his own. "All of those assembled here, as your *frienden* and family in Christ, and I, as your bishop, wish you the blessing and mercy of *Gotte*."

There were shouts of "Amen" and "Praise *Gotte*" and even "Hallelujah." Rachel gazed up into Caleb's eyes and felt as if his love was showering over her, covering her, blessing her.

"Go forth in the Lord's name." Bishop Joel turned them to face their guests. "You are now man and wife."

Her *mamm* was crying. Miriam was trying to shift baby Stevie to her left arm and clap at the same time. Becca and Clara were practically hopping up and down, and Ethan and her *dat* looked proud enough to bust a button. Ida was crying and John had his arm around her.

They walked back down the aisle, through the gathering of family and friends, and Rachel knew that this was a day she'd never forget.

After the ceremony and before the luncheon, Caleb whispered into her ear, "Care for a walk in the garden?"

Which was exactly what she needed to hear.

Her mother's vegetables were knee-high, and the flowers were a sight to behold.

As soon as they turned the corner in the garden, Caleb pulled her into his arms.

"I love you, Rachel Yoder."

"Rachel Wittmer now."

"I love you, Rachel Wittmer."

And those words were all she needed to hear to make her day the perfect memory. Their first Christmas together would be one that she would always remember, as was their first meeting, when she didn't know who she was and Caleb hadn't a clue as to how to deal with a pushy, moody stranger. But her dreams and hopes and prayers were filled with their future together— future Christmases, possibly dark days and certainly days of joy. The stuff of life, and she was ready, finally, to embrace it.

* * * * *